Praise for The Pri...

'A thrill-a-minute ride, with hea... that you'll never see com...

'It's smart enough to realize that for... in life isn't a... or something that bumps in the night. It's love. I... rrifying. And powerful. And unstoppable. And if... n't already know that, you're about to see why. ... *Priest's Graveyard* will haunt you – long after you want it to.'
Brad Meltzer

'Perfect entertainment. Beguiling, compelling, challenging, and riveting – fantastic gimmick-free storytelling. Don't pass this one up.'
Steve Berry

'Skilfully written, surprising, and impossible to put down . . . his best novel to date. This is an extremely well-thought-out novel, precisely plotted, and, like a good magic trick, deceptive and startling. A daring and completely riveting thriller.' *Booklist*

'An amazing novel, utterly compelling, the story of an abandoned girl and a strange, vengeful priest whose paths eventually cross – with terrifying consequences. Intensely readable, well written, and completely original.'
Douglas Preston

About the Author

The son of missionaries, Ted Dekker was brought up in Indonesia. He is the *New York Times* bestselling author of more than twenty novels. He is known for thrillers that combine adrenaline-laced plot̶ ̶with incredible confrontations between good and evil. ̶ ̶s in Austin, Texas, with his wife and children.

Also by Ted Dekker

Adam
Bone Man's Daughters
The Bride Collector
Forbidden

TED DEKKER

THE PRIEST'S GRAVEYARD

Northumberland County Council	
3 0132 02098541 7	
Askews & Holts	Feb-2012
AF	£7.99

HODDER

First published in Great Britain in 2011 by Hodder & Stoughton
An Hachette UK company

Copyright © Ted Dekker 2011

A CIP catalogue record for this title is available from the British Library

Paperback ISBN 978 1 444 72486 8
eBook ISBN 978 1 444 72488 2

Printed and bound by Clays Ltd, St Ives plc

Hodder & Stoughton policy is to use papers that are natural, renewable
and recyclable products and made from wood grown in sustainable forests.
The logging and manufacturing processes are expected to conform to the
environmental regulations of the country of origin.

Hodder & Stoughton Ltd
338 Euston Road
London NW1 3BH

www.hodder.co.uk

CONFESSION

"THERE IS NOTHING new under the sun, now is there, Renee?"

Father Andro's chair creaked as he leaned back. "Whatever you've done, I'm sure God can forgive you." He brought his steaming teacup to his mouth, took a sip, then set it down on his cluttered desk.

I had called three days earlier and asked to see him alone, but only if he could spare the entire evening. Maybe several evenings. By his silence I knew he thought the request strange, especially coming from a woman with an American accent. But for Danny's sake as well as my own, I had to unburden myself.

"Before I tell you the whole story," I said, pulling the old, brown journal from my bag, "I have to know that you can appreciate Danny's past. He wrote this entry when he was in the United States, several years ago. I don't think many people would understand why he did what he did there."

Father Andro looked at me over his round spectacles and took the old journal from me. "But you think I can?"

"If a priest in Bosnia can't forgive him, nobody can."

"I'm not sure I feel comfortable reading another man's confession without their being present."

"You must. I'm begging you."

The father's eyes held steadily on mine. "You would like me to read it now?"

"Yes, please. It's only a few pages."

"Wouldn't you rather tell me—"

"Please, let's just start with what you have in your hand."

Father Andro nodded. "All right."

He lifted the journal, cracked its cover, and began to read Danny's handwritten confession.

The Confession of Danny Hansen

I can only remember one time in my life when I begged for another person's screams to continue.

The screams were my mother's and I was sure that the only reason she'd stopped was because she could no longer breathe. I was still only a boy and I sat in the corner of my bedroom, knees hugged to my chest, praying for her to make another sound, any sign of life, even if it was a scream.

Now, much older, I hear those screams far too frequently and I beg them to go away. I don't know if I'm an angel or a monster anymore.

It's two in the morning right now and storming outside. I've laid in my bed for three hours, staring at the ceiling, and, despite my own vow of silence, I must write what happened that day in 1992, hoping that my confession here will finally earn me enough peace to bring sleep.

I grew up in a small town in northern Bosnia, and was fifteen when the civil war between the Croats and the Serbs began in earnest. There were many reasons for the war, but the only thing I came to care about was that Orthodox Christians were killing Catholic Christians.

My mother, my two sisters and I were Catholic. Good Catholics who attended mass at least once a week and said our prayers every day. For as long as I can remember I was convinced that I would become a priest when the time came.

My father had died of lung cancer four years earlier, leaving my mother to care for myself and my sisters, Marija and Nina. Within two years of Father's passing we had adjusted to life without him and took comfort in our love for each other.

On that fall morning, the weather was still warm and the leaves had not yet fallen from the trees in our valley. We were all seated at the table for a breakfast of muffins and oatmeal in our house on the village's southern edge. I can picture every detail still.

Mother had made the porridge with milk instead of water that morning, so it was smooth and creamy the way I liked it. Marija preferred more oats and Nina suggested more milk so that it could be eaten like a soup. I objected with a sour face and this made Marija laugh. Encouraged, I offered up a few more examples of how I could twist my face and for a few minutes my oddities made us all laugh.

Mother was still dressed in her sleeping clothes, the same pale yellow flannel night-dress she always wore. Her long, black hair was pulled back into a bun to keep it out of her face. My sisters had also come to the table in their pajamas. I was the only one who'd dressed (slacks and the same gray button-down shirt I'd worn the day before) after rolling out of bed at Mother's call for breakfast.

We were still laughing over my fourth or fifth facial contortion, this one involving screwed up lips and crossed eyes, when someone banged on the door repeatedly. A harsh voice demanded we let them in or they would break it down.

Our small town sat in a valley to the north of the fighting that had brought Bosnia to a standstill, but a hundred stories had reached us and each one seemed worse than the one before. Reports of terrible killings and rape, slaughters of whole congregations as they sat in mass on a Sunday, snipers hiding in the woods waiting to pop off anyone's head as they walked by minding their own business.

My mother stood slowly to her feet, face as pale as the porridge. The demand came again, with a curse this time.

Her eyes darted to me and then to my sisters. "Get to your bedrooms! Hurry!"

Marija and Nina fled the table in obedience, but I didn't want to go. Following my father's passing Mother had become my greatest source of security—besides the local priest, she was my only true comforter. I felt safe next to her. And I think I made her feel safe as well.

I started to object, but she cut me short with her finger, stabbing toward my bedroom.

"Now! Run! Climb out your window! Get your sisters and run to the priest!"

So I raced down the hall and was about to turn toward my sisters' room when I heard the front door crash open. I knew that from their vantage whoever had broken down the front door would see me if I ran across the hall toward Marija's and Nina's room.

I can't tell how many times I've relived that moment. It was the first in a string of choices that would eventually land me where I am today, a full grown man with a new name, living in America, courting madness.

Panicked, I slipped into my bedroom and eased the door shut, careful not to make a sound. I was halfway across my room, when my mother's first scream stopped me cold. Then the sound of a slap and running boots.

Afraid I would be caught, I ran to the corner, ducked behind my dresser, and dropped to my seat in the shadows.

The door flew open. Heavy breathing filled the room. Not my own because I had clamped my lungs as tight as a drum.

The door slammed shut. I was alone.

And then another scream, this one from Marija. Followed by the sound of another hard slap. I should have run for the window and gone for help, but even then my first instinct was to stay and save my mother and sisters, never mind that I was only fifteen and as skinny as a twig.

So I didn't run for help. I hid in the corner like a frightened rabbit, hugging my knees to my chest. Finally, the screaming stopped.

I knew they had missed me and I would be safe if I just stayed put, but I never was the kind to sit put. If you asked me to go one mile, I would go two; if you asked for one contorted face, I would give you four. I had already lost one father, and the thought that I might lose my mother or a sister or even all of them drove me to my feet, still trembling with fear.

The house had gone eerily silent except for the occasional muffled voice. Were they already dead? Or were they being killed, right then, while I stood doing nothing?

Maybe I could distract the Serbs. Or even lead them away from the house.

I don't know how long I stood there, anchored by my own terror, I only know that I became convinced that I had to know what was happening. So I walked to the door, breathless with fear. Slowly, I took the handle in my hand, and, when the house was silent for a few seconds, I eased the door open and pressed one eye up to the crack.

The hall appeared empty. So I pulled the door open just enough to give me a line of sight to my mother's bedroom.

I was standing in the six-inch gap, peering down the empty hall to my sisters' closed door, when a soldier in a green uniform filled my mother's open doorway, fumbling with his pistol belt. His eyes lifted and met mine. For a moment we stood still, staring at each other. If he had come after me straightaway, he would have been able to grab me and stuff me into a bag or shoot me before I got out of the window behind me. But he hesitated, stunned.

"We have a runt!" he roared. And he ran for me.

If I would have slammed the door and run for the window as any sane person of fifteen would have certainly done, I would be dead. He would have simply opened the door and shot me in the back.

Instead, I jerked the door wide open just as he lunged for it. His lumbering body hurled through the sudden opening. Off balance and carried by his own momentum he flew by me, tripped on my foot, and stumbled to his knees.

His pistol belt had fallen on the floor. I bent down, grabbed the gun and jerked it free. The man's bitter cursing was enough to propel me forward in a blind panic. But now a second soldier threw open my sisters' door and a third appeared at his shoulder.

"He's got a gun," one of them said, eyes darting down to my hand.

My father had taught me to shoot targets with a twenty-two gauge rifle when I was still a young boy. He said I was the most accurate eleven-year-old sharpshooter he'd ever seen. But in the hallway, I realized that if I took the time to shoot the man at my sisters' bedroom door, the man I'd tripped would reach me and kill me from behind.

So I didn't shoot the man. I acted as any sensible fifteen year old might. I ran. Down the hall in a dead sprint. Toward the front door. Leaping over a pack one of them had dropped.

It suddenly occurred to me that, although the way through the front door was clear, my back would be to them for the whole sprint down the path. I would be like a turkey in a fall hunt, with three hunters to shoot me down in the open.

So I spun to my left and ran for the kitchen.

A bullet slapped into the wood frame and I ducked. Maybe the shooter's choice to stop and fire slowed him down enough to give me the time I needed to get out the back door. Or maybe the deafening explosion was enough to give me inhuman speed, I don't know. Either way I was out and running toward the forest behind the house.

But I didn't run into the forest because it was only a thin strip of trees that opened up to fields on the far side. I would once again be a turkey to pick off. I only wanted to run into the waist-high grass that surrounded the forest, and I'd only run a few steps into that tall grass before dropping to my knees, scrambling to my left perhaps ten meters, and falling to my back, pistol at the ready above me, trying to control my breathing.

One of them swore. "He's in the trees."

They hadn't seen that I'd dropped short of the forest! They'd come out of the house looking north toward the burning town and by the time they'd turned in the forest's direction, I was down, leaving only some bent grass to show that I'd gone in.

Or so I hoped.

I recognized the voice of the one whose pistol I'd taken. "Your mother is still alive, you runt! Come out or I swear I'll go back and put a bullet through her head!" The machine-gun fire from the town sounded like popping corn. "I'll give you one chance. We have a whole army; your town is surrounded. Come out and we will let you live."

Their muffled voices approached as I lay there sweating, shivering with fear. But then they passed and faded. They'd gone into the forest?

I eased up, poked my head just above the grass, saw that they were gone and knew I might not get a second chance. So I stood and ran back to the house, praying with each step that I wouldn't be seen.

I raced through the kitchen and into the living room with my mother's name on my lips.

"Mama?"

She didn't respond.

Louder now. "Marija?"

I ran down the hall, still clinging to the pistol. Into my mother's room where I pulled up at the sight before me.

My mother lay at an angle on her bed. The sheets were soaked in blood. Her throat had been cut.

My heart stopped.

"Mama?"

Her head. It was barely attached to her body. Her dead eyes were staring at the ceiling.

Frantic, I tore from the room, down the hall, and spun into my sisters' room afraid I would find the same thing.

I did.

The only difference was that they were on the floor and both naked. Something deep inside of me snapped then, while I stood shaking, staring at my dead sisters. Then the pain came, like an erupting volcano. I dropped to my knees, then slumped to one side. There on the floor five feet from my sisters I began to sob uncontrollably.

I didn't care if I was found. I didn't want to live. If I had full use of my senses I might have put the pistol in my mouth and ended everything right there.

But I was lost in my anguish and for a long time I couldn't think straight. And even when I started to think again, my thoughts were strange ones that might make others wonder if I'd lost my sanity that day.

Thoughts like: *I will hunt down every last Orthodox Christian in Bosnia and make them pay for killing my mother and sisters.*

Thoughts like: *I will burn the house down with me and the soldiers trapped inside.*

Thoughts like: *I will take a stake and shove it through the eyes of the one who'd come out of my mother's room. Then gut the other two with the same stake.*

But out of that dark fog came a few more rational thoughts. In retrospect, I think the notion of becoming a priest who brought true justice into the world with the help of a knife and a handgun first began to take root as I lay there on that floor.

And then the memory of the pack that one of the soldiers had left by the front door entered my mind, and my eyes snapped wide. It was still there.

He would be back for it.

I sat up. My sorrow gave way to such a terrible need for justice that I was able to ignore my pain and push myself to my feet. I looked at my sisters' dead bodies one more time, then turned away, walked down the hall, and entered the living room.

There, I faced one of the most significant choices of my life. I could flee the house and make my way to the town to find help—surely there were many families who'd suffered similar tragedies that morning, milling about, helping each other.

Or I could provide what justice my mother and sisters deserved here, in our own home.

I chose the latter. It was a very easy choice.

The home's primary source of heat during the winter was a black pot-bellied stove that sat in the corner of the living room. After moving the green pack into the center of the room, I climbed behind that stove and carefully stacked firewood on both sides to protect my flanks.

Metal in the front, firewood on either side—I wasn't going to be the hunted this time. It was now my turn to hunt and that green pack by the front door was my bait.

I cleared the pistol, saw that it still had seven unfired cartridges, and chambered a round. Then I made myself as small as possible behind the metal stove and pointed the gun over the top.

They came to me about fifteen minutes later, single file, through the front door.

"Forget it, he's probably in the next village by now.

Even if they do listen to him, this kind of thing happens every day now. Get your pack."

"I don't like it. We agreed we wouldn't kill them."

"And you didn't, did you?" the first one snapped.

I could have shot then, they were in my sights. I would at least get one, maybe even two. But I didn't want to kill one or two. I had to kill them all.

So I had to think, which one would be most likely to stay and fight? Because that's the one I would shoot last, knowing he would not run. The one who would run, that's the one I would shoot first if I wanted to get them all.

The one who didn't like what they'd done was the most likely to run. I slowly angled the gun at him, and when the sights were lined up, I pulled the trigger.

The booming recoil knocked me back behind the stove, out of sight, as the man's body thumped to the wood floor. I quickly righted myself and took aim at the second one who was spinning around, trying to determine where the shot had come from. His eyes fixed on the stove. Then on me. And I shot him through his forehead.

This time I'd braced myself and wasn't knocked back. I turned the pistol on the third soldier who still didn't know which way the shots had come from, and I shot him as well.

The gun's echo faded, leaving only the sound of my pounding heart in my ears. There were six dead people in the house and most of me wished it were seven.

I dropped back down against the wall with the pistol loose in my right hand and my rage gave way to pain once again. But I had done some right to fix the wrong, hadn't I? I had done what was right for my mother's sake.

In some ways I took my first steps to becoming a priest

that day, and my own house was my first graveyard. Or maybe I have it all wrong.

That was how it all started, born in innocence when I was only fifteen. But that wasn't where it ended.

Dear God, have mercy on my soul…

Father Andro flipped through the journal and saw that the remaining pages were empty. He set the book down and closed the cover.

"I am so sorry, my dear. God forgive us all for the terrible tragedies of that war. Danny's suffering cannot be overstated."

"So you understand what he did? *Why* he did it?"

"Yes. I was here during the war—you must know that."

But would he understand the rest? The journal was only a litmus test of sorts, a way for me to determine whether I could trust the father with the rest of our story. Our story because Danny and I shared the same story now. We were both as guilty.

"And the rest?" Father Andro asked.

"The rest?"

"He writes here that this is how it all started."

"The rest happens in America."

"I assumed as much."

"You'll tell no one?"

"I'm a priest, Renee. Bound by my oath. There is nothing you can tell me that would change that."

I sat back and crossed my legs, suddenly eager to tell him everything. As he said, he was a priest. Who could better understand than a priest who had shared a similar history with Danny?

"The rest begins with me," I said in a soft voice.

"Then tell me about you," Father Andro said.

1

Eighteen Months Earlier

I CAN REMEMBER some things about myself but not everything. My name, Renee Gilmore, for example, is something I could never forget—how could I, after my failures had been so often pounded into my skull?

You're throwing your life away, Renee. You're screwing up, Renee. You're an embarrassment, Renee.

That much I could remember as I lay in the alleyway with my face planted in the concrete. I also knew that I was in my early twenties. That I was barefoot. That I was dressed in a T-shirt and jeans. That my mother and my father were both long gone or dead.

Mostly I knew that I had to get up and get moving if I wanted to live, although I must admit I was having some difficulty remembering *why* I wanted to live. A basic instinct, you might say, but when you're strung out on heroin, basic instincts have a way of feeling irrelevant.

These are some of the things I could remember then.

But if you had asked me in that state, I certainly couldn't have told you other things about myself that should have been as plain as day.

I couldn't have told you that I preferred to wear only silver accessories, or that my first kiss was with Tobias Taylor on a dare when I was six, or that my favorite food was a grilled hamburger with extra pickles and mustard but no mayonnaise, please.

An orbital shift had tilted my psyche off its axis during the last twenty-four hours. I was aware that I might be overdosing on the heroin that Cyrus Kauffman had helped me shoot up. But something else was pushing me.

I was seeing ghosts. Hearing voices. I was living through one long, uninterrupted panic attack. As a matter of fact, although I didn't know it at the time, I was suffering from a minor but real psychotic break that would only get much worse. My mind had finally crumbled under the weight of its circumstances.

I was on my face and my palms were on the wet concrete, pushing down as if they, along with my scrawny arms, expected to lift me up, too stupid to realize that even if I did get to my feet, I didn't have a clue where to run, assuming I could get my legs moving.

We're gonna eat you, Renee. The monsters were whispering. *When we get ahold of you you're gonna wish you had turned that trick for Cyrus.*

Fear came in waves, down my neck and back, to my heels. The rain on my back felt like stabbing icicles. *No good, no good, no good. He's gonna squash you.*

My body started to spasm, but I pushed anyway and managed to lift my belly off the wet ground. I dragged my knees forward, one at a time, and I shook like a rat stranded on a high wire.

Why was I here?

A few memories rolled around me like fog, but I wasn't sure if they were true. My dad left me and my mom in Atlanta when I was thirteen. My mother died in a car crash, and that was why I had come to California to go to school and make something of my life. Maybe.

I whirled back to see the monster who'd rasped that, but my head moved only a little. Then more, until the walls were spinning past me. I lost my balance and dropped to my right elbow but managed to keep from falling flat thanks to the brick wall next to me.

My dark hair hung over my face. No wonder my dad didn't want me. I was nothing but a scrawny mop head. A proper haircut at a real hairstylist in downtown Atlanta was the first thing I'd done with the money my mother had left me in her will.

I spent another thousand dollars on clothes, leaving me almost fifteen thousand of the twenty-thousand-minus-court-fees payment to apply toward a bus ticket, the deposit on my very own studio apartment, some living expenses for a while, and cosmetology school in Burbank. Beautiful Styles Cosmetology. I wanted to find a school in Hollywood because acting was my real passion, but the prices were too high.

The plan had been simple, something I'd talked to Mother about before the drunk driver slammed his black Dodge Ram into her blue Honda Accord.

"What about cutting hair?" I'd said one Sunday afternoon.

My mother, Susan, nodded absently. "Sure. Cutting hair is respectable enough." She was a cocktail waitress and made good tips.

"I mean, while I'm looking for a job," I said. "You know, acting."

Mother's eyes shot up. "Uh-huh." Only it sounded more like, *Yeah. Right. Fat chance.*

"I mean, in Hollywood. I could wait tables or something until—"

"Don't be ridiculous, Renee."

"Why not? I'm pretty enough."

"For starters, you don't even have the money to *get* to Hollywood. What're you gonna do, hitchhike?"

I should have dropped it then. But I've never been the kind to leave well enough alone.

"Maybe Dad's got some money."

Her eyes flashed. "Don't be an idiot. Even if we knew where he was, he's broker than a doormat. That much's a foregone conclusion. And if he does have a couple bucks, you'd be the last person he'd give it to."

That hurt. I couldn't just let the words sit there.

"So then he's not much better than you, I guess." I turned, knowing the words cut her deep. "I'll just find my own way."

I still feel guilty for the way I said it, and I certainly didn't mean for her to die so that I could get out to California. But that's how it worked out.

The plan was really that simple: Move to the land of opportunity, get a job waiting tables, and start looking for a way into acting. I wasn't stupid enough to think landing a role or modeling job would be easy, so I would be responsible and learn to cut hair as a backup.

Shaking in the alleyway, I couldn't begin to remember how I'd gotten from there—on top of the world with fifteen thousand dollars in my pocket—to here, enslaved by the most powerful pusher south of South Central, in three years. The last year of hard drugs had fogged my memory. My descent mostly had to do with running out of money and hooking up with a girlfriend to sell a bit of weed on the side. Was that it? Yeah, I thought so.

Like a magnet I had been drawn to my true, useless nature,

as if subconsciously determined to justify my father's disappointment in me.

I pushed myself up off the concrete again, and this time I managed to get one foot under me.

A voice yelled out. I knew the voice well and didn't have to look back to know that a black town car, window down, was at the alley's mouth. I'd seen Cyrus take out a woman's teeth with his fist. I'd seen worse than that.

But it wasn't Cyrus that terrified me. It was the voices.

The alley was closing in on me and the monsters—real monsters—were after me. Why they scared me more than the thought of Cyrus beating me, I don't know. Maybe because I had never heard them before. They weren't just in my head, right? They were the only detail in my world that was crystal clear.

I pushed off with my foot and lurched ahead.

"Around, around!" Someone was yelling again. "Go, go!" They'd seen me.

He's gonna step on you and break all your arms like you deserve.

My bare toes scraped the rough concrete, but the narcotics in my system numbed the pain some. I had to get out of the alley because the creatures there were reaching out of the darkness to grab me and pull me down.

And then I saw it directly ahead of me: a light hanging in the night sky, surrounded by soft sparkles of rain. I fluttered for that beacon of hope like a moth with wet wings. Deep inside I must have realized it was only a streetlight, but at that moment it was the promise of rescue.

The parking meters were there like sticks in the ground; cars were parked beside them like boulders, but my eyes were on that streetlamp looming. Nothing else mattered to me, only that warm halo of heaven in the sky.

I was in the street before I noticed the twin beams of a car rushing toward me from my left. More light? Closer light? And coming toward me. It stopped me dead in the center of the road. Maybe I was dying and this was the tunnel to heaven.

The choir sang, a high-pitched squeal like tires on asphalt, somehow beautiful. The lights swerved. The moment before the car hit me I remember thinking it wasn't the tunnel to heaven; it was a car.

The impact threw me through the air and landed me on my butt ten feet from the car, which had screeched to a stop. All I could see were the lights, glaring at me, and I thought this was the end, because it had to be Cyrus and he was going to break my arms and legs then give me to the gangbangers.

"Are you okay?"

The world was spinning and I was trying to crawl away. But my hands refused to cooperate. They clawed at the wet asphalt. I began to retch.

I fell to one elbow, threw up on the street, then toppled over, still heaving. Don't ever let anyone tell you that heroin is the drug of the gods. It has far more to do with vomit.

The driver of the car that hit me was frozen in his head-lights. A screech of tires from far behind him reminded me that Cyrus was still coming after me.

"He's...kill me...," I managed. However unintelligible, the driver seemed to understand. He spun back, saw the car sliding around the corner, scooped me up as if I were a crash-test dummy, and ran for his car.

I heard the bones in my left arm grating against each other as I bounced in his grip. Then I felt the pain and realized they were broken.

The man opened a white door and set me into the passenger seat. "Hold on, honey."

We were in a white BMW—I remember that as clearly as the light—and I thought maybe if angels really did exist, then he was an angel.

He slipped behind the wheel and ran the back of his hand over a sweating brow. "Stay with me."

Please don't let them rape me. Save me, please.

But I couldn't say it, because pain in my ribs and my arms made it hard to breathe. The car smelled like vomit. That had to be me, curled up on the seat, staring up at my savior who was dressed in an expensive black suit and a tailored shirt. His square, silver cuff links had crosses on them and held his sleeves neatly in place. He had large hands, and his fingernails were trimmed and buffed.

The car surged forward. For a brief moment I allowed myself to believe I was safe. But then I remembered who was after me, and I knew this rest was merely a delay of the inevitable.

Cyrus had a saying: Better die than be cheated. Thinking of that, I suddenly felt sorry for the man who'd run into me and then rescued me. He'd helped a cheater, which made him a cheater as well.

Cyrus would kill us both.

Something popped behind us. My rescuer glanced up at his rearview mirror and swore. Wind roared, and I knew the back window had been shot out.

Something hit my shoulder. Just a soft slap on my shoulder blade from behind. Either one of the monsters had reached through the seat and punched me, or it was a bullet.

The driver swore again, more urgent this time. Maybe he knew we were dead.

"Hold on, honey," he said. "Things are about to get a little bumpy."

He was a man of understatement, and for some reason that

comforted me. What could be bumpier than being in deep debt to a man like Cyrus with nothing but your body to make good?

We're gonna smash you up and crack the rest of your bones.

"Hold on!"

The car came to a screeching halt and I slammed into the dash, then crumpled to the floor, broken arm turned back at a sickening angle.

An arm hooked around my waist and pulled me out of the car and hefted me over his shoulder like a half-empty bag of sand. My savior had blocked Cyrus's car with his own and taken to the streets on the other side.

I think I began to fall in love with him then, while I hung over his strong back, bouncing and bleeding. The numbing heroin was maybe the only reason I didn't pass out.

Until the next bullet hit me and shattered my elbow. I remember thinking that my arm had stopped a bullet that would've hit the man carrying me—maybe killed him. He was trying to save me, but maybe I was saving him, too.

What neither of us could have possibly known was how soon he'd be dead anyway. Life can be full of cruel jokes, and the cruelest of them all would soon find us for its punch line. Had I known, I might have moved my arm, let the bullet take him through his back, and spared us both all that was to come.

He swore again. They were coming. I passed out.

2

AT THE PRECISE moment that Renee Gilmore lost consciousness during her attempted escape from Cyrus Kauffman, Danny Hansen stood in a gutted warehouse in Pasadena with his legs parted, three feet from heel to heel, gloved hands clasped behind his back, Ray-Ban sunglasses fixed upon the bridge of his masked nose, at ease and content.

He was oblivious of Renee Gilmore's fate.

He was not, however, unaware of Paul Birch's fate. The congressman was strapped to the folding chair ten feet from him. Paul would either come to his senses and present himself a changed man, or he would leave less pleasantly altered. Permanently.

The need for change was why Danny had subjected Paul to a powerful sedative, secured him in the back of the congressman's black Ford Explorer, and then strapped him to the chair in this abandoned warehouse where not a soul could hear or see them.

This task was Danny's calling, his duty, his privilege, his moral obligation, however unpleasant or challenging: to deliver justice where a broken system could not. Some would call him a vigilante. Some would call him a criminal. Some, an enemy of society.

He preferred to think of himself as a servant of the people.

If any man or woman saw Danny crossing the street dressed as he was now—minus the black neoprene ski mask and leather gloves—they might say, *There goes a pleasant dark-haired man of about thirty, dressed smartly in tan slacks and a light blue button-down long-sleeved shirt. No ring, so he probably isn't married, but he will be soon because he looks like a catch for any woman longing for a stable, upwardly mobile, kind husband.*

They would be right. Well, half right.

The other half was hidden from their view, the half that exposed the brood of vipers to the truth and—if they were not transformed by said truth—the half that delivered ultimate judgment.

To date, he'd killed three vile creatures ignored by a flawed system of social justice. The rest had seen the light.

The viper before him now was staring at him with dark, frantic eyes and, if not for the gray duct tape over his mouth, would undoubtedly be spewing obscenities. The man was still dressed in an Armani pin-striped blue suit. His yellow tie was askew, his shirt was wet with sweat, and his cuffed pants rode high over black socks and bared shins.

Now in his late fifties, Paul Birch was a hairy man—arms, legs, chest, and back. Nevertheless he kept himself well groomed, visiting the salon for a manicure and facial wax every Thursday evening. Although his nose was a little too broad for his face, photographs showed that he'd been better proportioned when he first entered politics and ran for a seat on the

San Francisco city council. Now fully entrenched, he, like so many politicians, could rely on power rather than charm, wit, and sound reasoning to keep him in his elected office, which happened to be the US House of Representatives.

Danny knew the man intimately, though he'd only touched Birch once, at a rally when they'd shaken hands. The rest of his knowledge had come from a careful two-month investigation.

"So pleased to meet you, Congressman Birch." The timbre of Danny's voice was low and soft. He clasped his hands in front of his chest. "You must be wondering why I've brought you here. Not to worry. I'll take the tape off your mouth when I'm satisfied you won't start barking up the wrong tree like a confused dog. Fair enough?"

No response from the man. Birch wasn't accustomed to being forced into a corner, much less tied to a chair.

"I want you to listen to me very carefully, Mr. Birch. When I think you've understood what I'm doing and why I'm doing it, then I will allow you to redeem yourself. Nod if you understand me."

The man hesitated, then finally nodded, and Danny knew by the look of defiance in his eyes that he would not change his ways. Danny considered cutting to the chase and making it a short night.

But no, he would follow protocol.

"You're undoubtedly wondering why you're here, so I'll tell you before you make your choice. A few years ago, I stumbled across a pedophile when one of his victims—a thirteen-year-old boy called Tigert by his friends because they said he was as wiry as a tiger—confided in me. As you may or may not understand, I was deeply concerned. It took some time, but the police finally arrested the guilty man and put him behind bars. A good thing, yes?"

Another slow nod. The man was clueless.

"Not so good. The man was out within a week. It turned out that he was somewhat insulated from the law. His father was a judge, and a crafty one at that."

Paul Birch just stared at him.

"Perhaps if that were the end of the story, you wouldn't be strapped to that chair. Unfortunately for you, the boy and I had become close during the whole ordeal. Tigert was like a son to me. A month later, he was killed in a hit-and-run. I was very upset. The police investigated but found no evidence to support a criminal case against any party. They let it go. I can tell you that I was very, very upset."

He paced in front of Paul Birch, searching for any sign of empathy. He saw only outrage at the man's own predicament.

"I couldn't let it go. So I traced the evidence myself, and it led me back to the pedophile. He'd killed my boy for exposing the truth."

Telling the story always filled Danny's gut with a bitter brew of sorrow and anger, and he took a moment to let the worst of it pass.

"My world changed that day. Something shifted in me. It took me back to a terrible pain I'd felt as an innocent boy, when I saw even worse atrocities in Bosnia. I was fifteen then and went by a different name, and there was war all around me. A part of me died when I was fifteen, but it came back to life when this pedophile killed Tigert. Have you ever felt that kind of pain, Congressman?"

Sweat raked the man's red face.

"It took me six months to work up the courage, but I finally did the only thing I knew to do, having learned some valuable lessons in the Bosnian war. I took that guilty abuser of human-ity off the streets and gave him one chance to see the light and change his ways. When he failed, I emasculated him. I cut off his penis." Danny lifted a finger. "And before you judge me, you should know that the apostle Paul suggested emasculation as an option for the wicked in his letter to the Galatians. So it wasn't my idea, you see. You'll have to blame Paul, I was merely being biblical."

A deep breath.

"It wasn't my intention to kill him, but I couldn't stop the bleeding. He was dead in fifteen minutes. I disposed of his body in the ocean, never to be found. He was my first. I want you to guess how many snakes like him I've taken since then." Danny approached his subject and ripped off the duct tape. The sound of the adhesive parting from flesh ripped through the gutted warehouse.

The fact that his name, Danny, meant "God is my judge" was intentional. He had selected it on purpose. He was, after all, God's judge on earth, at least for some.

"Guess."

"What are you doing?"

"Seven," Danny said. "Whether the number will go to eight after tonight is up to you. Do you know right from wrong?"

"What on earth is this? Do you know who I am?"

"Even more than you do. I've been watching you for a long time. You're a powerful congressman who lies for a living. You hide behind pork-barrel spending that lines your pockets. Your sole ambition in this life is to satisfy your desire for wealth and power, and you do it while pretending to fight for the small widow on welfare. In reality, you make your living by enslaving the poor with laws that keep them poor so they will do your bidding."

"I'm an independent. This is absurd!"

"You were also once a Democrat and once a Republican—that's not the point. Political parties are only a means to an end for you. You trample many to stand tall, don't you, Congressman Birch?"

The man had the audacity to glare, as if he were the schoolteacher and Danny the unruly student.

"None of this is why you're strapped to the chair. There are hundreds like you, and I wouldn't say they deserved to die for lying through their teeth. I'm here for another reason. But you already know that, don't you, Congressman?"

"What do you want?" Birch snapped.

"I want you to change your ways. Does the name Camilla Lopez mean anything to you?"

Hesitation. "Should it?"

It was all Danny could do to remain calm in the face of the man's bold denial.

"Let me help your memory. Do you know the name of Camilla's six-year-old son?"

"How could I?"

"Bobby. Bobby became a ward of the state when you sent Camilla to prison. He was admitted to a foster home. I have a soft spot for children whose lives are turned upside down like mine once was."

"This is utter nonsense!"

"Three months ago, Bobby tried to hitchhike a ride to the prison where his mother is being held. He never made it. I made every inquiry known to man in my search for him, but the child simply vanished. He is presumed dead. He left nothing behind but a weeping mother and a very upset me—that and a trail that led me back to you."

"Don't be a fool! I'm a man with responsibilities!"

"The fact is, Mr. Birch, you are Bobby's biological father, are you not?"

"Ridiculous."

"In fact, you raped Camilla Lopez dozens of times during her employ as your maid. She was nothing more than a sex slave to you, a convenience rudely sidelined by her pregnancy, thanks to your overstimulated libido."

Paul Birch kept glaring. He did indeed deserve the worst.

"I think you had the boy killed," Danny said.

Silence.

In the name of all that was holy, the man was pathetic.

"Are you as ignorant about the other women as well, Congressman? We both know that Camilla is only one of half a dozen you've 'employed' over the years."

Paul was starting to wheeze.

"I'll give you a shot at walking out of here, but you have to engage me reasonably," Danny said. "Are you willing to try that?"

"If you think you can bully someone by tying them down and forcing..." The man's face bulged. "What do you expect me to say? You can't do this!"

"I expect you to rethink some things, and the only way you'll do so is if you're tied to that chair. I want to present some thoughts that could make you question all that's familiar to you. Do you know right from wrong?"

"I...This is—"

"Answer the question!"

"Of course I do."

"Tell me, what makes something wrong?"

No answer.

"Let me enlighten you. There are two primary schools of moral thought on what makes an act right or wrong. The first is that an act is intrinsically wrong, so determined by religion or God or what have you, regardless of the consequences of that act. This is called *categorical* moral reasoning."

Judging by the blank look in the man's eyes, his reasoning had stalled. Like most ordinary minds, Birch's wasn't well equipped to think through moral reasoning, but Danny knew from experience that even the thickest person could eventually wrap his mind around basic truth.

"The second"—he paced to his left, hands clasped behind his back—"is called *consequential* moral reasoning, which is the belief that the consequence of an action determines its morality. Example: lying to the Nazis is the right thing to do, because it will save the lives of the Jews you're hiding. Lying, as well as killing, can be right or wrong depending on the outcome of those actions. Do you think the consequences of your actions matter, Paul?"

"This is crazy."

"If you subscribe to consequential moral reasoning, which most people do, then even if the law states that it's wrong for me to kill you, cutting your throat might actually be the highest moral choice I have."

"You can't get away with this."

"On the other hand, if lawful actions result in terrible consequences, following that law might be wrong at times, and breaking it might be right."

"You can't do this to me."

"The law's a decent guide, but the consequences matter far more. I have come to the conclusion that your actions are wrong, Mr. Birch. Terribly wrong. You rape and abuse women from across the border, and you do it with impunity because of your power. So now you have a choice to make. Your fate is in your hands."

"I've never heard anything so absurd in my life. You can't do this!"

"You keep saying that. And yet"—Danny spread his hands—"I am doing it." His mind ticked through his options in customary fashion.

Choice: Forever change Birch's life as planned now, or give him more time.

Consider: The man wasn't likely to change his ways, ever.

Consider: Countless women and children had paid a terrible price to feed the man's sickness.

Then again...*Consider:* A few hours more with Birch, no matter how disturbing or painful, was a small price to pay for the slight chance he might change.

On balance, the moral thing to do here was to give the man a fair shake, as planned.

"I'm going to give you some time to persuade me that you have changed, heart and soul. If you fail to convince me, then I will feel obligated to prohibit you from fulfilling your role as a congressman. That will mean forever altering your life."

Paul Birch was trembling. *He believes me,* Danny thought. *That's a start.*

"You have the floor," Danny said.

3

I COULDN'T HAVE been unconscious more than a few minutes, because when my mind crawled out of that dark fog, the man who'd swept in to rescue me was still running. How long could a man run while carrying a body, even one that weighed a scant one hundred or so pounds? I'm five foot two if I wear five pairs of socks, and I'm light as a toothpick, but even a world-class athlete would have trouble running with a body over his shoulder for more than a minute or two.

Unless, of course, he's an angel with superhuman powers, which I considered but doubted. I believed in demons because I had been hearing them all night, but I'd never met anyone who treated me like I imagined an angel might. Angels were the stuff of childhood dreams.

I was hardly lucid and unable to move, but I remember thinking that something had changed, and for a few long moments I couldn't place it. Then I realized that I was no longer hanging over his back, bouncing, but was cradled like a child in his arms.

The rain had lightened but I had to squint to keep it from falling in my eyes. His face came into focus. His jacket and shirt were soaked. A thick silver chain hung around his neck.

He twisted his head back over his shoulder and I knew there was danger behind us. But my mind was working slowly, and I was still captured by the look of this man who cradled me in his arms as if I were his Raggedy Ann doll and he wasn't going to let anyone touch me.

I saw it all in slow motion. His jaw was strong and his hair was trimmed neatly above his ears. When he swung his head back around, drops of water flew off his hair and there was a look of urgency above that flexed jaw, but he wasn't frantic.

I managed a feeble word. "Hello?"

He looked down, face stern. Dark brown eyes. "It's okay, honey. Just keep your head down."

Keep my head down? It was already in the crook of his arm. I didn't know how I could keep it down.

Pop, pop! Gunshots sounded like they'd come from cap guns. Maybe my head was sticking out past his arm where a bullet that just barely missed him could hit me in the ear.

I tried to pull my head in but it was hopeless. So I just hung there in his arms.

My angel veered around a corner at full stride, then ducked into an underground parking structure. He pulled up, panting, and glanced behind us.

I was in such a fog that half of these details could be completely wrong. They were moving around the edge of my mind like ghosts. I have to think hard to remember exactly what happened, but even those memories could be a hallucination because, like I said, I was overdosing.

I remembered my broken arm and wondered how it was getting along. "Are we safe?" I asked. I know it sounded stupid, but it was the question on my mind.

"Just hold on." His voice was soft but strong. "They'll see our tracks."

"I think I'm going to throw up," I said.

"Do what you need to, honey, just don't die on me."

He was hurrying now, headed for a side door, I think. But my mind was on what he'd said. My angel was giving me permission to throw up while he held me in his arms. I wanted to cry. If anyone had been so kind to me it had been a very long time and the memory was long gone.

I began to cry. The world was fading to gray and I was floating in his arms and crying.

In fact, I must have been crying loudly, because he hushed me softly as he pulled up next to a door with a small lighted EXIT sign above it. Then he pushed through, stepped back out into the rain, glanced both ways, and headed back down the same sidewalk we'd been on before.

He was retracing his steps?

We veered around the same corner and entered the same garage we'd just left, just as the far-side door slammed shut. Cyrus's men had followed our wet tracks into the garage and then back out. But now we were inside again and the ground was wet from many feet, so no one could follow our tracks.

At least that's how I remember the scene.

He slid around a car and ran along the wall, heading deep into the parking garage, all the way to the darkest corner, where he set me down behind a blue truck.

I lay on the concrete and watched him peer over the truck bed to see if anyone was following. Then he was leaning over me.

"Okay, we're safe for now," he whispered. He wiped my tears away with his thumb. "Are you still with me?"

I nodded. And I started to cry again.

"Shh, shh…It's going to be okay." He carefully lifted my broken arm off the ground and straightened it. "We have to take care of your arm. You took another hit."

His tone was all matter-of-fact, like he was a medic in a war zone, but I knew he was being brave for me. Or he might have been in the army for all I knew back then.

"I'm so sorry, sweetie. Can you hold on for me?"

Nausea swept over me and I began to shiver. I suddenly felt like I was going to throw up again. I turned my head away from him and retched. If I hadn't been in such a terrible state, I would have been mortified.

The man eased my head back toward him and wiped my mouth with his sleeve. "Just hold on, I'm going to get you out of here. I'll be right back."

He rounded the back of the truck in a crouch. I began to drift into a fog. Voices were yelling somewhere far away—but in the garage. They had found us?

The monsters were rasping in my ear again. *You can't throw us up, Renee, we're inside you and you can't just spew us onto the ground. You're sick on the inside, you filthy whore.*

It was over. My angel had left me in a puddle of my own vomit and the world was collapsing around me. The truck was my tombstone. It would roll over and smash me into the concrete and I would be dead. Or worse, trapped alive forever.

A shout broke through my daze. "They're at the back!" Wet shoes slapped the concrete.

Then my rescuer was back, muttering angrily under his breath. He motioned for my silence and scooped me up. "Sorry, honey, just hold tight."

He flew around the truck, head low. How he got me into the backseat of another car so quickly, I still don't know. Had he broken into it? But I was there on the backseat, lying face-down where he'd tossed me. My broken arm was folded under my belly.

The door smacked my heels when he shut it.

I heard the engine fire.

I felt the car jerk forward.

Bullets were smacking into the metal sheeting and my res-cuer was repeating his mantra—"Hold on, hold, hold on"—as the tires squealed and sped up the ramp.

Something thudded into the car. A body maybe.

We smacked through the wood gate and peeled into the street. One more bullet hit the trunk, and then we were flying into the night.

"Hold on, honey. Just hold on."

I mumbled the same command to myself. *Hold on, Renee. Just hold on.*

The night went black.

I DON'T KNOW how long I was in the back of the car. I was only barely hanging on to life and dreaming of floating in outer space. Angels were hovering over me, whispering, keeping me alive.

They wrapped my shattered arm in a glowing white cloth and poured a green liquid down my throat so I wouldn't throw up anymore. They washed my body in warm water and dressed me in a soft white gown, then laid me on a bed.

They brushed my hair and sang a beautiful chorus that made me think of Mariah Carey. It was as if she was kneeling over me, hands folded, singing about how beautiful I was. She kept singing the same refrain over and over.

"You are beautiful, don't let the devil tell you wrong; you are an angel in my eyes, so beautiful."

It was lovely, but it was also terrifying. I'd never thought angels would lie so blatantly, if at all. I kept wanting to tell her that she was wrong, that I wasn't beautiful, that they had the wrong girl. Stop lying, please. Please don't mock me with these kinds of lies.

I was the worthless one who had thrown everything away because I was so, so stupid. I was the one her father couldn't love. I was the one who shot up heroin and threw up in the alleys.

I was the one who washed out her underwear in the sink with a bar of soap because she was scrounging quarters for a fix.

I was the one who did whatever Cyrus wanted whenever he wanted because I was terrified of what might happen if I said no.

I was the one who owned only two pair of jeans, and one of those actually belonged to Sara, who was three sizes larger than me.

I was the one who cried myself to sleep before my tears had drifted away in the fog of hard drugs.

My name was Renee Gilmore and I was disgusting.

But the angel's voice kept washing over me, smothering me with such kindness that I thought maybe I had died and they really had managed to wash away my stains and make me beautiful.

I woke up once and saw that I was in a bedroom filled with soft light. A few images worked their way into my consciousness: a sheet pulled up under my chin; my bandaged arm resting on top of it. A moose was staring at me.

I wasn't in heaven. I was in a hospital. No. No, I was in someone's room. In a house.

Then I slipped into a coma.

4

THE RAIN HAD stopped, leaving the warehouse in an eerie calm disturbed only by the sound of water dripping down gutters.

"So this is your game?" the congressman asked. "To take people you think are guilty of hypocrisy and torture them? Who isn't guilty? You?"

"We are all guilty. I'm interested primarily in the Pharisees, though. The ones who are filthy inside and pretend they are not."

"And abusing my rights doesn't place you in that category?"

"I'm not abusing your rights. You gave those up willingly the moment you first raped your maid."

The congressman stared at him, then swallowed hard and cleared his throat. "So maybe you have a point. I may have my shortcomings, but I honestly do serve the country. That's my greater good."

"No, I don't think so. I've watched you and I would say you serve only lust, power, and money."

The congressman leaned back in his chair, eyes fixed on Danny.

The horrors of Bosnia crept into his mind. When his mother and sisters had been raped and killed by the enemy, he'd fled the house. *God, when will the pain end?* The fact that it had all happened in the name of religion only made the memory more bitter.

Not that Danny abhorred religion. Indeed, his life was in service to true religion, which was about love, for the greatest commandment was simply to love God and neighbor.

So here he was, administering his own kind of love based loosely on the practices of a perfect teacher. If he ever did learn that his actions were in any way immoral, he might rid the world of a monster by killing himself. He would certainly change everything and seek reconciliation with both society and God.

Paul Birch's face was beginning to twist up with some anguish. Perhaps he was understanding that his own heart was inconsistent with all he professed, that he did not know how to love.

"Paul," Danny said softly, folding his hands. "I'm sorry, but we are running out of time. I need to know if you're going to resign your seat and never take up politics again."

The man's face was red. He looked far too large for the chair to which his hands were tied, more so when he was so puffed up with rage.

"Pretend that I'm God for a moment," Danny said.

"You're not God!" the man shouted. His lips were wet and fat and spewed spittle. "You have no right!"

"I said pretend, Paul. I'm only a messenger, the lowest,

surely. But I can't bow out of my responsibility because you're upset about the consequences of your actions."

"You're no better than me."

"Perhaps. But I've changed my ways. Will you change yours? Will you step down?"

The man bit off his reply in a low, bitter voice. "Don't be a fool."

That's what I thought.

Danny walked over to a black briefcase that sat on a large folding table, the only other piece of furniture in the abandoned warehouse. He unclasped the latches and lifted the top of the case. Inside lay his instruments of choice: the necessary narcotics, a pair of garden shears, two silver scalpels, a pair of Vise-Grips, one twelve-inch butcher's knife, and a selection of tapes, bandages, and assorted items just in case, including a yellow spring-loaded clamp used to seal potato-chip bags so as to keep the contents fresh and crunchy.

His silenced nine-millimeter pistol was tucked away in a holster under his right arm.

He withdrew a syringe that he'd prepared earlier, removed the sleeve, and checked to make sure no air was trapped in the needle. Satisfied, he turned around and approached Paul Birch.

The man's eyes were round. "What's that? What are you going to do?"

Without responding, Danny injected the man in the shoulder and pushed the plunger home.

The congressman roared and jerked, then cut loose with a string of curses that made clear his fear of what might come next.

Danny returned to his briefcase and put the syringe away.

"Are you still with me, Congressman?"

The man gave him a groan.

"If you find a way to continue being unloving, I will come to you and I will make things much worse for you. The same if you talk."

He faced the man, who was sinking fast. "Did you hear me?"

The man's lips sagged as the drug relaxed his muscles. He nodded. And then his eyes slowly closed.

There, in a manner of speaking, sat the man who'd killed his sisters. The powerful sedative now flowing through his veins rendered him unconscious.

There slouched an esteemed congressman from California, fattened on the many lies fed to him by a corrupt system that had long ago embraced the law instead of love.

There slept a demon who would wake up forever altered by his encounter with a sword-wielding angel, who would be Danny.

Perhaps he should just kill the man, Danny thought. The politician would not change, surely.

Confident that Paul Birch was now under, Danny worked quickly to free the tape that strapped his wrists and ankles to the chair. The man was breathing heavily, dead to this world.

It took Danny a few minutes and considerable struggle to drag the limp body and hoist it onto the table.

There, he surmised, lay his eighth pupil, three of whom had not lived to tell of their lesson. If the truth was allowed in hell, they would be there now, spreading the gospel according to Danny and bemoaning their own very bad behavior.

He'd never administered his justice in a cruel way, because the point wasn't to torture the poor saps. The point was to change their behaviors by altering their life situations—or removing them from life altogether.

Also, he wasn't a man who relished a physical struggle.

After the ordeal involving his mother and sisters in Bosnia,

Danny had shadowed a doctor who patched up the wounded, mostly civilians. When he came to the United States to pursue higher education in his late teens, he maintained his interest in healing, and when he decided to take on the vipers, he engrossed himself in surgical techniques. It was amazing what one could learn on the Internet.

To call what he did *surgery*, however, would be unfair to the many physicians who'd devoted their lives to that fine craft. He preferred the term *procedure*.

Danny removed his leather gloves and pulled on thinner surgical gloves. He pried Paul Birch's jaw open with a dental wedge, which he placed between the rear right molars.

He pulled the man's tongue out using the Vise-Grips and cut off two-thirds of it with his garden shears. Blood flowed from the severed stump, and Danny worked quickly to apply the yellow chip-bag clamp.

It took him two tries, but in short order the man's severed stump was compressed and the bleeding nearly stopped. Drowning on the blood that had already exited the wound was still a concern.

Danny pulled Paul Birch's head to the table's edge and twisted down. Blood ran from his mouth and formed a small pool on the floor. Danny positioned the man on his side so blood would run out of his mouth rather than back into his throat, where it could cut off his breathing.

He hated the mess of it all, but doing the right thing was never a matter of having to love it. He replaced his tools in his briefcase and cleaned up.

The congressman would be without a tongue when he woke, but otherwise in the same physical condition in which he'd begun his narcotic-induced nap.

The same would not be true, Danny hoped, of Birch's mental

condition. He would certainly be screaming bloody murder. He might not be able to form words from a podium any longer, but one did not need a tongue to scream. Or to write. At the least, Paul Birch would hurry to the FBI and write down his full account, landing them even more evidence on the vigilante who was out there making their job easier by ridding the world of scum.

At the worst, Paul would continue his nasty politicking using his keyboard alone. If so, not for long.

The thought gave Danny considerable pause. He really should just let the man die in peace now and rid the world of a terrible thing.

He examined the warehouse space one last time to be sure he'd left no evidence beyond his shoe prints, the chair, the table, and Paul Birch himself. They might find the odd fiber from his clothing, but it would lead them only to a big-box store that had sold a hundred thousand shirts, slacks, and shoes of his kind.

The mask, the gloves, a long-sleeved undershirt, and long underwear would have kept any of his hair from falling to the ground. Even so, he could not linger. He had to get into a cold shower to wash away the sweat and general displeasure of his completed task.

But that was just it, wasn't it? His task didn't feel completed. The fact was, Paul Birch deserved to die. He would not see the light. Danny would only have to return to his home one day and end his life as promised.

Why not just finish the job now? Truly, not finishing the job might be immoral.

After a full risky minute of consideration, Danny did what he finally concluded was moral, all things considered. He pulled out his silenced nine-millimeter pistol and shot the congressman through the head.

Then he retrieved both bullet and shell, picked up his brief-case, and left the warehouse, confident that he'd done every-thing right.

Surely Bobby Lopez was seated in heaven with Danny's mother this very moment, smiling down on him.

5

LIGHT FILTERED THROUGH my eyelashes. My mind was blank, like a whiteboard. No dreams to remember, no sense of myself other than the fact that I was alive.

It took me a few moments to remember what the thing turning lazily through the air above me was called. A ceiling fan. One with white blades pushing the air, although I couldn't feel it stir.

The thing of it was, I couldn't really place where I was, or why I was there. I wasn't even certain *who* I was.

An ache throbbed down my right side as my heart pushed blood through my body. I could hear the sound of the pulse in my right ear. When I pried my eyes down to see what was causing the soreness, my eye sockets burned.

My arm was in a white cast. I remembered then that I had been on the brink of death and was somehow saved.

The room I was in was painted off-white, but the bottom

third of the walls looked like they were covered in pink leather. A large moose head was mounted on the wall opposite me, glaring at me with glassy eyes. Two stuffed foxes watched me from either side. I didn't feel like I had the strength to turn my head, but with a painful swivel of my eyes I could see that similar heads were mounted on the other walls.

I was being watched by all these dead animals, as if I were the one in the zoo and they'd each paid for entrance to see the human on the bed.

There were no windows that I could see. A dresser with a large mirror over it was painted with pink roses. So was a large armoire in the corner. The door leading out of the room was closed. It was painted white, too. However unique, the room's pink-and-white decor looked strangely beautiful to me.

Something clicked on my left and I listened. I thought I heard someone breathing. After a long pause, a door closed.

"You're awake?" His soft voice reached into me like a powerful narcotic, flooding me with relief. It was him. Although I couldn't remember the details, I knew immediately that I was alive because of the man behind this warm voice.

Then he walked into my field of vision and looked down at me wearing a gentle smile. His face came back to me—that carefully groomed face, that blond hair slicked back, that strong jawline, those soft brown eyes.

He'd been dressed in a black suit when he'd first come to save me. Today he wore a pressed dress shirt open at the collar, and I could see a silver chain like a cord around his neck. His sleeves were folded back. A silver Rolex hugged a strong wrist.

He was tan. He was beautiful. It was as if God himself had stepped into my room.

"My name is Lamont," he said.

The name was familiar, like the scent of my mother's perfume.

"I've been telling you that for two weeks. Lamont Myers. Do you remember?"

I opened my mouth to say I thought so, but nothing came out.

He sat down on the side of the bed and brushed my cheek with his forefinger. "It's okay, save your energy." His eyes sparkled. "You're back with us, that's the important thing."

Had he said two weeks?

Without thinking, I lifted a shaking hand and brought it to his hand on my cheek. He took my fingers into his warm palm and squeezed them.

"How do you feel?" he asked.

I cleared my throat, determined to speak. "Fine," I croaked.

His eyes darted to a bottle of water on the nightstand. "I don't know what I'm thinking. You must be dying of thirst!" He spun the lid off, inserted a straw in the neck, and pressed the tube against my lips.

I took a long sip, keeping my eyes on his the whole time. Maybe I was afraid he would vanish again. The cool water felt good in my throat.

"Better?"

"Yes," I rasped, and I was. "Two weeks?"

He set the bottle back on the nightstand. "You've been in a coma for two weeks, Renee. The doctors didn't think you'd make it. I insisted that you stay here, where I could keep an eye on you after the surgery on your arm. They put up a fuss as you can imagine, but I had a private physician sign a release. You weren't carrying any ID."

"You know my name?"

"I do now. I hope you don't mind. Mr. Kauffman was kind enough to fill me in on a few details."

The name gouged into my memory like a pitchfork. *Cyrus.* My eyes must have shown my shock.

"Don't worry, he won't be bothering you any longer."

"He's going to come after me."

"No. I can assure you that Cyrus Kauffman will never be coming after you."

"How do you know?"

He frowned but his eyes twinkled. "I have my means. There isn't much money can't buy. But enough about me. You should rest, and if you're feeling up to it, you might try some soup. I had the doctor remove a temporary feeding tube this morning after he expressed concerns about infection. He'll be back later."

"What happened?"

"You don't remember?"

"I was..." The whole ordeal was still foggy. Emotion choked me.

"It's okay, honey." He leaned over and kissed my forehead. "You're going to be okay now. I promise."

I nodded and held on to his fingers. "Don't leave me," I whispered.

"I won't." He paused, then spoke my name as if tasting it for the first time. "Renee Gilmore." His eyes searched mine. "You have no living relative that I could find."

"No?"

"No, dear. Your mother passed away in a car accident three years ago."

Yes, I remembered that now.

"Your father is presumed dead."

"Dead?" Was that a shock? I forgot whether he was alive.

"Unfortunately, yes. No aunts or uncles who know you. No living relative who has any connection to you legally. I'm so sorry."

He said it as if my solitude in this life were a death sentence. All I'd had was Cyrus, and in that moment I wanted to go back to Cyrus. He wasn't so bad, right? I'd managed with him.

But the moment I thought it, I felt my bones begin to tremble. It was as if my body knew more than my mind and was rebelling at the idea of rushing back to the man who would as soon break all my bones as give me a fix.

Lamont put his hand on my shaking body. "Your body's craving heroin. But I don't think it's a good idea. Do you?"

At the mention of the drug, I wanted it. My need was so powerful that tears came to my eyes.

"No," I said.

"Good."

I was suddenly very tired, and I couldn't get my body to stop shaking. He got a wool blanket from the armoire and put it over me. Then, although I didn't want to, I fell asleep.

I must have slept a long time. When I woke, a man in a white pin-striped shirt was leaning over me, peeling my eyelids open. I blinked, and he lifted his hand.

"There we go. She's awake."

The man who'd saved me...*Lamont*. Lamont Myers. Lamont hurried to the bedside. My pulse quickened when our eyes met.

He took my hand. "You're awake! Thank God. How are you feeling?"

How long had I been sleeping?

"Sorry, this is Dr. Barry Horst, the physician I mentioned."

The doctor smiled. "You're a lucky one." He was taking my pulse. "I'm not sure you were comatose after all. Your vitals are still strong as a horse. How's your throat?"

I cleared it. "Hurts."

"It'll be sore for a couple days, normal. Let's take a look, shall we?"

He stood, peeled down my sheet, and I saw then for the first time that I was naked.

Lamont turned away and walked toward the door. "Excuse me, I'll be right back."

The doctor asked me a dozen questions about how I felt, everything from my arm, which ached, to my bladder, which felt fine. It wasn't until he carefully helped me into a sitting position that I became aware of the catheter.

"Oh, yes, I'll remove that if you think you can urinate. Do you want to try?"

"Yes."

It took us a few minutes, but I finally found my legs. He helped me to the bathroom, then back to the bed, by which time I was exhausted but robed and feeling a little less helpless.

"I've given Mr. Myers my recommended diet. Liquids only for a day, I'm afraid. If you keep it all down, we'll get some solids in you. Fair enough?"

"Where am I?" I asked.

He looked caught off guard by the question. "You're in Lamont Myers's house. In Malibu. And I think that makes you a very fortunate person. He seems very taken with you, my dear. You're in the best of hands."

The door opened and Lamont walked in. "How are we doing?"

The doctor straightened his collar. "She's doing well." He lifted his coat off an armchair in the corner. "Page me if you have any more questions. Liquids only for now."

"And the drugs we spoke about?"

The doctor nodded. "I'll call the prescriptions in."

"Thank you."

I saw the doctor only once more, the next afternoon, when he came to check on me. To this day I've never found any record of any doctor in Southern California named Barry Horst. I'm certain that he was part of the whole cover-up that would forever alter my life, and Lamont's.

The rest of that first day passed with me drifting in and out of sleep. With each waking I felt stronger. Lamont was the perfect gentleman, nursing me as my own mother might have. I was in my twenties and he was in his thirties, he said, and I never thought of him as a father figure. My initial attraction to him was undoubtedly influenced by his tender care of me as I came back to life.

I started taking the blue pills that would allow me to break my addiction to heroin completely, he said. Two a day, just like the doctor ordered. My mind was in such a fog from all the abuse it had taken, but *patience* could have been Lamont's middle name.

It wasn't until the third day after my waking that I began to wonder if something was wrong with me. Why was I sleeping so much? How long would it take to get back on my feet?

Not that I minded being treated like a queen. I was in heaven lying in that bed, safe from life's cruel jokes. I still couldn't believe I was there, being waited on hand and foot when I had no right to be alive at all.

But I asked Lamont about the daze I seemed to be stuck in.

"My dear..." He tilted his head down and offered me a gentle smile that I was already getting to know well. I couldn't help but smile myself. "Who can say what the drugs did to your mind. You have to realize that your psyche suffered a very severe shock when it shut down. Comas are tricky things. They're hardly understood by the medical community."

He rubbed my arm. "The doctor says it could take you a year to recover completely. Let's just pray there is no permanent damage."

"Okay." I think I giggled then. I was so delighted to be in his company.

Ten minutes later I sank back into a deep, dreamless sleep.

Mornings, afternoons, nights—they were all one to me, marked only by Lamont's cheerful *good morning*s and *how's your evening*s when he came in to check on me. We never talked more than a few minutes before he hushed me and let me rest.

After several days, which felt more like one in my state, Lamont woke me and helped me to the bathroom as he always did. But when I came out he presented me with a chrome, wheeled walker as if it were a gift.

"Hmm?" he said with a grin. "What do you say?"

"What do I do with that?"

"You're ready to venture out. I'm dying to show you the place."

I looked at the contraption that would support me as I pushed it a step at a time. "Couldn't you just help me?" I asked.

"Of course!" He pushed the thing aside and rushed up to my side to take my waist. "Of course."

I put my arm over his shoulder and sort of hung on him as he led me out of the room. It was the first time since he'd rescued me that I felt the firmness of his arms. He stood a full foot taller than me, a really strong man who must have worked out daily. Two hundred pounds I would say. I'd lost weight, so I was probably only ninety-five. Next to him I was hardly a toothpick.

He held me as if I were a delicate flower.

The moment I stepped out of my pink-and-white bedroom I pulled up, staring.

"You okay?"

"Uh...yes," I said. The house wasn't like anything I'd ever seen. All the walls were glass framed by brushed aluminum, so I could see through several rooms at once. "This is yours?"

"The house? Do you like it?"

"It's all glass?"

"I like to see where I'm going," he said, then laughed. "Come on."

He led me down a long hall to what looked like a living room. All the furnishings were square, covered in black and white leather with chrome and stainless-steel trim. The walls were double-paned glass, each pane a full inch thick. Only the white doors and a marble-tiled floor appeared not to be glass.

"You live in a glass house," I said.

"Not all of it. The bedrooms and kitchen are private, naturally. And my suite is one floor down. But yes, I guess you could say that. Let me show you the best part."

He led me through the living room, past a large black table on which sat a silver bowl filled with red apples, to a panel of black buttons on the wall.

"I often keep the blinds down at night, but…" He pushed a button.

As one, the white blinds all around us began to rise. Glass walls, from floor to ceiling, looked out over a rocky beach and an endless ocean.

I gasped as the scene was revealed. Jagged cliffs punished by silent foaming waves rose on either side of the house. The sky was a brilliant blue with a few fluffy white clouds scattered about. The house was built up on stilts, and wooden stairs circled down to the beach.

I felt giddy. Paradise was right there in front of me!

"I take it you approve?" he asked.

"Do I approve?" I hugged him as tightly as my frail arms could. "It's beautiful! Can we go outside?"

Lamont chuckled. "No. It's far too dangerous."

"Dangerous?"

"You're just out of bed, my dear." He cupped my chin when he said it, and for a moment we looked at each other. He was tender, he was masculine, he was wealthy, he was holding me. I wanted to crawl up into his arms.

He kissed my forehead, then started to say something, but I reached up on my tiptoes and kissed him on the lips. "Thank you," I whispered.

He blushed, then turned to the ocean. "Please, don't do that."

I was confused. "I'm sorry, I—"

"I don't want to take advantage of you." He looked at me, then took my face in both of his hands. "Do you understand? Don't get me wrong…I…"

He leaned over and kissed me. I felt a tremble in his hands as he gently took my lips in his.

Flushed, he stood back, releasing me. I reached for the glass wall to steady myself, but he intercepted my hand before I could touch it.

"I'm sorry," he said. "I wasn't thinking."

We stood in an awkward silence for a moment. I didn't know if he was sorry for kissing me or for letting me go.

"Here, sit." He led me to a white leather sofa, and I eased myself down. "Better?"

"Yes."

An elaborate display of electronics covered the wall to our left. Seeing my interest, he went to it and punched a few buttons. Orchestral music filled the room.

"Beethoven," he said, turning back. "Over a thousand albums, and they're all yours to listen to. If you choose, that is."

"It's beautiful."

"Would you like to?"

"I love the music."

"Well…" Lamont returned and sat down next to me. "I was thinking of something else. Where are you going to go? When you're better?"

"I…I don't know."

"You could stay here."

"I could?"

"You don't have to, of course. The choice is entirely up to you."

"You mean…"

"I mean you could live with me. Here."

"Really?"

"We'd have to establish some rules. I don't exactly lead an ordinary life, and I'm very particular about some things, but yes."

The idea excited me more than I would dare show him. It occurred to me that I didn't know much about the man who'd rescued me and brought me into his home. He was wealthy, that much was obvious. He was a beautiful man both physically and spiritually. He'd rescued me, and the monsters hadn't made an appearance in his home. The very thought of leaving terrified me.

"Of course," I said. "What do you do?"

"I work in international investments. My partner's the devil and I swear that one day one of us is going to kill the other, but sometimes that's the price one must pay for wealth. He's twice my age and still has twice my ambition." He chuckled.

I laughed with him. "Does this devil have a name?"

He grinned. "Jonathan Bourque. Used to be a priest, if you can believe it."

"I take it you don't like this so-called priest."

"Former," he corrected. "Let's just say that he has his grave-yard and it's full of his victims."

The world was a twisted place, I thought.

Lamont grew more serious. "Your living here might present us with a rather complicated relationship. It's a dangerous world out there, and I'm obsessive about security." He looked at me. "I told you that Cyrus would never lay a hand on you?"

"Yes."

"I have to confess, I might have spoken out of turn."

"He's after me?" I was alarmed.

"Not as long as you're here. No one can touch you here, I'm absolutely certain of that. But short of killing the man, which is not in my nature, I can't keep him from being who he is."

"But you talked to him?"

"An associate of mine had someone approach him. To say that he's upset about having lost you would be a gross understatement. Which is why I think you'll be safer if you stay here."

"Okay."

A grin pulled at the corners of his mouth. "Just like that?"

I shrugged, and he shook his head. "No, you have to be deliberate about this decision. I wouldn't want you to think that I'm taking advantage of you."

"I would never think that. I like you."

He blushed. "I like you, too. That's what I'm worried about."

"I'm not a little girl," I said.

"No. Now, that I do know."

Lamont stood and paced thoughtfully. "I'm a little OCD, you know. I have my rules."

"OCD, that's like...anal?"

"No, it's more than anal. Everything has its place." He motioned around the room. "The doors all have two locks and a dead bolt. The house is dustproof—no door leads directly outside. The glass must never be touched. I prepare my food in a certain way. To the average man they're just quirks, but for me they're necessities. Why else do you think I live so far out of the mainstream?"

"I'm a bit quirky myself," I said.

"I'm gone for days at a time. I'm not sure you could handle that."

"I'd miss you. But you'd come back, right?"

At this point, I was hardly lucid. My mind was spinning and I was overwhelmed by my surroundings. His cleaning habits and travel schedule were trivial compared with the prospect of living in such a wonderful, safe environment.

"That's not what concerns me. While I'm gone I would need to be absolutely confident that you and the house were all right. It's just the way I am and you might grow tired of it. I wouldn't want you to leave the house alone, at least not until we were sure the world outside those doors was safe for you. And I would need to know that you aren't spilling beans on the floor or otherwise making a mess in my absence."

He looked at me apologetically as he said it, then he shrugged. "Sorry."

"Sure." I had no interest in leaving the house and I wasn't messy.

"Sure? You're very sure?"

"Are you forgetting my alternatives?" I asked.

"True. But you might get lonely. Are you sure you could handle that?"

"Trust me, I've had enough of the streets to last me a lifetime. As long as I have food, music, and television I'll be fine."

"Unfortunately, I don't have television. We could get it just for you. But my idea of controlling or messy might be different from yours." Lamont took my hand and kissed it. "Are you sure?"

"Yes!" I laughed weakly, not because I wasn't delighted, but because I suddenly felt so tired.

"Then I think we should celebrate tonight. Our first meal together, what do you say?"

"Can I sleep first?"

I did sleep, and for most of the day.

That night Lamont bounded into my room with gifts. Seven pairs of white slippers, one for each day of the week. Seven pairs of matching cotton gloves, in case I didn't want to avoid touching the glass, which he personally cleaned once a week. The gloves weren't mandatory, just a suggestion, you know, in case...

The slippers, on the other hand, had to be worn at all times. He pointed to the matching black pair on his own feet. He'd already cleaned the floor of my tracks where I'd tread in bare feet that morning, he told me.

His antics made me laugh. Looking back, I think I may have fully fallen in love with Lamont Myers then, when he was explaining how important it was that I not step off the bedside rug without a pair of slippers on my feet. He was on his knees, pointing out my tracks. When I donned the footwear, he breathed a sigh of relief.

We ate dinner by candlelight at a table overlooking the dark, foaming ocean. I had to keep pinching myself to be sure that I wasn't on another acid trip. I even wondered at the possibility that I was dead and this was heaven, but I knew people like me don't make it to heaven. Never have, never will.

I ate bland food—bread and water and some peas, a little chicken soup—because the doctor said that my stomach was still too weak to eat steak. I had never really cared for red meat anyway.

My mind was still foggy, but in a pleasant sort of way, like a soft pot buzz. I saw the best of everything around me, and that contented high was unlike any drug I'd ever tried.

"Why did you come to my rescue?" I asked, watching him cut his steak.

"Is that what happened? I remember you running out in front of me. I had no choice but to get out of my car. The moment I saw you sitting there so helplessly, obviously strung out, I knew I had to save you." He placed a neatly carved cube of meat into his mouth. "I should ask why you ran out at me."

"The monsters were chasing me. They were telling me they were going to kill me. I saw the streetlight. I was going for the light, I think."

"Monsters?"

I told him about them.

"Well," he said, then took a drink of red wine. "Those monsters can never enter this house. Stay inside and you'll be safe."

A shiver passed down my neck. I was certain that he was right. "They can't get in?"

He looked at me with those big brown eyes—my blond angel of strength—and he smiled. "No. I see everything that happens in and around this house. I will always protect you."

If I hadn't truly fallen in love with Lamont Myers while he made his case for slippers, I did as soon as he spoke those words. You might say I was easy pickings, but I wasn't. He found me because I'd rejected Cyrus and gone on the run. Lamont had risked his life when he picked me up off the road that rainy night. The cost to him of finding and saving me was significant.

Now he would protect me. No one had ever protected me before. As long as he lived I would love him, no matter how obsessively compulsive he was, no matter how strange his rules.

He had many rules. Rules about touching the walls. And washing my hands. And eating only what was good for me. And wearing only the clothes that did not disturb him. And a hundred other laws, but more on that later.

Lamont means "the law" and I suppose it was appropriate, but to me he wasn't the law. He was my savior and he quickly became my lover and I cherished every waking breath with him.

6

One Year Later

I CAN REMEMBER some things about myself but not everything. My name, Renee Gilmore, for example, is something I could never forget—how could I, after Lamont's constant affirmation?

You're a beautiful girl, Renee. You're the light of my world, Renee. I'm not sure I could live without you, Renee.

That much I could remember as I lay on my white bed in the pink-and-white room. I also knew that I was in my early twenties. That I was dressed in the same checkered pink flannel pajamas that I almost always wore. That the one man who loved me more than I could possibly love myself would soon be home after a long day at work.

There were other things that I knew about myself. I was no longer addicted to heroin. I never went hungry or lacked anything I needed to live comfortably.

The thought that I might have to run down an alleyway to

escape brutal men no longer entered my mind. I was safe as long as I stayed in the house. If I ventured out alone, I might not be so lucky.

But that didn't matter because I had no intention of leaving the house alone, at least not until I was ready. I hadn't set foot outside without Lamont once in the last year, and I had no desire to do it now.

Outside was where the monsters were. Outside was where the Cyruses of this world lived. Outside was where I was useless to my dead mother and father.

After two decades of hell, I wasn't interested in anything but this slice of heaven. Yes, there were some challenges. Lamont's obsessive-compulsive disorder sometimes about drove me mad, I will admit. But his need for order and perfection was something I had learned to tolerate, then appreciate.

Had he been any other man, one less loving, less tender, less caring and affectionate, I might have rebelled. Sometimes I was tempted to wonder what living with a different man might be like, but the thoughts didn't last long. The moment he walked in at the end of the day, I knew my lover had come home, and any small price I might pay because of his quirks was insignificant compared with the love he showered on me.

I loved Lamont with all of my being.

A chime pulled me from my lazy thoughts. I jerked upright—he was in the driveway!

My head spun with a sudden surge of adrenaline, and I sat frozen for a moment. Then I dropped my feet to the ground and stood, dazed. What to do, what to do? But I knew what to do. I did it every time he came home.

I suddenly forgot whether I'd finished preparing the food. I had to make sure the kitchen was clean, because if Lamont found a mess, even a small one, he would immediately clean it up on his own rather than ask me to do it. It was inconsiderate of me to leave such a mess, knowing how it bothered him. I certainly had all the time in the world to accommodate his need for cleanliness.

I started toward the door, felt the cold marble floor under my feet, and jumped back onto the rug. I dropped to my knees and, using one of my slippers, wiped up the tracks of moisture my feet had left.

The room hadn't changed. The one armoire easily held all my clothes because I preferred pajamas most of the time. One nightstand, one dresser, one bed, one chair, and one bathroom.

Naturally, I slept in Lamont's bed when he was home, which was about half the time. Lamont was old-fashioned in that way and wanted to be sure I was fully respected in every way. We agreed that I should keep my own bedroom if it made me feel more comfortable.

Sometimes I did sleep alone, even though we had been married. He called me his wife and I called him my husband. We had to have a ceremony, of course. Lamont did everything by the book. He bought me a white dress and he wore a black tuxedo. We lit candles and said our vows in the living room with the sea foaming outside the windows. It was perfect.

I pulled on my white gloves as I hurried down the glass-walled hall. The chime was the part of the security system that alerted us to someone opening the outer gate. Of course, that "someone" was always Lamont, which meant I had about three minutes to clean up.

What if it was someone else?

The thought stopped me in the living room, and I considered the terrifying possibility that one day Lamont wouldn't come home. My heart thudded at the prospect. It had become my greatest fear and I didn't know why, because Lamont always, always came home.

I noticed that all the amber and green lights on the music system were lit up but there was no music playing, which was sloppy, wasting all that electricity. I flew to the glass encasements and turned up the volume. Mozart's strings filled the room, and I sighed. Two magazines I'd paged through earlier lay on the leather sofa. I scooped these up and set them square on the sofa table.

I didn't know what had gotten into me. Normally I cleaned up after myself as I went. It was just easier that way. But I'd left a trail of broken rules behind me today, including, I realized, a smudge on the white leather.

I wasn't going to make it! I still had to clean up the kitchen! So I spit on my finger, wiped the smudge clean with my saliva, then rubbed the leather dry with my sleeve.

The first lock on the front door clicked and I hadn't touched the kitchen. The second, the dead bolt, clunked open and I ran. I was the one who'd suggested he put locks on the outside of the doors so that I couldn't mistakenly wander from the house if I ever was confused or forgetful. I still had those moments.

Blood roared in my ears, something that happened whenever I exerted myself. Lamont said this was a side effect of my medications.

I hit a chair as I rushed past the dining table. Panting now, I spun back to set it straight. The third and fourth locks opened. He was in a hurry tonight, opening them quickly.

I slipped on the smooth marble floor as I hurried into the kitchen, but I caught myself on the counter. I could see it all then with one glance: the carrot neatly cut up on the cutting board, the sliced cucumber next to it laid out in a perfect row, the cubes of tofu stacked in a pyramid the way Lamont preferred. Not a peeling or a wasted drop of juice to be seen.

But the lettuce…I'd left the full head on the counter and hadn't yet shredded it. Worse, the plastic wrap it had come in was on the floor. This would give Lamont heart failure. Had I done this?

I couldn't remember touching the lettuce, much less unwrapping it. In fact, I had only a vague recollection of preparing any of what was now on the counter, though I always prepared food for Lamont.

My memory still wasn't what it should be. The heroin had affected my mind more than the doctor had initially thought, and I faced a long road back to full health. Thank goodness Lamont was patient with me.

I had taken my first step in the direction of the lettuce mess when the door to my right opened. Lamont walked in, glanced at me, then closed the door behind him and engaged two of the locks.

I wasn't sure what to do, so I just stood there, feet planted in a stride.

He turned, ran his hand back through his hair, and sighed, eyes settling on me. Something was concerning him, and I hoped it wasn't the lettuce.

"Hello, Renee."

"Hello, Lamont."

He looked like the same angel who'd swept in to rescue me a year earlier. That light blond hair, those soft brown eyes, his strong shaven jaw and large hands. He still favored black suits worn with tailored shirts, collar open.

He smiled and crossed the kitchen. Then he took me in his arms and held me tightly. You see, this was why I loved Lamont so much. He was quirky with all of his laws, sure. But he kept me perfectly secure and held me close.

"Hmm. You feel so good, darling."

I smiled and wrapped my arms around his midriff. I was still only a hundred pounds—it was important that I not gain too much weight because of my medical condition—and enfolded in Lamont's muscular frame, I was like a twig in God's fingers.

"So do you."

Then he saw the lettuce wrapper and his body stilled. But he didn't complain as he might have. He simply released me, walked to the plastic wrapper, picked it up, and dropped it in the garbage.

"What do you say I cook us some meat tonight?" he asked.

"Meat? I can't eat meat."

"Once won't hurt you."

"Are you sure?" It wasn't like him to break rules. Had something happened?

"Of course I'm sure."

"I cut the cucumber and carrot, and the tofu—"

"I need a steak and some wine," he said. "And please, darling"—he faced me, looking worn and exhausted—"join me. Just this once." A thin smile curved his lips.

"Okay."

"You've taken your pills?"

"Yes."

"And you've cleansed your system?"

"Yes. An hour ago."

"Then you should be fine." He came over, lifted my hand, and gently brushed his thumb over the purple bruise where my knuckles had hit the door frame in my bedroom two days earlier. "Does it still hurt?"

"Not really," I said.

He kissed my injury. "Why don't I finish up here while you make yourself presentable?"

I felt like a schoolgirl being asked out on her first date. "I would like that, Lamont. Thank you."

He smiled. "Hurry back."

It took me half an hour to shower, dry and fix my hair the way he liked it, and slip into his favorite white dress. I was so excited not only to have him home, but to eat meat and drink wine. I wanted everything perfect. What did the doctor know anyway? I was so good most of the time. Lamont was right, a little meat wouldn't hurt my digestive system.

But the big surprise came when I returned to find that Lamont had set up the table on the deck overlooking the ocean. I stared, dumbfounded.

He walked out of the kitchen holding two glasses of red wine. "What do you say? I thought a little air might do us good."

I rushed up to the window and peered outside. He'd placed two red candles on the white tablecloth and set a pink rose between two settings of our white china. I'd been on the deck with him many times, of course, but never to eat and certainly not to eat such an extravagant meal.

This was the kind of man Lamont was, caring for me even if it meant bending all the rules. I was what mattered to him.

"It's...Oh, Lamont! It's perfect!"

He chuckled, and I followed him out onto the cedar deck. The waves crashed a hundred yards down the beach. Sea breezes gently brushed my skin. The candle flames danced seductively against a black sky of bright stars.

When I took my first bite of meat I was sure I was living in a dream. I'll admit I was a bit dramatic about it all, but I was a simple girl easily impressed by simple pleasures.

Lamont smiled and nodded, but he seemed distracted and I hoped I hadn't done something to concern him.

"Is anything wrong?" I asked.

"A hard day."

"Sorry." I ate another bite of meat, but now I couldn't enjoy it as much. "Do you want to talk about it?"

Normally he would dismiss his troubles. He rarely discussed his work with me. I knew he was in some kind of partnership that funneled a lot of money among international organizations, and that the transactions were mostly related to investments and charities. I knew that he was a shrewd accountant who made millions for other people. And I knew that he worked with the Bourque Foundation, named after his partner, Jonathan Bourque. But that was all I knew.

So I expected him to wave off my question, but he set his fork down and rested his elbows on the table.

"I stumbled across some information today," he said.

"Really? Something bad?"

He looked out at the ocean as if trying to decide whether to tell me.

"I've learned that the man I work with is involved in some very disturbing business. Something I find appalling."

"Oh no. Will you stop him?"

His eyes settled on me. "I wish I could. He knows that I know."

"He does?"

Lamont leaned back in his chair and closed his eyes. I'd never seen him so upset, and this frightened me.

"Is there going to be a problem?" I asked.

"He knows that I know and yes, that could be a problem. He's a brutal man who would think nothing of cutting my feet out from under me. I wouldn't put it past him to kill everyone who knows."

My tower of strength was crumbling before my eyes. I didn't know what to think, much less say. I set my fork down.

"Kill?"

"What do you do? You build everything up around you to keep out the wolves, then one sneaks in and just like that"——he snapped his fingers—"it's over."

"Don't say that!"

"You see, this is where the law fails. I should know, right? Me and all my rules and laws." He used his hands to make his points. "Don't do this, don't do that. Do it like this, do it like that. The law, the Ten Commandments, the police, me. And what's it worth in the end? Nothing! A man like Bourque can run circles around the law. He can come in and snuff out someone like me with one pinch of his fingers."

"Please don't say that!"

"Sometimes I think the vigilante has it right. I'm tempted to reach out and teach Bourque a lesson myself."

"What vigilante?"

"Some guy in the news. The point is, there comes a time when the law fails, and then you wish you could set things straight."

"Nothing's going to happen," I objected. "You're just talking, right?"

He looked at me, then nodded and offered an apologetic smile. "You're right. I'm just blowing off steam."

Relieved, I tried to laugh.

"You're right," he continued. "We have rules for a purpose. They keep us safe. Like religion, the law plays a vital role in people's lives. And you, my reborn, are the greatest benefactor of that law."

I raised my glass and toasted the air. "Then to the law."

"To the law."

We drank.

"But if the system ever fails you, Renee, then forget about the law and go after the pig with both guns blazing."

I stared.

He flashed a grin, brown eyes bright beneath that halo of blond hair. "So to speak."

"I'll fry Jonathan Bourque on a spit and bury his bones in the ocean," I said.

Lamont blinked at my boldness. "I don't think you can fry on a spit. That would be roasting."

I lifted my glass. "To roasting," I said.

"To roasting."

He laughed, and we toasted.

"Would you like to join me in our bed tonight?"

Our bed. Not my bed or his bed. *Our* bed. Regardless of how I felt, there was only one polite response, particularly after such a wonderful treat.

"Yes."

He nodded. "Wonderful. You should cleanse first."

"Yes."

Lamont sighed and stared out at the stars. "Such a beautiful night."

7

TODAY DANNY WOULD kill Cain Kellerman, his twelfth offender, nine of whom had been snuffed out.

The mounting death toll was starting to give Danny nightmares. This was his cross to bear. Like a father committed to disciplining his child, he did not relish the punishment itself, only the good that would come of it.

Danny sat in his Chevy Malibu at the curb just outside his cul-de-sac home in Lakewood's Brentwood Estates. His modest single-story brick house was one of a hundred built in the tract around five models, and it was a perfect fit for him in many ways.

For starters, the neighborhood was serene and beautiful compared with the war-ravaged Bosnia he'd left when he was eighteen, three years after his mother and sisters were brutally murdered by the likes of Cain Kellerman. Every day he thanked God for the blessing of such a beautiful country as this. Truly, most Americans did not know how fortunate they were to live in such luxury, free of Kellerman, who would be dead by the end of the day.

Danny studied the three-by-five photograph of the dark-haired, blue-eyed man wearing black-plastic-framed glasses and felt not a hint of pity.

Kellerman's sin was offing young prostitutes after using them up. He trolled the streets for his victims, took them to a hotel, had his way with them, killed them, and then disposed of their bodies in landfills.

Danny first learned about Kellerman when he'd confronted his eleventh subject, Keith Hammond, about his nasty habit of pummeling his wife. Danny convinced Hammond that he would get a first-class ticket to hell if he ever again so much as frowned at a woman. So far the man had not relapsed.

During the confrontation, Danny learned disturbing details about the attorney who'd defended Keith on a charge of spousal abuse. This lawyer, one Cain Kellerman, had threatened Keith's wife with the lives of her children if they did not recant their stories of their father's abuse. Naturally, they changed their stories, and Keith was acquitted.

Danny had begun his investigation into Kellerman the very next day, and what he learned convinced him that the only hope for such a vile creature was surely a bullet to the head.

He slipped the photograph into his bag and dropped the Chevy into gear, lost in the consideration of the facts. A loud *thump* from behind startled him.

He twisted his neck and saw that he'd backed into another car. Ellen Bennett's gray Lincoln crowded his own.

He shoved his gearshift back into park and jumped out as the older woman pushed her door open. "Are you okay?" he asked. No damage to their bumpers that he could see. "I'm so sorry, how careless of me!"

"It's you, Danny!" Ellen stepped out of her car. "Dear me, I didn't see you!"

"No, it was me who didn't see you." He took her hand and guided her a few steps from the car. "The important question is, are you all right?"

"Of course. It was hardly a tap." The midday sun turned her white curls into a halo. She'd become a mother figure to him, which suited him well because he had no other family in the United States. It was good to have a neighbor to care for, even if that care amounted only to mowing the yard once a week and making the occasional repair around the house. Ellen's husband had died four years ago, at about the same time Danny moved into the neighborhood.

She chuckled. "My, my, what a fright that was. You sure there's no damage?" She eyed the kissing bumpers.

"Maybe a scratch, but that's it."

She looked him up and down. "You're smashing today. Hal used to wear khaki slacks, too." She reached for his hair and touched it gingerly. "Have I told you his hair was as dark as yours before it went gray?"

"Yes, more than once."

"You're not working today?"

I have work to do that you'll never know about.

"I have an appointment," Danny said. "Just an errand to help out a friend."

His name is Cain Kellerman and he is a viper.

"Good for you. I have to make this up to you. Let me make you lunch."

"No, there's no need—"

"I insist! I practically demolished your car!"

Danny hesitated only a moment. "Well, if you insist." He offered her a wide smile and dipped his head. "I would love that. I could join you tomorrow."

Ellen looked back at the cars and shook her head. "My, my, my. I think I'm getting old." Her eyes darted up to him. "Tomorrow? No, my dear, now! I put out a fresh jar of sun tea this morning, and I can make up some sandwiches in a jiffy. Have you eaten? It's past noon."

"No, but I really should—"

"Please, it would make me feel so much better."

Choice: A bite with Ellen, or directly to the scene to kill Cain Kellerman.

Consider: Once Ellen got something in her head, it was easier to go with her than to change her.

Consider: Danny's plans could accommodate a quick lunch if it brought the woman peace of mind.

Consider: He liked Ellen very much.

"You talked me into it. Let me just pull my car into my drive."

"Wonderful."

Ten minutes later, he was seated at her kitchen table, marking the condensation on an ice-cold glass of tea with a lazy finger as she told him yet another story about her late husband, Hal, who had gone completely senile two years before his death.

"You should have seen it, Danny." She set down a plate bearing two club sandwiches made of American cheese, ham, and turkey. "He was out there in the backyard at midnight dressed in nothing but his pajama top and socks."

"No underwear?" Danny bit into his sandwich and took a sip of tea to wash it down.

"No! Butt as white as a split volleyball. A flat one at that."

"And you just left him out there?"

"Well, for a little bit, sure. It was too precious a moment to ruin—Hal out there wandering around muttering and me in here watching him. I couldn't stop laughing. Hal had a sagging white butt, I'm telling you."

The image, however humorous, momentarily suppressed his appetite.

"I assume you eventually rescued him?"

"Of course. I called to him from the deck, and he turned to me and asked if I noticed that the sprinklers weren't working. He'd been going on for a few days about the grass getting brown, but our sprinklers came on at night, and he'd gotten it into his mind that they needed to be checked."

"Every good man wants to give his lovely wife a green lawn."

"Well, he obviously thought so."

"Why was he naked?"

"I'm getting to that. When I asked him why he was in his socks, he said it was so he could tell if the grass was wet. When he saw me staring at his waist he looked down, stared at himself for a bit, then looked up at me with an impish grin that only Hal could do. 'Wow,' he said. 'I'm naked. You horny?'"

Ellen slapped her knee and laughed until Danny thought she might split her side. He joined her.

Moments like these—moments when pure goodness put to shame the selfish ambition of abusers—compelled him to do what he did.

Danny lived and killed so the Ellens of the world could grow old with their husbands and laugh when those old men wandered into the backyard wearing only socks and pajama tops.

He and Ellen ate their club sandwiches while she dug up a few more stories that made Danny laugh, one in particular about the time a porcupine got stuck in their chimney. Hal was the self-sufficient type who would work a challenge to its bitter end before calling for help. On that particular day, his temperament earned him a blackened face full of quills.

Whenever Danny spent time with Ellen, his convictions grew stronger and his compulsion to cleanse the world grew more urgent. Truth be told, if this sweet woman was ever victimized, Danny would likely forget his vow never to draw out his subject's pain in anger or for revenge.

He kissed Ellen on the cheek and left her house half an hour later, eager to resume his task. Slowly he piloted the car south toward Long Beach, then west toward the hills of San Pedro, reassured of his calling.

IT TOOK HIM an hour to arrive and position his car behind an oil storage container on the bluff above Kellerman's house. Another ten minutes to work his way down the hill.

Danny had spent a full week figuring out how to disable the security system. He'd subsequently been in the house on three separate occasions to observe the layout and search for incriminating evidence. As a result, he knew precisely how he would gain entrance on this day: through the closet window. He had cut the glass along the frame two nights earlier.

A firm bump with a gloved hand now popped out the glass. He crawled in, then replaced it.

If he'd learned one thing as a young assassin, it was that the only skill more important than combat was mission preparedness. Surveillance. Intelligence. Positioning. These were nine-tenths of any victory. The rest came down to flawless execution and ruthless violence, both of which he'd mastered despite his youth.

Danny let his eyes adjust to the darkness, then set his bag

down and withdrew his syringe. He readied the needle and squatted in the corner behind the closet door.

Patience.

Like many successful individuals, Kellerman was a person of habit. Indeed, it was the man's predictability that had enabled Danny to follow him to a hotel one night, where he'd slaughtered a prostitute and then returned her to his van in trash bags. Danny had watched through night-vision glasses as the man buried the body parts in the desert landfill east of the city.

It was an open-and-shut case, the first and last time Danny felt any need to tail the man. How such a successful attorney who traveled so broadly for a living could be this demented was beyond him.

Danny was so sickened that he'd begun looking for the first opportunity to take the man out. Each week of delay meant another dead woman. Why weren't the police on this? Perhaps they were.

Either way, Danny would end it tonight and wash his mind of the man.

The few times Danny had observed Kellerman returning home, presumably from work, the lawyer arrived around six. Traffic must have held the man up this night, because his entry door didn't open until six thirty-five.

Danny stood and waited in the dark closet.

The man walked about the kitchen for a while before coming back to his bedroom. He did his business in the toilet and flushed. Washed his hands. Burped. Twice.

All of this, every footfall indicating that the vile creature still lived, disgusted Danny to no end. The temptation to skip the usual procedure and kill the man now felt nearly overwhelming. Why waste the drugs on him? Danny had no intention of giving this one a choice.

So why go through all the motions?

His thoughts were cut short by the opening closet door.

Danny felt no anxiety, only calm. His advantage over the man was insurmountable. Even if Kellerman had a black belt in tae kwon do—Danny didn't know, because he hadn't gone that deep into the man's history—it would not affect the outcome.

The man turned on the light and walked in. Danny waited for him to cross into his field of vision before reaching out and injecting him with the drug.

As expected, Kellerman snorted like a bull and crashed back against a line of hangers, half of them empty.

"Hello, Mr. Kellerman," Danny said. "I'm here to settle the score for the women you've killed. Think of me as your Grim Reaper."

"What?" He drew his hand away from his neck, bloody. His face went red and he swore.

"That wasn't the dying apology I was looking for," Danny said. "I'm sorry, but your time is up."

Danny pulled out his gun, silencer already fixed in place, and pointed it at the man. He wasn't going to mess around with this one. Truthfully, Kellerman had made him wait longer than anticipated in this stuffy closet, and Danny was anxious to be done. He still had to clean the scene and dispose of the body, which would take the better part of the night.

Cain Kellerman dropped to one knee as the drug started to kick in. The full effect could take anywhere from seconds to minutes, depending on how much Danny had managed to inject.

"Hold on..." The man's face was now white; he held out a trembling hand, palm out. "Just hold on!"

"I have what I need," Danny said.

"I can give you more...This is Bourque? He sent you?"

The Bourque Foundation. Kellerman's employer, who had lured him away from criminal law some years ago. Danny knew little about the man behind the foundation.

"What about him?"

"Jonathan Bourque. He's cleaning house, isn't he? Killing off the people who know what he's up to? His attorneys? So now he's after me, too?" The man's breathing started to thicken. "I can pay you more than he can."

"I'm not for hire. I'm here because you're a killer. A sick snake who abuses women in the worst way."

"Getting Bourque will get you the sickest snake of them all. They think he's clean, you know. He used to be a priest...but the bodies of his victims could fill a graveyard. I can get him for you."

"I'm here for you, and honestly, I can't imagine anyone worse than you, no matter how many bodies he's buried."

"Who am I? Just one more on a list of people Bourque's killed this week. Who are you? Just one more killer on his pay-roll."

"You're misunderstanding," Danny said. "Your employer, Jonathan Bourque, did not send me."

"I can pay more." He reached out and grabbed a hanging belt to steady himself. "Name your price." He ripped the glasses from his face. Blue eyes glistened with tears of desperation. "Please, I'm begging you. I don't deserve to die. I'm a nobody over there. I just do what they want us to do with the cash. I...I don' wan' die."

"Why did you kill the women, Cain?"

His face wrinkled up. He was pathetic.

"I'm notta bad man I..."

Danny shot him twice in the chest to save them both any prolonged agony. The man knelt as if made of stone, then top-pled over face-first.

Silence filled the house. Only the cleanup remained.

Jonathan Bourque. The name hung in his mind. Took up occupancy in a secure place there.

Danny would have to see about this man who apparently was killing off his attorneys to protect himself. What kind of man would do that?

What kind of priest?

8

THE DAY LAMONT vanished from my life began just like any other day in the glass house by the sea.

He was gone for three days on a quick trip to Japan, and he would return Thursday, which meant he would be home by Thursday evening at the latest. I was certain to treat every day as if he might return early, because he sometimes did.

The sun was already well over the house when I climbed out of bed that Thursday. I had been very careful not to make any messes. In fact, after the way Lamont had treated me to a candlelight dinner overlooking the sea, I was determined to make his return very special.

I went through my normal daily activities—showering, cleansing, taking my pills, dressing in a clean pair of flannel pajamas, making my bed, wiping out the shower, wiping out the sinks, polishing his shoes, dusting the electronics, rubbing off any marks from the glass, and cleansing once more to be sure—but because I wanted to treat Lamont, I set out to do more.

Using a gallon of warm water and four ounces of vinegar, I carefully cleaned the marble floors until they were as shiny as a mirror. I polished the stainless-steel refrigerator and the stove-top, then all of the appliances, until they sparkled like stars.

Lamont's bedroom was one level down, in the basement, and it was the one room that I normally did not clean because it would upset his flow, as he put it, and I did not like it when his flow was upset. But on that Thursday I dared to sneak down and dust his nightstand and his dresser. He had a trophy room off his bedroom, but I did not go in there.

The exertion made my head dizzy, so I had to rest a few times, once for a full hour when I accidentally fell asleep on the leather couch. By the time I finished everything, the sun was going down. I decided to take another shower so I could be spotless for him.

Freshly dressed and squeaky clean, I prepared some food—a cucumber salad with olives and mayonnaise, some sliced salami, crackers, and tomato soup—so he could have a snack after his drive from the airport.

I checked and rechecked the entire house twice to be sure everything was just perfect, then sat down to wait.

When the living room clock chimed seven, I started to wonder why he was so late. I checked the digital clock on my nightstand to make sure I was reading the right time. Seven oh two. He must have hit traffic.

When the clock struck eight I grew worried. The cucumber salad would be getting rubbery and the soup would be cold, so I busied myself by preparing them again.

By nine I was biting my fingernails. By the time ten o'clock came and went, I was climbing the walls.

Had he been in an accident? Anything could have happened. If there was a problem, the authorities would visit the house to tell me, right? There was no regular phone in the house, not that I knew of. Lamont used his cell phone for everything.

He'd given me a special black-and-yellow cell phone preprogrammed with his number for emergencies only. I'd called him on it once when I was lonely, and he rushed home. But that was the only time I'd used it. It was important that I use it only for dire emergencies.

At eleven o'clock I decided this was a dire emergency. I hurried to my nightstand, pulled open the drawer, and withdrew the black-and-yellow phone. I couldn't get it to come on, so I had to charge it.

My head was throbbing with worry and I had to mutter comforting words to myself to remain calm. *This will all work out. This will all work out.* Everything always worked out with Lamont. He was the only thing in my life that had *ever* worked out.

But my concern swelled like a volcano. I couldn't live without him! What if he was dead? What if Jonathan Bourque had killed him? What if his plane had crashed? What if a truck had slammed into him on the Pacific Coast Highway and pushed him over a cliff?

I tried the phone again, and this time the screen lit up. *Please let him answer. Please, please.*

He didn't answer. It rang ten times then went to his recording. "I can't get to the phone right now. I will call you back." My fingers began to tremble and my eyes filled with tears.

I called the number twelve times over thirty minutes and got nothing but his message. I was frantic. Something was terribly wrong and I was completely lost.

In my mind, Cyrus was at my door, waiting for me to stick

my head out so he could throw a noose around it and haul me away to finish what he'd started.

The monsters were hiding behind the shrubs on either side of the driveway. *We're gonna kill you, Renee. You just wait, we're gonna cut you open and suck the blood right out of you.*

None of my worrying set off the chime that announced a car in the driveway. No amount of staring made the black-and-yellow phone ring.

It didn't occur to me until two or three in the morning that all of the doors were locked from the outside, including the door that led out to the deck, which Lamont locked as part of his ritual. Not that I wanted to get out, but if I did, how would I open any of the doors?

Even the windows were sealed shut. One less thing to worry about, he'd said. He'd spot-welded all of the latches long before I came to the house.

We'd covered this, but I couldn't remember what Lamont had told me to do if I ever had to get out. I was on a psychotropic drug and also a sedative to help me cope, and loss of short-term memories was one of the side effects. Memories like how to get out of the house.

I did not sleep that night. By the time the horizon turned white with the new day, my frayed nerves were starting to shred. I was mumbling at the monsters, daring them to keep Lamont away. I began to curse Jonathan Bourque profusely, certain that he was behind Lamont's disappearance.

I paced the kitchen and living room, my fierce eyes fixed on the door, begging it open. "Please, please, please, please…" It remained closed like the door to a vault.

I called the number on the special black-and-yellow cell phone repeatedly, and each time heard only his message: "I can't get to the phone right now. I will call you back."

The phone was one that could only place calls to numbers programmed by the owner, who was Lamont, and 9-1-1. The latter would bring the police. Did I know the address? I couldn't remember. Mail never came to the house, but to a mailbox down the street. Maybe authorities would know the address by the 9-1-1 call.

The thought of police terrified me, though. If Jonathan Bourque was behind this, and I was sure he was, he would have the police under his thumb. What had Lamont said? Something about how corrupt the law was. I should take the law into my own hands, like that vigilante did. Meaning don't trust the police, right?

But I was no vigilante. I was a scared girl who weighed only a hundred pounds, and I was all alone in a big glass house by the sea. I started to cry.

With tears running down my cheeks and exhaustion overwhelming my body, I finally collapsed on the leather sofa and fell into a dreamless sleep.

It was afternoon before I woke and sat up, wondering why I was in the living room. But then I remembered, and I began to run through the house calling Lamont's name. He wasn't in my room, nor the kitchen, nor the billiards room, nor the storage room, nor his bedroom.

My world was crumbling, and I was powerless to prop it up with sound reasoning or comforting thoughts. My predicament was painfully simple.

Lamont had vanished.

I was alone.

I had no way to get out of the house.

This last matter was a mere bug on the screen of my mind. I was preoccupied by loss, not self-preservation. In the absence of any reasonable alternative, I set my jaw and resolved to wait until Lamont returned, no matter how long it took.

I had plenty of food, enough to last for weeks, for all I ate. I had clothes, a bed, music, water, everything I needed until Lamont came home.

By nightfall I had convinced myself that my anxiety was all a mistake. Something very simple was keeping Lamont away. I'd misunderstood him when he'd said Thursday.

I hummed and sang to pass the time. I ate. I cleansed. I cleaned. I took my medication except for the sedative, because I didn't want to sleep. I embraced denial as if it, not Lamont, was my savior.

My determined resolve collapsed on Saturday at midnight, when I remembered with perfect clarity that Lamont had indeed said Thursday. He'd said Thursday, and it was now five minutes past twelve on Sunday and he wasn't home.

Lamont was either gone or dead. Just like my dad.

I fell to my face on the shiny marble floor and wept. I scolded myself for being the kind of person who always ended up alone. I begged Lamont to come and get me. I cried out for my mother even though I knew she was dead.

Slowly my tears ran dry and I lay there, facedown, for quite a long time. Then I pushed myself to my feet, retreated to my bedroom, and climbed under the covers.

I did not clean up the mess I'd left on the floor from all my weeping and slobbering. That would have to wait just this once.

I rose Sunday morning and, not bothering to put on my slippers, drifted through the house like a ghost, knowing I wouldn't find him. Still, I looked. Even under the beds this time.

My heart was lead in my chest. My face felt like it might fall off my head. Each step felt like a step farther into hell.

I didn't bother to shower on Sunday—I just couldn't. I couldn't listen to music. I couldn't prepare food or clean. I could hardly think.

So I sat on the stuffed leather chair in the living room and stared out at the ocean for most of the day, clinging to a fading hope that at any moment the door would fly open and Lamont would crash in to rescue me as he had once before.

He didn't.

MONDAY MORNING WAS like Sunday morning in every way except this one: I accepted that I was alone. Not just in the house, but in the world. Someone had taken Lamont from me, and I would have to go on without him.

The thought was overwhelming. For four days, I'd focused on Lamont, on my concern for his safety and on my loss of him. Now I was forced to start thinking about Renee.

What was I to do? How could I live? Would I have to leave the house? Who would buy the groceries? Who would pay the bills? Did I have any money?

Was Lamont really dead? Would there be a funeral?

I paced in front of the big window overlooking the ocean, hands on my cheeks. *Think, Renee. You have to pull yourself together. You have to figure out what to do.*

The house wasn't in my name, I was sure of that. To my recollection, he'd never mentioned anything about a will or arrangements other than how to get out of the house, and I couldn't even remember the details of that conversation.

I stopped pacing and made my first decision. I had to find a way out of the house. I couldn't stay cooped up in here forever, could I? The food would run out eventually. What if I knocked over a candle and set the place on fire? How would I get out then?

I had to get out!

Frantic with this new problem, I ran to the front door, quickly unlocked all the latches, and tugged. It didn't budge. I screamed at the door and jerked as hard as I could, but I might as well have been tugging on a solid concrete block.

I flew to the other doors and found them no more responsive, as expected. Without functioning doors, the most obvious way out was through a window, but they were all welded shut and I wasn't about to break a window. Lamont would have an absolute fit.

I would have a fit if I had to break one of those beautiful windows that I'd shined so dutifully all these months. Besides, the glass panes were thick, I wasn't even sure I could break one if I had to; besides, Lamont had said not even a shotgun blast could blow one out.

Still, I ran through the house, checking every window just to be sure that none of the welds had cracked. There weren't many because, except for the wall facing the ocean, the rest of the outer walls were made of solid brick.

The doors were locked. The windows were sealed. I was helpless!

There was a pull-down attic ladder at the end of the hall. I'd poked my head up there once, saw nothing but insulation, and made a hasty retreat. But now I wondered if there could be a vent in the space.

A shower of debris fell to the floor when I pulled the ladder down, and I ignored the temptation to sweep it up. I climbed the ladder, found a light switch on the frame at the top, and studied the attic by the dim light of one incandescent bulb.

Past mounds of pink insulation, through a maze of cross members, in the attic's farthest wall, rays of light angled through the slats of a square vent.

I stared for a while, considering the challenge of navigating my way to the vent. Maybe I was light enough to walk on the ceiling without breaking through. No. No, I couldn't risk that. If

I crashed through to the floor below and broke my legs I might die in the house, alone.

Getting to the vent wasn't the only challenge. I had to get it open, and even then I didn't know how far it was above the ground.

What else could I do? I had to pass through the darkness ahead if I wanted to reach the light beyond.

Teetering on one of the main beams, I made my choice. The wood was solid and several inches wide, so I moved quickly and crossed the attic with surprising ease. I reached the square attic vent, gripped the slats with my fingers, and peered out, feeling elated.

I could see the driveway and the bushes on either side, but the ground looked too far down for me to jump. A large palm tree swayed in the wind ten feet away. I couldn't jump ten feet!

The slats bent in my hands, so I tugged at one and was rewarded with a crack. Like a woman clawing at the face of a thug in a dark alleyway, I attacked the thin wood with both hands and tore the slats away, one by one, until I was panting and dizzy enough to fall.

A heavy metal screen protected the vent from the elements, and the moment I put my hand on it, I knew there was no way I could break through the barrier. But I could see the screws that held the screen in place. If I could unscrew them, I would have a clear escape path.

Rope.

If I had rope, I could climb down. Then I could unlock the dead bolts on the front door. Once the house was open, I could come and go as I wanted, which would only be when I was absolutely desperate for food or supplies.

I had to find a screwdriver and some rope. There was only one place where those might be.

I scurried back to the attic door like a wheezing rat, lowered myself into the hallway, and took the stairs at the end of the hall down to Lamont's bedroom.

I ran into his room, hit the overhead light switch, and hurried to the trophy room door. Locked. Naturally. But the key was on the dresser. I knew it well.

Thirty seconds later, having unlocked both dead bolts, I stood in the doorway to his inner sanctum. I hadn't had this much exercise in over a year, and my arms were trembling.

Hold it together, Renee. Don't collapse now. Find a screwdriver and some rope and get out of the house. That's all you have to do.

I nearly turned around and ran back to my room then, because I really didn't want to leave the house. I was lost without Lamont, a ghost without a home. All of this was pointless.

And yet I walked into the trophy room and looked around. The room smelled like Lamont. His desk sat on the near wall, an ornate wooden antique that had three drawers on each side. His papers were neatly stacked on the surface, everything in its perfect place, screaming his name.

Two of the walls were lined with mounted heads, like those in my own pink-and-white room. These were my protectors when he was gone, Lamont said. I knew the ones down here well: a water buffalo that was too large for the room, two gazelles, a zebra, a boar, and a fox, all from Africa.

I saw their glassy eyes staring at me now, filling me all over again with the weight of my loss. He'd always meant so well for me. However quirky all his compulsions were, he was the only one who loved me.

Move, Renee. Get out before they come.

The new thought sharpened my sense of urgency. If Lamont had been killed, wouldn't the men who'd done it come to his house to clean up anything that might point to Bourque's illegal activities?

The rope was easy to find. Three lassos hung from a hook on one of the walls. I took down the thickest one, though the thinnest would likely hold my weight.

The screwdriver was a different matter.

I'd never been through Lamont's desk and I didn't want to do it now, but if I were him that's where I would have put a screwdriver. So I pulled out the drawers one by one and rummaged through their contents.

I found paper clips, several old cameras, files and empty notebooks, binoculars, various electrical cords and adapters, rubber bands, a pocketknife—which might have worked, though it looked too flimsy—and other assorted items, but no screwdriver.

The bottom right drawer was locked. Having run out of places to search for a screwdriver, I began to panic. I put my heels against the desk's legs and tugged with a grunt.

The old wood around the lock crumbled and the drawer flew open.

Stunned by my success, I leaned in. There was no screwdriver in the drawer. There was, however, a large number of neatly bound and stacked hundred-dollar bills.

Money. A lot of money.

Of course, this made perfect sense. Lamont was the kind of wealthy man who, not trusting any system but his own, would keep a stash of money for emergencies.

The ceiling above me creaked, and I caught my breath.

There it was again: the soft shuffle of a step and another soft creak.

My first thought was that Lamont had come home.

My second was that I had just broken into his desk.

I shoved the drawer shut without making any attempt to hide my breach of his privacy and flew from the room like a bird from a cage.

He called out when I was halfway across his room. "Hello?"

It wasn't his voice. I pulled up sharply and listened without daring to move a muscle.

The feet padded softly above me again. Whomever they belonged to, they were not Lamont's. The police, maybe? Or a friend of Lamont's who'd come to get me and take me to him?

Or the people who had killed him.

Four days of wild imaginations sliced through my mind again, severing the nerves that told my muscles to move.

If they were the police, wouldn't they have identified themselves? If they had come on Lamont's behalf, wouldn't they have called my name? I had left the ladder to the attic down, and the floor was littered with evidence that someone was or had been in the house.

The vent in the attic was broken.

Terrified I would be discovered, I acted without any plan whatsoever. I ran back into the trophy room, pulled the door closed behind me, and slid both dead bolts home. The key was in my pocket.

Feet continued to walk overhead, more than one pair, I thought.

I turned off the lights, groped my way into the corner behind the desk, slid to my seat, drew my legs close to my chest, and waited for them to force the door open and kill me.

9

MY WAIT DID not last long. I could hear the soft mumble of voices as the people above moved around on the main floor, and with each step they took, I imagined new scenarios, all of which ended badly for me.

When the sounds finally stopped, I was sure it was because they had left the main floor and were descending the stairs to Lamont's room.

I was right.

"It's empty," someone said.

"Check the closet." Another muffled voice.

The knob on the door rattled. "It's locked. Framed in steel with a dead bolt."

"Look for a key."

I could hear them opening and closing drawers, and I held my breath, praying they wouldn't find a second key that I didn't know about. If I knew Lamont, they wouldn't be able to bang the door down. I clung to that hope. A rotting desk inside a locked room was one thing. Getting into that locked room without a key was another.

"Nothing. Try the door again. Use force."

They spoke in the mechanical voices of men who used force for a living. But after a few hard crashes into the door, the man applying that force backed off.

"Not gonna happen."

"*Make* it happen! Bourque says *everything*, he means *everything*."

"It's gonna take a torch. Two bolts deadheaded into a quarter-inch steel plate."

The other man swore. "I'll get it. Check the rest of the attic."

They left, padding up the stairs.

Crouched in the dark corner, I no longer had to guess at my predicament. Lamont's instincts hadn't betrayed him. Bourque either had him or had killed him, and he somehow learned that Lamont wasn't living alone. They'd come here to eliminate me.

I had two choices that I could see, and both were terrifying. One: I could try to sneak out now, leave the house with nothing but my pajamas to my name, and wait for Cyrus to hunt me down.

Two: I could take the time to grab the money and then sneak out, hoping my delay didn't give them enough time to get the torch from their vehicle and return.

I didn't want to see Cyrus's face ever again, not unless it was at the end of a long shotgun firmly in my grasp. So I stood and hurried toward the light switch, banging into the desk as I went.

Ignoring the pain in my thigh, I dropped down by the bottom drawer and pulled it open. Now I had another choice to make. How much?

I thought about taking the whole drawer but rejected the idea immediately. I could make a sling of my flannel shirt front and carry as much as it would hold. Anything I stuffed into my waistband would only fall through my pant legs when I ran.

I glanced around the room for a bag or anything I could use but saw nothing. I had wasted valuable time; if I waited much longer it wouldn't matter how much money I took.

Standing, I slid my long flannel pajama pants off and then quickly tied a knot at the bottom of each leg. My top was long enough to cover most of me. I would have rather run outside in an oversize shirt than go topless.

I feverishly stuffed all the money packets into my makeshift bag, slung it over my shoulder, and, hearing no creaking or walking above me, unlocked the door to Lamont's bedroom.

Not until I was on the bottom step did I consider what might happen if they returned to find the door unlocked. They would hunt me down before I managed to get off the property.

I flew back, locked both dead bolts using the key, then ran up the stairs. It was now a race—either I'd get out the front door without being seen, or I was dead.

My heart was weak from the lack of exercise, and it was flopping like a waterless fish. I was sure they'd opened the doors from the outside, so I sprinted for the side door leading into the garage, thinking I could slip out the back of the garage and then...

I didn't know what then. I only had to get out of the house before they saw me.

The door was open. I yanked it wide and for the first time stepped into Lamont's garage. Light streamed in through two small windows near the ceiling. I closed the door behind me and allowed myself to breathe.

Lamont's BMW was gone. A white Audi sedan sat in the

third bay. As much as I would have liked to zoom away to safety in a car, I wasn't sure I could still drive well enough to navigate busy streets. Or, for that matter, lead a chase through those streets—they wouldn't just let me drive away. Besides, I didn't have the keys.

I tiptoed to a door that led out the back, twisted the lock, and pulled it open a crack. I recognized the terrain leading down to the rocky beach. No one blocked the way that I could see.

Now the challenge of getting away from the house unseen confronted me. My tender feet couldn't exactly blaze a trail through the underbrush, and running down the street in nothing but a flannel top, with a sack that look conspicuously like pajama bottoms stuffed with hundred-dollar bills, was hardly the way to slip into obscurity.

I stood with the garage door opened a foot, frozen by the thought that I had come so far only to go nowhere.

The Audi was there to my left. The Audi had a trunk. What if I hid in the trunk until they left?

I heard the solid *clunk* of a door closing inside the house, and that got my feet moving in the direction of the car. I only hoped that there was a way to open the trunk from the dash. And that the Audi wasn't locked. What if the Audi was locked?

The driver's door came open when I pulled the handle. Thank God. Thank God, thank God. I dropped my two-legged bag on the ground by the driver's door before slipping into the front seat. I pushed buttons and pulled levers, praying for the right one. The hood popped halfway; the steering wheel tilted up. Where was the trunk release?

I muttered something nasty in a raspy voice.

The lever that opened the trunk was located to the left of the steering wheel. I learned this when I jerked it and was rewarded with a solid *pop* behind me.

Elated, I dipped out, grabbed my makeshift moneybag, and ran to the rear. I threw the stuffed pajamas into the trunk and was starting to climb in when I saw that I'd left the driver's door open. Nothing I did was smooth, but at least I was thinking on my feet.

It took me five seconds to close the door.

It took me fifteen to get into the trunk, because when I had one leg inside, I realized I couldn't lock myself in. How would I get out? I pulled my leg out and stared dumbfounded until I saw the cord with a handle marked TRUNK RELEASE.

Of course! All cars must have a simple means of escape for stowaways. Moments later, I was in the dark trunk with my back to the money-filled pajamas, sweating profusely and breathing hard but otherwise alive and safe.

For the moment.

Hidden away in the trunk, I could hear nothing but my breathing, which gradually slowed until I was able to draw air through my nose. Then the real wait began. A dozen times I was tempted to pull that cord and see if Bourque's men had gone. How would I know?

I would wait until dark, I decided. Once it was dark, I could climb out and sneak around unnoticed. Then again, legs as white as mine would likely be noticed half a mile down the road. Maybe I could sneak back into the house and get properly dressed.

Or I could stay in the house until I figured out what to do.

A rumbling noise made my decision for me. It was pitch dark in the trunk, but I could not mistake the sound of the garage door opening.

"I'll lock up."

I blinked in the darkness. The voice was muffled, but I thought that's what I heard. They were leaving!

The car shifted with the weight of a driver climbing in. With a single beat, the engine purred to life and my heart nearly stopped. They were taking the car!

I groped for the trunk release and found it but stopped short of pulling the cord. Popping the trunk now would be the worst thing I could possibly do. They would see the skinny white girl tugging a two-legged bag from the trunk and then running across the driveway. Once they got over their shock, they would either gun me down or run me over.

The car was moving. Backing up.

Rock music blared from speakers behind me. I was trapped with Led Zeppelin singing "Stairway to Heaven."

It took me only a few seconds to conclude that my life was as good as over. I should have sneaked out to the beach and hidden behind a large rock. I could have hidden in the corner of the garage with a blanket draped over my head. I was a fool not to dig a hole in the sand and bury myself until they had left.

But now I was speeding away from the house, surely to a field where they would drag me out and kill me, or onto a ship that would be sent overseas, where stolen cars bring in good money.

Motion sickness overwhelmed me and I had to throw up once, but after I wiped my face on a cuff of my flannel money-bag, I felt better.

I tried to keep track of how long we were on the road. I wanted a rough idea of how far from Malibu we would end up, but time drifted and I lost track.

I had left my pills in the house, I realized. Without them, the monsters would return. The blue pill was the one that helped me deal with the trauma I'd experienced, and the sedative helped keep me calm. Honestly, I don't know why I took the sedative. I felt calm enough in the house, but now I wished I had brought both bottles.

My mind imagined a dozen scenarios of what might happen once that trunk opened.

I had lived with men who used violence to get what they wanted, and the memories came back to me in fragments, each one more sickening than the last. Screams, the crunch of bones, gunshots. They were bundled in a heroin-induced fog from long ago, but I was surprised by how real they felt as they surfaced.

I started to cry softly as I lay there on that hard trunk floor, and I resigned myself to the fact that once they opened the trunk, I would be executed. My last threads of self-control fell away when one of Lamont's favorite songs by Coldplay, "What If," played over the speakers.

It was a sad song about not belonging that he would sometimes listen to while drinking a glass of red wine on the balcony. "I hope you never leave me, Renee," he would say. "I don't know what I would do if you left me."

I would throw my arms around his neck. "I would never leave you, Lamont! Never!"

In the trunk, I began to weep uncontrollably at the memory. Somehow this was all my fault. I was leaving him now, wasn't I? Guilt racked my body and I shook with sobs. It wasn't logical, I see that now, but my anguish was no less real than if I'd spit in his face to thank him for all he'd done for me. If the music hadn't been playing so loudly, my sorrow would have alerted the driver and gotten me killed on the spot.

As the miles rolled by I began to settle, enough to start thinking more about the present than the past.

I concocted absurd little plans. When the trunk opened I would spring out and bite the man on his nose before he had time to react. When he grabbed at his bloody face, I would snatch my moneybag and fly into the woods.

Or, when they opened the trunk, I would play dead and bide my time until they were off guard and leaning over me to poke me. Then I would swing my arm and hit the man on his head with...something...

This made me think of a tire iron. I felt around for a way to get to the spare tire. It must have been under the trunk floor, because I couldn't find a latch to open any tire compartment.

What I did find was a small tool bag affixed with Velcro to the side wall. I unzipped it, fumbled around in the dark, and came away with a screwdriver.

A new plan formed in my mind. I could hide behind the moneybag, way back against the seat. It would be dark when they opened the trunk, and they wouldn't see me because all their attention would be on the flannel pajamas filled with hundred-dollar bills. As they gawked at the cash, stunned by their good fortune, I would fly out and stab them in the ears with the screwdriver before snatching the bag back and fleeing into an alley.

These were among my more reasonable plans fueled by a burgeoning rage at the men who had, for reasons unknown to me, forced me to leave the house. Who'd separated me from Lamont.

Jonathan Bourque. I imagined ways to deal with Jonathan Bourque. They were nasty and involved everything from boiling oil to machines with a thousand blades.

I was in the middle of just such an exotic fantasy when it occurred to me that the car had stopped for longer than the typical red light required.

The engine shut down. Startled, I went rigid. I wasn't ready! None of my carefully considered plans rose to the top of my reasoning as the way to go. In fact, if the men saw the screwdriver in my fist, they would likely shoot me.

The driver's door opened, then closed. The cooling car ticked. I pressed myself against the moneybag, mind blank with panic, expecting the trunk to pop open.

I shut down my lungs so as to not make the tiniest sound. Walking feet crunched past me, then faded.

The trunk did not open. I ran out of breath and exhaled, then sucked at the stale air. They had left me? I felt momentarily exhilarated.

I wondered if Lamont had come to my rescue again. Maybe he'd been on his way home, seen the Audi leaving, followed it here, and would take care of my abductors before coming to collect me. The trunk would open and he would swoop me out.

But I knew that was impossible.

It took me at least fifteen minutes of stillness to work up the courage to take a peek. I carefully pulled the trunk lever, eased the lid up, and saw that it was dark outside. The car was in a building with ribbed metal walls.

I was so relieved by my good fortune that I got out of the trunk without fully considering what other danger I might be in. By then it was too late. I was standing exposed in a large garage lit by one fluorescent bulb over an exit door. This was about twenty feet away.

But as far as I could see, except for about a dozen cars, I was alone in the room.

Move it, Renee! Move it, move it!

I reached in and grabbed the money, shoved it under my arm, and ran for that red EXIT sign. The concrete was cool under my feet, and that reminded me that I was naked below the waist.

I pulled up and scanned the garage. Benches with tool boxes

lined the walls. One of the cars was high on a lift. This was undoubtedly where they brought cars to modify them after stealing them. Had Bourque been involved in jacking cars?

Several overalls hung by hooks on one wall. I hurried over to them, pulled down the first pair, and stepped into it. The legs and arms were way too long, but with a little folding and scrunching it fit well enough for what I needed.

I headed back toward the door, then on second thought veered toward a tire machine and picked up a black crowbar.

The night was cool outside. I was in a warehouse district lit by a full round moon.

I stood there in my blue overalls with my money-stuffed pajamas under my arm, and I stared around in a wide-eyed daze. I needed to move, I knew that, but I had no clue where to go.

I didn't know what I would do when I got to wherever I went. I didn't really even know who I was. I knew only that I was alone, that if Lamont was alive he would have a difficult time finding me.

More than anything, I knew that I hated the man who'd done this to us. His name was Jonathan Bourque, but as far as I was concerned he was really Satan.

You have to go, Renee. You really have to go.

I wiped away my tears on the sleeve of the dirty overalls and stepped out into the night with nothing to my name but a shattered memory, a few scrawny muscles and thin bones, a pretty face, and a bag of money over my shoulder.

When I counted it later, I learned that the hundred-dollar bills added up to about three hundred thousand dollars. And that was enough money to do what I thought I needed to do.

10

Three Months Later

DANNY HANSEN STOOD at the back of the Long Beach Hilton's banquet hall waiting for Jonathan Bourque's introduction. Three large chandeliers twinkled over the banquet hall hosting the Cancer Research Fund's benefit dinner. The four hundred guests seated before the finest silver and crystal place settings were being served their choice of tenderloin, wild Atlantic salmon, or stuffed quail. Most of the men and women were dressed in black and white, like himself. They were the cream of society, unlike himself.

Yet so few understood.

Despite Danny's violent encounter with religion as a teenager, he knew that violence itself was a natural aspect of life that could be used for good or evil.

Angels and demons had both wielded violence and would again, surely. As would so-called God and the so-called devil.

Did not God make waves to crash violently on the coral? And

if that violent pounding killed a baby crab, did one blame God for making violent waves? No.

The same could be said for all the great sins decried by religion through the ages. All were condoned or embraced by God himself in given situations.

Had not Rahab the prostitute been called a great woman of faith for lying to save God's servants?

Had not Jesus taken up a weapon in anger to whip the merchants out of the temple?

Had not God blessed David with many wives and mistresses?

If any of these wealthy, tastefully dressed contributors to the Bourque Foundation's Cancer Research Fund knew of Danny's particular violence, they would undoubtedly grow red-faced and cry foul.

They had been bred, born, and raised in a system that bowed to a set of rules and laws, both religious and societal, that satisfied their need for a nice, neat box of moral understanding. In their minds, violence in general was immoral, and killing outside the law was diabolical, even when it truly benefited society.

Danny thought about that for a moment, wondering absently if he was wrong in his own understanding of the matter. What if, however absurd it seemed to him, all these thick-headed fools were actually right and he was wrong? Would God forgive him?

Either way, one thing was certain: While feeling smug for avoiding "bad" behavior, most people missed the point of morality.

Morality wasn't about following rules. It was about treating others with love. The box of rules certainly aided that cause, but only as a guideline. Danny's use of violence against the guilty was an act of love. For Danny so loved the world that he gave up his own dignity to cleanse the temple of snakes.

Like the one about to take the stage.

Crackling applause filled the room when Jonathan Bourque was introduced, and Danny shifted his attention to the man who stood from his table and strode toward the podium.

Three months had passed since Danny had taken his last subject, that being Cain Kellerman. He'd spent that time settling his spirit and examining his conscience, always mindful of his oath to change his behavior if he ever became convinced that what he did was immoral.

The ten weeks of rest had ended with affirmation. His mission to bring justice to his small corner of the world, regardless of the danger to himself, was sound. Inspired even.

Indeed, if he ever had to give his life to this cause, he would.

Jonathan Bourque was speaking in a deep, rich voice that conveyed confidence. Oratory was perhaps the gift that served him best as a priest, then as an attorney, and now as the founder and figurehead of the Bourque Foundation, which swindled unsuspecting charity donors of millions.

He was married to Cynthia Bourque, a blond woman twelve years his junior who had married him for money. She secretly hated him for many reasons, including his refusal to have any children because he privately despised children.

He stood six foot three. Six-four if you counted his black, slicked hair, which looked like it might break if tapped with a hammer. The man wore a mustache and goatee, which softened his ax-shaped nose. High cheekbones rose toward a forehead that sloped back to meet an arching hairline.

He was appealing in the sense that power and authority were attractive, but if one were to remove Bourque's social standing and sharp intelligence, he would not be considered handsome, at least not to Danny's thinking.

"Every dollar you contribute goes to work in industries

throughout the world, employing millions, before the profits are returned to charities like the Cancer Research Fund. In our last fiscal year, the Bourque Foundation returned one hundred eighty-two percent to its benefactors. I think it's safe to say that we have elevated benevolence to a whole new level, my friends."

Applause thundered. Naturally. Bourque was spoon-feeding these socialites his own special blend of manure, made to smell like strawberries and go down like a health-food smoothie.

Danny stood just inside the back door, one hand in his pocket, the other holding a glass of water. The ice was nearly melted. He took a swig, then set it down on the drink table to his left.

"Would you like another?"

He faced a woman in coattails named Kris, according to her Hilton server badge. "No thank you."

"A soft drink? Coke, Sprite, Dr Pepper? Anything?"

"A stiff martini, perhaps."

She glanced down at his jacket. "Tell me about it. These charity dinners are all the same."

"That they are. Still, as they say, it's more blessed to give than to receive."

"So they say."

"Hold the martini." He winked. "My work isn't finished."

She laughed. "The story of my life." She moved off.

Danny was willing to bear the weight of purifying the world for women like Kris, who served others in small ways that made God smile.

He sighed and returned his attention to the podium. Bourque's right hand rested inside the breast of his jacket as he talked. Without glancing down he slid long fingers into his pant pocket, slipped out a cell phone, and set it on the podium.

The information on the device could prove helpful, but people of Bourque's caliber almost always protected that information with densely encrypted codes.

Besides, the kind of information that Danny sought would be hidden in the minds of a very few people, not in a PDA. Indeed, if Cain Kellerman hadn't offered up disturbing details about Jonathan Bourque in a bid to extend his life, Danny might have already moved on, because nothing he'd found so far provided anything but circumstantial suggestions that Bourque was as evil as Kellerman had insisted.

It wasn't easy to distinguish the kind of snake that deserved crushing from the ordinary garden variety that filled half the room. In fact, the craftiest were chameleons, who could fool even the most astute observer.

Bourque finally glanced down at his phone. He'd come to the end of a sentence and his pause was natural. But for the briefest moment his eyes darted to the far entrance. If Danny judged the man correctly, there was some tension in his fleeting look.

He followed Bourque's glance to a man who stood at the other exit, PDA in hand. The head of the Bourque Foundation's security, Redding. Simon Redding. Though four inches shorter and at least as many thicker than his boss, he favored the same dark slicked-back hair. The man looked like Italian muscle from the streets of Chicago.

There was a connection between them, communication made with unspoken words, but nothing more than Danny expected, considering their roles here.

Yet if there was any one person who might unlock closely guarded secrets in Bourque's empire, it would be this man, Simon Redding. Upon seeing him for the first time that night, Danny felt his nerves tighten.

When he glanced back at Bourque, the man was talking

while staring down at the podium, nonchalantly sending a message.

"That reminds me of a joke," Bourque said, grinning. "A blonde and brunette were ushered to the gates of heaven."

When Danny looked back, Simon Redding had vanished through the exit.

"Saint Peter addressed the blonde first…"

Danny didn't hear the rest of the joke. He was moving already, slipping out the door to his rear, into the hall that ran the auditorium's length. No sign of Redding.

There was a choice to be made here, but it wasn't a moral choice. He could either return to the banquet hall and follow through with his intention to meet Bourque for the first time if the opportunity presented itself, or he could take a few minutes to perhaps learn more about Redding.

He would never put himself in the position to pressure Redding for information, naturally. Directly involving any person other than the subject presented unacceptable risks. What he learned from others about his subjects had to come in the course of ordinary encounters.

Then again, Redding might be the key to his investigation.

There were three doors in the hall. The man had to have taken one of them. Danny headed for the exit closest to the banquet hall, the one with a red-letter sign that indicated it was for EMPLOYEES ONLY. He pushed through the door.

Metal stairs. Ascending and descending.

The clap of hard leather soles on steps echoed below. Danny eased the door shut behind him, slipped off his shoes, and descended quickly.

A door closed below. From what he could tell, he was alone in the stairwell.

The steps ended two floors down at a door labeled UTILITIES.

He slipped his shoes back on and walked through, entering a short hall. To the right, two closets that he checked were stuffed with supplies: spare fuses, lightbulbs, coffeemakers, tools, and the like.

Unless he'd made a mistake and descended one too many floors, whoever had preceded him had gone through the door at the other end of the hall.

Danny was about to back out of the second closet when he caught sight of a black-and-yellow box knife with a retractable blade. The useful tool struck him as appropriate given the thuggish appearance of the man he was following.

He plucked it off the bench and dropped it into his pocket, then moved down the hall on the balls of his feet.

A sharp slap brought him up short. The sound was muffled but as undeniable as a cap gun on a winter morning.

His heart lodged itself in his throat and he backed to the wall. He might have stumbled upon a lovers' quarrel off the hotel's beaten track—two employees whose affair had been discovered and were sorting matters out rather violently. Or it might be something less ominous. Perhaps a magazine had fallen off a shelf and landed flat on concrete.

He didn't think so.

He slipped along the wall, up to a door with a glass window that peered into a darkened room. The sound he'd heard had come from farther in, perhaps from beyond the single interior door that allowed light to seep past the gap at its foot.

The knob turned in his hand and he eased into the dark room. Immediately voices reached him.

"I told you, I only wanted to talk to him." The voice sounded timid. Female.

The slap that followed surely wasn't female. Amazingly the woman did not cry out.

It took considerable control on Danny's part to remain calm. He couldn't barge in without jeopardizing both the woman's health and his cover. He had to think. Feeling exposed, he stepped to the wall beside the lighted door.

"Mr. Bourque's a very powerful man. He has enemies." Danny assumed the low voice belonged to Redding. "It's my job to make sure he's never in danger. You're trying my patience. I need to know what you think you know that is so damaging to him."

"Let me talk to him," she said. "I'm sure it's a misunderstanding."

"You can tell me."

"I'm sorry, I can't do that."

"Why not?"

Hesitation. "I swore not to involve anyone but Jonathan Bourque. But I have it all written down in a safe-deposit box, and if anything happens to me, the truth will go to the press."

Danny doubted this. It was a television cliché that had little usefulness in the real world.

Feet shuffled on the concrete floor. "I don't think you understand your predicament," Redding said. "I should turn you over to the police and press charges. They are good friends with us and would agree to uncovering your intentions. Or I could—"

"I have a bloody lip," the woman interrupted.

"Heroin addicts found facedown on the street often have blood on them."

She didn't fire back so quickly.

"I'm not an addict. That's not me."

"But it will be you if I choose to turn you over to the police. I'll shoot you up, beat you down, and drop you off." He paused. "My other choice is to ask you again, politely, who you are and what your interest in Mr. Bourque is."

Danny's mind spun with the implications of the exchange.

The woman wasn't known by Redding but claimed to have information that threatened Bourque. The fact that Redding took the threat so seriously suggested Bourque indeed had much to hide, some knowledge that he would protect with force.

"The thing about heroin addicts is that they can do some pretty strange things to themselves without really knowing what they're doing," the man continued. "I knew one who cut off his nose to stop the itching. The police would think nothing of a strung-out girl coming in with a few missing fingers."

"You're going to cut off my fingers?"

"Not all of them."

This territory was familiar to Danny, and he knew two things already. One, Redding—assuming the low voice belonged to Bourque's man—would think nothing of carrying out his threat.

Two, the woman either was truly naive or knew how to play naive most effectively. She sounded like a child, not someone who could pose a legitimate threat to anyone.

"Only one of them?" the woman asked, still void of emotion.

Evidently her abductor was also taken aback by her fearless question, because he hesitated for several seconds. "I'll start with one, yes. Your thumb, up to the first knuckle."

Danny knew he meant it.

11

I COULD TELL you how I ended up in such a terrifying predicament, handcuffed to a chair in the basement of the Long Beach Hilton, but the journey had taken every second of three months, and dozens of missteps before this final, monstrous misstep, and all those details would fill a whole book.

The very short version is this:

I started my new life with one pair of pajama bottoms stuffed with roughly three hundred thousand dollars, the matching pajama top, a pair of pink-and-white underwear, an oversize pair of dirty blue overalls, and a spirit so crushed that I spent the first three days wondering if I had died and become a ghost trapped in the world.

The money saved me.

From that warehouse district, I walked for an hour on bare feet that started to bleed before I found any motels. You have to remember, I'd spent a year in slippers, protected from the elements in every way. My skin was lily white, my fingers were as soft as tissues, and my feet were like delicate creampuffs.

With each step in those wee morning hours, my bitterness grew, and I used it to push away the pain. I arrived with puffy, cried-out eyes and raw feet at a dirty motel called the Rendezvous. Although the night manager had undoubtedly seen his share of strange people, the sight of me made him blink.

I'd had the presence of mind to shove my stuffed pajama bottoms into a garbage bin outside the front door. When he said it would be twenty dollars an hour or fifty for the night, I handed over one of the bills I'd stuck in the pocket of the overalls.

That was how I spent the first hundred of Lamont's dollars.

If I hadn't been so exhausted I would have taken one look at the room's dirty orange carpet and smudged bedspread and fled. Lamont's obsession with cleanliness had rubbed off on me. I tried halfheartedly to clean the bathroom, but the stains in the toilet and sink were stubborn, and the linoleum squares on the floor were starting to peel away from the crusted concrete.

I finally gave up, turned the water as hot at it would go, and scrubbed every inch of my body under a steaming shower. But it didn't really get me clean, not really, really clean. No amount of hot water could wash away what had happened to me.

I sat down in the tub and wept while the water washed over me. Having lost Lamont, I was prone to crying those first few weeks.

My most embarrassing moment might have been my first trip down the street to the Walmart. I needed clothes. I couldn't very well go around in pajamas or dirty blue overalls the rest of my life. And I had to get some shoes. Even so, it took me two days to work up the courage to leave my room.

I washed out my pink-and-white pajamas with hand soap and let them dry over the air conditioner. When they went stiff,

I pulled them on. With some imagination, I reasoned, the pajamas might look like they were meant to be worn in public.

I carefully hid the money under the mattress, put two of the bills in my waistband, and headed out into the bright day.

How I got to the Walmart in such a state of terror I can't say, but I was soon inside. I had rehearsed a list of items to buy, but when I stood beside the cash registers, my mind went blank and all I could think of was shoes, jeans, and soap.

I don't know if it was the pajamas, the stark terror on my face, or my frantic darting around the Walmart, but everyone was staring at me. I wasn't blending in as well as I had dared hope.

In my rush not to be noticed, I spent my second hundred dollars poorly. Upon racing back to my dirty motel room, I found that I had purchased one pair of green slippers size 11 for men, a pair of Wrangler jeans that swallowed me, two boxes of Clorox bleach, a quart-size bottle of shampoo, and a tin of Altoids that I'd picked up at the checkout stand because Lamont liked the smell of mint.

Still, it was a start.

Emboldened by my limited success, I returned to the Walmart late that same night dressed in my new oversize jeans, my pajama top, and the monstrous slippers. This time I arrived armed with a thousand dollars. I bought a large rolling duffel bag and enough clothes and supplies to fill it half full. I had to leave room for the money.

I returned to the motel, stacked all of Lamont's cash on the pillows, and laid my new clothes on the bed. This was now the sum of my earthly possessions: two pairs of Quiksilver slim-cut jeans that fit me well, three T-shirts, four tops, six pairs of underwear, three bras, five socks, a cute leather belt, a pair of black boots, tan slippers that fit me, a pair of Nikes, some lip gloss—Lamont hated makeup but thought gloss was okay—and a black purse.

The supplies included duct tape, some string, and a screwdriver, none of which I had any immediate use for, though they had impressed me at the store. I also had one white plate, a set of flatware, and a glass so that I could eat and drink properly.

I began to hope. If I could buy stuff and rent a motel room on my own, I could surely track down and kill Bourque.

What was I thinking? I'll tell you: With every fiber of my being I was thinking that however naive I was or far I had to go, I would not stop until either he or I was dead.

Staring at my new possessions and the pile of money on the pillows, it occurred to me that I did have some options. For example, there was no need for me to spend another night in that dirty motel room. I could afford a better place. And I could certainly afford a taxi to take me to a better place.

The only question was where? The obvious answer came to me immediately: closer to the man who was responsible for destroying us.

The law was in my hands, and according to the law of Lamont, any man as evil as Jonathan Bourque could only deserve one verdict and one sentence. Lamont had told me as much in his own words. I was sure that the only reason I'd found his money was to use it to hand down justice.

Even though Lamont wasn't around, I was still his. So was the money. I would use everything in my power to honor him, or to give my life trying. I had no other purpose.

It wasn't revenge; it was justice.

The problem was, I had no idea how to go about finding much less killing a man like Bourque. I wasn't even sure how to live on my own anymore. If not for the money I would have ended up back where Lamont had first found me, in some alley, a heartbeat away from death.

That night I lay awake late and started to string together a semblance of a plan.

The next morning I returned to the store, bought hair bleach, and spent an hour becoming a blonde. My hair was short, because that's how Lamont liked it. With the blond I thought I looked quite different from the way I had a year ago. Not even Cyrus Kauffman would recognize me immediately.

According to the phone book, the Rendezvous motel I had stumbled upon was in Cypress, east of Long Beach. The headquarters for the Bourque Foundation, I learned, were located in Long Beach. Problem was, Cyrus was also in Long Beach.

I packed up all my belongings, called a cab, and asked the driver to recommend a cheap hotel with kitchens close to but not in downtown Long Beach.

Half an hour later we rolled up to the Staybridge Suites at East Anaheim Street near Cherry Avenue, where I rented a suite for eight hundred dollars a week. I felt guilty spending so much—Lamont would probably object—but I didn't want to be anywhere near Cyrus's operation on the west side. Then again, the more I thought about it, the more I became convinced that Lamont would approve of me renting a place with a kitchen so I could prepare my own food. Anything that could be ordered for delivery would undoubtedly poison me. Processed food was full of chemicals. Lamont had helped me learn how to eat only the finest whole foods—mostly raw, fresh, and local, without trans fats, preservatives, or sugars.

It took me two days and both boxes of Clorox to clean my new home. Then I spent the better part of a week settling in, though I never grew comfortable with the brown couch or the carpet, both of which looked clean but were dirty to the touch.

There was no way to clean them properly, and when I asked the manager if he would replace the carpet and exchange the couch for a leather one, my request was denied.

I did exchange the flowered comforter that came with the room for a pink one I found at Walmart.

I didn't have a driver's license and wasn't eager to go out and get one, not yet anyway. I didn't have my birth certificate, or any ID for that matter. The whole idea of legitimizing myself with papers and bank accounts and all the things required to function normally in society made me ill with nervousness. I didn't have time to fill out forms and take tests that I would fail.

Instead, I began to plot my journey to Jonathan Bourque's doorstep with a boldness that surprised even me. It all started with a few simple questions that I began to obsess over.

Basic questions, like: How do you kill someone?

Even more basic: How do you *find* somebody? And, having found him, how do you *reach* him?

I was surprised by how much thought these simple questions required. You would think anyone with a gun could just walk up to someone and shoot. While that may be true, other factors complicate even this simple action.

Getting a gun, for example.

Getting access to the individual without being tackled, for example.

Getting away with it, for example.

Each question led to other, more important questions. Did I want to get away with it? What did *getting away with it* mean? Did I want to simply survive or was it important to escape a prison sentence as well?

On an even more fundamental level, I had to answer the question of guilt. Was Jonathan Bourque truly guilty of the evil Lamont had pinned on him? More to the point, had he killed my companion, my lover, my rock, my husband, as I assumed he had?

These questions sickened me! How could I even doubt Lamont's word? And yet they wouldn't leave me alone.

How much evidence did I need to remove my doubt? How would I go about finding that evidence?

These were only a few of the questions that welled up in my mind as I gradually shifted my focus from functioning alone to the monumental task ahead of me.

My two greatest assets were time and money. The Bourque Foundation was housed in a fifteen-story Wells Fargo bank building on Ocean Boulevard, across the street from the Long Beach Public Library.

I purchased binoculars with the intent of watching the building to see when Bourque came and went, but the notion quickly proved absurd. For starters, I didn't know what my target looked like. Also, within an hour of perching myself across the street with my glasses trained on the towering building, it occurred to me that the stares I was getting from passersby likely had everything to do with the fact that the building was a bank.

I doubted that a bleached-blond ghost of a girl fit the typical bank robber's profile, but I got far too much attention for my liking.

The Long Beach Public Library—more specifically, the computers at the library—quickly replaced my binoculars as the better reconnaissance tool. I became a regular, although I couldn't check anything out without a library card, which required identification.

It occurred to me that the kinds of subjects I was looking up weren't exactly the kind I wanted people seeing over my shoulder. Searches for *kidnapping* and *poison* and *guns* done on the same computer as searches for *Jonathan Bourque* might lead to an undesirable outcome if discovered.

Two weeks after my return to Long Beach, I bought my own computer and hooked it up to the wireless Internet service at the Staybridge hotel. This saved me both time and cab fare.

One of the first things I learned was that the manner of foul play I was contemplating was best done by people who were physically fit. I might need to run away, or hit someone, or quickly grab a gun from them.

I had put on a couple of pounds since recovering from my addiction, but Lamont had been careful to make sure I was healthy, which meant I should stay thin. Although I was strong enough to clean the house and cook, I certainly didn't have the muscle required to swing a bat around or break someone's neck.

I decided that I had to start exercising. Not that I expected to enter any karate competitions, but as I looked at myself naked in the mirror, I began to see that I was fragile as a feather. Bourque might blow me away with a heavy sigh.

On the computer, I researched the kinds of exercises I could do without going to a gym or lifting weights, because I was far too shy to join a throng of half-naked, sweaty bodies, and I wasn't interested in lugging dumbbells through the hotel lobby. So I installed a clamp-on pull-up bar in the bathroom door frame, downloaded a file on calisthenics, and started a basic regimen of push-ups, pull-ups, sit-ups, and jumping jacks.

I'm sure I looked like an animated scarecrow doing the jumping jacks, but I could handle them well enough. The sit-ups were more of a challenge, but with some grunting I managed to string together ten. The push-ups were okay as long as I stayed on my knees.

But the pull-ups were evil. After tugging with all my

strength and failing to lift myself more than an inch, I walked away from the bar and didn't return to it for another month.

Most of my emotional energy those first two months went into normalizing myself. Fitting in. Adopting the psyche of a woman bent on bringing justice to her corner of the world. Embracing righteous anger so I could extract justice no matter what the cost.

You know, normalizing.

By nature I wasn't the vengeful type. I wasn't easily angered or quick to judge. But I had nothing in my mind except the complete ruin Bourque had brought to us.

I set my mind on his evil nature, and with each passing day and week my resolve grew. Time didn't settle me but only made me more anxious. Maybe I held out hope that Lamont would one day knock on the front door and sweep me off my feet, and maybe the growing realization that he was gone forever played into my bitterness. I don't know.

My ideas of what I might do to the evil Bourque became wilder and more developed as the days became weeks and then turned into months. Coming off a year in which I'd spent most of my days alone in a house with little to do but clean and exist in my slightly drugged state, I was completely occupied with a burgeoning imagination fueled by hundreds of hours surfing the Internet.

I decided early that I wanted to survive. And I did not want to spend the rest of my life in a prison, which meant I couldn't get caught. Which in turn meant that I had to outwit the authorities. The police. The FBI.

Those three letters terrified me. *FBI.* The FBI always won, as they should. They stood for the good guys, for the widows and the orphans and people like me.

But like Lamont had said, sometimes the law got in the

way of justice. I was actually on the same side as the FBI. I had to do their job because my hands weren't tied like their hands were.

This is what I thought about as I spent hours lying awake, staring at the ceiling in my suite at the Staybridge hotel. That and the fact that the FBI was smarter than me. Not that I was an idiot, but I wasn't the sharpest tack in the tin, my mother used to say, and that was before the heroin.

Consider how my days went and you'll get the picture. I usually got up around eight and drank sixteen ounces of bottled mountain-spring water to flush out my system. Then I took a very hot shower and cleaned the bathroom while steam still covered all the walls, the sink, the toilet, and the bathtub. Only when the entire room was squeaky clean would I dress and head back out to the kitchen.

There I made myself a healthy breakfast using vegetables and fruits cut into small squares and arranged neatly on a plate. No sugar, no breads, no eggs, no animal products of any kind. Lamont used to cheat from time to time, but I didn't dare. My body had taken a beating from the drugs, and I was obsessive about keeping it clean. He'd taught me well.

After I wiped down the kitchen and mopped the floor tiles using vinegar and warm water, I sat down at the desk and turned on my computer. This was usually around ten thirty in the morning.

The moment I began to research any topic, I would find so much new information to occupy my mind that it was impossible to stay on track. I would start with police procedures, for example, and upon learning that the police used stun guns to stop criminals, I would do a search on stun guns and soon be lost in an article on the electrical charges in such guns, which would lead me to the inventor of that device. I might lift my head at one o'clock having just read an obituary of a scientist in Lincoln, Nebraska.

None of this brought me closer to breaking Bourque's neck or kidnapping him and holding him in my closet for a month while he slowly confessed to every evil deed he'd committed. Worse, my memory was still a bit foggy, and much of what I might have learned about my initial topic—such as police procedures—seemed to evaporate in the haze of digital information.

Feeling hungry from my heavy research, I would make myself a salad, eat it with a fork, brush my teeth, check to be sure the suite was clean, and return to the computer around two unless I had some shopping to do.

Gradually I did learn, I suppose. Sure I did. I learned many things, but I'm not sure I learned in those first two months to be a very good criminal.

It was then that I decided to change my approach. Instead of reading about the ins and outs of the underworld, I would focus on the man I would bring to justice. I considered enlisting the help of Cyrus Kauffman, the dealer who'd first put me in this predicament. For a healthy sum he could show me the ropes and get me the lowdown on Jonathan Bourque. But I was quite sure he would rob me, let his friends rape me, and then shoot me full of drugs and kill me.

So I worked alone and started to peel back the layers hiding my target.

I might as well have tried to peel a pool ball. Public information about Bourque was readily available, naturally. But this was worthless. I quickly realized that if I wanted to get to the truth about the man, I would have to do it in person.

I had to meet people who knew him. And I had to meet him. I needed to look him in the eye and ask him about Lamont, because then I would really know. A flicker in his eye would betray him. A shadow over his face would confirm his knowledge of my husband's fate.

Meeting someone as secretive and protected as Bourque turned out to be even more daunting than pull-ups. I was sweating like a sauna the first time I set foot in the bank, pretending to be a respectable customer considering her options. I can't tell you exactly what happened, only that I spent five minutes wandering around in a complete panic, telling myself that my fear was silly. I had to do this.

But I did not belong in that bank building. I wasn't dressed right. I didn't speak right. I *did* have a carefully rehearsed cover story about representing a new charity for recovering heroin addicts, and I planned to use this when I eventually met Bourque, but there in the bank I stood out like a ketchup stain on a white tablecloth.

It took me two days to settle on an outfit I was comfortable wearing and that I thought would allow me to blend in at the bank. I chose a white blouse and a gray skirt suit from JCPenney that fit nicely around my thighs without hugging them too tightly. My legs were fluorescent white and I thought about wearing hose or trying a spray-on tan, then rejected the ideas. The thought of suffocating my legs or spraying them with chemicals made my skin itch.

The saleswoman, a nice lady named Kelly who had large breasts, insisted that if she could fit into a suit like the one I'd chosen, she would definitely wear black stilettos with it. But I perched awkwardly on the high heels she brought for me to try on, and I had a sudden and terrifying vision of trying to run away from Bourque and breaking my ankles. I settled for a pair of black flats.

The next time I went back to the Wells Fargo bank building,

I assured myself that I was only there to practice fitting in. I kept my eyes trained ahead, walked directly to the elevator, and rode it to the top floor.

There were two others on the elevator and neither stared at me. I looked like any other businesswoman coming to inquire on charity business. There was no reason not to be fully confident. Still, I was sweating, and although I wasn't wearing any makeup but the lip gloss, because Lamont insisted cosmetics detracted from my natural beauty, I was afraid someone might notice.

But no one did.

The foundation's lobby was furnished with a long marble counter, behind which sat a red-haired receptionist in a bright blue suit, answering phones and filling appointments. Two large brass doves sailing over waves and the words THE BOURQUE FOUNDATION decorated the rear wall.

"May I help you?"

It took me a moment to realize the question had been asked of me. I froze, then turned my head to the receptionist in the blue suit.

One of her eyebrows went up. "May I help you?"

I was stuck on the top floor with nowhere to flee but back to the elevator. All of my careful research and preparation vanished in a puff of proverbial smoke.

"Hi," I said.

She smiled. "Hi."

"Um...Does Jonathan Bourque...Is here?"

I was barely aware that I'd butchered the question. I was far more concerned with the fact that I'd asked it. I have no idea what I was thinking.

"And you are?"

I pushed through my panic and stepped forward. "I'm sorry, I'm just...Could I see him?"

"I'm afraid that's impossible. Mr. Bourque doesn't take unsolicited appointments. What did you say your name was?"

I knew I couldn't use my name, because he might see that I was Lamont's wife and kill me on the spot.

"Mary," I said. "I'll just come back."

The receptionist dismissed me with a half nod and answered a call. I descended in the elevator and exited into the lobby, where I stood for full ten seconds, realizing that I hadn't set fire to myself or the building. I had come, fit in, spoken, and now it was time to leave.

So I did, feeling elated. I caught a cab and rushed back to my room.

But as I paced the kitchen and thought about my first visit to the Bourque Foundation, it occurred to me that I really hadn't accomplished much. If anything, I'd only learned what I already knew, namely that Jonathan Bourque was inaccessible. I might have even ruined my chances of getting a meeting with him.

The next day, I called and tried to make an appointment, but again I was dismissed. Jonathan Bourque did not take unsolicited appointments. In fact, no one at the foundation did, not without a reference. Evidently there were far too many people looking for handouts, and being snobby was part of the foundation's screening process.

Two days later, I went back to the Wells Fargo building, rode up to the top floor, and this time spent three hopeless minutes trying to make a case for an audience with anyone at the foundation regarding my new charity, which I'd named Recovering Addicts Anonymous—a silly name in hindsight, but I thought it was pretty clever at the time.

Over the next week I tried on five different occasions to find a way through their firewall, as I began to think of it. But in their eyes I was only one of many bothersome advocates for worthy causes, and with each attempt I was simply sent away.

I was starting to think that Bourque was untouchable. I began to panic, and then I began to consider an entirely new approach.

Fitting in was no longer my concern. If anything, my problem was that I fit in too well. I was like every other gold digger out for an audience with the king. Maybe the only way *in* was to stand *out*—not as a nutcase, but as a potential threat. They would have to take me seriously then.

This idea was absurdly dangerous, of course, but the more I thought about it, the more I became convinced that if I really did want to force Bourque's hand, threatening him might be the only way to get his attention.

My harebrained scheme began with a trip back to the foundation's receptionist and ended with my captivity in the basement of the Hilton.

I presented the redhead with a note stating I had information that would hurt the Bourque Foundation. I demanded an immediate meeting with Jonathan Bourque. I was begrudgingly escorted to the Hilton and introduced to Simon Redding, who guided me with a steel grip down into the basement, shoved me into the chair, and began his interrogation as if I was a prisoner in a war camp.

This is the short story of how I came to be handcuffed to a chair while Bourque's right-hand man paced in front of me. I was terrified. I was sweating. I was a skinny recovering drug addict pretending to be someone else in a gray suit.

I was also furious, which surprised me a little—not because I didn't have a reason to be angry, but because of how it affected me. Instead of being shy or timid, my determination to defend Lamont's honor was absolute.

I finally had my proof, you see? I admit it: Up until this point, I hadn't been perfectly positive that Bourque was as evil as I'd imagined. But Simon Redding's threats exposed Bourque's ugly underbelly. In this regard, my plan was working flawlessly.

"You're going to cut off my fingers?" I asked, unsure if I understood.

"Not all of them."

"Only one of them?"

"I'll start with one, yes. Your thumb, up to the first knuckle."

The thought scared me enough to make my fingers tremble. But my mind filled with an image of this man standing over Lamont, threatening my husband with something even worse before eventually killing him.

They'd done it. I knew this all the way to my bones, and my fear gave way to outrage. Three months of obsession and frustration boiled over. I spoke without thinking clearly.

"Do whatever you need to do. You killed the only man who ever loved me!" My voice was tight and high and I was more shouting than speaking. "You can't get away with this! People like you will rot in hell, which is exactly where I would send you if—"

His hand slammed into the side of my head, nearly knocking both me and the chair over. "Keep your voice down," he said. "Who are you talking about?"

I spit blood from my mouth. "So you've killed more than one? You don't even know who I mean?"

"You obviously think I'm capable of doing some real damage. Listen to yourself. Be smart. Don't make me hurt you."

"You're just going to kill me the way you killed him?" I cried.

"Who?"

I wanted to shout Lamont's name, but it occurred to me that knowledge was my only leverage; knowledge was king in the underworld. They wouldn't kill me until they knew everything I knew.

"Kill me and you'll never know."

He stared at me for a moment, then pulled out a large pocketknife and extended the blade.

"Okay, honey. We'll do this the hard way."

Knuckles rapped on the door. "Hello?"

Redding slipped his knife into his pocket.

"Hello?" The door swung open and a man dressed in a black shirt with a white priest's collar stood in the door frame.

The priest's round eyes went from me to Redding, then back again. "What's going on?"

12

THE WAY DANNY saw it, he had two choices: to save the girl or to walk away.

In this matter Danny wasn't sure which choice was the moral one, because he didn't have time to fully consider the consequence of each choice. So he did what came naturally.

As a fighter in the Bosnian war, he'd learned a hundred ways to kill a man, and most of them involved leveraging tactical advantage over brute force. Although Danny could wield a knife and handle a gun like few could, his keen mind was what had appointed him to the most difficult missions behind enemy lines.

He knocked on the door. "Hello?"

Before they could answer, Danny opened the door and took in the small room.

It was another utility closet. Redding stood over a young woman handcuffed to a metal chair.

"What's going on?" he stammered as any priest stumbling upon such a scene might.

The girl's eyes went to his collar. The fact that he was a priest rarely played to his advantage, but it might today if he played his cards correctly.

Upon immigrating to the United States, Danny had become a priest for one reason: to cleanse his mind of all the evil that kept him awake nights. The fact that he'd since gone from being a messenger of peace to a dispenser of justice was the fault of that pedophile whose penis he'd severed.

Although Danny was many things, chief among them a vigilante who killed the worst offenders, at that moment he had to remember that he was only a priest—a priest who'd heard sounds of distress and, like any priest worth his collar, gone to investigate.

"Hello, Father," Redding said, smooth as a good cognac. "I was expecting the police." He flashed an official badge that read PRIVATE SECURITY. "Just a small security situation. We're holding the girl until the authorities arrive. If you'll please excuse us, I'd rather this not disrupt the dinner, as I'm sure you can appreciate."

"Of course. Of course." Danny turned as if to leave but then looked back at the blood on her lips. "My goodness, does she need a doctor? She fall down the stairs or something?"

"If you leave, he's going to kill me," the girl said.

"She's high on something," Redding said with an apologetic shrug. "Kids today."

"You really should stay away from those drugs, dear," Danny said. For Redding's sake, naturally.

The young woman looked like she was in her midtwenties, skin as white as a lightbulb but spotless. No signs of abuse. She was thin though not emaciated like a junkie. Her hair looked too light to be natural, likely bleached. If he were to guess, she was a shut-in who rarely saw the light of day, not a woman battered by the street.

Redding nodded. "Thank you, Father. I have it under control."

"Sure." Then Danny said to the woman, "Could I get you a glass of water or anything while you wait?"

"Yes, please," she said.

Redding lifted a hand. "I'm sorry, Father, but really, it's my responsibility to secure——"

"She's parched," Danny said. "A glass of water given to the least of these honors God. Surely you're not worried she'll use it to escape?"

He'd stalled the man, but Redding was no fool. The wheels were spinning behind his dark eyes, weighing his options.

"I'm sorry, Father, but I'm going to have to ask you to go. I'll get her some water, but this is a security issue involving a sensitive situation. The police are on their way. I assure you, everything is in good order. Now please leave us."

Danny could have left the room, called hotel security, and waited outside the closet until they arrived. Redding wouldn't risk complicating matters by escalating the violence. But Danny saw an opportunity to better understand Bourque's machinery.

"Of course. Of course. There's nothing worse than injustice. I've always believed that those responsible for it should be brought to their knees even when they come in small, frail packages."

"Then you should stay, Father," the girl said, staring directly at him. "The injustice here isn't mine, it's theirs."

"Oh? And what is your name, young lady?"

"Renee," she said.

Redding's face darkened a shade. "You're overstepping your bounds, Father."

"Am I?" Danny took a step closer. "Perhaps I could offer Renee here some spiritual counsel while we wait for the police to arrive. She looks properly restrained. I'm sure neither of our lives is in jeopardy."

"That isn't necessary."

"But I insist," Danny said. "Why do you do drugs, Renee? You see what kind of trouble it brings you?"

She spoke quickly before Redding could object again. "If you cared anything about justice you would demand he uncuff me. My only crime here is that I have accused Jonathan Bourque of killing the man I love. They're afraid of what I know."

"Enough!" Redding thundered.

Danny looked at the man. "What are you going to do, cuff me to the chair as well? It isn't the first time that Jonathan Bourque has been accused of injustice." He let the comment sink in, then backpedaled just enough to give himself an out. "The world is full of crazy people who mistake kindness for wrongdoing. In the end, we will know them by their fruit, isn't that right?"

Redding's jaw was firm. His suspicions had been piqued.

"You think I'm crazy?" Renee asked Danny. There was a certain naïveté about her voice.

"I think you're cuffed to that chair because you're meddling in affairs you should leave to others," Danny said.

"If you don't leave now, I will be forced to restrain you," Redding snapped. "I have a job to do."

Danny held up a hand. "Let's just calm down. As you said, the police will be here any minute."

"You should take your own advice," Redding said. "Leave matters like this to the proper authorities."

"Is that a threat?"

No response.

"Sir, I only opened the door at the top of the stairs looking for the bathroom, and I heard the commotion here. However unusual it might be to find a woman restrained in a basement, your explanation makes perfect sense. But now your threats make me wonder if you're being entirely honest with me. Speaking may not be your strong suit—you should think before opening your mouth."

That stalled the conversation completely. Perhaps Danny had been too strong.

Redding walked to the door and faced them, scowling. "Stay here. Both of you. I didn't get your name, Father."

"Hansen. Father Danny Hansen."

"She'll tell you all kinds of stories. Believe what you will, but I have an obligation to my employer and to the authorities."

With that Redding exited the room, closed the door, locked it, and was gone.

"He's gone?" Renee asked.

"Apparently. Smart man."

"But he just left us?"

Danny faced her and lowered his voice. "What you said, it's true?"

"Of course it's true! I—"

"Keep it down, please."

She did, but barely. "You believe that thug over me?" she said. And then as an afterthought, looking at the door: "Why's it so smart to leave us?"

"Because he saw that I wasn't going to leave. There are no police coming, and that would have quickly become obvious and awkward. His only other choice was to threaten me, which would complicate matters for him."

She stared at him. "Really? What's he doing now?"

"He's getting orders."

"To do what?"

"To either let us go or take us both out."

She stared, aghast. "How do you know?"

"I'm a priest. I read people better than most."

"Then you have to get us out of here!" She stood, dragging the chair.

"Sit down!"

She sat.

Danny pulled a thin black bundle from his coat pocket. He rarely carried any kind of weapon on his person—though he did have the box cutter he'd lifted from the other closet—but he kept his lock-picking pack with him at all times. So much of his work involved retrieving information under lock and key.

He withdrew a shim pick from the five-piece kit. "I heard some things before I came in. They're true?"

"I told you, yes," she said.

"I don't know what you thought you could accomplish by confronting him, but I suggest you leave well enough alone and disappear for your own sake. Let the authorities handle Bourque."

"You don't understand. The authorities can't touch him."

"Neither can you. And I do understand. I'm going to get you out of here, but I want you to promise me you'll disappear. If you know something that truly threatens these people, they'll come after you. I would consider leaving the state, maybe finding a new identity."

She was dumbfounded, but he didn't have time to persuade her. Redding would have his answer quickly. Even if he set them free, issuing apologies, he would establish a tail on the girl and deal with her later in the night.

Danny dropped to one knee, inserted his shim into her cuffs' locks, and sprang them open. Then he went to work on the door using another pick and a small torque wrench. The knob was locked from the outside, but the lock was keyed on both sides.

"There's another closet at the end of this hall. I want you to hide inside for five minutes, then climb the stairs and get out. Don't look back."

"What are you going to do?"

"I'm going to find Redding and explain what happened."

"And what did happen?"

He had a vague notion of what he would say, but he was still working on it. "Let me take care of that."

The lock disengaged.

Danny eased the door open, stuck his head out into the hall, saw that it was empty, and waved her forward. "Hurry. End of the hall. Give me five minutes. You got that?"

"Five minutes."

She hurried down the hall, got to the closet door, then turned back and stared at him with large, questioning eyes.

He motioned her in. "Inside."

She nodded, then vanished behind the door and pulled it closed.

Danny took the stairs quickly, paused at the door that led out to the main hall, and stepped out. The keynote speaker droned on in the adjacent banquet room. He had to get to Redding while the man was in a public setting.

He entered the dining hall and pulled up. There, not ten feet from the door, stood Redding with his back to Danny, talking to Jonathan Bourque. Danny could not have been blessed with a better gift. God was indeed alive and well and had his eyes on his faithful servants.

He hurried up to Redding and tapped him on the shoulder. Redding turned and, caught off guard, took a step backward.

"Mr. Bourque, excuse the intrusion. So happy to meet you."

Before the man could return his greeting, Danny turned to Redding. "I think there's been a mistake, my friend. You shouldn't have put me in charge of holding the woman. I'm a priest, not a prison guard. It's none of my business, really. I assure you that I want nothing to do with your affairs. You'll find her downstairs where you left her. I hope that's okay."

"I'm sorry, you are—?" Bourque asked.

Danny wanted to say, *I'm the man who is going to kill you.*

Instead he said, "A priest."

"Clearly." Bourque offered Redding an amused look, then put his hand on Danny's shoulder and guided him toward the door. "Look, Father, I'm a bit confused about what's happened, but I want to offer my sincerest apologies for your trouble."

Danny wasn't interested in entering the hall, where at any moment Renee would fly out of the door that led to the basement. So he stopped and forced Bourque to turn back.

"No problem, sir. If there is one thing I know about human nature it's that we are all prone to error, albeit some more than others. You might consider giving your man a few pointers on kindness. He seemed just a bit rough from my perspective."

Bourque smiled. "Security people—what can I say? Simon has the best intentions, but your point is taken."

Danny took the man's elbow. "I think he may have made a mistake with the girl as well. She seemed quite innocent to me."

"Noted." Bourque's smile broadened generously. "I like you, Father. And I can assure you that this has all been a dreadful mistake."

He was good. Good enough that had Danny not heard Redding's interrogation of Renee, he might have wondered if he'd misjudged the man.

Danny nodded and was considering how he might stall the

man another minute when he heard the soft whoosh of a door closing in the hall beyond. Renee had made her getaway.

"Good. Thank you, sir. Do you attend Mass, if you don't mind my asking?"

"Actually, I'm Protestant. It's strictly church for me."

"Oh? I thought I'd read somewhere that you were once a priest."

"That was a long time ago. I've mixed things up a bit since then, though I assure you I have the highest respect for all."

"Well, that's just as good. I don't think God cares what the building looks like on the outside. As the Good Book says, it's the inside that matters, yes?"

"Just as I've always believed."

"Indeed."

Danny had given her enough time, he thought, so he dipped his head and bowed out. "Nice to meet you. Oh, and I let the girl out of her cuffs." He held up his lock pick. "Little trick I learned when I was a younger man. She was bruising and promised me she would stay put."

Bourque's grin held firm. "I'm sure she will. Nice to meet you, Father."

"So nice."

13

I WAS A neurotic mess who'd been taught by Lamont that everything pointed to some greater purpose. After meeting the priest, I became that much more convinced that everything Lamont had said was true, not that I'd ever doubted him.

Here is how I thought about it: I was lost and God sent Lamont to save me. My name is Renee, which means "reborn" in French, as Lamont also liked to point out, and I was indeed reborn in his house of laws. Then I became lost again, and he showed up—a priest named Danny Hansen.

I looked up his name. Danny is from Daniel, which means "God is my judge." So you can understand why I couldn't sleep that night. For the second time in two years I had been saved from death by a man of the law, so to speak.

This could only mean that I was on to something, that I had a purpose, which I assumed had to do with delivering justice. Being the judge where the law had failed, as Lamont said.

The priest's words circled my mind like buzzards, whispering and calling to me.

It isn't the first time that Jonathan Bourque has been accused of injustice...

I do understand...

They'll come looking for you...Leave town...

The next morning I tracked down Father Danny Hansen. As it turns out, priests are public servants who apparently live open, transparent lives. Unlike Jonathan Bourque.

Danny Hansen was one of several priests at the Saint Paul Catholic Church on Long Beach Boulevard. He was a parochial vicar in charge of benevolence who served under the pastor, Bernard Lombardi.

The parish receptionist was a sweet woman named Regina who was enthralled with my somewhat modified story of recovery from heroin addiction. When I explained that I needed Father Danny Hansen immediately and had lost his number, she was happy to provide it.

I found his address through a reverse-directory search on the Internet. He lived in Lakewood, in a subdivision called the Brentwood Estates, a middle-class neighborhood in which most of the brick homes looked like they had come from the same mold.

A Yellow Cab driver delivered me to the address shortly after noon. I paid him and stepped out of the car into a cul-de-sac ringed by five homes.

The house directly in front of me was number 3005. This was God-is-my-judge's home, a single-story red-brick house with brown trim, bordered by a green lawn, like the rest of the houses.

Not a soul besides me was around that I could see. The quiet was a bit unnerving. I wasn't used to this kind of neighborhood, having lived first on the street, then in an ocean mansion, and now in a hotel.

I walked up to the cement landing and stopped in front of the door. A clay pot with a leafy green plant sat to one side. The doorbell button glowed orange, and I wondered if I should push it or just knock. It was early afternoon and I had no idea if the priest was even home. I reached up and pushed the button.

When no one responded to the faint sound of the chime inside, I tried again. Still nothing.

I had already decided that if the priest wasn't home I would simply wait, but standing there alone on the porch, I felt completely exposed. Maybe it would be better if I waited in the back, where neighbors peering through their windows would be less likely to notice me. Surely Danny wouldn't mind if I sneaked into his backyard.

I stepped onto the grass and walked to the side of the home, then through a wooden gate. At the back of the house, sliding glass doors stood behind a small porch with a table and two chairs. A set of blinds blocked my view of the interior. I looked around his small green lawn, then slid to my seat next to the door and waited.

What if I was wrong about Danny Hansen? What if he didn't know more about Bourque than I'd convinced myself he did? What if in my obsessive state of mind, I'd read him wrong?

And yet everything the priest had said seemed to suggest more than the actual words—maybe only to me, to my own craziness, but what if I was right?

What if Danny Hansen knew much more about Bourque than he let on? What if he hadn't come into that basement by accident? What kind of priest would suggest I leave town, if not one who knew precisely how dangerous Bourque really was?

Either way, I had to know, because this could be my first real break. My simple plan had all gone wrong, but I just might have found my guardian angel.

The previous night's pacing and fretting caught up to me. The next thing I knew, I was slumped over between my knees, climbing out of a foggy sleep. I opened my eyes to dusk and jerked up. I wiped some drool from the corner of my mouth, alarmed that I had slept so long.

"Welcome to the land of the living."

I flinched and saw that Danny Hansen was seated on a chair with his legs crossed, nursing a beer. He wore jeans and a pale blue button-down shirt with short sleeves, looking more like the priest's twin than the man who'd rescued me the night before.

I clambered to my feet, nearly tipping over in the process.

"Want a beer?" he asked. His voice carried a very slight and quite pleasant accent that I couldn't place. Maybe European.

I stared at him, not sure what he expected me to say. Did he know I didn't touch beer? When Lamont let me drink it was only wine, and then only the best, not the grape juice that teenagers and NASCAR fans sucked up, as he put it. Was it a trick question?

"Why?"

He shrugged. "Because you're thirsty?"

"Oh."

"Would you like one? I have Fat Tire and Corona."

"No. Thank you."

He nodded then took a pull from his bottle of Fat Tire. He indicated the empty chair. "Have a seat."

I slid into the chair across the small round metal-mesh table and folded my hands, feeling awkward. I'd rehearsed what I would ask him, but my mind was now blank.

Danny looked at the horizon and took another drink. His

arms were well muscled and his hands were large. A scar ran from his right thumb over his wrist. Maybe he'd gotten it dragging a victim from a car wreck or rescuing an unappreciative cat from a tree. But somehow I didn't think this priest spent his downtime patrolling the neighborhood for car crashes and stranded kittens.

"I see you didn't take my advice," he said, eyes watching the dimming sky over his neighbor's roofline.

"To get out of town?"

"Yes."

"No."

He drank again, just a sip, as if he needed time to think.

"I couldn't sleep," I said.

"You were sleeping when I found you."

"I mean last night."

"That's understandable, I'm sure you had a lot to think about. You were fortunate I came along when I did."

"Thank you."

Danny set his bottle down and turned his eyes to me. "I meant what I said. You shouldn't be here. And I mean in this town, in this state. You can thank me by leaving. You need some money?"

"No, I have some."

"How did you find me?"

"You're a priest, your life is transparent."

He didn't respond to that, but he broke his stare and looked back at the neighbor's house. There was much more to this priest than what showed on the outside, I thought. The line of questioning I'd rehearsed finally came to me.

"Where did you learn to pick locks?" I asked.

"Why did you come to me, Renee?"

"You remember my name? Thanks."

"You're welcome, but that doesn't answer my question."

"Because I need to know where you learned to pick locks," I said.

"A quick search on the Internet will tell you all you need to know, if you want to learn how to pick locks."

"I'm more interested in you. You're a priest who knows how to pick locks and handle criminals and come up with clever escape plans quickly. I want to know who you are and where you learned to do what you did."

He eyed me suspiciously. "What I did was only natural. I meet rough people every day in my line of work."

"I'm sure you do. Maybe I'm wrong, but I think God might have sent you to save me."

"Then be saved," he said. "Leave town. And stay the heck away from men like Jonathan Bourque."

"I can't leave town, not until he's dead." Had I just said that? I had. So then I was committed. "So you see, I still need saving."

He looked at me for a long time, and I spoke again, thinking I had no choice now but to trust Danny Hansen completely.

"If I tell you where I come from, will you tell me how you learned to pick locks? Never mind, I'll tell you anyway. I was rescued from the streets by a man named Lamont Myers. I was overdosed on heroin and as good as dead, and he saved me. He took me into his house and brought me back to health. We fell in love and then were married. Not officially."

I wasn't sure why I added that last comment.

It was the first time I'd ever talked to anyone about my love for Lamont, and I was surprised by the surge of emotion that welled up in my chest. Tears sprang to my eyes and I thought I might begin to fall apart, right there on Danny Hansen's back porch.

"Lamont was like an angel to me. I took care of him and he loved me. We listened to music and we danced. We drank wine and we watched the Malibu shores under the moonlight. I was lost but Lamont found me. You must understand that, Father. He was everything to me."

He looked at me with soft eyes and I saw only empathy and goodness in them. "I do," he said. "Call me Danny. Please."

"Well, Danny, you should know that Jonathan Bourque killed Lamont." My throat knotted painfully. I swallowed but that didn't help. "And he would have killed me last night if I hadn't escaped."

Danny averted his eyes. I think he was about to say something, but I wasn't done. I was desperate to speak. This was my confession and Danny was my priest.

Bitterness crept into my voice. My face was hot and my breathing was thick and I wanted to scream. I tried to remain calm but I didn't do it well.

"You're probably thinking that I'm mistaken, but I know that pig killed my husband. Lamont worked with him, and my husband told me how evil Bourque is." The words came out like nails. "Lamont found out something that he wasn't supposed to know, and he told me he was afraid for his life. The next day he disappeared."

Tears leaked down my cheeks. Danny watched me with steady, kind eyes.

"I waited for him for three days. Two men broke into our house then, and I heard them talking about Bourque while I hid in the corner."

Then I settled down a little and told him everything.

I told him about the money I'd stuffed into the pajama bottoms. I told him about climbing into the trunk and escaping to the warehouse. I told him about renting the room at the Staybridge hotel in Long Beach.

I told him much more than I had intended, but I was speaking for myself and I couldn't stop. The whole time, he just listened.

When I finished I wiped my cheeks with the back of my hand and we both sat in silence for a moment.

"I have to kill him, Danny. Is that so evil?"

"I'm so sorry for your pain, but it's not your place to decide," he said.

"Who then? Will God decide? I think God wants him dead!"

"Then he will see to Bourque's death, either here or in hell. But believe me, you won't survive that kind of confrontation with a man like Bourque. He'll crush you."

Danny said it calmly, without any passion or deep conviction, but he said it, and I immediately pounced on his admission.

"So you agree Bourque is a ruthless man."

"I didn't say that."

"You did! And you said as much last night before you even knew my story. Why else would you be so adamant that I get out of town?"

He hesitated, and I embraced the pause as a statement of affirmation.

"Aren't you jumping to conclusions?" he asked.

I hardly heard his denial. "I don't think you were there by accident. In fact, I think you have a problem with Bourque. You followed that man down into the basement. Who in his right mind would look for the bathroom through an employees' door? And how did you know to tell me to hide in the other closet—unless you'd already checked it out?"

I'd caught him flat-footed.

"Will you help me?" I asked.

It was getting dark, but I was sure I saw his face go a shade lighter. He didn't know what to say. I was right about him.

"This is absurd," he said in a soft voice. Then, with a little more intensity: "Listen to yourself. It's true, Bourque has a reputation and I wouldn't put foul play past him. I've seen my share of ordinary people doing horrible things. But I'm not above the law. I'm a priest! I'm so sorry for your loss, I really am. Injustice infuriates me to no end. But if you think I'm in any position to actually help you get your revenge, you're terribly mistaken."

"I don't think so. I think you're the only one who *can* help me. Tell me where you learned to pick locks."

"What?"

"I saw the way you handled yourself, and you're not like any priest I've ever heard of. Tell me, and maybe I'll believe you."

He stared at me, mouth parted.

"Go on," I said. "Tell me."

Danny closed his mouth, leaned back, and stared off at the horizon again. It seemed to be his escape. He sighed. "This is ridiculous."

I noticed that his hand was trembling, only a tiny bit, but it was on the table right in front of me and there was a tremor in his bones. I suddenly felt a deep empathy for him, maybe because I thought he might have suffered as much as I had. Maybe that's why he was a priest.

I reached out and put my hand on his. "It's okay, Danny," I said. "You can tell me."

He glanced at my hand, but I didn't remove it. I couldn't help thinking Danny needed me, and I was desperate to be needed. Also, I can't say I wasn't pleased with the small amount of power I felt in taking control of the situation. It was as if we'd switched roles. And I had done that!

"Tell you what?" he asked.

"Tell me how you were so deeply wounded," I said.

For a long time neither of us spoke. I realized that my hand on his was making him uncomfortable, and I suddenly felt awkward, so I removed it and folded my hands in my lap.

"I suppose we've all been deeply wounded at one time or another," he said. He shrugged. "I grew up in Bosnia. I saw some things there that left an impression on me. I'm sure you've heard of the Bosnian war, 1992?"

"No."

He gave me a strange look. "They say it was an ethnic war between Croats and Serbs, but it was just as much a religious war. Bosnian Serbs, mainly Bosnian Orthodox Christians, adopted a policy of ethnic and religious cleansing—the relocation and slaughter of Roman Catholic Croats and Muslims. It escalated into the systematic rape of women and the mass killing of non-Serbs, all done in the name of Christianity. They came into the small valley my family and I lived in. We were Croats."

Croats? The Catholics who were cleansed? My breathing stalled.

He shook his head. "I don't know why I'm telling you this."

"Because I want to know," I said. "Because you need to tell someone. Because maybe we are the same."

He chuckled, but it was a nervous reaction. I didn't let him off the hook.

"So tell me," I said.

The muscles along his jaw firmed up. "My mother and my two sisters were raped and killed by Christian Serbs because they were Catholic. I was fifteen."

"Oh no!"

"As you can imagine, my life was shattered. I joined the militia and learned how to fight. After the war I came to the United States, determined to honor the death of my family by being a good Catholic priest. And here I am."

I didn't know what to say. I felt such a bond with him in that moment, because he'd faced what I had faced. Worse! Much worse!

"So you see, Renee, I do know what it means to suffer and lose something precious."

"But you became a priest? Serving God, who let you down?"

Danny nodded. He closed his eyes briefly, then unfolded his legs and stood. "Would you like to come inside for a moment? Have some hot tea?"

"Tea?"

He slid the door open and stepped into his house. I stopped at the entrance and looked around. His house was furnished simply: a kitchen table, one leather couch, one stuffed leather chair, two floor lamps, and an armoire, which held a big-screen Toshiba television. The floors were covered with wood and tile—no carpet.

It was clean. Not as clean as I would have liked it, but cleaner than I expected.

"Coming?"

He was at the stove, heating a pot of water.

"You're clean!" I said.

Danny grinned. "I am? Tea?"

"Tea. Yes, I can have tea as long as it's a fresh bag with boiled water."

Three minutes later we sat around a small oak table with steaming cups in front of us.

He looked down at his tea. "So. I became a priest. To do God's work—true religion. Cleansing the world of evil and serving orphans and widows. If people knew my story, they might question my occupation. Even I do sometimes." He lifted his eyes. "I'm not a typical priest, I assure you. And I could leave it all if I felt so compelled. I'm sure that day will come. But for now, serving God suits me."

I thought I understood and I said so.

"Then maybe you can also understand why I spot the evil in people like Jonathan Bourque so easily. Faith isn't about a list of rules and regulations, it's about love."

I wasn't sure where he was headed, but I let him talk because he had done the same for me.

"But I am deeply offended by injustice, if by your actions you abuse the rights of another. This is what I learned in Bosnia as a teenager. Innocent men, women, and children lost their right to life, in the name of God."

"Lamont was innocent. Jonathan Bourque killed him," I said.

"God will be his judge."

"Do you believe in the death penalty?"

He answered slowly. "Yes."

"Then why can't you help me? I'm an orphan *and* a widow. I need help. I need to kill the pig who killed Lamont."

"That is not for us to do. You and I should concern ourselves with loving others, not extracting revenge."

"Surely God uses people to carry out his will. Would you kill the butchers who killed your mother if you had the chance?"

"I believe I did."

"Really? When you were fifteen?"

He hesitated. "Yes."

"And did God approve?"

"I believe he did."

"But you won't help me——"

"Please, Renee! You're trying to convince a priest to help you kill someone. I might have an obligation to turn you in to the authorities."

"You won't. If you wanted to involve the police, you would

have done it last night."

"You're missing the point. You are on a dangerous path that will end badly for you. These are youthful fantasies, and however much I might empathize, you have to forget them! Look at you!"

"Maybe I should be God's servant, too," I said. "If you killed the men who killed your mother, why shouldn't I do the same for Lamont?"

"Because you'll only be killed yourself!"

He had a good point. What if Danny did turn me in?

"You're young, naive, and inexperienced. Bourque will crush you with one blow."

I took a sip of tea, feeling deflated. But even then I didn't waver in my resolve to end Bourque's life. My convictions ran too deep. I suddenly wanted to leave.

"I don't mean to hurt your feelings, Renee," Danny said softly. "And I won't betray you to the authorities. I won't need to, because you're going to leave the state."

"I can't."

"You must. I've seen enough people around me die."

Now he was telling me I was going to die and he couldn't—wouldn't—help me stay alive. I felt terrible and small. What had I been thinking, coming to a priest to help me kill a man?

It only showed how ridiculous I was. Maybe the heroin had wiped out more of my mind than I'd realized.

"You're right." I stood. "I should be going."

"I'm sorry, Renee," he said, standing. "I'm begging you, forget this."

"Yes. Of course. I don't know what I was thinking. It's stupid."

"I can still help you. I can put you in touch with good people who will take you in."

"No. No, I'm good. I can leave town on my own. I'm not *that* stupid."

"No. I'm sure you're not."

We stood like that for a moment.

"Can you call me a cab?"

"Nonsense, I'll give you a ride."

"No, you've done too much already. I'd like to take a cab."

"Are you sure? It wouldn't be a problem. It's the least I can do."

"No. I like cabs."

He watched me.

"Okay. But promise me you'll forget all this nonsense about Bourque. Let God deal with him."

"I promise," I said.

I was lying through my teeth.

14

THE WORLD'S ORBIT, once in a constant rotation that could not be altered by anything even as cataclysmic as an encounter with a massive comet, had faltered. Perhaps even stalled. A young bleached-blond woman who couldn't weigh more than Danny's left leg had smashed into it and forever altered its course.

At first Danny couldn't understand why Renee's visit made such a devastating impact on him. After the Yellow Cab took her away, he'd gone about his business, determined to shrug off their meeting. He washed the cups and wiped down the counter and prepared himself a Cobb salad and watched some news.

But after thirty futile minutes of not hearing what was said on the tube, he gave up. The matter was fairly simple. Renee had managed to enter his mind and was refusing to leave.

In a matter of minutes they'd bonded. She'd simply walked

through the barriers he'd carefully built around himself as if she were a ghost who could walk through walls.

He'd sat listening to her talk about her husband, but his mind was preoccupied with fending off an insane desire to grab her hand and tell her everything.

You're right, Renee. I know you're right because I'm just like you. You're like me. We're the same, you and I. Your life has been ruined by a beast who will only ruin more lives if we let him live.

At least three others in Bourque's organization had gone missing that very month.

Now one more had come to light. Lamont Myers, who was evidently farther up the food chain. Bourque would have cloaked his disappearance with special care, but he hadn't taken into consideration the widow left behind. Renee.

Danny's and Renee's paths were already inseparably linked.

She was idealistic enough to believe, truly believe, that she was meant to destroy Jonathan Bourque. Even more, she believed that she was morally obligated to kill him. Looking into her eyes, Danny had known beyond the slightest doubt that she would not be dissuaded from that conviction.

In this way, she was his twin.

He lay awake trying to remember precisely what he'd said to her, what words he had chosen, and whether those words would betray him in any way.

He'd said too much, far too much. Without meaning to, he'd given her all the moral reasoning she needed to feed her obsession. Though he'd insisted she was foolish for even thinking of going after Bourque, was it enough?

That depended on how intelligent Renee was. Where at first he had seen only naïveté and idealism, he understood she possessed a simple logic that cut through all the fog that kept most people scratching their heads.

It was no secret that most people were like sheep, content to eat the grass at their feet and join the herd at a shepherd's beck and call. This was why whole nations followed the smooth tongue of a dictator. This was why good men and women massed to salute Hitler as he rode by in his motorcade. This was why decent people had raped and slaughtered their neighbors in Bosnia.

Danny managed to fall asleep sometime shortly after two in the morning, but his rest was fitful. When he rose at eight, the matter seemed even more dire than it had during the night.

He could not just dismiss his encounter with Renee.

He slipped on his clerical collar, studied his image in the mirror, then grabbed an apple from the kitchen before heading to his first appointment, a dreaded budget meeting with the administrative staff.

He had a clear choice, one fraught with moral implications.

Consider: Renee was like him in too many ways for him to ignore.

Consider: She was directly involved with Jonathan Bourque, his own target, and could prove to be an invaluable source of information.

Consider: He liked her. In fact, in some ways he liked her very much, in the same way he imagined he might like a soul mate. This sentiment surprised him, because he hardly knew her.

Granny Smith apple in hand, Danny climbed into his white Chevy Malibu and backed it out of the garage.

Consider: Renee was in danger. The thought of harm coming to her disturbed him considerably.

Consider: She might have an insight into him that could undermine his objectives.

Consider: The mystery that surrounded her had become a serious distraction to him.

The moral implication was quite clear. He had to know more both for her sake and for his.

Danny stopped his car at the end of his driveway and made a decision. He picked up his cell phone, selected the church's number from the list of contacts, and called Regina. She answered on the second ring.

"Good morning, Regina."

"Well, good morning, Danny. You're on your way in?"

"Actually, no. I've had an emergency come up and can't attend the budget meeting. I'm needed. Please extend my apologies and tell them to go on without me."

"Oh? Is everything all right?"

"Yes, yes of course. A personal matter, actually."

"No problem. I'll let them know."

"Thank you."

He pulled back into the garage, hurried to his bedroom, and reemerged wearing jeans and a black polo shirt. It took only a few minutes to find the address of the only Staybridge hotel in Long Beach. He left the house and headed south, objective clear.

He called the hotel and asked for Renee Gilmore's room. From what he'd learned the night before, she left her room only to shop or to conduct surveillance, however ill advised and amateurish, on the Bourque Foundation. He had to give her credit, though; she had more of a backbone than she might realize.

She picked up on the tenth ring.

"Hello?"

Danny disconnected. She was home as expected. He would have to wait, but waiting was a task with which he was well acquainted. At least he knew where she was. He doubted her enemies did. The fact that she lived in a hotel was to her advantage.

Twenty minutes later, he parked his car in the strip mall across from the Staybridge and settled down with a full view of the front entrance. A quick drive around the property had revealed two other exits, but when she emerged it would be to take a cab, her preferred means of transportation, and she would meet it at the front.

No doubt the money she'd spent on cabs these past few months could have purchased her a car. He didn't know how much cash she'd packed into the pajama bottoms before escaping Lamont Myers's house, but she obviously wasn't concerned with small details like money. She existed solely to bring justice to Jonathan Bourque's doorstep.

His wait lasted three hours.

She stepped out dressed in a pink T-shirt, her shoulder-length bleached hair blowing in the wind, and walked toward a Yellow Cab that had pulled up five minutes earlier.

He had to admire her nerve, so great for such a tiny thing. Renee might step on a ladybug and not have the weight to crush it. She seemed to float more than walk.

The cab door shut with her safely inside and motored away.

Danny exited his car and hurried across the street. There were a number of ways to learn the room number of a hotel guest, and though all were quite simple, none was easy. It often took more than one attempt.

He approached the front desk, relieved that the man on duty was young with black hair that flopped over his left eye. It was always easier to convince a rebellious spirit to bend the rules. Older people who'd grown comfortable in their boxes were the worst.

"Can I help you?"

Danny held out the manila envelope, on which he'd written Renee's name. "I hope so. I'm from the law offices of Morton and Laurence and I have a document that must get into the hands of Renee Gilmore as soon as possible. I understand she's a guest of yours."

"She just left."

"Ah."

"But I can take it for you."

He pulled the envelope back. "Sorry, state law. I can't actually deliver it into the possession of any other person. But I could slip it under her door. Or I could put it in her mailbox. Anything as long as I don't physically give it to another person. I know that sounds crazy, but that's California for you."

A whimsical smile crossed the clerk's mouth. "We don't have mailboxes. She has a slot, but no door on it."

"That could work. Show me."

The young man walked to a bank of slots to his right. "Right here." The slot that belonged to Renee Gilmore was marked 232.

"Should work," Danny said. "Just make sure no one but her touches it. You think that's okay?"

"Not a problem."

He handed the envelope over the counter. "Do you mind?"

"Sure." The manager slipped the envelope into the slot.

Danny thanked the young man and left. He rounded the hotel, walked in past a guest who was leaving through the back entrance, and made his way up the stairs to the second floor.

Three minutes later, he sprang the lock on number 232 and stepped into Renee Gilmore's current place of residence.

The room appeared hardly lived in. It was, as the name of the hotel claimed, a suite, with a door that led into a bedroom. One couch and one chair bordered a scratched but polished coffee table. A laptop computer sat open on a small desk in one corner, and next to that desk, a new red Dirt Devil vacuum cleaner.

The worn carpet had the telltale markings of a recent vacuuming. The kitchen counters, bared of all but one sparkling glass half full of water, were spotless. Clean.

She'd been pleased that his house was clean. Even in this way they were similar.

He walked into the kitchen and opened the refrigerator. Small bottles of pomegranate juice filled the top shelf in perfectly aligned rows. No milk. No butter. No cheese. No meat. No condiments. Two opened boxes of baking powder occupied the bottom shelf, one on each side. Vegetables filled both of the bottom drawers. Renee was clearly a vegetarian.

He closed the door and opened the cupboards, one by one. Again, all plates and glasses were crystal clean and perfectly ordered in rows and stacks. Even the sink was spotless, not just clean but wiped down and dried. No dish towels or rags in the open—they would attract mildew and germs.

If Danny were to guess, he would say that Renee suffered from a mild obsessive-compulsive disorder. Had she always been so orderly?

He left the kitchen and walked to her bedroom, noting that he would have to allow for time to vacuum the carpet. She would spot the indentations from his shoes immediately.

The bedspread was white with pink flowers. Two pillows had been fluffed and positioned at the head of the bed, not a wrinkle on either pillowcase. Three books, one about the FBI and two true-crime paperbacks by Ann Rule, were neatly stacked on the nightstand.

Danny walked up to the books and picked up one of the true-crime paperbacks. It was titled *The Stranger Beside Me*, a familiar account about a serial killer named Bundy. It was there, standing by Renee's bed and holding that small book in his hands, that Danny felt his heart begin to break.

How often had Renee read late into the night, identifying with the accounts of these innocent victims? How often had she cried herself to sleep as she mourned the loss of the one man who had given her meaning and life?

It was as if Danny held his own shattered heart.

So few people thought about those left in the wake of injustice. When Bourque killed Lamont he'd also killed Renee, not once but a thousand times, night after night, with each recurring nightmare.

Danny knew this. He had been one of those victims. His pain returned now, suddenly and with a vengeance, like the fist of God.

He set the book back on the nightstand, slowly lowered himself to the bed, and fought to control his emotions. But the pain he'd barricaded in the deepest part of his soul raged to the surface, and he could not stop himself.

His mother was there, in the house, screaming to be saved. But he'd let them all down.

And now you will run away from another victim?

Danny pushed himself up. He'd stepped on holy ground here. He'd violated Renee's space.

He hurried to the bathroom, turned on the faucet, and splashed cold water on his face, thinking only then that he was making a mess. The carpet, the bed, the sink—he'd practically ransacked her suite!

He worked quickly, retrieving paper towels from the kitchen to wipe the sink.

He would not peruse the contents of her computer as he had planned. He'd lost track of time. For all he knew, she was walking down the hall at this very moment.

He had to vacuum the carpet to erase the indentations from his shoes, then get out, even though he'd learned nothing new from his visit. Unless she invited him, he would not return to her home.

Danny headed for the living room but paused at the sliding doors of the closet. He pulled one of the doors open and stared at the shelves carefully lined with what were surely Renee's most prized possessions.

Jeans, T-shirts, a gray business suit, and several blouses hung from a rod to the left. Socks and underwear were carefully stacked in color order on the bottom shelves. Shoes and slippers neatly lined the floor.

But it was the contents of the top four shelves that arrested his attention. Two pairs of binoculars—one small, one large. A night-vision scope. A pair of handcuffs. A pair of nunchaku. Three knives, one of which was longer than her arm. A set of lock picks. A camera. A pair of brass knuckles. Wire cutters and flexible wire, the kind that might be used for a garrote. A box of rat poison. At least twenty books similar to the ones on her nightstand.

And a Browning nine-millimeter pistol.

This was the treasure trove of an amateur obsessing over the perfect crime. As he paired the contents with an image of the young woman who'd asked him to help her kill Jonathan Bourque, Danny's heart melted.

It was both tragic and endearing at once.

The sound of the front door opening jerked him from his thoughts. She was home? So soon? He hadn't vacuumed!

Frantic to avoid embarrassment, Danny stepped into the closet and pulled the sliding door closed as quietly as he could. He stood between her T-shirts and blouses, breathing in near-perfect darkness.

What had he been thinking?

15

THE MOMENT I opened the door to my suite, I knew that something was wrong. I saw it clearly right there: The carpet had been stepped on.

I was already in a bad place. The night before, I'd left my embarrassing encounter with Danny Hansen and was filled with a new fear that he was right—I didn't stand a chance against my evil enemy. My mind worked furiously and I could not sleep as I conjured up all kinds of nasty endings to my own life.

Now I saw proof-positive evidence that my enemy had entered my room and was waiting in the bedroom to kill me. The thought almost made me drop the bag of hygiene products I'd purchased.

Instead, I tightened my grip on the plastic bag and stood perfectly still, studying those prints on my carpet. Maybe I'd walked on it before leaving. Of course that had to be it.

The prints were fairly large, however. Much larger than

mine. A man's prints, I thought, and if I hadn't been so freaked out I might have felt some satisfaction for that piece of detective work. But I was far too preoccupied with the possibility that someone was in my suite.

I almost ran back out the door. Down the hall, out into the street. But then what? While I ran down the street with nowhere to go, whoever was here would take all my files and money and maybe turn me over to the police. Or wait for me to come back so he could kill me then.

For all I knew, the person had already come and gone. Or maybe the manager had come in to set a breaker or something. With the door open behind me I had an advantage, right? I could make a quick escape from this position if I needed to.

Heart banging away like a woodpecker on speed, I carefully set my bag down. I gripped the door frame to give myself leverage to hurl myself backward if anyone with a gun or knife suddenly bolted out of my bedroom.

"Hello?" My voice was high-pitched and shaky, not the kind that might frighten anyone, especially not a man with a gun. No one responded.

"Hello? Who's there?"

Still no answer.

I weighed a dozen possible scenarios, some taken directly from my many books that detailed crimes of passion and murder. Instead of running, as the intruder would likely expect, I should play it smart and call his bluff. I could hide myself and wait for him to leave.

The thought of going in while someone with a gun or a machete was lurking in my bedroom made my pulse peak, but I had read so many accounts of people doing stupid things in the heat of the moment, things that could have been avoided with a little thought. Like bolting.

Redding had said he had ties with the police. If he found any incriminating evidence against me, like the suitcase full of cash under my bed, he might send them to investigate. Running away would only leave me looking over my shoulder in a fog of fear. Someone had found out where I lived, and I needed to know who and why. The best way to do that was to stay put.

All of this flashed through my mind in a few moments while my heart tried to tear itself free from my chest.

The drapes (which I detested because they were green, heavy, and hard to clean) hung next to the sliding glass door, which led out to a tiny balcony. If I could get to them undetected, I would be able to hide in the corner where they were bunched. I was thin enough, and the drapes hung all the way to the floor, so my feet wouldn't stick out.

But I would leave my own marks on the carpet. The intruder might see the tracks, follow them to the drapes, and stab his machete through the material.

Unless I went over the couch.

I started to move, then hesitated as another thought hit me.

"Okay," I called, loud enough to be heard in the whole suite. "I'm going to get the manager. I'll be right back!" Then I slipped out of my shoes and closed the door firmly behind me.

Snatching up my shoes, I tiptoed to the couch and walked along the cushions, down the length toward the sliding glass door. If it had been a sleeper couch, the springs might have given me away, but I could hardly hear myself. I stepped on the carpet at the end, just one step far off the beaten track. I was now committed.

I slipped behind the drape and snugged my heels into the corner, making only the softest of bumps when the shoes in my hands knocked the wall.

Calm down, Renee. Breathe quietly.

Light filtered through the drape but I couldn't see the room. I couldn't peek without risking being caught. I wondered if I'd be able to hear the intruder shuffling around; the drape was heavy. I could only wait for the sound of the door opening and closing.

Nothing happened. No shuffling, no creaking, no heavy breathing, no door opening and closing.

SHE WAS STILL in the suite, Danny thought. He could not be sure, but as he pressed himself against the back of the closet he'd heard a distinct bump along that same wall.

She'd cleverly called out and shut the door in an attempt to make him think she'd gone to find the manager, but then she hid behind the drapes along the back wall. This was his guess.

He could remain where he was and wait for the silence that would assure him she was in fact gone. Or he could slip out now and risk being seen if she had any line of sight through a break in the curtains.

On the other hand, now might be his only chance to leave undetected. If she was behind the drapes, she would more likely be staring at the back of the curtains, terrorized, than boldly peering out to catch the intruder.

Then again, she'd shown herself to be surprisingly bold.

The thought of her seeing him was so disturbing that it incapacitated him. He, a priest, caught violating her space? If he were in anyone else's room, his decision would have come quickly, but his empathy for her was befuddling and frightening.

He was about to slide the door open and take his chances when another thought presented itself to him. The bathroom was more often than not a person's first destination upon returning from an errand. His only better chance of escape might come when she entered the bathroom to use the toilet. For a few seconds, any sound he made running from the room would be masked by the sound of rushing water.

If he could remain hidden until that moment, he was sure he could get out unseen. To that end he'd made a mistake when he entered her closet. She would surely check it first. She would throw open the shower door. She would press her face on the carpet and look under her bed. She might very well check them all ten times.

But there was a small balcony off the bedroom as well. And sliding doors with drapes. He couldn't go outside, though. He wouldn't be able to hear the toilet flushing and then make his escape.

Statistically speaking, however, drapes were the most often overlooked hiding place in a house, because people tended to view them as an extension of the wall.

If he hid behind the curtain as she had—

A loud bump from the next room cut his thoughts short. She was moving.

I WOULD SAY it was my inexperience that made me panic, but it could just as well have been because the heroin had destroyed half my brain cells and left me a little stupid, like Lamont sometimes said.

I don't know how much time passed, but to me it felt like a lifetime, and I suddenly thought I had made a terrible mistake. Whoever had entered my room might have already left and taken all my money and files with him! The police might show up at any moment with handcuffs!

Or, if the intruder left now while I hid behind the drapes, he would escape with my stuff and then send the police. Either way, I couldn't just hide here! I had to know the truth, so I could escape. Or I had to stop him from leaving.

I couldn't think past this sudden realization, and so I threw the drapes aside and ran out, bumping the wall with my elbow as I did.

If anyone was in the suite, they must have heard me, so I didn't pretend any longer.

"Okay, I know you're in here, okay?" The sound of my voice gave me a little confidence, so I continued, storming into my bedroom. "I saw your tracks on my carpet. I have a gun! I swear I'll blow your head off if you don't come out with your hands up!"

I shoved my hand under my blouse and pointed my finger like a gun. I didn't know how else to hide the obvious fact that I had no weapon.

The room was empty. But there were tracks all over the carpet. And my bedspread was rumpled as if someone had sat down—I would never have left it such a mess.

"Out!" I screamed. "Get out here!"

FOR THE FIRST time in a very long time, Danny was having difficulty thinking clearly. Renee had done the unthinkable by barging out of hiding, and by doing something so unexpected, she'd played her hand brilliantly, intentional or not.

His indecision had cost him precious minutes. He was now immobilized and at her mercy.

Part of him wanted to rush out, fall to his knees, confess all, and beg for her forgiveness. Part of him wanted to melt into the wall behind him, hoping against reason that she would go into the bathroom before checking the closet. Maybe even flush the toilet.

All of him wished he was in the budget meeting rather than in her closet.

Danny pressed his hands against the wall at his back and breathed a pointless prayer.

I WAS YELLING not because it was a smart thing to do, but because I was terrified and furious at once, and because no one was coming out with his hands raised in the air. I took my hand out from under my shirt. It was ridiculous anyway.

He was gone. Or he was hiding. But why would anyone like Redding hide from me? It made no sense. I could hurl all of my hundred pounds at a man like Redding and maybe, if I was lucky, put a dent in his shirt.

Which could only mean the intruder was no longer here.

I rushed to the bathroom door and spun in. Empty. I raced to the shower and pulled the curtain wide. Untouched.

I ran back to the bedroom, dropped to my knees, and bent low to look under the bed. Nothing but the suitcase I kept my money in. It hadn't been moved. Relief flooded my mind. If they hadn't taken my money... Well, that was a good sign. Maybe the manager had come in to check on a maintenance issue. He'd done it once before, explaining when I complained that it was his hotel.

That left the closet.

I stood and stared at the sliding door. The more I thought about it, the more I realized that it made no sense for anyone like Redding to hide from me. He would want to intimidate me, not sneak out on me. He would be the one with the machete, not the one hiding in the closet.

But still, there was that closet. It was always the closet.

I walked across the room, and just to be safe I gave one final warning to offset my fresh surge of fear.

"I told you, I have a gun and don't think I won't shoot. I have a hair trigger. And I'm ticked."

I held my breath, hesitated a few long moments while tingles washed down my neck, and then I shoved the sliding door wide. They were all there, all my carefully placed possessions, set where I'd left them on my shelves. Not one had been touched.

I glanced to my left, at my shirts, which hung from hangers so they wouldn't have any creases in them. But the shirts were not the only thing there.

The priest, Father Danny Hansen, who'd thrown me out of his house last night because he thought I was such a silly little girl, stared at me from between two pink shirts at the back of the closet.

My heart stopped. Was it his ghost?

Then his ghost blinked and I took a step back.

"Hello, Renee," he said.

I couldn't speak. I couldn't even breathe.

He brushed aside my shirts, stepped past me, and stood with his arms by his sides, staring at me. He looked like a boy who'd been caught with chocolate on his face ten minutes before dinnertime.

"Father Hansen?" I said.

"Call me Danny," he said. "I'm afraid I don't make a very good priest."

My relief at seeing him rather than anyone else was so profound that I lost my mind for a moment. I rushed up to him and threw my arms around his neck.

"It's you!" I cried. "Oh! Thank goodness it's you!"

He stood still without returning my embrace, and it occurred to me that my reaction might be somewhat startling. I released him quickly and stepped back.

"I'm sorry...Thank you. I mean that it's you and not someone else."

"I'm so sorry, Renee. It's not what you think."

I began to think about that. He'd been in my stuff and his

face looked a little different than I remembered, like he'd been crying maybe. What if Danny Hansen was some kind of pervert?

"What are you doing in my closet?" I asked.

He spread his hands apologetically. "I'm sorry, I had no right. I...Our conversation last night was bothering me. I...We said some things. I was thinking that maybe I was a little too quick to judge you."

My heart skipped a beat.

"So you'll help me?"

"I didn't say that. I——"

"Did you touch any of my stuff?"

"No."

"Did you sit on my bed?"

He hesitated. "Well, yes. I was...I'm sorry, I just——"

"Are you some kind of pervert?"

"No! Oh no, oh no! It's not like that."

"Then tell me what it is like, Father Hansen who wants to be called Danny? Tell me why you broke into my house and snooped around my closet. Tell me why you were on my bed. Did you go through my food, too?"

"Food? No!" Then he added, "I looked in your refrigerator."

"Why?"

"I'm trying to tell you, if you'll just slow down and let me explain!"

I crossed my arms. "Fine. Explain. I want to know why a priest is so good at breaking in and snooping around. Because I have some thoughts on that."

"I had to know how sincere you were about all that you said. I had to know if you really did plan on going after these people. I had to know, because I really do think you're putting yourself in real danger."

"Well, now you know. You saw my gun. I'm going to shoot Jonathan Bourque dead. Satisfied?"

He turned away. "I see that. And no, I'm not satisfied."

"Why not?"

He swiveled to me, angry. "Because I like you!"

You see, I was right. God had brought Danny Hansen to save me, just like he'd brought Lamont to save me. Three months ago, I might have thrown my arms around him again, but I was older and wiser now. I was someone to contend with.

"That's nice, Danny. I like you, too. And you obviously know much more about this kind of thing than I do. So why won't you help me?"

"Because I'm not going to help you *kill* a man!"

"Then at least help me find out more about him. Help me expose him. Help me find the whole truth about him. That wouldn't be so bad, would it?"

He didn't answer.

"You want to know what I think?" I said. "I think that you're much more than just a priest. I think you're here because you're more like me than you admit. I think you'll do anything to stop a man from killing innocent people. You did it before, when you went after the people who killed your mother, and maybe that wasn't the last time."

His eyes widened, just slightly, but I was sure that I had said something that took him off guard. He looked at me for a few seconds, then ran his fingers through his hair and started pacing.

"This is crazy. You're right, I have my reasons for wanting to help you, but it's not what you think. I have a terrible weakness when it comes to self-righteous dogs who destroy others for their own gain. Yes, I'm sure it has everything to do with my own experience, but that doesn't mean I could possibly stand by and support you in this crazy crusade of yours."

"So why are you here? Why do you want to help me?"

He was prowling like a lion in a cage.

"I swear, you can trust me," I said, suddenly hopeful.

"You don't know how much danger you are putting yourself in."

"I was facedown in an alley dying, just a year ago. Don't tell me I don't know about danger."

"Going after someone like Bourque will get you killed."

"My only reason for living is for justice, and if that gets me killed, oh well."

Danny turned his face up to the ceiling. "Dear God, help us."

"No. *You*, Danny. *You* help *me*."

He lifted a trembling finger. "Not to kill. Not that! And you must also promise me you won't try to kill him or do anything so absurd."

It was all I needed to hear. The mere thought of bonding with someone who would help me was overwhelming.

"Thank you." Tears flooded my eyes. "Thank you, thank you so much. I swear I won't let you down."

"We'll do a simple investigation, nothing more. Promise me."

"I promise! I promise you with all my heart. I just need to know the truth, that's all. I just…" My voice froze up with emotion.

"I thought you already knew," he said.

"I do. I just want to really know, you know. So I know I'm not crazy."

"You'll have to do exactly what I say. Nothing more. And no one can know. Not a soul."

I stepped up, wrapped my arms around him, and hugged him. "Thank you, Danny." I could hear his heart pounding in his chest. This time he put one hand on my shoulder.

"It's okay," he said.

"Okay."

I felt like I had come home. Like I was lost and had been found again.

I finally pulled back and wiped my eyes.

"I should go now," he said. "Come to my house tomorrow at noon. Can you do that?"

"Yes."

"Okay."

Then he turned on his heels and left the room.

16

THE NEXT THREE days were the happiest days of my life.

Looking back now, I can say that with complete confidence. A brilliant light had blazed into my dark world.

I'd had so many happy days with Lamont, of course, but my early days with him had been fogged by heroin and blurred by the new drugs prescribed to deal with withdrawal symptoms. In their dulled state, my emotions couldn't match the level of intensity that I felt bonding with Danny after three months of isolation and uncertainty.

I remember the first time I got a real Christmas present. I was seven. My father hated the holidays because he said the whole thing was just a lie made up by big corporations to sell junk that no one needed. He called it robbery. All of the neighborhood kids got gifts, but I didn't, so I hid out in my house over Christmas.

But for one Christmas, that changed—I still don't know why. I think my father wanted to appease my mother, who'd caught him cheating that December. Whatever the reason, when I woke up that Christmas Day there was a new red bicycle with a white bow on it in the living room.

I could hardly stop jumping up and down. I rode the bike up and down the street all day to show the other kids that my parents could be cool, too.

Two weeks later I ruined our neighbor's rosebush by crashing into it by mistake. To punish me, my father broke all the spokes on the bike. But for those first two weeks, I was in heaven.

That's how I felt going over to Danny's house that first day, like I'd gone from having nothing to having everything in just one day.

I was so excited that my hands were shaking when I knocked on his door. I wanted to rush in and throw my arms around him when he opened the door. I didn't, of course. I just said, "Hello, Danny," and walked in. But we were both smiling.

He had a pot of tea ready, and my first question had nothing to do with killing people. "Why do you like tea so much?" I asked as he poured the steaming tea into two white porcelain cups.

"In Bosnia, my mother used to serve us tea twice every day, once in the morning, once in the afternoon. She said tea had medicinal value. I guess the habit stuck."

I lifted my cup. "Then we will drink to your mother," I said. He smiled. I think he liked that.

"To Mother," he said. And he sipped his tea.

"So, when do we get started?" I asked.

"We have already," he said. "If we're going to work together, we need to know a little more about each other. I need to know what you do and don't know about Jonathan Bourque. Infiltrating the enemy's a dangerous business, and if you're not prepared it will get you killed. I would like to avoid that."

"Good thing I wasn't an enemy yesterday," I said. "I could have killed you in my closet."

"Touché." He smiled, but I think he was just being gracious.

We were soon sitting and talking very comfortably, as if this sort of thing was common for both of us. He wanted to know everything—where I'd come from, why I'd gotten into drugs, how Lamont had rescued me, what life was like living by the sea. And I didn't hold anything back. After all, he was trusting me by taking me into his confidence, so I was eager to do the same.

We talked about so many things over so many hours those first three days. I can't begin to explain it all. Although we first met at his house, we spent the rest of our time at a park on the east side of town where our meetings would be less conspicuous. His neighbor, an older widow named Ellen Bennett, would undoubtedly sit him down and interrogate him for long hours if she saw him coming and going with a beautiful young blonde, he explained.

I was like an apprentice, and Danny was the wise, experienced master. He was thirty-two, not really much older than my twenty-four, but he'd been to hell and back, whereas I had only been to hell (not counting my year with Lamont). He, the priest, would help me find my way back. At least that's the way I looked at it.

In some ways, he did seem like the perfect priest. He spoke with a sure voice and listened with those kind blue eyes. He oozed such an unwavering confidence that it was impossible for me to imagine we could do anything but succeed, never mind his insistence that exposing Bourque would be dangerous.

"Of course," I always said to that. Of course, of course. But I was thinking that Danny had eaten danger for breakfast. I felt like he and I could conquer the world.

During our walks in the park, he told me about growing up in Bosnia, about the war, about the brutal deaths of his loved ones, about his path to justice. Hearing Danny tell the story, my heart broke for him.

The laws in Bosnia were a shambles, so he took the law into his own hands. After killing those who'd raped and murdered his family he'd joined the militia and learned how to fight like a man. By the time he was seventeen, he was leading an entire squad of scouts, assassins who killed enemies in their own homes.

Like I said, Danny ate danger for breakfast. He began to methodically teach me some of the fundamentals of hunting an enemy—surveillance, planning, preparation, execution.

In a private corner of the park sheltered by oak trees and dense greasewood shrubs, Danny taught me about weapons. Though I had learned a fair amount about the basics, Danny was the Zen master of personal weapons.

"Here, let me show you," he said on the second day as I practiced wielding a large bowie knife.

"Sure." I handed him the knife. He effortlessly flipped the blade over and spun it once. He wasn't showing off. In fact, he hadn't even started to demonstrate what he wanted me to see. He was simply examining the blade by rote.

But he had me there, at the grip of his strong hand on the hilt of that blade, the flex of his forearm as he spun it, the perfect balance and control he had over the weapon.

He caught my look of adoration. "What?"

"Nothing," I said. "Go on."

I forget what he showed me. I was too enamored with his command of that blade.

Danny owned only seven guns, which he let me see and handle, but he knew every firearm currently in use, or so it seemed to me. And he could palm a pistol like a gunslinger.

He demonstrated much more than I could possibly remember those first few days, but more than the weapons, he talked always about love and true religion and his longing for justice. He only wanted what everyone wants, he said, and the reason everyone wants justice is because God is just.

These were the truest words anyone had ever spoken to me, because I, too, only wanted God's justice. They gave me hope. Danny's hatred of injustice began to flow in Bosnia and now spilled out on the streets of Los Angeles. He had many beautiful faces, but his love of justice was his most attractive to me.

Danny would cross the street to help a woman pick up a dropped bag of groceries. Or stop traffic to give an old man time to cross. He would sit with widows and pray for a husband and he would take time to bounce a ball with an orphan boy. I could see it in his eyes, he loved them all.

And he hated anyone who stood against them.

Many other things Danny said drifted over my head, especially when my mind was focused on the way he was handling a gun. But I tucked away the rest like a secret treasure.

He left Bosnia after the war and came to America to start over thirteen years ago. Changed his name to Danny Hansen to make the break clean, entered seminary, and set out to be a true man of God, to atone for the many so-called Christians in Bosnia and the rest of the world whose sins spit in God's face.

At the same time, he seemed nothing like a priest. He never wore his collar when I was with him. He said that he wanted children one day. Even more, he didn't strike me as a very religious man, but more of a philosopher. His occupation seemed to be more of a convenience than a calling.

According to Danny, it was the rules set down by religion that most often got in the way of truly loving people. Religious authorities made it too easy to feel good about following those rules, regardless of love, and to frown on people who didn't follow the rules.

True religion, he said, should be about love. This is what he learned in Bosnia, and this is what he had set out to prove to himself here in America. Justice was a supreme act of love.

He was very eager for me to understand this, and I assured him that I did, although I think he could tell that I was distracted. I was itching to go after Bourque, an act that didn't require quite so much philosophy.

I admit that I was a little distracted by Danny himself. After Lamont, I'd thought I could never look at another man with even mild interest, but Danny was different. I can't say my thoughts were necessarily romantic, but I'm not sure how else I would characterize them.

I was in awe of him. He was a beautiful man with a strong jaw and soft eyes. He was very kind and smiled a lot and, even more endearingly, he actually laughed at my antics. I could tell that he liked me, and I think he could tell that I liked him.

We were so different from each other, he being a priest and me a recovered junkie. He being a man who stood nearly six feet and solid as a steel beam, me being a woman just over five feet, weighing in at about half his size. He growing up in Bosnia in a loving family that had been killed, me growing up in Atlanta with two parents who didn't love me enough to stick around. He being a meat eater, me being a vegetarian.

But in other important ways we were similar, I thought. We both valued cleanliness. We both loved people. We both hated injustice. We both listened to jazz and classical music as well as pop and rock.

We both had an interest in Jonathan Bourque.

I was surprised to learn that Danny was actually at the fund-raiser where we met *because* of Bourque. He'd started his own investigation into the man, having stumbled on information from an attorney named Cain Kellerman, evidently one of Lamont's co-workers.

My suspicions had been right—Danny had purposefully followed Redding into the basement that night.

I wondered why a priest would start his own investigation rather than turn the matter over to the police, but when I asked, Danny just shrugged and said he had a thing for exposing injustice. At any rate, he hadn't learned anything more than I already knew.

"So when are we going to do this?" I asked while we walked in the park on the second day.

"We are doing this," he said, hands clasped behind his back.

"Of course. But when are we going to ... you know ... go after Bourque?"

"We're not going to go after Bourque. We're going to let Bourque come to us."

I never could quite understand the difference between the two but I let it slide.

"When are we going to start our surveillance?" I asked.

"When the time is right."

Danny was as steady as a rock, but I wasn't sure I had the patience to watch a rock. I was more interested in picking up that rock and slinging it into Bourque's head.

Most of our time was spent rehearsing what I knew, what I didn't know, and what I should know in regard to how to conduct myself in the field: choosing methods of surveillance, tracking subjects, breaking into secure locations, avoiding detection, foiling security systems. It was a kind of hopscotch approach to fieldwork primarily because I kept changing the subject.

As he drove me home from the park after our third meeting, my mind was rattling with facts.

"Fieldwork," I said, thinking of the Ann Rule books I'd read. "Seems more like FBI talk than war talk."

"Like I said, I was with a militia. We were hunters with personal weapons who blew up bridges and infiltrated the enemy. My primary duties involved finding key targets and neutralizing them. It was a different kind of war."

I hesitated, wanting to get past the war to more personal kinds of killings. "How did you kill the men who killed your family?" I asked. He glanced at me, and I wondered if I'd overstepped a boundary. "Sorry, I didn't mean it like that."

"I shot them that same day. There were three of them."

His confession surprised me, not just because he'd made it, but by the way he said it. So matter-of-fact. It seemed so real, and yet so...I don't know, maybe so *sur*real at the same time. It wasn't as if he was gripping the wheel of the Chevy with both hands and sweating profusely as he broke down and confessed. He just sat there with the wheel between three fingers and said it as if he were shrugging. I tried to imagine his hands covered with blood.

"It was crude," he said. "I was young. I wouldn't do that again."

"Would you ever kill outside of a war?"

He hesitated. "If I thought it was my moral obligation."

I was leaning back in the passenger seat with one leg folded under the other, but in my mind I was on the edge of my chair.

"When is it morally right to kill someone?" I asked. "I mean, outside of war?"

"Now you want me to help you justify your desire to kill Bourque."

"Yes," I said. "I do."

Danny turned the corner and headed down Cherry Avenue toward the Staybridge. "Are you sure you want the answer to that?"

"Yes. A simple one. I'm not that smart."

"You're wrong about that. The problem with any philosophical consideration is that once you open a door in your mind, you can never close it. Once you learn something, you can never convince your mind that you didn't learn it. If you learn the world is round, you can never fit in with a world that thinks it's flat."

"My world's like an amoeba," I said. "It changes shape every day."

He laughed, and I couldn't help but smile.

"So," I said, "when's it right to kill?"

Danny took a breath. "Said very simply so that even a child can understand? Not that I'm suggesting you have the mind of a child."

"Yes, said very simply," I said. "I want to be able to kill Jonathan Bourque without the slightest confusion about why I'm doing it."

He grinned. He liked me, I thought.

So he told me, using phrases like *consequential moral reasoning* and *human rights to life* and such. I found it all fascinating and, even more, I found Danny to be a perfect gentleman who was as patient as he was smart.

Then I asked what I really wanted to know.

"So have you? Ever killed someone outside of a war, I mean."

Danny remained silent, and I knew that he had. The priest beside me might have a whole graveyard full of skeletons for all I knew.

"You don't need to answer," I said. "If you have, I'm sure it was the right thing to do. Just like I'm certain that killing the man who killed Lamont is the right thing to do, and nothing will ever change that."

"Renee—"

"Please, I don't want to talk about this anymore."

"I have to tell you—"

"No, Danny, please. It was a stupid question and really, I don't care. It's none of my business. I'm sorry."

"Okay."

And that was it, at least for the time being. We drove in an awkward silence into the Staybridge parking lot.

"What are you doing tonight?" Danny asked.

"Reviewing my moral obligations," I said.

"We had an agreement. You assured me that you would forget the whole business of taking the law into your hands. What we're going to do is strictly expose the world to the truth about Jonathan Bourque, nothing more."

"That was before you gave me the moral reasoning I needed to justify killing him."

He said nothing, but a soft grin formed on his face when he saw that I was smiling.

"I'm serious," he said.

I winked. "So am I."

He pulled up to the lobby entrance and looked at me. "Tell me what you learned about where most people hide their secrets."

We'd talked about this yesterday. "In their homes," I said.

"Why?"

"Because that's where they spend most of their time in private, which is where most hidden things are done."

"And where in the home?"

"Office, safe, computer. Or basement, if they have one."

He nodded. "So if you want to find Bourque's secrets, where would you look?"

"In his home office."

"Would you like to do that?"

My heart jumped. "Are you serious?"

"A window of opportunity has opened," he said.

"When?"

"Bourque left for Atlanta this morning. His wife is speaking at a fund-raiser in Hollywood tonight. She'll be staying at a hotel for the night to avoid the long drive home. If you don't mind setting your moral deliberations aside for a few hours, I was thinking we might take a look."

This was it. This was the culmination of it all!

"Yes!" I cried. "Yes, yes, of course, yes!"

"Okay then."

"You're serious?" I still wasn't sure he meant it.

"I am."

"When?"

"You tell me. We covered this."

"Two in the morning. "

"Good. Then two in the morning it is."

As I said, those first three days were the happiest of my life. A brilliant light had shined into my dark world. But the sun was going down on the horizon; darkness was coming, and those three days were about to end.

17

SIMON REDDING SAT in his Suburban at midnight watching the Staybridge across the street. His task was simple, one he'd accomplished many times over the past five years. This time his employer had crossed a young woman, one with connections to Lamont Myers, Bourque had said.

She was likely as innocent of wrongdoing as he was guilty. But that no longer concerned him. She was a problem; his task was to eliminate problems.

Before a problem could be eliminated, it had to be identified. Then located. And then, when the time was right, dealt with.

It had taken Redding four days to identify and locate Renee Gilmore. The fact that her only mode of transportation was by cab had rendered the motor vehicle registration search useless, which had stalled him. But it had taken only two days using his contacts at the cab companies to flush out information on a bleached-blond girl who weighed a scant hundred pounds if she was wet.

Cabbies talked. Put the word out that a five-hundred-dollar tip was in the works for anyone who could locate a particular fare, and they would, especially if they believed the subject in question was a runaway who needed help.

Although he could have taken her in the Staybridge, he needed to know what she knew before silencing her. Hotels were not suited to the task of coercion.

Better to wait for her to exit the building and climb into a Yellow Cab.

Redding sighed and picked up a bag of sunflower seeds. He sometimes thought that the five years of medical training he'd put himself through were a complete waste, considering his present profession. But the money was good and the benefits were far too generous to ignore. Bourque did not believe in thugs, preferring trustworthy men with brains over brawn, and he was willing to pay for those brains, especially if they came with some brawn. In this way, Redding was uniquely suited for his occupation.

Thirty minutes later, Renee Gilmore exited the Staybridge. But she did not climb into a Yellow Cab.

She was picked up instead by a black BMW.

FOR THE FIRST time since the war, Danny Hansen found himself on a mission with a partner, and the camaraderie brought some comfort. But only a little, because this time, the objective was different.

By the time he was seventeen, he had two years of field-work under his belt and had gained a broad reputation for being the kid who could get anywhere. "Injun," they called him. He frequently took small bands of three or four on hit-and-run missions. They all had endured rigorous training, all knew how to kill, all faced death, and all were in excellent physical shape. They were warriors who knew they might not return alive.

Renee Gilmore, on the other hand, had never killed, had endured no real training in the field, and would be lucky to do half a pull-up on the bar she'd installed in her bathroom door frame.

She was without question a liability.

But Danny hadn't brought her along to help him break into Jonathan Bourque's house. He needed no such help. Rather, he would help *her* break in. Renee needed to find justice, and he had decided to help her find it. For her sake.

If he could help her do what she needed to do, and at the same time rid society of the worst kind of menace, he would do well.

Bourque's ten-thousand-square-foot Greek-styled mansion stood on the cliffs of Rancho Palos Verdes, off Palos Verdes Drive, overlooking a stunning view of the Pacific Ocean under moonlight.

He'd rented a black BMW 7 Series, knowing from several previous trips to the neighborhood that there was no place to hide a car as conspicuously non-European as a Chevy Malibu. A BMW would fit in like a pea might fit its pod.

The house loomed against the dark gray sky, a monstrosity presumably purchased with blood money. Other than Renee's inexperience, Danny's greatest concern had been how to interrupt the security system. To that end, he spent two hours earlier in the night meticulously tracing the circuits that led to a single dish on Bourque's roof.

The ADI system employed its own power source independent of the city's grid. The dish attached to this private source communicated with the security service via a satellite signal that, if broken, would alert the company of a potential security breach.

The satellite's signal cable was mounted on the roof. Danny cut this line, and the security service was alerted. He had five minutes to complete the task and clear the property.

Working quickly, he clipped a powered circuit loop to the wire he'd cut. The matchbox-size device would supply the dish with a duplicate signal to be broadcast, and the security service would see that the signal had been restored. They would nevertheless dispatch authorities to the house, find the system fully functional, and assume that a power burst had temporarily interrupted service.

Safely in the trees to the east of the house, Danny waited for the police to arrive, check the house, and leave before returning to his car. The alarm system was still fully operational through the phone system, but when he cut the phone service to the house just before breaking in, the constant signal from his bypass device would keep the security service in the dark.

"So what now?" Renee asked, crouched beside him in the dense shadows of some trees.

They were both dressed in black—slacks, long-sleeved shirts, ski masks, and gloves, all provided by him. He'd mistakenly purchased Renee's two sizes too large, but she didn't mind. Fashion wasn't at the top of her list.

Bourque was.

He glanced at his watch. Three AM. "Now I cut the phone line and we go in."

"How, through a window?"

"Through the front door. Better not to leave a trace unless you want them to sweat. In this case, we don't. Don't move from this spot. Stay low. I'll be right back."

"Okay. I'll stay low."

He had to smile. She was so...cute. She had the intelligence to pull this off. Her years on the street had prepared her emotions for violent encounters. Her loss had given her the motivation. And now her connection with him had given her the opportunity.

Danny checked the street, saw no sign of the security car that made its rounds every hour, and made his way quickly toward the west side of the house where the phone service kept its box.

There was more to Renee's relationship with Lamont Myers than she'd shared, he thought. He'd done a quick search on Lamont Myers and found no mention of the man in the Bourque Foundation's public records, which meant that Lamont was indeed well connected, a high-level man who could afford a house in Malibu—unlike Cain Kellerman, a lower-level employee who was still listed on the foundation's Web site as one of their attorneys.

There was a Lamont Myers, however, listed as the sole mortgage holder on a house by the sea in Malibu, which was in foreclosure for nonpayment.

All of this was consistent with what Renee had told him and raised no alarms. It was the way she spoke of her late "husband" that made him wonder how anyone so perfect could exist.

Her memory of the man had been whitewashed by tragedy. He knew how easy it was for the faults of the deceased to fade. Although Renee represented Lamont as a strict man suffering from a severe case of obsessive-compulsive disorder, she didn't seem to remember a single incident when he'd been anything but loving to her.

Then again, Renee wasn't exactly in a position to think clearly about the past. She'd been taking prescription medications until Lamont's passing, and she didn't know exactly what kind. She'd likely suffered a psychotic break the night Lamont had rescued her. It only followed that her memory of the man was gilded.

Danny could never live up to such a memory.

He had just severed the phone lines when that thought cut through his mind. He paused for a moment, surprised that he thought of himself as a potential replacement for Lamont.

But he didn't. He couldn't. One day, with a girl like Renee, perhaps, but not now. Not while in such a dangerous relationship, one focused on the death of another man.

He quickly corrected himself. The *exposure* of another man.

Danny returned to the trees where he'd left Renee and dropped to one knee beside her.

"Get it?" she asked.

"Got it."

They sounded like two kids spying on their neighbor. What was he doing?

"Now what?"

"Now we go in."

She jumped to her feet, and he immediately grabbed her shirt and pulled her back down. "Stay low. Follow me."

He cut to his right, stooped, aware of her hand on his hip as they ran. There was little danger at this point—breaking and entering was easy when the premises were vacant and unsecured. But he had to keep his mind on the objective and off Renee, a task that was proving more difficult than he'd anticipated.

They glided up to the front door and he started on the locks, ignoring her heavy breathing and darting eyes. On her own, she wouldn't last a week out here.

"In." He pocketed his tools, pushed the door open, and stepped inside with Renee pressing in close behind. He motioned silence and listened.

Nothing other than her breathing.

It took them three minutes to locate Jonathan Bourque's office and another two to unlock its door. The time was now three twenty-two in the morning.

Danny removed his ski mask, grateful for the air. He pulled a thick plastic sheet and two chip clips from his bag. Standing on one of the chairs, he clipped the plastic over the window drapes—a simple safeguard that would ensure no stray flashlight beam would escape. Satisfied, he nodded and faced Renee, who stood in the middle of the room watching him, having followed his lead and removed her ski mask.

"That's smart," she said.

"That's why I'm alive."

She was a little starstruck by him, he realized, and it wasn't off-putting.

"Now what?" she asked again.

"Now we look. But I don't want you to touch anything."

"Why not?"

"Because we can't leave any trace that says we were here."

"But we have gloves on."

He was thinking more of knocking things over than of leaving fingerprints, but he didn't want to suggest she was a klutz, so he nodded. "Okay, but put everything back exactly, and I mean exactly, where you find it. If there's dust, don't touch the dust."

"Okay."

The office walls and ceiling were lined with rich cherrywood paneling. Long bookcases were built into one wall. It was a typical office, really, with a bear rug, a sitting area with leather chairs, and a six-foot-wide desk crafted from a dark, exotic wood Danny didn't recognize.

Using his picks, he unlocked the desk drawers. "Go through the files," he said. "Look for the kind of information we talked about. Payoffs, offshore banks, personal notes . . . anything."

She began to rifle through the first drawer, pulling out one manila file at a time, flashlight between her teeth as she'd seen him do while picking the lock. It was unlikely that Bourque would have any useful information in his paper files—computer files were much easier to safeguard. Unless, of course, he was old-school, mistrusting electronic data that could be snatched through thin air.

He traced the bookcases with his light, scanning for decorative boxes and compartments favored for personal effects, particularly if the boxes had locks.

He opened seven such small boxes, all empty. The eighth one was locked. He pulled it off the shelf, set it on a lamp table, and worked on its lock.

What most could not know about searching offices, unless they had executed such searches themselves, was that the process took time. Like searching for a contact lens dropped on the bathroom floor, one had to assume it might be anywhere. If an initial search did prove unsuccessful, it was best to start at one end of the room and carefully search every square inch, because contact lenses could bounce surprising distances and come to rest in unlikely places.

He sprang the lock and looked inside the box. A small USB flash drive lay at the bottom. He scooped it out and pocketed it. Gold. If Bourque—

"I knew it!"

Renee stood behind the desk, holding an open file in one hand and the penlight in her other, staring at the contents.

"I knew it!" she cried again.

"Shhh!"

But he saw she wasn't likely to hush. If anything, she looked like she might start screaming.

"What is it?"

"Lamont! He"—her eyes shot up—"he ordered a hit on Lamont!"

Danny bounded over, reached across the desk, and snatched the file from her hand.

"I knew it!" She was frantic and yelling. "He killed him, I told you he killed him!"

"Keep your voice down," he snapped. "The whole neighborhood will hear you."

She gripped her head and paced, suddenly sobbing, beyond control. Danny scanned the page she'd found. It was a schedule of monthly fifty-thousand-dollar payments made to a bank account under the name Lamont Myers. Not unexpected. After all, Lamont had worked with Jonathan Bourque.

A red marker had struck through the last three payments on the schedule, with the word TERMINATED printed at the top of the page. Not exactly definitive evidence.

A crash jarred Danny from his thoughts. The green desk lamp lay shattered on the desk where she'd smashed it.

"What are you doing? You can't do that!"

"Read the note!" she said, thrusting out a trembling finger.

"What note?"

"The Post-it note!"

Then he saw the small yellow note on the desk. The Post-it had fallen from the page when he'd grabbed the file. He plucked it up and saw what had caused Renee to lose herself.

Five words, written by hand: *Take care of this problem.* Just that, no more.

His mind spun. True, taken with the larger body of evidence they had regarding Jonathan Bourque and Lamont's disappearance, the note made a statement. But it wasn't conclusive.

"You see that?" she demanded. "That pig killed him!"

Renee's recklessness was so disconcerting that he wasn't immediately sure how to respond. If Danny had replied, his voice might have masked the soft thump that came from the hallway.

It was a soft sound, an elbow on a corner molding perhaps, or a foot bumping into a baseboard. And the moment Danny heard it, he knew they were not alone.

He spun toward the door. Closed, as he'd left it.

But then the door swung open. Simon Redding stood in the frame.

He had a gun and it was trained on Danny.

18

MY WORLD CRASHED in on itself when I read those words on the yellow note. I don't know what I expected to find after all our sneaking and breaking in; maybe nothing. After all, Bourque was the kind of man who hid in the darkest corners—surely we wouldn't go in and find his sins printed on the walls. Besides, Danny had said it would be tough.

Honestly, I was just so excited to finally be on the job, doing what I'd dreamed about doing for so long. After three months of imagining, I wasn't only getting closer to my goal, I was reaching it with a master by my side. Danny might be a priest to his neighbors, but to me he was the fist of justice, and I was safely in his grip.

Yet when the flashlight played over the Post-it note and I saw Lamont's name, the sound of Danny picking at the box faded. I couldn't hear anything, not even my breathing, not even my own voice.

Something seemed to pop in my head. I stared at the file in my hand as a flood of realization crashed into me, washing away the doubt in the corners of my mind.

Jonathan Bourque had killed Lamont.

My next response was perfectly normal, I thought. Where I had hated Bourque before, I'd also feared him. More accurately, I'd feared what my hatred would bring to me—capture and torture and maybe even death.

But with the last reservation washed away, I was left with only raw hatred. The fear was gone. I wanted to kill that man in whatever way made him dead, preferably by a method that put him through terrible agony and sorrow first.

I cried out.

Danny took the file from me.

I smashed the lamp.

Then the door swung open and the man who'd threatened to cut off my fingers at the knuckles stood there with a silenced gun pointed at Danny. He flipped the light switch on.

For a moment no one moved.

"Hello, Mr. Redding," Danny said.

The man's eyes darted between us. A faint smile tugged at his mouth.

Danny spoke in a soft, sincere voice. "It would be a terrible mistake to pull that trigger," he said.

Simon Redding tried to appear relaxed, but small beads of sweat had popped out on his forehead. There was something about Danny that could unnerve anyone, even when a gun was pointed at his head. Maybe it was his confidence, something I decided then and there that I would emulate. I think I fell in love with Danny in that moment.

"The priest is more than he seems," Redding said.

"Aren't we all?"

The man's right brow lifted and my faith in Danny's confidence fled. Sweat aside, Simon Redding looked too relaxed for my liking. And he had the gun.

We were finished, Danny and I. There was no way out.

Then again, the fact that Redding didn't deny killing Lamont was as good as a confession to me. I stood rooted to the floor, torn between the realization that I hated this man as much as I hated Jonathan Bourque, and the fear that he might kill Danny.

Redding swiveled his gun and pointed the barrel right between my eyes.

"She's just along for the ride," he said. His eyes flitted to Danny. "You're the professional here, she's just a tagalong. What do you do, track down people you don't like and turn them over to the authorities? You're some kind of masked marauder who goes by the name of priest?"

"Take your gun off her," Danny said.

The authority in his voice helped me regain some confidence, but the effect was only momentary. After all, there was a gun in my face.

"No, I don't think so," Redding said. "I think you love this girl. I think you'll tell me everything to save her life."

I finally found my voice. "That's the most stupid thing I've heard in my life," I said. "We just met the other night."

His eyes turned to me. "Really? How about we start with your fingers?"

"Go ahead, just try!"

I was blinded to everything but my own rage. I didn't see how Danny got his gun out from under his belt at his back. I just heard the soft *pop* and saw a quarter-size red spot appear on Simon Redding's forehead. Blood sprayed the wall behind him.

My jaw dropped open.

The sight of him standing tall, unblinking with surprised eyes, gun pointed at me, was completely surreal. It was also terrifying, because even though I was quite sure he was already dead, his hand was still shaking.

I thought, *That gun's going to go off!* I cried out and dropped to one knee behind the desk.

Phftt! The bullet slapped into the bookcase behind me.

Then Redding staggered back, crashed into the door, and toppled to the ground like a felled redwood tree. The whole house seemed to shake when he hit.

I stood up, trembling from head to foot. But not from fear, I knew that even then. It was adrenaline. I didn't feel a moment of fear once I saw that the brute was dead and bleeding on the stone tile, half in, half out of the office. If anything I felt elation, because, although Jonathan Bourque had given the order, it was probably this man who'd actually pulled the trigger and killed Lamont.

I shouted out, a victory cry, something nondescript that sounded a little like a shriek, a little like "yes!" but was neither.

Danny looked at me. I didn't know what else to say. Here we stood in our black outfits, and there lay a dead man.

So I said, "He's dead."

Danny swore and hurried to the body, shoving his gun behind his belt as naturally as he'd withdrawn it. He leaped over the man, grabbed him by his shirt, and pulled him out into the hall.

"What are you doing?" I asked.

"Keeping him from bleeding on the carpet. We've got to get out of here."

"What about him?"

Danny flipped off the light. "Do me a favor, will you? Take the plastic off the window and get it under him. I have to get some things. Be right back."

He raced away, leaving me with Redding's dead body bleeding onto the tile just outside Bourque's office. To my recollection, it was the first dead body I'd seen, and he hardly looked dead. If not for the pool of blood spreading by the head, I might think he was only sleeping.

I whirled around and jerked the plastic off the drapes where Danny had clipped it. He wanted me to get it under the body to contain the bleeding, I thought. That way we could haul Redding out of the house without drizzling a trail of blood.

I laid the black plastic beside Simon Redding's body, grabbed his shoulder, and tried to roll him. He was a large man, heavier than I guessed, and it took a tremendous tug to get his torso to cooperate. Even then I didn't manage to get the body all the way over before my foot slipped in his blood, dropping me to my seat.

Now I had his blood all over my leg. His body rolled back to its original position. I swore. This was the dirty side of killing, I thought. Nothing was as easy as it seemed in books or movies. The little details always made the whole business messy. But if that's what it took, so be it.

Eager to get the job done before Danny returned, I pushed myself back up, stepped over the body, grabbed his shirt at his side, and pulled, this time shoving my heel against the wall for leverage.

"What are you doing?"

Danny had returned.

"Get your foot off the wall, please," he said. "You can't leave boot prints on the wall like that."

"Oh, sorry. I slipped."

He stared at me for a moment, then he set down a black bag and hurried up to help me. Together we rolled Simon Redding's dead body onto the black plastic sheet.

Danny didn't stop with that. He grabbed a box of black lawn

bags and some gray duct tape from his bag and began to tape bags along the edges of the plastic sheeting. I couldn't begin to guess what he was up to, and I was about to ask when he gave his next order.

"Go to the kitchen. Find a mop and a bucket. Fill the bucket with water and soap. We're going to need to get this blood off the floor."

"Okay. He deserved it, anyway," I said. "And he hardly felt a thing, right?"

Danny glanced up at me but said nothing.

"Actually, it might have been better if he'd felt something. A little pain," I said.

"Please hurry," he said.

"Okay. What about my boot? It's got blood on it."

He saw where I'd stepped in the blood. "Take them both off. And don't step in any more blood."

"Okay."

I followed his directions eagerly, elated to be an integral part of such a noble thing. I couldn't get my hands to stop shaking.

Did I feel bad about Simon Redding? No. Maybe I should have, but we had just stopped a man from killing other innocent people. He'd given up his right to life a long time ago, as Danny would have said. We had done the world a great service.

And when we did the same to Jonathan Bourque, which we would, we would do the world an even bigger service.

The sound of a motor running made me think Danny was vacuuming up with a wet vac before I mopped up the last traces of blood. He was careful like that. The best. I could learn so much just by watching him.

It took me ten minutes to find a bucket, a sponge mop, and some Ajax in the laundry, to fill the bucket half full with water, and to return to Danny. He was leaning over the body.

"Got it!" I said over the whine of his machine.

I saw what he was doing and I pulled up. Danny wasn't using a wet vac. He had some kind of electric saw out, and he was cutting away at the brute's right leg, six inches below his hip. He'd taped the plastic in such a way to catch any flying debris. Two arms and the left leg were already off and stacked up beside the torso.

It was dark, thankfully, so I couldn't see all the flesh and red blood, but the sight still hit me hard at first. Danny didn't seem to know I was watching him. He was leaning and sawing and making quick work of that leg.

But it was only a dead body, right? Simon Redding wouldn't care if we sawed his leg off after he was dead. Danny obviously knew what he was doing. In the next minute I knew why he'd gone to all that trouble.

He finished cutting off the leg, set it next to the other appendages, and looked at me. "Sorry, I should have warned you. But we have to get this body out of here, no traces. The only way to do that properly is to seal it in bags. The plastic won't cover the whole body, and even if it did, trying to stuff a body this big into a trunk is too risky. Rip the plastic and spill blood and you leave evidence in the trunk; that could be a real problem down the road."

I was impressed. "Smart," I said.

"No evidence, right? That's the first rule. Help me get these in their bags."

The legs and arms were easy enough. I held the bags while Danny placed the limbs inside. The torso was harder, but we managed with me holding it upright while he slipped a bag over the head and shoulders then down to the ground.

Now we had one large bag and two smaller bags. Following his careful direction, I mopped up the mess on the floor and wiped down the walls while he cleaned up the office. This was something I was good at, and I made sure not a speck of blood or bone remained anywhere. Meanwhile, Danny hid the bullet hole in the bookcase and put everything back exactly as we'd found it, minus the desk lamp I'd foolishly broken. Live and learn, I suppose.

After the scene was cleaned to Danny's satisfaction, it took us ten minutes to get out of the house. He carried in both arms the large double bag containing Redding's torso. I carried Danny's tool bag. I tried to carry the two smaller bags as well but couldn't hold them along with his tool case, so he set the arms and legs on the lawn for a second trip.

"I'm assuming you can drive?"

"Me? No, I don't have a license."

"But you can drive?"

"Sure."

"Good. You're taking the BMW."

"You're staying behind? I can't drive!"

"I'm taking Redding's car. Leaving it out front will only raise an alarm. The streets are empty, you can follow close."

Smart.

Redding's car was a Suburban, and I wondered if we'd wasted energy carving up the body. We could have just shoved the body into his mammoth vehicle without tearing the bag. Danny said no. It would be easier to dispose of the body in pieces. The larger the body, the more buoyant it would be. Smaller pieces sink easier. I would see, he said, as he placed the bags into the Chevy.

We left Jonathan Bourque's mansion in Palos Verdes after Danny repaired the phone lines, checked the house for any sign we'd been there (other than the missing lamp), and locked the front door.

In the Suburban, Danny led me west; I hugged his taillights

in the rented BMW. It had been a long time since I'd been behind a wheel, but it came back to me after a few corners.

I was ecstatic. We had broken in, found the evidence we needed, eliminated a problem, and escaped without any additional complications.

But as I followed Redding's body parts, I began to think about the fact that we hadn't touched Bourque yet. Until the man who had killed Lamont was dead, I could not, would not, did not want to rest.

I wondered if I could do this for a living. Danny did, didn't he? Simon Redding had accused him of taking the law into his hands, and Danny hadn't offered any denial.

He hadn't come right out and said he killed people, naturally. Who would? People would put him behind bars if they knew what he did. I understood his need to lie.

Danny was a very special kind of priest who had done this sort of thing before. And I thought I might be quite good at doing the same kind of thing.

Maybe that's why I'd been saved from the streets. Maybe all my suffering would produce some good after all. Maybe Lamont's death wouldn't be wasted.

At the very least, I was now more confident than ever that I would learn whatever I needed to know to kill Lamont's killer. The idea of it made my head tingle with a strange mix of nervousness and anticipation. Maybe it's the kind of feeling that comes right before jumping out of a plane for the first time.

I followed Danny to a dirt road that ran half a mile toward the ocean before ending at the top of a sheer rock cliff. Climbing out of the BMW, I hurried to the edge, where he was studying the breaking waves a hundred yards below.

"You're going to throw the bags over the cliff? Won't they just float?"

"Not the bags. The body parts. Give me a hand."

He headed to the back of the Suburban, opened the rear door, and pulled out the three bags.

"Won't the waves just wash the body parts up onto the shore?" I asked.

"There is no shore in this section, only cliff. The tide's heading out. We'll give each piece some added weight and let the ocean do its thing. Within a day, the fish will have Redding stripped to the bone. Even if he does wash in, it's highly unlikely anyone will spot his smashed bones way down there. Here, help me out."

We pulled the body parts out and strapped large boulders to each using rope. We shoved each bundle over the cliff and watched them splash into the waves, then disappear beneath the surface.

Shark food, Danny said. He retrieved his power saw and dropped that over as well.

He explained how he would burn the bags and clean his other tools to rid the world of the last evidence linking Redding's disappearance to us. We'd both worn gloves and left no prints; we'd vacuumed and washed away all stray hairs and fibers from the house; we'd been careful not to leave any forensic evidence in the cars. There was evidence of a break-in at the house, perhaps, but not a killing. The missing flash drive would create some havoc, but Danny could live with that.

Now all we had to do was drive Redding's Suburban to a warehouse that specialized in stripping cars for resale on the black market, and we would be done.

On the cliff with Danny, facing a gentle sea breeze, I felt a numbing sense of appreciation and accomplishment. We'd done it. Together. Danny and I.

The long arm of Danny's law had rescued me in the same

way Lamont's had. I was saved by the law, our own law. The full, just, unbending law. A law that called to task all those who acted nice on the outside but trampled innocent victims without a second thought.

It didn't all make perfect sense to me yet, but I was sure that complete understanding would come. Danny had been thinking on this for much longer than me.

I hooked my hand around his elbow and stared out to the sea. "It's beautiful, isn't it, Danny?"

"Yes." He didn't react to my hand on his arm. "It is."

"I used to stare out at the ocean when I lived with Lamont and dream of what it would be like to get on a boat and sail away forever."

"Dreams are a gift," he said.

"Like that song 'Come Sail Away,' by Styx."

"Good song."

I don't think there's anything quite as intimate as saving the world with another person. I wanted to hug Danny and thank him for this gift.

"Do you know what I dream about even more than sailing away?" I asked.

He hesitated. "You do know that what we did tonight was an accident. Redding was a devil, but he wasn't properly vetted. I don't want you to think I kill like this. It was a terrible mistake."

"You don't kill people like Redding?"

"Not like Redding, no," he said. "Tell me your dream."

"My dream is to kill the man who killed Lamont. After he's been properly vetted." I liked that word. *Vetted.*

"That's some dream."

"Will you help me?"

He'd been adamant about only flushing Bourque out, not

killing him. Now my heart pounded with the realization that Danny was rethinking our relationship.

"It wouldn't be easy," he said.

"And he would have to be properly vetted."

"You're way too green."

"Then make me ungreen!" I faced him, slightly wounded. "I did good tonight, didn't I? I distracted him so you could shoot—"

"I don't think that was intentional on your part."

"I'm perfect for this! I have what it takes. And I know how to clean up, you can't deny that."

"True. You're a very good cleaner."

"So then you'll take me under your wing?"

"Meaning exactly what?"

"Meaning you'll teach me how to be like you."

"A priest?"

"A vigilante who kills the scum of the earth."

There, I'd said it. And I continued quickly before he could object or try to pretend he didn't know what I was talking about.

"Even if you're not that, I think I am. I've sworn to kill the man who killed Lamont, that much we both know. But also I think I'm meant to do more. With or without you, I'm committed."

"Hmmm..." was all he said.

"I'm right about this," I said. "Please don't lie to me."

"It's that obvious?"

He was confessing? I was so honored that he would confide in me that I wanted to cry. I pulled his arm tight against my side and held on to it with both hands.

"It is to me. And I couldn't be more proud of you."

Danny stared out at the sinking moon and shook his head. "Listen to us. They would think we're absolutely crazy."

"Only because they don't know what we know. They haven't lost a mother, a sister, a husband. They haven't seen what a failure the system is when it comes to justice. Like you say, they don't even think about, much less follow, strong moral reasoning."

He slipped his hands into his pockets and kicked at the dirt with his toe. "And do you? Or is this just revenge for you?"

"I may not be the smartest girl in California, but with Lamont's help and now yours, I think I see more than most. And I know what I feel. Redding is dead because he signed up to be dead, and as a consequence, innocent people who didn't sign up to be dead won't be. And that's a good thing."

"You do realize that things have just gotten infinitely more complicated."

"How so?"

Danny set his stare out to sea. "For starters, you have blood on your hands."

"Guilty blood," I said.

"The kind that sends people to prison for the rest of their lives."

"I'm already in a prison. But with your help, I can avoid the kind with bars."

"It's not that easy."

"Which is why I need you."

"You'll have to move," he said.

"Move? Why?"

"We have to assume that Redding was on to you, and that Bourque knows where you live."

I didn't know what to say. The thought of leaving my sacred den terrified me.

"Does Bourque know about you?" I asked.

"No. Redding was surprised to see me in the house. But when Redding turns up missing, Bourque will come after you."

"Then you *have* to help me! I'm as good as dead!"

He didn't disagree. And he didn't say he wouldn't help me, either. The more I thought about it, the more I realized that I was lost without Danny.

"So you will?" I asked, now on pins and needles.

"You'll have a lot to learn first. You can't just go after Bourque."

"I'll do anything you say."

"And *only* what I say."

"I swear!" I turned into him, pulled both of his hands out of his pockets and took them in mine. "And I won't disappoint you. Please, Danny, teach me everything you know."

"I deal with killers," he said. "It can be nasty business."

"You kill killers. I saw you kill one tonight. And I love you for it."

"You do?"

I was so caught up in the moment, I hardly knew what I was doing. I stood on my tiptoes and kissed Danny on his lips, lightly, for maybe a second.

"I want you to teach me how to kill someone," I said.

He stared into my eyes, then took a deep breath.

"We'll see," he said.

19

IT WAS ONE thing to engage in a behavior driven by a carefully crafted moral philosophy. Behavior like killing vipers for the good of humanity, for example.

It was something entirely different to lead another person into that same behavior. But faced with precisely this conundrum, the choice was fairly clear to Danny.

Six days had come and gone since he'd killed Redding, cut up the man's body, and tossed the remains over the cliff, all with the fervent aid of his new protégée.

During that time he had focused every waking hour outside of his religious duties on helping Renee grasp the fundamentals, which would help her stay alive and out of prison. When his confidence in her solidified, he finally yielded to her demands that he show her how to do what he did. She meant killing, of course, but, as he repeatedly explained, "what he did" had more to do with remaining free than pulling a trigger.

His was not a suicidal mission, but truth be told, she was less concerned about staying alive.

Dressed in black clerical clothes and a white collar, Danny passed through the vestibule, considering the fact that it was harder to reconcile his double life of priest and killer than it once had been. His lying, like his killing, was justified by the results of his actions, but his intricately laced web of deceit had grown so tenuous that he found himself avoiding the church so that he didn't have to account for himself.

If he was ever found out, Saint Paul Catholic Church in Long Beach, California, would draw the world's attention like a desert fire attracted hyenas. He had no desire to see the church thrown into scandal. Perhaps it was time to back out of the priesthood gracefully.

Not that he intended to get caught. If anything, his attention to remaining free was more acute now with Renee under his wing. But taking on the responsibility of a collaborator also focused his attention on the consequences of getting caught. He was more concerned with the price the church would pay than any he would pay.

"Mother Evelina is asking for you, Father."

He turned and saw that Regina had walked into the vestibule. "Oh?"

"Yes. I told her you were still here. I hope that's okay."

He glanced at his watch and saw that it was just past six. He had agreed to pick up Renee at seven outside the Diamond Shamrock three blocks from the Super 8 motel she'd moved to the day after Redding's death. He'd set her up with a new identity under the name Mary Wilcox, complete with a driver's license, and set her on a path of legitimacy. She was unabashedly delighted.

Today was the day Renee was going to finally do something

on her own. Knowing her, she was probably already waiting near the gas station, pacing in anticipation.

"Do you know what she wants?" Danny asked.

"I'm sorry, no. She's waiting for you by the confessional."

"Thank you."

He turned into the sanctuary and looked across the pews at the dark wood confessional with its twin black curtains both pulled open. Mother Evelina stood in her white coif and habit with her back to him, arms folded in her sleeves, staring at the large cross bearing a crucified Christ. She was a slight woman who walked with the timid steps of one whose legs were wearing out. Eighty years on concrete would do that to a person, Danny thought.

The reverend mother had come to them only yesterday from a community in Nepal where she served the blind, maimed, and all who were physically disadvantaged. She had come to California on behalf of a charity for cataracts and blindness, then planned to visit her sister in San Francisco before returning to Nepal. She had spent the day with Father Lombardi, an old acquaintance from days they'd spent in Rome.

Danny had talked to her twice, briefly, and found her both genuine and kind.

She heard him approach and turned, perpetual smile fixed on her small face. Her eyes spoke only kindness, understanding, and empathy.

"There you are, Father."

He dipped his head. "Here I am." He clasped her ancient hand and returned her smile. "And here you are, Reverend Mother."

"I was wondering if you might do me a favor, Danny."

The ease with which she said his name took him aback for a moment; then the surprise passed. He preferred the simple name, and here was a woman who seemed to know this about him already.

"May I call you Danny?" she asked, one brow arched in a face wrinkled from decades of smiling. Her light blue eyes were like passageways to God himself.

"Of course. What is it?"

"I would like you to hear my confession."

Danny expected someone of her stature to seek out a more senior priest such as the pastor, Father Lombardi. But Danny couldn't deny her request, and he certainly wasn't about to beg off because he had to get to his apprentice. *Dreadfully sorry, Mother Evelina, but I have someone to kill tonight.*

"Your confession?"

"Yes. You do know how to hear an old lady's confession, don't you?"

He had to smile. "Of course. I would be honored——"

"Because I can see the darkness in your eyes, and I would understand your reluctance."

"No," he said. The remark made him ill at ease, and he couldn't hold her eye contact. "Yes, that's fine. Fine."

Danny entered the confessional, closed the curtain, and opened the sliding door to the small square screen that masked his view of the adjacent booth.

He cleared his throat. "Please, you may begin."

"Bless me, Father, for I have sinned. It has been seven days since my last confession. Generally I like my position before God, but coming to this country has filled my heart with temptations that I fear could destroy me."

She stopped.

"It can be a frightening place," Danny said.

"Yes. They tell me you came from Bosnia. You must know."

But this was about her, not him. "Please, continue."

209

"Yes, well it's not the kind of temptation you might normally associate with the West. I'm too old to want young men and too wise to covet luxuries. My sin is far more sinister than either of these."

"Go on."

"Well, Danny…" Danny again, not Father. "Everywhere I look, people seem to be made of porcelain and wood, like dolls engineered to do all the right things. Have you ever noticed this?"

Interesting observation. "Yes. I doubt that God takes issue with your observations, Reverend Mother."

"That isn't my sin, Father. It's the fact that I stand in judgment of them. I find myself judging everyone I see, and I find that it's driving me mad."

"It's your job to understand people," Danny said. "I don't think God will blame you for discerning the true nature of others."

"It's not our place to judge. Let him without sin cast the first stone. Judge not lest you be judged. My judgment of others *is* my sin. If I clean my heart so that I can judge, it dirties again the first time I judge again. I am on a terrible path with so much judgment in my heart."

He wasn't sure how to respond.

"Are you ever tempted to think you're better than they are, Father? Are you ever tempted to judge?"

"I think we all are."

"Pray for me, Danny."

20

DANNY'S HOUSE CONSISTED of three bedrooms. He slept in one of them, the master, which contained a queen bed with a quilted brown comforter imported from Bosnia, a dresser, two nightstands, and one stuffed chair next to a large window that looked out to the backyard.

He used the second bedroom for a guest room, simply but comfortably furnished with another queen bed and two decent lamps with forest-green shades purchased from Target. Renee had crashed in the room on two occasions.

The third bedroom served as his study, a private enclave that only he had ever entered. The blinds on the window had never been opened. The corduroy-covered guest chair had never been sat in. Only his feet had left prints on the brown carpet.

But now here she was, pacing in front of his desk while he eyed her. Renee wore the black shirt he purchased for her and a pair of tight-fitting yoga pants she'd found at a sporting-goods store. Watching her bounce around the room, he had to suppress a smile. She was adorable.

Tell her something once and she knew it. He repeated himself only to be cut off with, "You've told me that." Her mind was a trap.

And her appetite for life was a vacuum, sucking in all it could. She had none of the caution that kept most people living vicariously through the fantasies of others rather than pursuing their own.

This was why Renee had left all and come to California.

This was why she had become a heroin addict.

This was why she had so unreservedly embraced Lamont as her savior—and now Danny as her teacher, her confidant, her soul mate.

If he wasn't mistaken, she was falling in love with him. And in the most honest of moments, he had to admit that he was drawn to her like an unstoppable tide. He wasn't sure what to think, except that it gave him one more compelling reason to leave the priesthood.

Absurd, of course. But there it was.

He stood by a large corkboard that covered one wall. It was the kind with side panels that folded in to form doors, which he kept locked. The board was now empty.

"I got it," Renee said. "Reconnaissance only. I'm not going out there to kill some guy. That would compromise everything we've talked about. I get it. You've told me that three times tonight."

"We can't be too careful."

"Yes, yes, yes." She waved him off.

"There's no indication that our target needs to be handled with any severity."

"But he's evil, right? It's not like you just pulled some guy off the street."

"As you'll see, there's more to my selection of this mark than the dark nature of his character."

The reverend mother's voice whispered through his head. *Are you ever tempted to think you're better than they are, Father?*

"So he *is* male," Renee said.

Danny opened the manila file on his desk, pulled out a picture, and pinned it to the board. The image was of a middle-aged man with brown hair, short on the sides and slicked back. A dark mole stood out on the right side of his forehead, exposed by a receding hairline. Thin face, dark circles under hazel eyes.

"Meet Darby Gordon. Age thirty-four. Married with two children. Rents in a low-income tract in San Pedro."

"This is him?" Renee stepped up to the board, eyes wide like saucers. She slowly brought her hand up to the photo. "Darby Gordon?"

"The man drives a blue Chevy pickup truck and works in the port when he's not working muscle."

"What's he done?" She stared at the picture, fascinated. "I can see it in his eyes. He's sick, isn't he?"

"Not physically. He's been arrested for domestic violence four times."

"I knew it!"

"No, you can never know anything by looking at someone. You know them by their fruit, nothing else."

"Of course."

"That's why you're paying him a visit."

"So how did you find him?"

"He was in Simon Redding's wallet, under a list of men Redding evidently called on when he needed help. What he knows about Redding may help us learn more about Bourque. Nothing is random, Renee. Ever. Our objective here is ultimately Bourque, don't forget that."

"Trust me," she said. "Never."

She didn't know Danny had palmed the thumb drive in Jonathan Bourque's office, and he'd decided not to share its contents with her until she was ready. The data detailed three years of payoffs and strong-arm operations in a dozen countries. It included names and dates and, worse, recordings of conversations.

This was Bourque's insurance. With the information contained on the drive, he could threaten anyone who tried to bring him down, including a surprising number of government officials and politicians around the world who'd turned a blind eye or pushed grants his way in exchange for favors and money.

Danny had spent two mornings poring over the data, cross-checking it with the figures made public by the Bourque Foundation. The organization raised money for many charities, and it appeared that most of those dollars were handled correctly as a cover for Bourque's more profitable business—his own operations, which were cleverly mixed with third-party relief organizations.

While he delivered nicely for a host of reputable parties, winning their applause and trust, Jonathan Bourque was running dozens of smaller charities, mostly international, that raped the donations of benefactors for his own gain.

In a typical charity operation, at least eighty cents of every dollar donated ended up in actual aid to the needy. Sometimes this figure was as high as ninety-five cents.

Danny doubted that more than a third of the money the Bourque Foundation raised for its own international charities ended up in the hands of those who needed it. The bulk went to covering up the skimming of large sums, often with the application of threats and force. To that end, the man had no scruples.

Bourque was the worst of the worst, a true Pharisee who

used his history as a priest to attract hundreds of millions in do-nations, much of which ended up in his own pocket.

There was no direct evidence that he'd ordered Redding to kill Lamont, but Bourque was guilty nonetheless. Danny had already decided that Bourque would either change his ways or die.

But not until Renee was ready. Not until she followed her own trail that led to him, under Danny's watchful eye and care-ful guidance.

"It's important for you to establish Bourque's unquestionable guilt in Lamont's disappearance. Starting with Darby Gordon."

She turned her head and looked at him with fiery eyes. "I'm paying him a visit alone? Tonight?"

"That's the idea, yes."

"Under my new identity?"

"No. As Renee Gilmore. Making Bourque nervous, should he learn of your visit, isn't a bad thing at this point. And I don't want you to blow your new identity."

Her face was flushed with excitement, but she was otherwise calm. Eager, but not nervous.

"How do I get to him? You want me to break into his house tonight?"

"Not this time, no." He glanced at his watch. Seven forty-five PM. "By nine o'clock you'll be in his living room, drinking a beer with him, peeling back the layers that hide his secrets."

"I will?"

"You will."

"How?"

"It's really quite simple."

DANNY SAID IT was quite simple, but standing on Darby Gordon's porch at nine fifteen, I thought *insane* might be a bet-ter word to describe what I was doing.

But then so was jumping out of a plane for the first time, he'd said, and he was right. The first time was always filled with anxiety.

The house was a tiny box, with only two windows facing the street on the main floor, and one above, from what might have been a small loft or an attic. The gray wood siding was in bad need of fresh paint; the lawn was scraggly and worn to the ground in some sections. A plastic Big Wheel tricycle with a broken pedal lay on its side next to a frayed garden hose. The light on the porch was out, probably busted. Mini-blinds blocked most of the light filtering out through the two windows.

Danny was in his car a block down the street, waiting to step in should anything go wrong. He'd given me a small Panasonic recording stick, which I stuck in my bra, where it would capture my conversation with Darby Gordon. If I ran into trouble of any kind, I was to press a small button on the pager in my pocket, and Danny would come.

That was the plan. But I had no intention of running into any trouble because this was me, the meek mouse, here to ask a few questions, close the case on Bourque, and feel out my instincts for doing this sort of thing on my own.

It had only been six days since we'd killed Redding, but I felt like a changed person. I had been born into my new self that night with Danny, and then baptized by blood. Sure, it was Redding's blood, but that was fine by me. He was the goat on the altar, and we did sacrifice him pretty good.

Things changed after that night. Danny took me seriously I think. He spent hours with me, preparing me by rehearsing interrogation techniques, evasion strategies, law enforcement practices, that sort of thing. It was all about tricks, really, the art of illusion, methods of making people think one thing while something different is going on. Better to trick them into the truth than coerce them, Danny said.

Particularly if you're not much over five feet and only a hair over one hundred pounds, messing with someone who could flick you in the neck and break your spine.

I think Danny had a crush on me. I could tell by the tenderness in his voice, by the way his hand sometimes lingered on my arm or shoulder. I could tell by the way he talked to me in that soft voice and even more the way he looked at me when he listened. We were poring over critical ideas and details that sent people to jail or worse, but we were also speaking to each other, holding each other with our eyes.

I was becoming like Danny, and I didn't want it any other way. Because, truth be told, I was falling in love with *him*. It was strange to feel attracted to a man besides Lamont, especially a priest, but I was sure that in his absence, Lamont would have wanted that for me. I knew that Danny didn't take all of his priesthood vows seriously. After all, he killed people for God.

I pushed Darby Gordon's doorbell and took a calming breath. *Here we go. Don't mess this up, Renee. Just act normal.*

That's what I told myself, but then I began wondering what *normal* really was in this world.

The door flew open and Darby Gordon stood in the frame. He was shorter than I imagined and wiry, with a sloped forehead that made him look like a snake.

He was dressed in a plaid shirt with the sleeves rolled up to expose a large tattoo of a skull on his forearm. He looked like he was about to snap at me, then thought twice as his eyes flashed up and down my body.

Danny had asked me to change into jeans, and I was glad I had. I figured I looked at least a little hot in denim, and I didn't mind the advantage a little sexiness might give me.

"Darby Gordon?"

A thin grin twisted his flat lips. "Depends who's asking."

This was it. "My name is Renee. I was sent by Jonathan Bourque. Do you mind if I come in?"

Danny and I had discussed exactly what I was to say and do, and standing there on the dark porch, it all came quite naturally to me. I watched Darby's eyes close and looked for whether he recognized that name.

If he knew Bourque, he wasn't showing it. "Do I know you?" he asked.

"No. But you know Simon Redding, and Mr. Redding works for Jonathan Bourque. I'd rather discuss this inside, if you don't mind."

I saw the jitter in his eye when I said *Redding*. He looked past me, then stepped to one side. I went in. The door closed behind me with a *thump*.

I stood in a small living room with a large green sofa. This faced a big-screen television that was blaring an action movie with foul language. The carpet was worn and the place smelled like a dirty dog, although I didn't see any pets. Half-filled plastic glasses and plates dirtied with tomato sauce—maybe from spaghetti—sat on an oak coffee table in front of the couch. A pair of boots with mud on them had been tossed to the floor next to an old crusted jacket. Clothes were draped over the back of three wooden chairs, which seemed to have been set around haphazardly. Lint, matchsticks, and a few cigarette butts littered the brown shag carpet.

The place was a mess by any standard and a toilet by mine.

But I held my blanching in check and focused on my first objective: understanding the theater of operation, as Danny called it.

Okay then. There was a door to my right that probably led

into the bedroom. Through a lighted passage on my left I could hear clanking that led me to believe Emily Darby was in the kitchen, hard at work.

Two children, a boy about seven with bleached-blond hair and girl maybe two years older with long stringy hair, stared at me from the couch.

"Out!" Darby snapped.

The two kids scampered away like rats.

"And stay out if you know what's good for you." His words chased them through the left passage, where they hooked right and pattered up a flight of stairs.

"Alicia?" A cautionary voice, timid with a hint of a tremor, called out the name. This was the wife reacting to her children's flight up the stairs, wondering what was wrong. There was no response.

The stuffy room fell silent. A nauseating sense of déjà vu sucked the blood from my head. The TV was still blaring, but I hardly heard it. I couldn't put my finger on what caused this reaction. Maybe it was pity for a mother so frightened for her children in her own home; maybe it was empathy for the children, whom I immediately imagined were being beaten and starved by their father; maybe it was the plight of the woman trapped under the cruel thumb of spousal abuse.

It all struck me as being about *me*, somehow.

But I ignored the hot rage flushing through my face, stepped over the dirty boots, walked to the middle of the living room, and faced Darby Gordon, who still stared at me from the door.

"Hey!" he yelled toward the kitchen. "Get in the bedroom!"

A slight woman with her dirty-blond hair haphazardly pulled into a ponytail hurried into the room, drying her hands on a dirty shirt. No makeup, white as a ghost. She was wearing pink sweats and a pale blue sweatshirt.

She offered me a sheepish smile, then her eyes darted away and she slipped into the bedroom and carefully closed the door.

"What do you want?" Gordon said, approaching, face flat.

"I need to know when you last spoke to Simon Redding." These were my lines.

"And who are you?"

"I think you know who I am."

"No. As a matter of fact, I don't. Tell me."

He had a harder edge than I'd anticipated, though I don't know why I expected anything different. "Jonathan Bourque sent me," I said.

"And that's supposed to mean something to me?"

I knew then that the direct approach meant to take him off guard wasn't going to work as smoothly as we'd hoped.

"Please, man, don't pretend with me." *Man?* I was sounding stupid, so I cleared my throat and bore down with more authority. "We both know that you've done work for Simon Redding. Don't tell me you don't know who he worked for. Redding's missing, and if we don't get to the bottom of this, the whole house of cards is going to come down."

He glared at me for a few seconds, and I was praying that he would break that stare and smile or laugh—anything that would suggest he was just testing me.

"I don't have a clue what you're talking about," he said.

I lost track of what to do next. Were we wrong about this guy? No, Danny was sure about Gordon's involvement. It was me...I wasn't breaking him down the way Danny probably could. He'd have this punk in tears in a matter of seconds, begging for his life. I might not be able to use the same approach, but I wasn't about to leave without proving that I was more than worthy to work side by side with Danny.

I forced myself to relax. "You have any beer?"

Still no smile. "Sure." He walked toward the kitchen. "This way."

I didn't know why I had to follow him. Couldn't he just bring me a beer? I followed him anyway, thinking maybe I could regroup in the kitchen.

But the moment I stepped into that nasty room wallpapered with dirty-yellow flowers, the sight of piled dishes and half-eaten food accosted me and I lost track of myself completely. If the living room was the toilet, here was the sewer. I could practically feel the grit and grime crawling up my legs, the microscopic bugs flowing into my lungs as I breathed.

I clamped my mouth shut, and that was when Darby Gordon moved, before I could shift my attention from the ungodly mess back to him.

He snatched my wrist, spun me around, and slammed me up against the wall. I managed to turn my head, but my cheekbone and chest hit the greasy wall in a dish-rattling impact.

"Now you're going to tell me who you really are, you little skank."

I panicked and spoke without thinking. "Ouch! You have no idea who you're messing with. He's going to kill you, man. You have no idea!"

"Then give me an idea!" He jerked my arm up behind my back to make his point. Pain flashed through my shoulder.

"You're dead," I said. "When he finds out you messed with me, you're dead."

"Who?"

"Are you deaf? Bourque! The man Simon Redding works for."

He breathed into my ear, pressing in close from behind. "That's not good enough." His breath smelled like beer and pepperoni. "Redding would never send a scrawny kid to check on me."

"Redding's dead, you idiot!"

That got him. But only for a second.

I was completely lost, but I didn't let up. "I'm here to find out if we can trust you."

"Is that so?" He grabbed the skin on my belly and squeezed hard enough so that I thought I might pass out from the pain. "No one comes into my house and threatens me."

"You don't know Jonathan Bourque," I managed.

Darby jerked me around and pinned my wrists against the wall. A wicked grin on his face defied any fear. "Well now that's the problem, sweetie. I do. And I got the call from him two days ago, asking if I'd seen Redding. I know Bourque. The question is, who are you?"

I was frozen. My cover was shot! Several thoughts crashed through my head: I should knee him in the groin and run, but he was pressed too close for that. I should smash my head into his face and break his nose, but I knew he wasn't the kind who would let go.

I had to get to the pager in my pocket!

My eyes must have darted downward, because Darby followed my glance. He saw the small lump in my jeans, held one forearm against my neck in a choke hold, and fished out the pager, which he tossed into a pot of water.

"You a cop?"

"No! You're making a mistake..." I sounded like a bad movie.

"You wired, too?" He fished his hand up my shirt, found the tape recorder, and yanked it out. It went into the pot as well.

"Okay, okay," I squealed, mortified by the fear in my voice. It wasn't supposed to go down like this. "I'm FBI. Let go, I'll explain. Just let go!"

"Is that so? FBI? Do I look that dumb to you?"

I wanted to say yes, but the forearm against my throat argued for a more thoughtful response. My mind was blank.

"This isn't FBI equipment," he growled. "And you're not from Bourque. Which means I caught me something. Here's what we're gonna do, honey. You're going to tell me everything you know about Jonathan Bourque and Simon Redding. You're going to tell me, because if you don't I'm going to hurt you real good in ways that only women can be hurt, you hear me?"

At that point I could have gone one of two ways. I could have lost it completely, started flailing and screaming the way most would at the prospect of suffering underneath that dirty weasel. Or I could dig deep, push aside all thoughts of scratching his eyes out, and play ball until I found a way to flip the tables.

I chose the latter. Base instincts will get you killed, Danny liked to say. After months of thinking scenes like this through, I was smart enough not to do what I wanted to do.

"Fine," I croaked. "But what I said stands. If you hurt me, you'll be dead by morning. If you think Jonathan Bourque is—"

His palm crashed against my cheek and I cried out.

Darby shouted over his shoulder. "Emily! Get out here!"

"Please..." I wasn't able to stop the trembling that had come to my arms and legs.

"Shut up. Emily!"

His wife appeared in the doorway. I could hear the faint sounds of one of the kids crying above us.

"Come here, honey," he said.

When she didn't move, he shouted, red-faced. "I said, come here!"

She came, hurrying like a mouse. But she didn't make it, because he backhanded her with enough force to send her reeling.

"Get upstairs. And keep those brats quiet."

She whimpered and fled up the stairs.

Then Darby Gordon grabbed my hair and propelled me back into the living room. Past the living room, pulling my head back with my hair.

We were headed toward the bedroom. Darby Gordon was going to hurt me and hurt me bad. The room began to spin.

21

THE BEDROOM WAS a pigsty. Under different circumstances I would've had to exercise significant self-control to avoid launching into cleanup mode, but at the moment my focus was on the unmade bed.

Darby gave me a shove and I sprawled on the dirty sheets. He was chuckling.

Those base instincts that I'd wisely refused to obey earlier now raged to the surface, and I lost myself to them completely. The mission was shot. All I wanted to do now was survive.

I scrambled to the far side of the bed and rolled off, spinning back to where Darby stood, blocking the exit. I thrust both arms toward him, palms out.

"Stay back! Just stay back!"

"Yeah? Or what?"

"Or I swear I'll claw your eyes out, you freak!" I screamed.

He seemed amused by that. "You got spunk, I like that." He

walked to the dresser, pulled a gun from the top drawer, and faced me, smile now gone. "There's a couple ways we can do this. I can shoot your leg now so you won't be tempted to claw my eyes out. Maybe have a little fun before I kill you and dump your body. Or I can let you talk a little while I decide what to do."

"Then let me talk. Just take it easy and let me talk!"

He looked me up and down then gave the gun a little wave. "Talk."

"Put the gun down."

"Talk!" he roared.

I flinched. "Okay, okay." I had to get hold of myself. My mind was blank and I wasn't sure what to say. "I'll talk, just don't shoot me."

He grinned like a serpent. Danny's voice echoed in my mind: *It's all an illusion, Renee. Sleight of hand, sleight of mind. Get them thinking about anything but your objective.*

My objective was to live. And to get out. Through that door behind him and out into the street. Everything had happened so quickly. Danny wouldn't know to come to my rescue, not yet, not before it was too late.

I lowered my hands. "Okay. The truth." There was a closet with a sliding door to my left, like the one I'd had at the Stay-bridge Suites. "Okay, so I'm not with Bourque. You're right, he didn't send me. That was just a cover, and okay, so it didn't work."

He just grinned at me. My mind started to settle.

"But I know about Simon Redding, right? You have to ask yourself how I know he's dead."

I waited for him to respond, because I realized I had just made a very good point. Could I just tell him the truth? What would Danny think about that? What did it matter? My life was at stake here, I had no doubt about that.

"Nobody said he was dead," Darby said.

"I did. He's missing and Bourque's probably freaking out, thinking his number one man's gone to the feds. Right?"

"Just talk."

He wasn't going to let me take control of the conversation. I let my shoulders relax and took a step forward to ease the tension, but my heart was pounding and my palms were wet with sweat.

"We were lovers," I said. "Jonathan and me. No one knew. We met in New York and I followed him out here."

Darby didn't object. The idea was probably totally unsurprising to him. Why not? Jonathan likely had a dozen lovers stashed in a dozen different cities.

"But he crossed me," I said. "He treated me like dirt. So I stole some money from him, and that set him off."

I stopped, refusing to continue until Darby engaged me. *Get them talking*, Danny said. *The more they talk, the more they hear themselves. The more they hear themselves, the less they focus on you.*

"You stole from Bourque," Darby said doubtfully.

"I did. Why else would he send Simon Redding after me?"

The man shrugged as if to say, *A hundred reasons.* He gave only one. "To get rid of the evidence. No one steals from Bourque."

"Exactly. But I did. And I still have the cash to prove it." *Talk to me, you freaking dog.*

"That so, huh? How much?"

"Enough."

"How much?" he snapped.

"Put the gun down," I said. "Quit acting like I'm some kind of thug who's going to shoot you in the gut. I'm just a little skank without a gun."

He hesitated, then his lips twitched and he lowered the gun. "You got balls, I'll give you that. How much?"

"Three hundred thousand dollars," I said. "In cash. Hundred-dollar bills."

"You stole three hundred thousand dollars from Jonathan Bourque," he said, still doubtful.

"When he found out, he sent Simon Redding to kill me. I know that because Redding tried. Instead, I killed him."

"Is that so? You killed Simon Redding." He said it, but the words came out more like a question.

"And I cut up his body and threw it in the ocean," I said. What did it matter? They would never find the parts anyway.

He eyed me, trying to decide if he should pay any attention to my claim. This was good. In less than five minutes I'd gone from lying on the bed to making him think twice, and I took courage from my victory.

I took two steps closer and continued. "I have the money, all of it. But I don't care about the money. I want the freak who ruined my life, and I'm willing to pay for it."

Darby scoffed. "You're nuts."

"Maybe. But you have to think about your options. I came here to check you out. I had to know whether you could get close to Bourque, and whether you would rather make some serious money or end up dead like Redding."

"Even if you did kill Redding like you say, you're in my house now."

"If you kill me, you'll never see the money. Worse, Jonathan Bourque will have you killed when he learns that Redding's dead. He won't leave you around to tell what you know. You have enough information to bury him."

There were probably holes in my hobbled logic, but I was thinking on my feet and making him think long and hard.

Even in that state of fear I imagined that I was pretty good at this.

"You don't have a clue what I know," he said. "This is all crazy."

"Maybe. Maybe not. Why would a pretty little thing like me come waltzing up to your door at night? I'll tell you: because I need your help and I know that you're in trouble. Tell me you don't know that Bourque's behind the hits you've made for Redding."

A slight tic bothered his right eye. He said nothing. I stepped closer, now only four paces away from him.

I spoke in a soft, sincere voice. "Please, Darby, you have to help me. You can have all of it. I just want Bourque dead. And you know he's going to shut you up eventually. He knows you know about him. He can't let that go."

"That's not the way it works," he said.

The anger I felt toward this man suddenly raged to the surface. "No? Then tell me, you stupid thug! How does it work?"

"His reach is longer than you realize, honey." His use of that endearment made me cringe. "Even if I did kill him, which I wouldn't—not for any price—I would end up dead or worse. He's got his end covered. You, on the other hand, are already dead. Just a matter of time."

"That's what Redding said."

"Simon Redding's no Jonathan Bourque."

A chill snaked down my spine.

"So here's what's gonna happen. First I'm going to hurt you pretty bad." His gun came up slowly and his grin was back. "You're going to tell me where the money is. We're going to get it. And then maybe, if you're real nice to me, I might let you go."

My confidence was derailed. I began thinking about that closet again. It had two overlapping sliding doors.

"Get on the bed," he said, motioning with the gun.

"Do you know anything about a hit on a man named La-mont?" I asked.

Darby Gordon blinked. He wasn't a blinker, I'd noticed that. He stared for long seconds without a break. But when I said my late husband's name, he blinked, and I knew that this man had been involved in Lamont's death.

I almost screamed and threw myself at him then. But that would have only gotten me killed. I managed to hang on to that realization.

"You're sick," I said. "You beat your kids, you molest your wife, you kill anyone for money without any thought about who might be left behind."

He seemed surprised by my sudden outburst.

My fingernails were biting into my palms. I shoved a trem-bling finger at his face. "You're a demon!" I screamed.

Darby Gordon's face flushed red and twisted into a knot of rage. He made a grunting sound and started toward me.

Run!

The word filled my mind. I feinted to my right half a step, just enough to get him leaning that way, then I threw myself to my left. Toward the closet with its sliding doors.

I crashed into the door, grasped the frame and shoved it wide. Plowed inside. Slammed it shut.

If he wanted me alive to mess me up, he would have to come in after me—I was counting on it. I would make my move then.

"You stupid, stupid..." Darby didn't finish the insult, intent on opening the door.

But I was already at the other end, fumbling for a grip on the edge of the second sliding door. *Hurry, hurry...*

My nails caught the molding. *God, help me.* It was a sincere prayer I think.

The moment I heard him slide the first door, I shoved the one at my end of the closet open and bolted out into the bedroom. Darby was leaning into the closet with his gun arm leading, looking for me, just now realizing that I had exited the other end.

Now I was pushed by survival instincts, not anything as calculated as determination. I sprinted toward the door.

"Hey! Get back here!"

I had no intention of complying. Darby hadn't locked the bedroom door—his wife and children were no threat to their cruel master. He was a pig.

And I was a mongoose, streaking for the front door as fast as I could run. I got my hand on the knob as he spun into the living room.

"Hey!"

I threw the door wide, ducked out, and raced up his driveway. Was I going to make it?

But I was certain a bullet would slam into my back. I started to weave, like a drunken mongoose now.

Darby's stocking feet padded on the concrete behind me.

I didn't stop to look back, but ran to the corner and into the street, straight toward Danny's car, fifty yards away. All the way, pumping my arms.

The lights on his car suddenly blazed. He'd seen me!

I reached it in a dozen more long steps and dived into the backseat, not wanting to run around the car.

"Go, go, go!"

Danny didn't go. Not right away.

I stuck my head up over the seat and saw that Darby Gordon had stopped at the edge of his driveway and was staring at our lights.

"I take it things didn't go as well as hoped," Danny said.

Why wasn't he driving? Then he was, in reverse, and I understood. As long as the glaring lights were in Darby's eyes, he wouldn't be able to identify the car or its driver. Danny hooked one arm behind the passenger seat and backed all the way to the intersection, swinging onto the crossing lane and then speeding away.

"Whooooeeee! Boy, that was close!"

My hands were still shaking, but I was elated. I'd made it. And I'd found out what we needed to find out, hadn't I?

I threw my arms around Danny's seat, leaned over and kissed him on the cheek. "Thank you. Thank you! Ha!"

"What did you do?" he said.

I wanted to jump up and down and cry for joy, but it occurred to me that this wasn't what skilled vigilantes did in their getaway cars. So I took a deep breath, climbed into the front seat next to him, and told him.

"I got what we needed, Danny. I have proof."

22

DANNY LISTENED TO Renee tell her tale. She had tricked Darby Gordon into confessing his involvement in her husband's murder and then escaped after cleverly luring him into one end of a closet while she escaped out the other.

Her exuberance faded before they reached her hotel, replaced by a deep sorrow about the finality of Lamont's death. She'd always assumed him dead, but now she believed she had firsthand confirmation of that fact, and it robbed her of the thrill.

Her descent into sorrow was so quick, in fact, that Danny didn't have the heart to tell her he didn't consider the mission successful. She'd done almost everything wrong and placed them both in far more danger than he was willing to accept.

Indeed, based on her terrifying tale—in which she'd surely avoided rape, torture, and death by the slimmest of margins—he was tempted to reconsider his commitment to help her become a version of himself.

It's her, Danny. You are falling for her. She means too much to you.

He pulled his Chevy to a stop half a block from her hotel, thinking she should move again in a few days. Bourque would blanket the city with inquiries the moment he heard from Darby Gordon. For all they knew, the call had already been made.

"I could kill him, Danny," she said bitterly, staring past the hood. He studied the fine lines of her jaw, pale now under the halogen streetlights. Her other cheek was red from Gordon's blow. The thought of such a snake laying a hand on her was nearly too much to stomach. Such a delicate creature, so violently abused.

Danny had made his decision the moment he'd seen Renee's cheek: He would return—perhaps tonight in the early hours, maybe tomorrow night—and he would kill Darby Gordon after assuring himself that Renee had judged his guilt correctly.

He would do it in part because the man qualified to pay that price. He would also do it because the man had abused Renee. *You've fallen in love with her. You're endangering her life and your mission.*

He couldn't quite admit these truths to himself. But he had to consider them, and he did, as he watched her in silence.

"You should have seen his wife." Her jaw flexed. "How could anyone treat another human being like that? He's an animal!"

"He is." Danny turned his eyes to follow her blank stare. A slight drizzle had begun to fall. The forecast called for rain by the early hours. "Stay away from him. This wasn't a good night for us, you have to realize that."

She faced him, eyes wide. "What do you mean? I thought I did pretty good."

"You did. But you almost didn't, and that's not acceptable."

Her jaw dropped. "Not acceptable? I pulled it off, and all you can say is *not acceptable*?"

"Please, Renee, that's how this business works. If you want to stay alive and——"

"I know, you've told me. No mistakes. Zero tolerance for errors, all that Bosnia wartime mumbo jumbo. Sorry, I didn't mean it like that. I respect it, I do. But tonight I went in there and I came face-to-face with that scum and I got out alive. Not to mention I learned what we needed to know."

"And that's good, although he didn't directly confess."

"Sure he did, just not with words. I know a guilty man when I see one."

"Regardless, you came too close to failure for my comfort. I don't know what I would——"

"For *your* comfort? I've been *dying* ever since Lamont was killed! Tonight was the first time in three months I've lived, really lived! This isn't just about staying alive to do it again, Danny. Not for me. It's about doing what's right. I'm going to kill the man who killed Lamont. I want to, I have to, I will. Period. I don't care what it costs me!"

"Then at least care what it costs me," he said.

She faced the windshield speckled with tiny drops of moisture. "Don't worry, I won't get you caught. I didn't say a word about you."

"That's not what I'm talking about."

"Then what?"

He hesitated, then said it plainly. "I don't want to lose you."

She looked at him, silent. Her face softened. Danny felt a knot gather in his throat and looked away, uneasy with his own emotions.

As much as he could no longer avoid his growing affection

for Renee, he couldn't displace a brooding sense that he was watching himself in her.

"I know what it's like, Renee," he said. "Losing someone precious to you is a harrowing thing, and it storms the emotions with a desperate need to set things right. What you're feeling after losing Lamont, I've felt for years. I get it. It's a beautiful thing in some respects. But it's also crippling. I see you and I see a precious person who's crippled by her own need to make things right. Like me."

The car filled with silence, as if it had been poured in through the retracting sunroof. He could smell the leather-scented freshener. Renee's deodorant, a musky antiperspirant she preferred to wear without any other perfume, hung softly in the air.

"You love me?" she said.

He didn't know what to say.

"You love me, and the thought of losing me drives you crazy," she said. Her hand rested on his knee. "I think that's beautiful, Danny. I think I love you, too."

Dear God, what am I doing? The knot in Danny's throat had become a fist. The distress had come out of nowhere and swallowed him, and if not for her presence in the car, he would have let himself go.

But here with her now, he could only share so much of his own pain. His role was to bear her pain, not burden her with his—to give comfort, not take it, because it was more blessed to give than to receive.

"But you're not going to lose me, Danny. I'm not going to let that happen. I just have to do this one thing. Okay?"

"There's a fine line between the killers and us," he said, finding his voice. "In the war I often wondered if I was as guilty as the enemy I killed. I don't want to turn you into a beast, Renee. And I don't want to lose you."

After stretched silence, she leaned forward and kissed him

lightly on his cheek. "That's the sweetest thing you could say. When this is over, we should run away to a small house in the Swiss Alps and tell each other sweet things."

He chuckled, in part because her spontaneity drew it out of him, in part because he was desperate to break the tension.

"Okay," he said.

"Perfect, that's our plan then. But you'll have to give up being a priest first. I wouldn't want to just sit around whispering and sipping hot chocolate."

"No, that wouldn't do."

"I would be cleansing myself all day if all I did was drink sugar like that."

She was trying to be funny, but her mention of cleansing struck Danny as odd. Just how deep did her obsessions reach?

"In the meantime," he said, "please, stay out of sight. We should move you again in the next few days just to be safe. Bourque will—"

"Kiss me, Danny," she whispered into his ear.

When he turned his head, she was right there, gazing at his eyes. He didn't really intend to kiss her, but he did. He leaned forward and kissed her warm lips gently.

When he pulled back, her eyes were closed. They fluttered open and her lips parted in a soft, teasing smile.

"That was nice," she said. Then she leaned forward and kissed him again. She took his jaw in her right hand, pulled his face into hers, and kissed him hungrily, deeply, with a passion that made his heart pound.

"I like you, Danny," she said breathlessly. "I really do like you." And then she flew out of the car and was gone.

I LEFT DANNY in his car and I felt triumphant and I might have skipped back to the hotel if it didn't strike me as a silly thing to do. I had completed my first mission. I had entered the brood of vipers and come out without a bite, not counting the one slap.

And I had been kissed by Danny.

I really was falling in love, I was sure of it. We were finding meaning and love in each other. Becoming like one. See, that word *triumphant* was a word that Danny would have used. I was sounding a bit like him now.

Triumphant.

The feeling started to fade before I entered my room on the third floor. The thoughts I'd lived with for three months started to come back, only now they had a face.

Darby Gordon's narrow features. Sharp chin. Beady eyes.

There was still Bourque, but I'd always known that he hadn't pulled the trigger himself. Now in my mind's eye I was sure: Darby Gordon had. At the very least, he'd been involved and knew exactly who had pulled the trigger.

I got to my room sobered by this thought, fixed myself a glass of cranberry juice, changed into my pajamas, and sat down in front of the television with my legs curled under me. I was wound up and needed to settle. There was no way I could sleep.

Danny loved me and I had done well, but only well enough to learn who had killed Lamont. Now what?

The late news was on, something about the Middle East. I didn't really care about a war across the ocean; mine was here on the streets of Southern California. I was about to change the channel when the picture changed and caught my attention.

A bomb had gone off somewhere, and a jerking camera showed people running as smoke boiled to the sky. The women and children on the screen were from Beirut, but I was seeing the two children and the woman who'd fled upstairs in Darby Gordon's house.

People would think nothing of blowing the responsible terrorists to kingdom come. Wasn't that what Danny was doing? Going in and dispatching the guilty to hell if they deserved it? Defending the innocent?

Wasn't that the whole point of what I was doing? And it wasn't costing the taxpayers a million dollars a bomb. People like Danny should be national heroes. They should hold parades for priests like him. We were like God's angels.

I realized then that what I needed to do wasn't just about my vow to defend Lamont's honor. It was also about those two innocent children crushed by a useless man who called himself a father. It was about Darby Gordon's wife, Emily.

The thoughts made my face hot. It was hard to see the television. My mind was clouded by images of Darby glaring at me, twisting my arm behind my back, breathing obscenities into my ear. The sound of his hand smacking into his wife's face shot through my memory like the crack of a small-caliber pistol.

My breathing was heavy. I took my glass of cranberry juice into the bedroom, set it on the nightstand, and walked into the bathroom. It had taken me three days to clean the place, and a sanitized smell still hung in the air, not quite cut by the lemon-fresh deodorizer I'd used.

I took my time brushing my teeth, washing my face, combing my hair. But the whole time my mind was on Darby Gordon, and I was imagining what he would have done to me if I hadn't outfoxed him.

What was he doing to his wife right now? I imagined that his children were crying themselves to sleep, begging God to take away their daddy.

I decided I needed a hot shower to clean the stink of Darby's place off my skin, and I emerged fifteen minutes later, red as a lobster but squeaky fresh.

Thoughts of Darby Gordon's wickedness ran circles around my brain like rats on a wheel. I had to relax and turn my mind to other matters, like Bourque. Yet I was having difficulty thinking of anything but Darby Gordon.

Spotless as a baby lamb on the outside and dressed in newly laundered pink pajamas with yellow butterflies, I climbed under my covers and tried to lose my mind in a book by Ann Rule. Perhaps if I focused on other people's problems I could put my own out of mind.

This might have been a mistake, because the book launched right into a scene of a woman's carefully plotted revenge against her husband, who'd run off with all their money.

I immediately began to think up ways to deal with Darby Gordon.

I imagined his death and the freedom that his death would bring his wife and children in at least a dozen different ways.

Did he have life insurance? Probably not. He didn't care about those he left behind. But I had some money I could give them. I wouldn't miss fifty thousand dollars.

I had the book in my hands, reading by a single lamp's light, and I got four pages into the chapter before realizing that I had no clue whatsoever what I'd just read. My eyes were following the words dutifully, but my mind had switched to more important matters.

I started the chapter over, and this time the thoughts that crept into my mind were of a slightly different nature. This time I began to imagine more than Darby Gordon's death. I began to detail clever ways that I, Renee Gilmore, could, would, or at least *should* kill Darby Gordon.

Not all of them were particularly inspired, and some were outright absurd. Like renting a wood chipper and feeding his bound and gagged snake-self into the part used to shred trees and such. I'd seen this in a movie called *Fargo*, a detective story set in (no surprise) Fargo, North Dakota.

But as my mind spun through various scenarios, discarding those that were either stupid or beneath me, I began to wonder what it would be like to actually go over there to that devil's house and kill him. Just slit his throat, for example.

Assuming I could break in.

Did he have an alarm? It was an old house, and he didn't strike me as the electronically savvy kind of person. Could I burrow under his foundation with a shovel and come up in the closet?

No, I could easily go through the window in the kitchen. The kids were upstairs and used to crashing sounds, and the viper was on the other end of the house. I could break in, I was sure of it. We'd broken into Jonathan Bourque's house, a fortress by comparison.

I finished the whole chapter and closed the book with very little memory of what I'd read beyond the first two paragraphs. Turned the lamp off. Hugged my pillow and willed myself to go to sleep.

It was then, in the darkness, that I relived each moment I'd spent in Darby Gordon's house. His hot breath, his twisted grin, his terrified children, his battered wife, the cigarette butts on the carpet, the sweat on his face—all of it. The look in his eyes when I'd asked him about Lamont.

The way that he treated his wife gnawed at me like a ferocious animal. That was me, you see, battered by Cyrus, abused and used up and left for dead before Lamont rescued me. I cringed to think of that poor woman.

I was lying in bed trying to sleep, but my body was coiled like steel springs. I would kill Darby Gordon. I had to, if it was the last thing I did. I would kill that man who'd killed Lamont.

My mind skipped a thought.

What if I did kill him?

My eyes snapped open.

Kill him now. Tonight.

The fist of God himself was pounding on my chest as the thoughts came alive in my mind.

Why not? This wasn't about Danny, it was about Lamont. I, not Danny, had to avenge Lamont's death. This is what I was living for.

But it was more than that. The thought of such a vile creature breathing even more breath sickened me. He was there, snoring in his bed, and Lamont was in a shallow grave somewhere. Or cut to pieces and lying at the bottom of the ocean.

I sat up, fully awake and trembling. It was the perfect time. He would never expect me to return, not after I'd run like a mouse.

Could I really do it? I'd never actually killed a man with my bare hands. I'd helped cut up Redding and throw him over the cliff, but only after Danny had shot him.

A gun, I thought. I had a silencer for my gun now. Killing that viper would be a simple thing for me. Just sneak in, press the barrel up to his head, and *pop*. One bullet in his temple while he slept next to his wife, who was probably dreaming of ways to poison him.

I slipped onto the floor, shaking like a twig in the wind, and I paced next to my bed. I could do this. I would delight Danny with this. I would finally be able to sleep in peace. Lamont would love me for it.

It was this last thought that got my feet moving toward the box in my closet, where I now kept all my tools, including the gun.

My decision was final. I was going to kill Darby Gordon, and I was going to do it tonight.

23

I REACHED THAT dark, nasty house at two o'clock in the morning, and it took me twenty-five minutes to leave the shadow of the tree where I'd had the cab drop me off. Because I could still back out and call Danny for advice. Because I knew I had to rid myself of my emotion first, if I wanted to avoid mistakes. Because I had to be perfect, absolutely perfect, if I really wanted to impress Danny.

I was dressed in black, from my Puma runners to my long workout pants to my long-sleeved pullover. After the cab pulled away, I tugged a black neoprene mask over all but my eyes. Every other inch of my body was covered—no skin cells or hair would fall off me as evidence for a forensic team. Even my small leather tool bag was black.

Finally satisfied that I was calm and that the street was empty, I casually strolled down the sidewalk toward the house I'd fled hours earlier.

There were no streetlights. The neighbors had darkened their houses. The rain had stopped. My shoes made a sticking sound as I walked over the wet asphalt. The hot air from my lungs was already making the mask humid, like breathing in a sauna.

But these things were distant to me. I was homed in on the Darby house. More precisely, on getting *around* that house, where I could work in secret.

It was a rough neighborhood, but not even these folks could kill the greenbelt that ran behind the string of houses. My back would be covered. I had to concern myself only with being spotted from the front, and from what I could see, there was no one to spot me.

Heart pumping like a steam engine, I cut left and sprinted on my tiptoes toward the back of the house. Careened around the corner. And came face-to-face with a high fence.

A dog fence.

The thought of a pet was new. I'd forgotten about the smell of dog hair in the house. But I was quick on my feet and sprang back around the corner before any canine could sound the warning.

No sound at all. Darby had probably killed the children's pet in a fit of rage and then barbecued it for dinner in front of them.

Trying to still my breathing, I carefully poked my head around the corner and eyed the back of the house. An old doghouse sat in the corner of a fenced lot that could have passed for a yard if it had any lawn. Tufts of wild grass grew in spots on otherwise barren ground.

I picked up a pebble and tossed it at the doghouse, then jerked back and listened for it to hit the roof. It missed, so I tried again and this time was rewarded with a soft *plop*.

No bark. No nothing. So probably no pet. To be sure, I

sent another stone sailing toward the doghouse and this time watched for any sign of a dog. There was none. Spot had been eaten by his master, and that was no surprise.

I flung my bag over the fence and hoisted myself into the yard, thinking that if properly motivated I could vault this thing and sprint for the car.

I had contemplated a number of ways to execute body disposal, as Danny called it, if I got to that point, and I had decided that the safest way would be in the black bags I'd brought. But the moment I landed on the bare ground and saw the shovel leaning against the back wall, a new idea popped into my head.

I stood there for a full five minutes running this idea through my grid of possible downsides, as Danny had taught me to. My eyes remained on the doghouse, because that was the deal: What if I was to bury the body under the doghouse?

Assuming I could move the wooden structure, which looked pretty heavy. Assuming I could dig a hole large enough to fit a body. Assuming I could cover it up properly and drag the house back over the disturbed earth.

There were no tree roots to make digging impossible, which would probably be the case out in the greenbelt. No wild animals to dig up the body. Even if the house was eventually sold and the doghouse tossed, no one would know there was a body buried there. Even if they did eventually find the body after years of rain washed away the dirt or something, they would only assume Darby Gordon had been knocked off by some nasty criminal, he being one himself.

I was not a nasty criminal. I was God's merciful angel. Danny, my priest, my savior, my new soul mate, had his own private graveyard. Now I would add to it here, in San Pedro. The idea was intoxicating.

I grabbed the shovel and ran over to the doghouse at the back corner. A blanket of clouds provided a cover of darkness. If I was caught, I could throw the bag over the back fence, leap over, and vanish into the greenbelt.

The doghouse wasn't anchored into the ground, and although it took even more muscle and huffing and puffing than I had expected, I managed to push/pull/drag it to one side. The earth was hard, and there was no grass to keep the base from sliding.

The hole was another matter because, although it was clay and dug up quite easily, I realized that after I put a body in the mix, the dirt wouldn't all fit back into the hole. So I began to toss every other shovelful over the back fence.

A man like Darby Gordon would notice the fresh dirt strewn along the ground beyond his fence, but with any luck he wouldn't be around. His wife and children might see it but wouldn't likely make the connection. If they did, they would only rejoice.

I pulled my ski mask up so I could breathe, then dug for half an hour, until my back was breaking and my palms were blistering. Without my gloves I wouldn't have lasted ten minutes. I was a puff cake, not a construction worker, albeit a puff cake that could cut life with a knife when needed.

My mind spun with each thrust of the shovel. If Lamont could only see me now. I missed him terribly.

Would anyone believe me if I told them I was digging for treasure at three o'clock in the morning?

I loved Danny, but I missed Lamont. I could do both, right? And I could kill Darby Gordon for both of them.

The hole wasn't long enough to lay a body in, but I had to keep to the doghouse dimensions, so I went deep instead of long—a good three feet deep. Satisfied that I could get Darby into the grave if I broke him up a bit, I pulled my mask back down, grabbed my black bag, and ran to the kitchen window.

I was still clean, see? I could still make a run for it. But I didn't because I didn't want to. A part of me was trembling, but a part of me would die if I didn't see this through. The feeling wasn't so different from how I'd felt searching for a fix when I was addicted to a different kind of high.

The thought stopped me for a moment as I stood at the window with the glass cutter in my hand. I had tasted the blood of vengeance once, and I wanted it again.

Was a good person's addiction to doing good, bad?

I might have just broken the glass with a towel wrapped around my hand like they did in movies, hoping no one would hear, but Danny had explained the foolishness of it. Instead I took the time to painstakingly cut a one-foot hole in the bottom of the glass, wide enough for me to reach in and release both locks that fastened the window to the sill.

With a single shove, the window jerked up, gaping eighteen inches at the bottom. I stood, listening. I heard the distant hum of a transformer; a ticking sound that came from inside the house, maybe a clock; my own breathing. Nothing else. No sound of Darby creeping around to intercept me.

At the moment, my crime was limited to property damage, but the second I climbed through the window I would be guilty of breaking and entering. So what? Neither compared to cutting up a body and throwing it in the Pacific Ocean. I was ready.

I withdrew my silenced nine-millimeter gun from the black bag, shoved the firearm behind my waist, hoisted myself into the open window, and slid over the sill onto the floor of the kitchen's dinette.

I did not land in perfect silence. My gun fell out and *thump*ed on the linoleum floor.

To me it sounded as if a bomb had been detonated in the house—there was no way Darby could sleep through such a racket! He was probably grabbing his shotgun and rushing out to shoot me.

I snatched up my gun and scrambled to the edge of the kitchen cabinets. I crouched there, trying not to breathe, with my weapon cocked and ready to fire the moment he stepped out. A dozen thoughts crashed through my head, all of them about one kind of disastrous ending or another.

It took a full minute, which felt more like ten, before I realized Darby had either slept through my thumping or was waiting for me in the bedroom.

Once you go, go. Danny's voice came back to me. *Keep them off balance. It's all about maintaining the advantage, surprise, illusion, sleight of hand. Speed and stealth are your closest friends.*

I'd already blown the stealth bit, and I wasn't doing so well with the speed thing, but I could change both now, right?

So I moved forward in a crouch like a ninja, gun ahead of me. I crouched/tiptoed/rushed out of the kitchen and through the living room, which was barely lit by one night-light on the far wall.

The bedroom door was open. I poked my head around the corner, gun by my chin now. The room was dark, but I could make out one lump curled up and another sprawled out, snoring softly. That would be the beast, lost in nasty dreams.

I froze by the door, knowing it was a bad time to freeze up, but I couldn't help it. I was now guilty of property damage, and breaking and entering, but I still hadn't done the deed. And doing the deed wasn't going to be as simple as shooting Darby in the head and running. The knowledge in that head was too valuable to waste. Killing him outright would be unforgivable.

Danny favored drugs. Incapacitating the target was the best option, he said, and who could disagree? I'd become fascinated with the idea that a simple needle could reduce any thug to a lump of flesh, and I practiced with a poor cantaloupe until Danny was satisfied I could sling a syringe with the best of them.

His drug of choice was propofol, which when injected directly into the bloodstream would typically render any subject unconscious in seconds.

Still crouching, I hurried around the bed to where Emily was curled up in a dead sleep. Kneeling so that only my head poked above the mattress, I set my gun down on the carpet, withdrew one of two syringes in my pocket, and removed the protective sleeve from the needle.

Poking someone in the neck with a needle and injecting a drug into their jugular is much harder than most people imagine. Too shallow or too deep and you miss the vein. Either way, Emily would wake. The idea was to quickly, and I mean very quickly, inject the drug and get the needle out before she could interrupt the procedure.

I carefully guided the needle to her bare neck so that it hovered in line with her vein. Then, taking a deep breath to steady myself, I jabbed the needle in, shoved the carefully measured dose into her bloodstream, withdrew the syringe, and dropped to the floor.

Emily gave a short cry and slapped at her neck, jerking up onto one elbow. Beside her, Darby grunted. Finding no gargantuan mosquito hovering over her bed, Emily scratched her neck a couple of times and sank back to the pillow.

On the far side of the bed, Darby rolled over. It was a shame I had to hurt her, but try as I might, I couldn't think of a better way to deal with her without exposing myself. No matter what I did with Darby, she would probably wake up and identify me, if not in the bedroom, then later when she peered out through the window as I buried his body in the ground.

Drugged, she would sleep soundly and wake in a few hours, groggy and with a bruise on her neck, but otherwise ignorant and safe.

I waited several minutes on the ground beside the bed, then reached up and poked Emily's arm. When she did not respond, I jabbed harder in her side.

She was out. Now I could do my deed properly.

I sneaked over to the lamp, turned it on, and then stood back as Danny had instructed so that Darby couldn't easily reach me. The man was still snoring. I started to speak, then stopped to clear my throat and spoke with a trembling voice.

"Wake up, you lousy viper."

They weren't the most clever words, and Darby didn't wake up.

"Get up!"

He jerked upright and twisted toward his wife. Uttered an unintelligible word.

"This way," I snapped. "Make any sudden moves and I'll pull the trigger."

He swiveled his head and stared in my direction. "What?"

"Turn over on your stomach and keep your arms spread," I said.

His eyes widened as his head cleared.

"Now! On your belly. Now!"

The man's face darkened. "What do you think you're trying to do?"

"I'm trying to give you a chance to live, you stupid schmuck. Turn over like I said!"

I almost pulled the trigger then, because instead of showing fear, he actually sneered like he was daring me to kill him. But I didn't want to leave blood on the sheets or shoot a bullet in the wall.

So I said, "I'm going to count to three. One...two..."

His sneer softened and he lifted his hands. "Okay. Calm down."

"On your face."

"You have no idea who you're dealing with."

"I'm dealing with a fool in his underwear. Turn over!"

He clenched his jaw and finally turned onto his stomach. "What do you want?"

"Arms wide."

He stretched his arms out, a frail little man at my mercy, face turned so that I could see it.

"Tell me how I can get to Bourque and I'll let you live," I said.

"You're mental! You think I have any access to Bourque? He's going to kill you, you know that. No one crosses him and lives."

"Tell me why and how you killed Lamont."

"I didn't, you fool! I have no idea who he is."

"Don't lie to me. Jonathan Bourque had him killed and I want to know why and how. Tell me!"

"I am telling you! I don't have a clue who—"

"He worked for Bourque. We lived in Malibu. Blond hair, handsome man. You killed him."

"And I'm telling you, you have the wrong man. I've never heard of him."

"You're denying that you've killed people for Jonathan Bourque?"

"No. I'm not denying that. But whoever this Lamont is, I wasn't involved."

I stood in silence. He was telling the truth? He said it with such conviction that I was tempted to believe him. This wiry snake had killed for Jonathan Bourque, but maybe Lamont wasn't one of his hits.

"You're lying."

"Why would I lie?"

"Then who did?" I asked.

"I have no idea. I've never heard of the man. Now are we done here?"

"No."

My mind was reeling. Part of me was saying that he *wasn't* guilty of killing Lamont, so I *didn't* have the right to kill him and all my work digging his grave had been wasted.

But another part was telling me that Danny would kill Darby regardless. He was the lowest kind of human, abusing those closest to him for his own gain. If there was any man who deserved justice, it was him.

I imagined the children upstairs, cowering in the beds, and I felt rage boil in my face. I admit that my anger was probably partly motivated by the fact that I hadn't uncovered Lamont's killer, but anyone who physically abused his wife and children without showing the slightest remorse did not deserve to live.

In fact, now that I was able to put Lamont's death out of the picture, I saw that this ugliness in Darby's character was worse than the role he played for Jonathan Bourque.

I wasn't prepared for the emotions that overtook me then. My hands began to shake and for a moment I thought I might fall.

"Face the other way," I said, eager to get his eyes off me.

He stared at me angrily.

I felt frantic. "Turn the other way! Turn toward your wife, you pile of vomit. Turn your head!"

"What are you going to do?" The first signs of concern crossed his face.

"Nothing, just turn. Turn away from me!"

He turned his head and swore. I jerked out the second syringe, pulled the sleeve off using my teeth, and rushed up to him. "Will you just settle down? I—"

It was as far as he got. I stabbed the needle into his neck and shoved the plunger home. I did it without taking time to think.

Darby Gordon roared and came up like a tiger, clawing at the needle still stuck in his neck. I jumped back, gun level with his face. "Shut up!"

But I'd missed his vein. It would take longer for him to go under and he wasn't shutting up. He flung the syringe across the room, cursing bitterly, demanding in the vilest terms possible that I tell him what I had done.

"Shut up!" I cried. The whole neighborhood would hear if he kept this up! "Shut up!"

"You thupid…"

His eyes clouded as the drug began to reach into his mind. Grunting like a cow, he lunged from the bed, took one long step toward me, and collapsed facedown at my feet.

I stood over him, shaking from head to foot, gun still pointed at the bed where he'd been lying only a minute ago. Emily slept on in peace. The house had gone completely silent.

I had killed him? But the rise and fall of his back said he was alive.

No one rushed in to arrest me. The kids were not standing in the doorway wondering what all the hollering had been about. It was just Darby and Emily in a deep sleep, and me standing over them with a gun.

Now what?

The moment the question crossed my mind, I knew the answer.

24

DIRECTING THE SACRAMENT of penance would be the least missed of all Danny's duties when he left the priesthood. This much he'd known from the first time he'd taken up position in the confessional and heard an older woman named Betty confess that her obsession with chocolate at two in the morning was the real reason for her obesity. But he'd missed two dates with the box in the last two days due to his preoccupation with Renee, and Danny felt obligated to make an appearance today.

"Bless me, Father, for I have sinned. It's been two months since my last confession." A middle-aged female had taken the booth. Danny made a point not to identify those who bared their secrets to him, because he had no interest in the paltry sins of the flock. Stealing, cheating, lying, fornicating, masturbating, overeating, gossiping, jealousy, anger, et cetera, et cetera, et cetera—the common sins of the masses, so banal, so human—were utterly predictable, and inevitable, no matter how hard people tried to avoid them, no matter how many prayers they uttered.

What was the point? Go and sin no more, he would say, but they would. It was impossible not to.

"But you are here," Danny said softly. "God will reward you for that."

"I have thoughts, Father. They scare me."

Take this woman speaking in a timid voice now. If her thoughts were about hating and abusing others in a premeditated, purposeful way, he might find her confession more interesting. But to date, he'd never encountered such a person in this box. He'd met plenty outside the law.

"Go on."

"It's my mother-in-law. She's coming for a visit and I hate her. My husband and I have fought for three days and I can't take it." She sniffed once.

"Well, you don't plan on killing her, do you?"

The woman uttered a short gasp. "No!"

"Good. That wouldn't be wise."

She recovered and went on, and he listened dutifully, but he only heard the broad strokes. His mind drifted to the matter of Renee, who hadn't called today and didn't answer his call two hours earlier, at noon. She'd probably lain awake half the night thinking about her first solo effort. He had found sleep fleeting himself.

It was unlike her to sleep in, but last night had been no ordinary night. It could have gone worse, much worse. At least she hadn't done anything stupid, like attack the man, which Danny wouldn't put past her. They would have to work on her impulsive nature.

Such an enigma. So simple and innocent, yet so complex. World-wise in a way that drew him like a moth drawn to the flame. The fact that he might be burned wasn't lost on him, but he couldn't seem to help himself. Killing the man who'd ended Lamont's life was Renee's obsession. Renee was his.

He heard two more confessions, both from women—no surprise, 80 percent of all confessions were given by women—both involving paltry sins. He was about to call it quits when another person entered the booth and sat still, unspeaking. Perhaps a man. Men tended to be less forthcoming.

"You'd like me to hear your confession?" Danny asked.

"Bless me, Father, for I have sinned. I put two bullets in a man's head last night and buried him under the doghouse in his backyard."

Renee's unexpected voice came to him like the sound of an angel.

What she said robbed him of breath.

"Are you mad at me?" she asked meekly.

"I…" Had he heard correctly? He couldn't move. They were in the church where, however unlikely, voices could carry! She'd killed a man?

Now she spoke hurriedly. "I'm sorry, Danny, but I had to do it. You have to understand that."

"You…Who?"

"Him," she said.

"You went back?" he whispered.

She gripped the latticework between the booths with both hands and spoke with hushed excitement. "He's dead. He was the worst of the worst. He—"

"Not here!" Danny abruptly stood, sliding the gate between the booths closed as he did. "Meet me at the Starbucks two blocks down in fifteen minutes."

Then he walked out of the booth and strode for the offices without looking back. What had she done? What had she done?

THEY SAT AT an outside table half an hour later, Renee staring at her herbal tea, Danny watching her over an untouched vanilla latte.

There was no one within earshot, but that could change. "Go on," he urged. "All the details. You're in their room. Both are sedated…"

Her eyes flitted up, bright, eager. The eyes were called windows to the soul, and he was already deep inside of hers, cohabiting. Their common character, their interests, the raw attraction…all of it had pressed them into the same mold. Even now, in the wake of her breaking sacred trust with him by going off on her own, he felt an inseparable bond with Renee.

"I couldn't leave them," she said. "I don't think he was involved in Lamont's death, but when I thought about the demonic way he treated his wife and children, I just couldn't leave him, right?"

"Actually, you could have."

"Would you have?"

He thought for a moment, scanning the area without moving his head. The strip mall's parking lot was nearly empty. Danny often treated those in need at this Starbucks. Drug addicts, hardship cases, single mothers—the coffee shop was more of a confessional than the one in the church.

"Maybe not," he said.

"That's what I thought. So I—"

"Hold on."

A car pulled up to the curb and two teenage girls piled out, laughing. This wouldn't do. Renee was too volatile to trust in any public setting, and his nerves were wound too tight for his own comfort. Meeting her here was a mistake. He wasn't clearheaded around her.

"Let's go for a ride in my car."

"Okay." She stood without hesitating.

Danny wore the collar now, and some might raise an eyebrow at the sight of a priest giving such a beautiful young woman a ride, but it was nothing new to the regulars here. The disadvantaged were often without wheels, and they were sometimes beautiful.

He was overthinking the situation.

He steered the car down Long Beach toward Ocean Boulevard, headed to Bluff Park on the beach. It would be nearly deserted at two in the afternoon on a Tuesday. She rode in the passenger seat, waiting for his direction like a good understudy who knew she was about to be reprimanded—already at work on him in her own subtle way, and unaware of what she was doing. She was smarter than she realized, he thought. Raw and undisciplined, but a natural. Perhaps even more gifted than he.

He turned the radio on. A pop station was playing one of Beyoncé's latest singles. "Okay. Now tell me."

She picked up exactly where she'd left off. "I couldn't leave them, Danny. I just couldn't. Her, of course, but not him. But I couldn't kill him in the house, either. I knew I would leave evidence of a break-in because I'd cut a hole in the kitchen window, but that's not exactly bloodstains on the floor, which is what I would have left if I'd killed him in the bedroom, right?"

She was looking for his approval. "Go on."

"So I opened the bedroom window, dragged him over, and shoved him out into the backyard. Then I locked it, made sure there were no signs of a struggle, and went out to the kitchen, where I left the note."

"The note?"

"On a piece of paper using a Sharpie I found on the counter."

"You left your handwriting?"

"No. I wrote in block letters."

"Wrote what?"

"He's gone. Breathe a word to the cops and you'll be next." There was a twinkle in her eyes. "But here's the smart part. I signed it Jonathan Bourque."

He grasped her reasoning immediately. There was a connection between Bourque and Darby Gordon. In the unlikely event that the wife went to the cops, Bourque would learn about it. He'd leverage his relationship with the authorities to shut down any investigation, keeping the note tying him to Darby Gordon from surfacing.

"Smart," he said.

"I thought so, too."

"Then what?"

"Then I dragged the body to the grave and shoved it in."

"He fit?"

"I had to jump on him a few times. Something broke, I think his legs." Her voice had grown soft and she was looking ahead at the street now. "It made me queasy. But I just kept thinking about his wife and children."

"Then you shot him?"

"Yes. I shot him twice in the head."

She went silent. He let her process without further coaxing. Danny had killed his mother's killer a year after her death. Even then, in a time of war, after planning the kill for so long, taking a man's life had bothered him far more than he could have imagined.

"It hurts," he said.

"It's strange," she said. "I actually felt sorry for him. Not that he didn't deserve it. I would have felt even more sorry for his children and wife if I hadn't killed him. It was the right moral choice."

She turned to him. "Leaving him alive would have resulted in much more destruction than killing him. And his abuse of them took away his right to life. He was the worst of the worst, Danny. I promise you that."

"Did I ask for justification?"

"No. But you're thinking it. I should have called you first, I know, but I was afraid you'd say no. And I wanted to surprise you."

"You're right, I would have advised against it. And you did surprise me. I hope I'm not creating a monster."

"What? That's what you think of me?"

"No, I didn't mean it like that. Just a figure of—"

"Was God a monster for killing the Philistines? Were soldiers monsters for bombing Berlin?"

The reverend mother's voice whispered through Danny's mind. *Are you ever tempted to judge, Father?*

"No, they're not monsters, and neither are we."

"So." And that was that.

They rode in silence for a few minutes, approaching the park on the left. What had he been thinking, bringing her into his way of life? Surely this could not end well. They were playing with the trigger of a bomb that could go off with the slightest misguided movement.

"What did you do after you killed him?" he asked, breaking the silence.

"I shoved the dirt back in, flattened it all down, and scooted the doghouse back over the grave. You can't tell, if that's what you're worrying about."

"You left nothing behind?"

"I put everything back exactly as I found it, drove home, fell into bed, and slept like a baby for the first time in months." Her voice was subdued.

Danny pulled into the park's lot, aware that she was struggling between two poles pulling at her soul. Death, regardless of its form, had that effect on any healthy human.

He slipped the car into park, quietly let the air out of his lungs, and stared at the ocean across the street. Other than a Corolla on one end of the lot and a Nissan pickup truck behind them, the spaces were empty.

"Well...It's done," he said.

She didn't respond.

He turned to face her and her tears then. Two watery tracks glistened down her cheeks. Her eyes were closed and she was trying to be brave.

No, Renee! It's okay, I didn't mean to hurt you! He'd been too callous with her. She'd been up a mountain that few had the stomach to climb, and he offered her no support or appreciation.

Danny reached for her shoulder and rubbed it with his thumb. "It's okay, Renee. I cried like a baby after I killed my first, even though he deserved it. He'd raped and killed my mother."

She leaned into him, wrapped her arms around his stomach, and pulled herself close to his chest as the floodgates broke. Sobs began to shake her body as she cried into his shirt.

He held her gently, suppressing his own emotion. "It's okay, Renee. Really, it's okay. You did well. I'm proud of you."

That only brought more tears, buckets of emotion that had pooled for months. His eyes misted, but he could not allow himself to break down.

Danny was dressed as a priest and he was holding a woman in his arms, but he didn't care. For so many reasons Renee was far more important to him than any obligation or reputation related to the church.

He comforted her, and her sobbing slowly subsided until she was able to sit up, wipe the tears from her eyes using her thumbs, and make fun of her own puffy eyes.

"Take a walk with me?" he suggested.

"Yes." She laughed, a short chuckle that was born of release, not humor.

They strolled along a cement path bordered on both sides by bright green lawn, Danny with his hands clasped behind his back, Renee with her hand on his elbow until he suggested it might not be such a good idea in public. A quickness had entered her step.

They walked and talked for an hour, interrupted by only one call—the office wondering if he was going to make a four o'clock meeting with the board. No, he wasn't. His apologies.

Renee took several steps, thinking, eyes on the concrete path. "But he didn't kill Lamont."

"You're sure?"

"As sure as I can be."

"I think you're right."

"So... When can we go after Bourque?"

He chuckled, but the comment unnerved him. "Slow down, dear. The blood isn't even dry on your hands."

"No, not that! Of course not. I mean, in general."

He stepped off the path onto the lawn and stopped, put his hands into his pockets. "Then let's agree on one thing. We let this lie for a few days. Time is our friend, not our enemy. It's critical we sit back and see what Bourque does now. Nothing proactive on our part. Fair?"

"Of course! Yes, fair."

"No exceptions."

"No, not even one."

"All in good time."

"Exactly. In good time."

"Besides, you need to move again."

"Out of sight, out of mind."

"Good."

She looked at the sea. "Maybe we could do dinner."

"Of course. I would love that."

"Maybe you could take that collar off and we could go to San Diego or something."

He laughed. "We'll see. Just promise me, no Bourque."

She held up two fingers pressed together. "Scout's honor. No Bourque."

"Good. We'll let it rest for a few days."

"We'll let it rest."

Danny smiled and sighed with relief.

He had no intention of letting it rest.

25

THERE WAS A time to be discreet; there was a time to be direct. The time for the latter had arrived. This, Danny reasoned, was because the more he thought about Renee's fixation on Jonathan Bourque, the more he became convinced that she could not deal with the man without a significant probability of failure, *failure* being defined as her getting caught or being killed, neither of which he could live with.

Furthermore, he was no longer convinced that killing Bourque was a wise course of action, not even on his part. He still had no irrefutable evidence the man had ordered a hit on Lamont, and Renee's safety was now far more important to Danny than his personal missions.

Two days had passed since Renee's breakdown in the park. She'd moved, resecuring her anonymity as Mary Wilcox. Danny had met Renee for lunch on both days, and he'd done his best to keep the discussion on them and off Bourque. He'd otherwise kept his schedule stacked, knowing that his first opportunity to deal with Bourque would be today, when the man returned from a trip to Northern California.

The Wells Fargo bank building that housed the Bourque Foundation stood tall against a blue afternoon sky. Danny parked his car, checked his collar in the rearview mirror, and strode toward the elevators as a priest.

Given more time, he would have chosen a more cautious approach, but under the circumstances his need for information outweighed his need for caution.

Consider: He had to know if Bourque had tied him to Renee.

Consider: He had to know if Bourque suspected him or Renee in the deaths of Redding or Darby Gordon.

Consider: He had to determine if Bourque's connections to Lamont's disappearance were as real as Renee assumed.

Conclusion: It was time for a direct approach. If Danny's discoveries turned out to be negative, he would insist they abandon interest in the man either forever or until a later date. Damage control was as important a part of warfare as any confrontation.

He rode the elevator to the top floor with a carefully groomed man who was dressed in a blue Armani suit—not the kind one typically associated with nonprofit charities. But that was no longer Danny's concern.

The reception area was occupied by only one other patron and the receptionist, who was on the phone. Stacked blond hair, crisply pressed suit, all business and alert. Naturally. The big man was in town.

Smiling as any good priest comfortable with his calling might, Danny approached the desk and waited for her to clear the line.

"May I help you?"

"I hope so." He put his hand on the counter. "I know this is unexpected and I don't have an appointment, but I was hoping to see Jonathan Bourque."

"I'm sorry, but he's tied up in meetings at the moment."

"No problem, I can wait."

"Actually, he'll be tied up the rest of the day. Would you like to make an appointment?"

"No, no appointment necessary. I'm sure he'll want to see me. If you just—"

"I'm sorry, sir, but Mr. Bourque's a very busy man and doesn't see guests without appointments."

"It's Father, not sir," he said. "And if Mr. Bourque learns that you turned me away, he will undoubtedly fire you. I suggest you interrupt whatever meeting has him so occupied and tell him that Father Danny Hansen is here regarding Simon Redding. I suggest you do it now, before you lose your nerve."

The receptionist blinked, clearly unaccustomed to such a bold demand.

"Please, darling, it's for the best." He smiled again, offering her an olive branch as such. "Make the call."

She finally stood and excused herself. "One moment please."

Two minutes later, Danny was ushered into a corner office with walls made of glass overlooking the Pacific Ocean. "Please have a seat. Mr. Bourque will be right with you."

"Thank you, my dear. Thank you so much."

But Danny did not sit. The room had a similar decorative feel to Bourque's home office, favoring rich woods, antiques, and exotics over the contemporary decor found in so many high-rise work spaces. If there was a single piece of incriminating evidence to be found here, Bourque would never have allowed any guest to be left alone. The gesture confirmed Danny's estimation of the man's lofty criminal intelligence.

He glanced at his image in a large, ornate, gold-framed mirror that hung over a credenza. Black shirt, black pants, white clerical collar. His wavy hair could use a bit of tidying, but it was short enough to pass as free-spirited rather than shaggy. Still, he raked his fingers through it to smooth a few loose ends.

"Father."

Danny turned to see that Bourque stood in the doorway to his office. "Mr. Bourque." He extended his hand, which the man took. Warm, very large hands. "Thank you for interrupting your day for me."

Bourque closed the door, walked to his desk, and eased himself into the leather chair. "So, Father Hansen. Tell me what this is about."

"She didn't tell you? It's about your thug Redding."

The man watched Danny with eyes set deep in a chiseled face sharpened further by his mustache and goatee. His dark hair was greased back, cut short in the back above a starched white collar. He wore a black suit with a burgundy tie that screamed of dominance.

"She did mention Redding, yes. Please, have a seat, Father."

Danny sat and folded one leg over the other, hands clasped in his lap, eyes on his host. "I know you're busy. Let me get straight to the point. I mention Redding only because I assumed that would gain me an audience, but I'm not really concerned with how you conduct your security. Good people sometimes need to flex their muscles to achieve their objectives. Even the Vatican has its guards."

Bourque's left brow arched. "And what concern is so pressing that you insisted I break from a meeting?"

"It's the girl I set free. This Renee Gilmore, whom your man Redding had handcuffed to a chair in the hotel's basement."

"An unfortunate misunderstanding," Bourque said.

"Yes. But you should know that it's my job to work with the

disadvantaged. Young misguided women like Renee. I asked her to pay me a visit at the church, which she did, the next day."

"Good. I trust she's doing well?"

"Actually, no. In fact, she seemed quite distraught over the disappearance of her husband three months ago. A Mr. Lamont Myers. She claimed that he worked for you and vanished after a run-in with you. This, she claimed, was why Redding had detained her. And she seemed quite concerned for her own safety."

"I believe she was detained because she was making threats." He waved his hand. "But that's behind us. No harm, no foul. Like I said, a misunderstanding."

"Yes. But now Renee has gone missing. She was supposed to meet me a week later and failed to make our appointment." The misdirection was a critical element in removing suspicion from himself. It was important that Bourque not feel threatened by Danny. "So I tried to get in contact with Simon Redding, thinking he might know something. It's what I do, you understand, chasing down the wayward so that I can offer them my help."

"Of course. Not so different from what we do here."

"When I failed to reach Redding, who has evidently left your employment, I tried to track the young woman down at her hotel, then through the cab company. I used every means at my disposal, but she's vanished."

"I'm sorry to hear that, Father. I'm not sure what this has to do with the Bourque Foundation."

"Nothing necessarily. But before I closed the book on the matter I felt obligated to look into the disappearance of her husband, Mr. Lamont Myers. I learned that he had indeed worked as an attorney for you before disappearing three months ago. So you see, all this disappearing makes me nervous. I need to clear my head of any inappropriate suggestions."

Enough of the truth to do the job.

Bourque watched him for a few long beats, then sat back, crossed his legs, and sighed. "I appreciate your concern here, Father, though I can't quite understand why you made such a play to see me today. This could just as easily have been handled over the phone."

"Exactly, but I prefer to look people in the eyes. I need to know, Mr. Bourque: Do you have any idea what might have happened to the young woman?"

"Believe me, if I did, I would have no reason not to tell you. Having been a priest myself once, I know exactly where you're coming from. I support your work like few can." He folded his hands.

"And why did you leave the priesthood?"

"There is only so much one can do in the church," Bourque said. "I felt I could do more out here. I imagine you know what I mean."

Danny thought silence would be the wisest reply.

"Now, as far as Lamont Myers is concerned, I'll tell you what I know. He worked for me, as you say. He was an attorney who oversaw the foundation's international legal affairs. At least that was what I was led to believe until I learned the truth."

"Which was?"

"That Lamont Myers wasn't as he appeared to those of us who knew him."

Danny's interest was piqued. He hadn't expected to hear details about who Lamont was. In fact, he'd never had more than a passing interest in understanding the man beyond his role as Renee's so-called husband, her soul mate for whom she would willingly die.

"In what way?" he asked.

Jonathan Bourque shifted his gaze out the window toward

the horizon. "I can assume your confidentiality, yes? It's a rather sensitive subject. Lamont Myers is missing, as you say, but if he were to surface and learn that I've been saying things..." Bourque turned and drilled Danny with a stare. "Well, let's just say that I wouldn't put anything beyond that man."

"Of course. But please don't feel like you have to share anything that might break a confidence between you."

The man offered him a shallow grin. "I think I can trust you, Father."

Quid pro quo. They both played their games with casual mastery, Danny thought, dipping his head. *Go on...*

Jonathan Bourque's mouth flattened. "Lamont Myers—we'll call him that although he had several aliases—was one of the best lawyers who ever worked for me. But he was unscrupulous. Vicious even. I began an investigation into him when complaints of certain brutalities in an operation in Kenya came to my attention."

In part true, perhaps, but if so, those brutalities were ordered by a brute named Jonathan Bourque, Danny thought.

"What I learned made me sick," Bourque continued. "To say that the man led a double life would be an understatement. He had more than one house, and while he was perhaps the consummate attorney here, he was the devil everywhere else. The web of lies he wove to protect himself would astound you."

Danny wasn't prepared for this. This characterization of the man Renee had loved so dearly had to be Bourque's own fabrication. Even so, he pronounced it with surprising authority.

"This is Lamont Myers?" Danny said.

"Lamont Myers. And you'll have to forgive me, Father, but if he hadn't gone missing when he did, I might have been tempted to deal with him myself. I can't tell you what happened to him, only that when I sent my men to check on him, he was gone. Not a sign of him since, not even at his home in Malibu, which has since gone into foreclosure. He just vanished."

A warning bell went off in Danny's head, but he wasn't able to trace its source. Something wasn't right. The man Bourque was describing was nothing like the Lamont that Renee admired. Was it possible she'd been wrong about him?

No, not that wrong. Not unless—

"He had his own sex slave," Bourque said. "A woman stashed away in his glass house by the sea. The man was sick."

"That's not possible." Danny said it, but he hardly heard his own words. "How...?" He lost track of his question.

"But it's true. She wasn't an actual slave, of course, but a young woman he kept locked in the house to serve his every need. He kept a secret room in the basement—whips and chains, the whole bit."

If the words were a sledgehammer to Danny's stomach, he might have felt less pain. He couldn't breathe, he couldn't think. He could only see Renee hanging from the wall in a secret basement room. Nausea swept through his gut.

A strange light had come on in Bourque's eyes, taunting.

"I'm surprised you didn't notice anything amiss in your dealings with her, Father. It is my understanding that this young woman, Renee Gilmore, is likely the woman in question."

The room faded, and for a moment Danny thought he might throw up, faint, or both. He'd been here before, when he was fifteen in Bosnia, with his mother and his sisters.

It couldn't be! Renee was naive and impulsive, fun loving and eager. She wasn't a battered woman staggering through life under the burden of horrific abuse.

But even as Danny denied the possibility, he knew he could have misread all the signals. She was obsessive-compulsive. She'd suffered a psychotic break. She was irrationally committed to protecting her image of Lamont and erasing any mark against him in her loving memory.

What if this behavior was a powerful subconscious device to protect herself from cruel memories?

He had to go to her. He had to hold her. It was all that mattered now! He had to hold her and tell her that he loved her, and that nothing that had happened to her changed his love for her.

"I didn't mean to disturb you, Father," Bourque said, but his words were laced with irony.

"Thank you for your time."

Danny pushed himself to his feet, no longer concerned with the Bourque Foundation or the man who ran it. Assuming what he'd just heard proved to be true, he could only be glad that Lamont Myers had vanished—with any luck, into hell itself.

Assuming...

He's lying to you, Danny. He's playing with your mind.

"You can check the evidence for yourself, Father. It's all still there."

"If you'll excuse me." Danny turned without offering his hand or any other salutation. He had to get out and get out now, before he did something embarrassing.

He left the office without turning. Crossed the reception area without a word of gratitude. Descended in the elevator without acknowledging the two women who joined him on the eighth floor.

He couldn't go to Renee and hold her now, he realized. To do so would only beg for an explanation. If she had been the subject of abuse, she had completely shut it out of her mind's eye.

For her, it had never happened, and anyone who suggested it had might become her bitter enemy. This was how the mind protected itself.

What did that beast do to her?

No, he wouldn't go to Renee now. Instead, he would retrieve his tools, go to the glass house in Malibu, and see for himself. Then, no matter what he found, he would rush to Renee and hold her.

If he found that she had been abused, he would never tell her. How could he?

26

I HAD BECOME slack and dirty over the two previous weeks, being so caught up in my new life with Danny. In fact, I'd only cleansed once a day at the most, even skipping a few days here and there because the thought of vomiting up *impurities*— Lamont's word for unsuitable or extra food—had somehow become less urgent to me than it had been when he was alive.

Part of the duty of any good wife was to make sure she took care of her body and didn't become a slob, Lamont used to say. And he was right. Keeping the body clean and healthy was as important as keeping the house or the mind clean.

With his patient help, I'd become nearly perfect at doing all three. I have to admit that learning to think Lamont's way was difficult for me at first. I don't remember how difficult, because the change happened over many months, and the blue pills that Lamont gave me to help wean me off the heroin had fogged my mind.

I learned that everything in life—preferences, love,

beauty—was a matter of perception. That's what he always used to say. Pain, ugliness, hate—the mind could block anything out with enough encouragement. Mind over matter.

For example, although I once loved meat, I learned that I could love tofu just as much if I just tried hard enough.

But I hadn't been taking my blue pills for over three months now. And Danny didn't seem the least bit interested in whether or not I ate a certain way or cleansed the impurities from my body. I once asked him if he thought I was getting fat because I'd gained two pounds. He only laughed at me. It took me a few minutes to realize that he wasn't mocking me but actually thought I was being silly.

That was the difference between Lamont and Danny. Lamont knew what was good for the soul, the body, and the mind. He was the one who had taught me what was right and what was wrong.

Danny knew which people needed to be judged. But unlike Lamont, he wasn't caught up in rules and all the little laws.

Still, I owed all that I was to Lamont, so after skipping two full days of cleansing I walked into my bathroom on Thursday afternoon, stuck my finger down my throat, and cleansed myself of all impurities.

It was like saying a confession, cleansing myself inside and out. I stood from my knees, flushed the toilet, scrubbed out my mouth with my toothbrush, and left feeling much better.

This was the third day after I had broken into the Gordon house in San Pedro and killed the monster who'd preyed on his wife and children. With each passing day, my craving to get on with it, to deal with Bourque, grew.

I know I've said this before, but I really felt like I had in the old days of my addiction to heroin, only in the best of ways. The fix is good, but after a few days I was dying for another one.

Not that I was dying to kill. Please, no, that wasn't it at all. If I had felt that way, I might have been concerned for myself. Danny talked about how important it was to avoid becoming pathological, like a pathological liar or serial killer who can't control his need to lie or kill.

Not at all. If anything, Danny and I were the exact opposite, carefully controlling our need to do what was right for the sake of others, not ourselves.

Still, I was feeling more eager to get back to Bourque as the hours ticked by. It's what I now did, right? I was this new creature, and I needed to act like it.

Which is why—after cleansing that afternoon on the third day, after calling Danny at home and at his office without reaching him, after sipping a glass of prune juice for an hour, after vacuuming and scrubbing the tiny floor in the Embassy Suites, after calling the church again and learning that Danny had left for the day—I decided that I would visit the Wells Fargo bank building downtown.

That's all it was supposed to be, a simple trip past the Bourque Foundation's offices. Going *by* wasn't exactly going *after* Bourque, which I had no interest in doing without Danny anyway. But after three months of dogging Lamont's killer, I couldn't just sit still, drinking prune juice.

So I dressed in my black skirt and a white collared blouse with short sleeves, slipped into my only pair of heels, and picked up my key card. I had come a long way since the days of flannel pajamas and slippers.

Danny wouldn't mind, right? He never told me where I could go or what I could eat—that was Lamont.

I paused at the door, then headed back into the bedroom for my bag. I was going out to a place of some danger, it would be best if I took my kit out with me. The black leather bag held my silenced gun in a custom case that Danny had made me, two knives, some nylon rope, my gloves, lock picks, and a variety of other tools that might prove useful. The basic tools that anyone in my position needed to do their job correctly.

The weight of the bag in my hand gave me some comfort walking down the hall. If they only knew. But who would suspect a short, thin blonde dressed in proper business attire as having any thoughts besides impressing her boss on her mind?

Well, maybe seducing their boss. But certainly not *killing* him.

I couldn't take a cab. That might have been how Redding found me the first time. But I'd become quite familiar with the bus routes and knew I could get downtown by taking two buses. It would take me longer, but better to be safe. Besides, I had more time on my hands than I knew what to do with.

I caught the first bus a block down on Anaheim and sat in the back with my black bag in my lap. The trip took almost an hour with all the stops and the switch on the Pacific Coast Highway, and the whole time I couldn't help but worry that I was being foolish. I really didn't know what I was hoping to accomplish.

I was practicing. That's what I kept telling myself. I was just putting the miles in, learning to move around in full gear. But I still felt awkward, riding around in a bus, so out of place in my business attire.

It was almost four o'clock by the time I stepped off the bus in front of the Wells Fargo building on Ocean Boulevard. There I was, standing on the corner with my bag hanging in my hand, blending in like a wart on a witch's nose.

I almost turned around and climbed back on the bus. I should have. If I hadn't come so far, I would have. But I didn't.

Instead I walked down the sidewalk, eyeing the towering bank building across the street. My own history with the Bourque Foundation edged back into my mind: the hours I'd spent casing the place. The run-in with the receptionist on the top floor. My abduction at the Hilton. The night Danny had come into my life.

Breaking into Jonathan Bourque's home.

Cutting up Simon Redding's body.

Shooting Darby Gordon.

I stopped and stared, suddenly unconcerned about whether I fit in with the other pedestrians on the sidewalk. Because it all came down to that top floor, didn't it? It had been more than three months since that monster had killed Lamont, and I still hadn't come face-to-face with him.

And I probably wouldn't anytime soon. Danny wasn't going to let me. Every time I mentioned Bourque, he changed the subject. It wasn't that I didn't trust him; I did. But my needs were different from Danny's when it came to confronting and killing Lamont's killer.

If I was infected with any pathological disease, it was my vow to honor Lamont.

I should cross the street now and take the elevator up to the top floor and shoot Jonathan Bourque.

I should sneak into the parking garage, find the black Mercedes that Bourque was driven around in, then shoot him when he made his way to the car.

I should take out one of the hundred-dollar bills in my bag and give it to a messenger to deliver a note to the offices on the top floor: *I'm gunning for you, you viper.*

I should...

My thoughts were cut short by the appearance of a black Mercedes. The one I had just thought about.

Jonathan Bourque's ride nosed out of the underground garage and came to a stop directly across the street.

I might have turned and walked away then, but I'd frozen solid. I couldn't even move my eyes off the car. Its left-turn signal was blinking, *left, left, left,* and I was staring right into the front window.

For the first time in my life I saw Jonathan Bourque in the flesh, sitting in the rear seat, talking on a phone. I was completely unprepared for the storm that rushed my mind.

If the traffic had been any thinner, the Mercedes might have turned and been gone before I could move. But the car waited for a count of ten, maybe twenty, and it was still facing me when a taxi emptied its fare at the curb beside me.

The Mercedes started to move and suddenly so did I. Straight to the Yellow Cab. Without waiting for the driver to acknowledge me, I pulled the back door open and slid in with my bag.

"Follow that car," I said, jabbing my finger at the Mercedes.

The driver, a burly man with a beer gut, twisted in his seat. "I need an address."

"No, you need money," I snapped. "And I have two hundred dollars that says you can stay on the tail of my husband's car without being obvious about it."

He glanced at the Mercedes now pulling away, then back at me. A thin grin pulled at his mouth. "That bad, huh?"

"That bad."

He flipped his meter off, signaled to enter traffic, and eyed his side mirror. "Strap in, honey."

DANNY PULLED UP to the house by the sea in Malibu at four forty-five, parked his car at the top of the driveway, and stepped out. The address of the foreclosure was a matter of public record and had been easy to find. Dark storm clouds were gathering on the horizon over the Pacific Ocean. It was the fourth day in a row that had either brought or threatened rain.

Before him on the edge of a short cliff, which met a rocky shore twenty feet below, stood a white stucco mansion with a red-tile roof. A three-car garage jutted out to the left of the main house with a sloping driveway and apron bordered by tall, swaying palm trees. The blue-and-white sign in the front lawn announced that the house was still for sale.

A lone seagull cawed as it drifted overhead, eyeing the property.

Danny studied the house, taking note of the windows, which were all shut and blocked by interior blinds. Americans were obsessed with privacy, cocooning themselves in brick and mortar that hid their passions, their habits.

Their sins.

No one would drive by this mansion in its neighborhood of similar mansions and think, *Inside that house there is a woman being held captive to serve a psychopath.*

If it was true...

Danny stood still, pushing away the dread that had haunted him since leaving Bourque's office. He'd seen his share of horrors, but there was nothing quite so disturbing as the violation of unwitting innocence.

Bourque could have been playing him. He desperately hoped so. More than once he'd almost turned the car around and headed home, wanting to avoid the prospect of finding anything ugly here, in this house. But now here he stood at the top of the sloping driveway, feeling like a fifteen-year-old boy returning home to find it had become a slaughterhouse.

His memory of that day, brought to life by the prospect of what he would find inside of this house by the sea, made him want to cry.

Holding his bag loosely in his right hand, he walked down the driveway and up to the front door, a large wooden entry with decorative panels, now secured with a combination lock-box that held a key for Realtors.

It took him only a minute with his picks to spring the lock-box, withdraw the house key, and open the front door.

The house sucked in fresh air as the door's seal broke. And then Danny stepped into Lamont Myers's house by the sea.

27

WE DROVE WEST. I don't remember the street names or the highway we entered then exited ten minutes later. My eyes were glued to the back of the black Mercedes, and my mind was crammed with Danny's voice: *Stop it, Renee. Tell the driver to make a U-turn. Drive back home. Stop a few blocks away from the Embassy Suites. You don't want any cabdriver to know where you're staying.*

I sat in the middle of the backseat and watched the car ahead of us, hugging my bag with both arms.

"He's headed into a secure warehouse district," the driver said. "You sure you want me to follow him in?"

The large steel warehouses were lined up in rows like self-storage units, only much larger. Did I know this place? "Yes. Follow him."

"Because I'm just saying, not too many cabs come this way. We could be spotted."

"No! He can't see us, stay back!"

The driver glanced at me in the rearview mirror. "You sure you're okay?"

"I'm okay. Yes." But my tight voice didn't sound okay, and it made me wonder if he might realize he'd picked up a serial killer and feel compelled to call the cops.

"You can't call the cops," I said. "Please, it's okay. He's got a thing going and I need to see for myself, that's all."

"No need to explain, honey. I'm just being sure. Looks like they're going in through the gate. I can't drive in there."

The Mercedes pulled up to a steel gate, where a security guard was waving them through. Was it normal to have security at a fenced warehouse complex? 'Course it was. With Bourque it always was.

Pins and needles pricked my hands, because I was at one of those crucial junctures Danny talked about. If I lost Bourque now, I could either go home (which I just couldn't) or get the driver to wait for him out here (which would surely get us noticed).

But following them in was like walking into a lion's cage.

"You can't get in?" I asked. "I'll pay you more."

"Even if we did go in, someone's going to notice. Look, I brought you this far—"

"Another two hundred dollars," I interrupted. Something about this place struck me as strange. There was something I should know but couldn't remember. "If you can get in and park close, behind a building or something, and wait for me, I'll pay you five hundred."

"It's secured—"

"A thousand," I blurted. "I have it right here. Please, just try."

He eyed me. "A thousand?"

"A thousand if you get me back out."

"That's not what you said."

"Okay, two thousand if you can get me back out and where I need to go."

"Where's that?"

The Mercedes disappeared around a warehouse to our left.

"Just go, you're going to lose him!"

He hesitated only a moment, then turned the cab and gunned for the gate just now beginning to close. "Two thousand, honey. Don't forget that."

I'd forgotten it already. My mind was on this warehouse complex, and suddenly I knew why it struck a bell in my brain. This was where I'd climbed out of the trunk and made my escape in the blue overalls. Only it hadn't been fenced then.

"Tell them you're here for the Bourque Foundation," I said, reaching over the front seat, nudging the driver in his shoulder. "Tell him."

"No guarantees this is gonna work."

"Just use that name. The Bourque Foundation. Got it?"

"The Bourque Foundation."

I noticed the driver's name for the first time. His face stared at me from a protective plastic sleeve below his radio. RAYMOND PAULSON.

Raymond slowed at the entrance, rolled down his window, and spoke to the guard. "Delivery for Bourque," he said. "I have a daughter here who wants to surprise her father."

The guard glanced back at me and I flashed him something of a smile, but I'm sure I looked more like an alien baring its teeth. Still, the guard waved us through.

"Where do you want me to wait?"

"Find the car."

He followed the route the Mercedes had taken, up the center

then to the left, just in time to see Bourque's car hook a right at the far end.

"I don't want to get too close." Sweat beaded his forehead.

"I just need to see where he parks. Don't lose him!"

In my frantic state of mind I had only one thought: Bourque's men had brought Lamont's car here. Other than his money, which had made it possible for me to live these past months, I hadn't seen *anything* directly connected to Lamont. The urgency to know or touch or smell something connected to Lamont was irresistible. For all I knew, he was in that warehouse, bound and caged, but alive. Irrational, I know, but that was all I could think.

I felt like a hound closing in on its prey. I had to at least see which warehouse belonged to Bourque so that I could come back later.

The Mercedes had parked next to the second warehouse on the left, and as soon as Raymond saw it, he brought the cab to a halt.

"What are you doing?" I asked.

"It's right there." He had his eyes fixed on the car. "You want to get out?"

"Here?"

"I don't know, you're calling the shots."

"Just drive by slowly."

He hesitated, then pulled up.

"Not too slow," I said. "They'll notice."

The car surged forward.

"Not too fast."

"Make up your mind!"

Our lives hang in the balance of unpredictable situations, Danny had said to me once. *One minute you're driving down the road whistling a tune, the next moment the car right in front of you spins out of control and crashes. How you prepare for those unpredictable occurrences determines whether you live or die. Always leave an empty lane to your right or left for escape.*

Preparation was why you trained. It's why you took your time, approaching a target only when you had complete control of the situation.

That's why any vigilante with half a brain would *not* have followed Bourque into a fenced warehouse complex without knowing the lay of the land.

I watched a man dressed in a black suit walk out of a side door ahead of us.

"He's got a gun," Raymond said.

He held it down by his side, a big pistol with a silencer extending its barrel. I was too shocked to respond.

The man in black stopped, lifted his weapon with both hands to steady his grip, and aimed the barrel at Raymond.

"Go!" I screamed.

"He's got a gun!"

"Go, go, go!"

If he'd been in the movies, Raymond would have gone. He might have swerved to avoid the danger. He might have run the gunman over. He might have ducked as bullets slammed into his headrest.

But Raymond didn't go. He stopped.

"What are you doing?"

"Just calm down, don't do anything stupid," Raymond said to me, nodding at the man who was now at his window. Then that window was down and I was locked up solid in the backseat.

"Out," the gunman ordered.

Raymond held up a hand. "Whoa, man. I'm just delivering my fare. I just checked with dispatch—this is the right address.

Bourque Foundation, right? What's with this?" He glanced at the man's gun.

That was smart, because it forced man-in-black to assume that dispatch knew where we were. If we disappeared, someone would know where we were last seen. The cops would be all over this place like flies on rot.

At least that's what I thought the man was now thinking. Raymond was no pushover—that gave me some courage.

The man leaned over and I got a good look at his face, eyes covered by dark glasses, square and unsmiling jaw. He had a large mole to the left of his nose. "Get out," he repeated.

I knew then that I was going to meet Jonathan Bourque, the man I had sworn to kill. Anticipation broke my fear, and in a moment of clarity I realized it was important that the driver stay in the cab, as planned. I had to go, and I had to go alone.

I leaned forward and spoke out the window. "Is Jonathan Bourque here?"

Man-in-black wasn't ready for that.

"I can't tell you how important it is that I talk to him," I snapped.

When he didn't immediately respond, I knew that for a moment I had the upper hand. I grabbed my bag, scooted over, opened the door, and got out. I could do this if I just let my newly honed instincts kick in.

Just go easy, Renee. Just play your role. Sleight of hand.

"Tell him it's Renee Gilmore."

He eyed me for a few seconds, then waved his gun at me.

"Give me your bag."

THE INTERIOR OF the house by the sea was made of glass, giving any who entered a view, however distorted, of the ocean through two walls and a large picture window.

Danny stood in the living room, absorbing the chill. A thin film dusted otherwise untouched glass and white leather furniture. The polished marble floors were spotless, as was the kitchen to his left. The black dining table with high-backed chairs looked new.

Black, white, and clear—these were elements of Lamont's house by the sea. An architectural wonder to its creator, perhaps, but a sterile prison in Danny's eyes.

He checked the windows and found them all welded shut. Both doors had redundant locks, at least one on each of which was inoperable from the inside. They had been designed to keep someone in.

The outer walls were concrete as far as he could tell, plastered and painted bright white. The glass walls were several inches thick, not solid but airtight, like those found in glass office buildings.

On the main floor, only one room offered any privacy. Renee had talked excitedly about the room.

Lamont loved animals. He had them on the walls, you know, mounted heads, watching us. My room was pink and white. Do you like pink, Danny?

The memory of her voice made him want to cry. Did she know that the moose in that pink and white room had camera lenses for eyes? An untrained eye would miss the detail, but Danny had spotted it at first glance, perhaps because he assumed anyone who valued transparency so highly would find a way to look into the most private spaces of his house.

It all made perfect sense, of course. What good was Lamont's strict code of law unless he could monitor compliance?

The tales that could be told by these walls might bring a strong man to his knees. But then so could the walls of any human heart, if they agreed to speak of hidden secrets.

The fact that the house hadn't been stripped of its contents wasn't surprising—it would show as a cold grave without them. Even the elaborate entertainment system along the living room's northern wall had been left to be sold with the house.

Danny let his breathing work slowly, doing his best to keep his perspective clear. He hardly needed to find any secret room to know that the entire setup was all very wrong.

But these glass walls did not speak directly of abuse. Lamont had suffered from a severe case of obsessive-compulsive disorder. What Danny saw on this floor reflected that much, nothing more.

The stairwell leading to the basement gaped ahead of him. If there were secrets to be told, they waited down that dark flight.

He picked up his bag, took a deep breath, and walked to the stairs.

28

MAN-IN-BLACK USHERED ME into the ware-house, and my fear made a comeback the moment I stepped through the door. I'd had no choice but to hand my bag over as if giving it up was of no concern to me. But now I was naked, stripped of the only tool that might give me an advantage over Bourque. My gun. I felt like a sheep being led to the slaughter.

But no, that wasn't true. *Your mind is your greatest weapon.* Danny had drilled that into me every day. If ever there was a time for mind over matter, it was now. *Mind over matter, mind over matter.* Wait. That was Lamont, not Danny.

I plowed ahead, fearful as a mouse and determined not to show it. I was so focused that I forgot to look around the ware-house as we crossed one corner, then walked through a side door that opened onto a short hallway with four doors.

"That's far enough." The man stepped past me, knocked

on a door, and stuck his head inside. I could have attacked him then, when his back was to me for that moment, which showed me that he didn't feel threatened. But of course he was unconcerned. What was a small girl like me supposed to do with a thug like him? Knock him out with a punch to the back of his neck and run? I was defenseless. All I had was my mind.

And that gun in my bag.

The door swung open and the man in black set my bag down on the floor just inside the room. "Take a seat."

I walked into the office and stared across a gray metal desk at Jonathan Bourque. The door closed behind me.

I can't say how I felt coming face-to-face with that monster for the first time, because my emotions were all muddled up and overwhelmed at the same time.

My first thought was, *He's just a man.* He was watching me, eyes dark, mouth straight, one finger stroking his goatee. But he didn't look like the epic beast I'd created in my mind.

"So, the young woman with a chip on her shoulder emerges," he said. "Sit."

I looked at the two cushioned chairs facing the desk, then walked to one and sat. The office held nothing unexpected: a bookcase, some tall steel file cabinets, four chairs in total, a poster of a red racing car on one wall, one large potted plant in the corner, and the desk.

Just an office. And just a man.

There was one more thing in the room, and it sat against the back wall. My kit was behind me. And in that kit was my gun.

But I was at a loss about what to do now that I sat across from him. So I crossed my legs to show that I was completely at ease here, which I wasn't, and returned his dark stare. His face slowly took on a look of amusement.

"My, my, my. You do get around, don't you?"

You would know, I thought. He was just a man, but the memory of just how vile a man edged back into my mind.

"What is it exactly that you want?" he asked.

"To talk to you," I said. "That's all."

"That's all? The priest's looking for you. You do realize that, don't you?"

"Danny?" I said it too quickly.

His brow arched. "Danny, is it? So you're friends. Maybe more than friends. And yet he insists that he hasn't seen or talked to you in two weeks."

"You spoke to Danny?"

"He's my priest," Bourque said. "He's been my priest for three years. It's important to have close friends in high places, and that includes the church."

The man was lying, of course. I knew it immediately, but that didn't stop my mind from racing back over the last few weeks, wondering if Danny had been completely honest with me. I was sure he had, and the fact that this monster thought he could trick me so easily infuriated me.

"The reason I'm alive and not dead is because I'm smarter than you think I am," I said. My voice wasn't as strong as I intended, but I was starting to gain some steam. "And I know much more than you think I know."

His face didn't change, so I continued. "As for the priest, I couldn't give a rip. You're the one I need, not him."

"I'll be sure to tell him. I'm guessing he's at the house in Malibu as we speak."

That struck me as odd. Danny? At Lamont's house? Another lie.

"I don't care where he is. You're here and I'm finally here, that's all that matters."

Bourque smiled, then stood and walked to a bottle of Jack Daniel's that sat on one of the bookcase shelves. He set two shot glasses on the desk and splashed some whiskey into both.

"Perhaps we should start over, Renee Gilmore. That is your name, isn't it? Drink?"

I almost said no, but he came around to the front side of the desk, leaned back on the edge, and offered me the shot. I took the glass and drank the whiskey in one gulp. The hard liquor burned my throat.

"This is a dangerous game you're playing," he said softly, sipping from his own glass. "I'm not used to being stalked. I can't stress how important it is that you tell me why you're so interested in me."

"Isn't it obvious?"

"No, not really."

"Lamont told me some things before he disappeared," I said.

"Lamont told you some things," he restated.

"You know, your old partner. Lamont Myers."

"Yes, I know Lamont."

"He told me to find you and ask for your help if anything ever happened to him. I'm a little lost without him." He was making me nervous, standing over me the way he was. "Would you mind sitting back down?"

He chuckled, then rounded the desk and sat in his own chair, smiling large, tapping his shot glass with a long finger. He drained the Jack Daniel's and set his glass down with a *clunk*.

"I don't believe a word you're saying," he said.

"Obviously. That's why you had Redding question me at the Hilton. That's why you sent him to kill me after the priest stumbled on us. And that's why I had to kill him. But that's not the way it should have happened."

His eyes showed no surprise. Then again, a man like this was a master at hiding his emotions. The fact that he didn't show any only confirmed that I'd struck a chord.

"That's a bold statement," he said.

"Is it? But I have nothing to hide from you, so I can afford to be bold."

"You expect me to believe that a woman like you killed a man like Simon Redding? I don't think so, darling."

"And Darby Gordon as well, if you insist on knowing. The real question is why you would go to such lengths to silence someone like me. You expect me to believe that a man like you feels threatened by a girl like me?"

"There's no need to believe I feel threatened by you. I don't. Although if what you say is true, perhaps I should."

"Darby Gordon was a thug, you know that as well as I do. He came after me, so I killed him. What else was I supposed to do?"

I knew this wasn't the most effective way to divert a threat, but I couldn't stomach the idea of Bourque thinking I was a pushover. The fact that Darby Gordon hadn't come after me no longer mattered—Bourque would never know for sure.

"Why did you send him after me?" I asked.

"I didn't."

"Then Redding did. Same difference."

"Not quite," he said. As good as a confession.

"Why did you kill Lamont?" I asked.

"I didn't." Not as good as a confession.

I leaned back in my chair and crossed my arms. "Let's start over. Let's start with the truth. Lamont told me that you'd help me. Well, here I am, Mr. Jonathan Bourque. So help me. Who knows? Maybe I can return the favor."

He looked me up and down. "As tempting as that might be, I'm not sure how I could help you."

"For starters, I'm without a home. Lamont was all I had, and I'm assuming he's dead. But he taught me a few things, and I'm looking for a way to use my new skills."

It wasn't until I'd stared at his wry, knowing grin for a moment that I realized he might have misinterpreted my meaning to be more closely linked with sexual favors than with assassination techniques. Fine. Any way to distract the man, however disturbing the thought.

"Look, he told me to find you," I said. "It's taken me three months and way too much energy to get here. Now, if you're gonna sit there and tell me to take a hike, I will. I'm sure I can find work somewhere else."

That grin was still plastered on his face, and it took all of my willpower to let him sit in such smugness. I wasn't as practiced as Danny when it came to patience.

"Just tell me what you know about Lamont's death," I said. "You owe me at least that much."

"Actually, I don't owe you a thing. If you did happen to kill Simon Redding, it's you who owes me. A great deal, I would say."

"Then let me work for you. If I can take care of one thug, I can take care of another. Right?"

"I run the Bourque Foundation, not the Mafia. Simon Redding has vanished, true, but he was only the head of my security, not—"

"Shut up!" I snapped. "You don't think I made him talk before I shot him? Don't be a fool. No disrespect, but you're as dirty as I am." Again there was room for confusion with that word *dirty,* but I let it slide. "The way I see it, you have three choices: One, you can take me out back and kill me, dump my body, and come up with a fancy explanation for the cabbie and dispatcher who know I'm here right now. Two, you can come after me later when you think the air has cleared, but I won't make that easy for you. Or three, you can give my request some serious consideration and let me work with you."

I don't think he'd expected the skinny, dumb blonde to come in and read him his options. I was beginning to think my ploy was working quite well. That smug grin flattened.

"I have many more than three options," he said. "And the one that's most attractive to me right now is to kindly ask you to leave. Vanish from my life and never reappear. What Lamont may or may not have told you is none of my concern. He was a vicious liar who deserved what he got, whatever that might have been. He was scum."

I blinked, infuriated by his casual character assassination.

"Then dismiss me," I snapped, knowing I was being far too impulsive for my own good. "But don't pretend you had nothing to do with Lamont's death."

"I don't need to pretend. But given the opportunity, I would have killed him, believe me."

His mug was looking more like the monster of my imagination now, and I wanted to smash it.

"How stupid do you think I am? You really expect me to believe that Redding would come after me with a gun, but not go after Lamont?"

He leaned forward and slammed his fist on the desk. "That's exactly what I expect you to believe!"

"You're lying!" I cried. He stared at me, disbelieving. I was slipping, I realized that, but I didn't care. "If you think I buy your nonsense about Danny working for you, you're as thick as a brick. I may be a skinny blonde half your height, but I'm beginning to think my brain is twice the size of yours." I was going way too far.

He sat back. "I'm sorry for your loss, but the fact is, I didn't kill Lamont. And I can't imagine why he would suggest you do anything but kill me if he went missing. He knew I was looking into his dirty laundry."

"Really? Maybe you have that backward."

"You really don't get it, do you? What he did with you up there—that was nothing compared with what he did to others. You got off easy, my dear. He obviously had a real thing for you."

I felt like I might explode, but I pushed my feelings down.

"That's not true," I said. "Lamont was a good man."

"Which Lamont was that? Because he had more than one identity. The swindler? The lawyer? How about the murderer? Or the rapist? Which one did you know, hmm? The one who lived in Malibu? Or one of the others?"

What happened next seemed beyond my control. I heard the lies spilling from that fiend's mouth, I felt my face flushing hot. Something in my head popped. My hands were trembling in my lap.

"You're lying," I said.

"No," he said. "Your precious Lamont was the liar. He kept you locked up in that glass house of his and—"

I didn't hear the rest because I was moving already. Around my chair. Two long steps to where my bag lay on the floor. The clasp flew open with a flip of my wrist; the nine-millimeter inside filled my clawing fingers.

I came up and spun with the gun extended at him. His eyes widened, and I thought I pulled the trigger then, but I must not have, because it didn't fire.

For a moment I just stood there, every muscle in my body vibrating like taut wire, shaking from head to foot, facing the one who had taken my love, my life, and now was trying to take my mind.

"Say it!" I said.

"Settle down." His hands were spread and that smug grin was gone for good. "What do you want me to say?"

"Say you're lying! Say you killed him!"

He didn't say anything right away. And that was good enough for me.

I shot him.

The sound of the gun firing was soft, like a pellet gun, but the smack of the bullet wasn't so soft. It thudded into his shoulder and jerked him to his left.

Bourque began to swear, but I cut him off.

"Shut up! The next one goes in your head, you filthy pig!" My voice sounded distant, as if another part of me was speaking, the part that was chased by ghosts sometimes. I was hardly aware of what I was doing. My mind had skipped off its track and was on a surreal trip.

His face twisted up into a blood-dark knot. "You shot—"

He wasn't listening, so I shot him again, this time in his belly. It sounded like a hard slap.

He grasped his stomach, aghast, then pulled his hand away bloody.

My mind cleared long enough for me to grasp what I'd just done. It hit me like a thunderclap. I'd actually shot the man! I'd shot him twice. Danny would kill me!

"You shot me," he said. "You stupid whore, you shot me!"

My impulse to shoot again was overwhelming. I wanted to make him eat my gun for spreading those lies about Lamont.

But my hands were trembling and I knew that something was wrong. I couldn't piece it together, but something wasn't right here. I should just shoot him. I'd waited three months, and I could finish everything with just one more piece of lead.

So I did. I pulled that trigger one more time, and this time the bullet took him between the eyes.

His head snapped back and he sagged on the chair.

The smell of gun smoke hung in the air. Silence settled around me.

I had to get out!

I lurched forward and stumbled to the window. I fumbled with the latches, finally flipped both open, and yanked the window up. A screen blocked the way and I tried to punch it out, but the thin wire mesh only bent and then broke where my fist had hit it. So I stood back and kicked the frame. This time the whole screen popped out.

I was halfway through the window, gun banging noisily on the metal framing, when I remembered my black bag.

Never leave your kit. Never.

Obeying Danny's voice, I retrieved my kit, rushed back to the window, flung the bag outside, and rolled through the opening after it.

If the cabdriver had turned tail and run out on his two-thousand-dollar fare, I would be on foot and caught within minutes.

Someone yelled inside as I came to my feet, bag in one hand, gun in the other. I shoved the gun into the bag and ran, not knowing where to, praying for that cab to materialize.

But I didn't have to pray. Raymond had parked directly across from Bourque's warehouse in the shade of another.

I ran at the cab, flailing one arm over my head. The engine roared to life, but with it came a curse from the window behind me. So I zagged, thinking zigging and zagging targets were harder to hit than ones running as straight as a bullet flies.

"Hurry!" I screamed.

The car squealed through a tight turn and skidded to a stop

in front of me. I plowed into the side, grasped for the door handle, missed, and was making a second grab when the car window exploded with the impact of a bullet.

"Up front! Up front!" Raymond had thrown the front passenger door wide.

I dived into the cab headfirst.

Pop! A second bullet slapped into the car's metal skin. It was all the encouragement Raymond needed. He swore, grabbed onto the back of my blouse to keep me from falling out, and floored the gas.

"Hold on!"

But he was the one who had to hold on, because my feet were still bouncing off the concrete drive. I grabbed for the thing that would give me the most leverage, which happened to be the steering wheel.

Hauling my feet into the cab, I managed to get the door closed just before we squealed around the first corner, as close to being on two wheels as a car can get without rolling.

Then we were out of the warehouses and flying past the gate, which was open on the exit side.

Three corners later, Raymond was still mumbling curses. But my mind wasn't on him. I was already up at the glass house. Something was wrong, I could feel it in my gut. Something didn't add up.

Bourque had said Danny was there, at the glass house by the sea. Now. I didn't know why. I didn't really care.

I just had to get to Danny.

And I had to get to him now.

29

IT TOOK DANNY five minutes to satisfy himself that the metal door at the back of the basement was the only other exit besides the staircase that led up to the rest of the house.

Oddly, the door was locked, barred by both a dead bolt on the bedroom side and a keyed lock.

It appeared as though it had been repaired recently. Someone, perhaps Bourque's men, had chipped the metal framing trying to get in, and the Realtor had done a patch job and called it good. The bank selling this house had elected not to replace the entire door. Too many houses on the market to fuss over them all.

The dead bolt was already open. He withdrew his picks, sprung the lock that was missing its key, slipped the pick set back into his pocket, and walked into the small room.

A ring of mammal busts prepared by a skilled taxidermist stared at him from two of the walls. Of these, a water buffalo's head took the prize for being the most disturbing, if only for its size. Lassos and whips hung from one of the other two walls. An old wood desk to his right, a closet at the back of the room.

An office. On the surface.

The frame on the desk's bottom left drawer was busted where the lock had been forced. Renee's account of finding Lamont's money wandered through his mind. She'd called the room Lamont's trophy room.

Danny set his case on top of the desk. Nothing incriminating supported Bourque's claims about the man. So then, perhaps Danny had been played. What he'd seen in the house thus far might be seen as incriminating—the pink room with its camera, the glass walls, the numerous locks, the welded windows. But any or all of these could also be merely the signs of a wealthy man driven by compulsive behaviors.

Danny walked up to the slatted accordion door on the back wall, pulled it open, and surveyed the contents of the tiny closet. It was just large enough to step into and maybe turn around in with the door closed. Its shelves were lined with books, mostly legal in subject matter. A few white file boxes on the top shelf might produce some interesting information about Lamont's private life, but nothing here exposed the kind of abuse that had haunted Danny's mind over the past several hours.

A copy of Charles Darwin's *Origin of Species* caught Danny's attention. It sat on the shelf to his right, slightly away from the wall to allow for a light switch. Odd. The light had come on with a hinge switch when he'd opened the door.

He reached in and flipped the switch. A hum sounded. There was grinding and scraping as the shelves at the back moved.

Into the foundation wall.

Danny stood back, stunned, watching as the wall formed a

three-foot opening into a dark space beyond before clunking softly to a halt. Fingers of dread tickled the back of his neck.

This was it. This was the place of secrets. This was where Lamont lived true to his basest self. Danny could not go inside.

He could not, but of course he had to. He had to because his life had changed today. There was Bourque, and there was the priesthood, and there were monsters who preyed on others—the world had not changed. But there was Renee, and today Renee had become the centerpiece for all that was wrong with injustice.

She'd stormed into his life and stolen his heart, and today his heart would break for her. He knew that already, staring at the hidden space beyond Lamont's office.

All Danny could think to do was snatch Renee away from her past and hide her somewhere safe. But he had to know what she'd suffered. He had to bear her burden, even if in complete silence.

His breathing was thick. *Easy, Danny. Easy.* He was only staring at darkness, and darkness was often far more frightening than what it contained.

He walked up to the opening, reached into the darkness, felt along the inside wall, found a switch, and flipped it on. An overhead incandescent bulb popped on. Low-wattage yellow light. Danny ducked his head and eased into a room slightly larger than the office behind him.

There was a bed with pink sheets there.

Shackles with padded wrist restraints hung from chains attached to padded walls.

Rows of prescription bottles lined a medicine cabinet with glass-panel doors.

A toilet squatted in the corner.

The floor was linoleum. Black-and-white checkerboard.

Danny saw it all in one sweeping glance, and in that space his muscles lost their rigidity. His legs began to tremble. The room spun.

He'd found Lamont's altar, and he knew that Renee had been the sacrificial lamb.

Renee, I'm so sorry...oh, I'm sorry. His lungs had stopped working properly and he had to inhale deliberately for oxygen.

There is a point one reaches when no amount of effort can fix a given situation. All that is left is to wait and endure the pain until it passes.

But this...

He wanted to turn and flee the house, and he might have done it, but he couldn't seem to turn his muscles on.

He wanted to shut down the part of his mind that yielded any imagination of what might have happened in this room, but his intellect had lost its bearings and didn't seem to know how to turn that switch off.

So he stood there on the black-and-white linoleum as terrible thoughts smothered him with a pain he hadn't felt since finding his mother dead.

Whatever had happened here, Renee's drugged mind had found a way to protect itself by erasing the memories until no significant evidence of them remained.

Here was the ultimate judgment for failing to follow Lamont's law. Here was a living hell for the unwitting victim.

I STAYED IN the front of the cab as Raymond drove west through heavy traffic to the address Danny had turned up two weeks ago after doing some research on Lamont. I didn't care about the wind that howled through the shattered window, and I ignored the questions from the driver, who wanted to know just what the heck had happened back there.

I couldn't tell him, of course. I hardly knew myself. Well, yes, I knew what had happened, sure. I mean, I hadn't been able to resist the temptation to look, just look, at Bourque's den of iniquity. Then follow him, just follow, to his secret place. Then I'd flipped my lid and shot him. That's what had happened back there.

What I didn't know was exactly why I'd flipped my lid. When I told Danny, which I would right away, he would say I'd made a dreadful mistake that proved I wasn't ready. The most important weapon is the mind, and I'd made it as clear as humanly possible that I didn't have control of mine.

Worse, Bourque was dead. His men and the law both would come after me with both barrels blazing. This, more precisely, was what I couldn't tell Raymond.

But it would have been worse if I hadn't killed Bourque, right? He would come after me himself. I'd rather have the FBI than Bourque after me.

Danny would be upset. I'd been a complete fool. I couldn't wait to beg his forgiveness.

To keep Raymond quiet, I finally told him that I'd shot my husband in the arm for having an affair with a man. Then I told the driver not to ask any more questions. Two thousand dollars was a lot of money, I reminded him, and it should pay for my privacy as well.

My foolishness wasn't the only thing that kept me silent as we inched toward the coast. I couldn't shake the things that Bourque had said about Lamont. Lies, all of them. Terrible, unconscionable fabrications concocted by a deceitful man. He was so accustomed to lying that he might even believe at least some of them himself.

You can tell when a man is lying, Danny said. And I thought I could. Jonathan Bourque didn't sound like the kind of person who knew he was lying.

See, there was something wrong there, just under the surface of my mind. Like a déjà vu that I couldn't quite grasp. And I don't mind saying that it bothered me quite a lot.

In one sentence, Bourque had thrown everything I knew about Lamont under the bus. It was like hearing for the first time that Santa Claus wasn't real, or that the world wasn't flat, or that your religion wasn't quite as flawless as you thought it was.

Absurd. Infuriating. I should have just shot that pig in the mouth before he finished. *I told you to shut up.*

But even the most loyal believer is allowed to ask *what if?* now and then. It took me half the trip to shut down that nagging question and focus on how to deal with Danny's disappointment when I told him what I'd done.

I sat and stewed and stared ahead in silence.

"What's taking so long?" I asked.

"Rush hour," he said. "We're almost there."

My palms were sweaty. This was the first time I'd gone back to the house by the sea. I had no desire to live through the tragedy of losing Lamont all over again.

But now Danny was there. I wasn't sure what he hoped to accomplish. He was probably just covering all his bases, learning more by visiting the scene of the crime so to speak. Gathering more incriminating evidence against Bourque. With what I'd learned, the case was closed, right? Danny would be thrilled. Sure, I'd broken our code, but...

Stupid! You're so stupid, Renee! I don't know what I was thinking, going against Danny like that.

How did Bourque know Danny was at the house? See, that was another nagging question, one I couldn't get rid of. The whole thing about Danny being Bourque's priest was a crock, I'd seen that in the man's eyes. But had Danny talked to him today? If so why? He'd broken our agreement, too?

What if Danny wasn't at the house? Or what if it was a trap?

"Excuse me, Raymond? Um…Do you mind parking down the street from the house? And waiting for me?"

His brow went up in the rearview mirror. "Waiting for you is a dangerous occupation, honey."

"I need to get a few things from the house and a friend may meet me there, but if not, I want to get out before my husband gets home."

"Uh-huh."

"I'll make it worth your while. If I need a ride, that is."

He only had to think a couple of seconds. "Okay. But you pay me the two grand before you get out. I'll wait for half an hour, and if you need a ride, it'll cost you another five hundred. S'long as it's local."

"That's extortion."

"That's what it's gonna cost to fix the holes in my car. Heck, the two grand'll barely cover that."

He had a point.

"Then I'll pay you an extra thousand."

"Now?"

"If I need a ride. Or I could pay you an extra five hundred now for waiting and another five if I need a ride."

"Works for me."

"'Kay."

Ten minutes later Raymond pulled over and put the car in park.

"This is it?" I stared out, trying to remember. I'd never seen my neighborhood except from the windows of the glass house. It was getting dark, and tall shrubs blocked my view. I couldn't even see the sea.

"You don't recognize your own neighborhood?"

"'Course I do. I meant, is this where you're going to park?"

I opened my bag, counted out twenty one-hundred-dollar bills, and handed them over the seat.

"Thanks, Raymond. You'll wait, right?"

"Twenty-five hundred?"

"Oh yeah." I dug out another five hundred.

He took the money. "That buys you half an hour."

"'Kay."

I climbed out with my bag and walked up the street, straining to see the house numbers, so nervous that my legs were numb. But I could hear the ocean now. *It's okay, Renee, you're safe. This is home. It doesn't feel like home, but this is home. Nobody's going to get—*

I saw Danny's car parked in the next driveway and my heart jumped. I walked faster, then stumbled into a half run, I was so eager to get to safety.

Then the house was there in front of me and I came to a dead stop at the top of the driveway.

This was it. But Lamont was gone. It all seemed so surreal, having lived in Lamont's glass house for over a year without leaving even once. Now I was outside the house, suddenly terrified to go back in.

I stood there for ten or fifteen seconds, frozen by a horrible collision of emotions and ideas. Lamont, drinking wine on the back deck. Me, preparing him tofu, purging, taking my pills, polishing the floors, cleaning the walls. Danny.

I was a different person now, but still the same. I was afraid to go back inside and remember. The pain of my loss would eat me up.

But Danny was inside.

I ran, afraid I would lose my nerve. Down the driveway to the front door. The knob twisted in my hand and I pushed the door in.

The house was dark. And cold. As silent as a coffin.

"Danny?"

My voice sounded like it was in a box, and the first thing I thought of was that the glass-walled hallway had always sounded a bit boxy. I should clean those glass walls while I was here. Lamont would like that.

Lamont's dead.

"Danny?" I cried his name, gingerly stepping in.

Why was the house dark if Danny was here? Had he already gone? But then why was his car still in the driveway?

The light switch was on the wall to my right; I set my bag on the floor, reached for the switch, and flipped it up. Fluorescent tubes popped to life on the ceiling above the hall. The door to my pink room, the only room upstairs without glass walls, was open, and a stab of anger sliced through my nerves.

Who'd been in my room? I would kill him!

But no, it wasn't my room anymore. And Danny was here. I would love Danny to see my room!

I started down the hall. But I'd left the door open behind me. Dirt would get in. Thieves and murderers.

The thought was ridiculous, but that didn't stop me from thinking it. Or from turning back and closing the door.

Thunk.

Once more I was sealed in the house of the law. I could feel Lamont in the air that I breathed.

Heart hammering, I hurried to the open bedroom door and peered cautiously around the corner, half expecting to see Danny sitting on my bed or in the corner, although I don't know why. He would have answered my call if he were up here on this floor. He had to be in the basement.

My pink bed and the moose head with big eyes was there in my bedroom. The sight of it was so painful that my head spun—a physical reaction to my loss. An image of me purging in the toilet crashed through my mind and for a moment I thought I might throw up.

"Danny?"

The house was quiet. So quiet.

I tiptoed out to the living room and saw that the kitchen was dark, as was the wall of electronics that would normally be lit up with amber and green lights. But there was a soft glow at the bottom of the stairwell to my right.

Danny was in the basement. In Lamont's bedroom. Maybe in his trophy room.

I didn't know why that last thought flushed me with panic. Well, yes... I did know. Lamont's inner sanctum was very special to him. No one, including me, was ever allowed inside his trophy room without an express invitation from him. Even though Lamont was gone, Danny had broken the rules.

Instead of calling out again, I went down the stairs on my toes, trying not to make any sound. I had to warn Danny.

I had to get him out before it was too late.

30

THE BREW THAT triggers the most potent of human emotions is sometimes as simple as death. More often it's a complex cocktail of events that leaves a wife curled up catatonic on her bed, or a husband slumped in the corner, weeping.

For Danny, the convergence of events that led to a shift in his paradigm was fairly simple. He'd become that boy of fifteen again, crushed by his failure to stop terrible injustice. He hadn't been able to save his own mother and sisters from brutal death.

He wasn't able now to save Renee, either. They were all doves in his mind. Perfect innocence violated by evil men.

Such stark proof of Renee's tortured past was compounded by the fact that she had blindly followed her master's laws, thinking it was the right thing to do. Lamont was Renee's religion, and his laws had delivered her here, to this pit of restraint. Like all devoted followers, Renee hadn't even known that law was killing her.

And there was nothing he could do to stop it. His own attempt to be the hand of God, to compensate for his failure to save his mother, was itself a failure. That realization had come into full view here, in this basement.

Have you ever been tempted to judge, Father? The reverend mother's words were simply an echo from history, but they pounded in his mind as if they'd been newly formed and spoken for the first time.

Judge not, lest you be judged.

Your judgment will not make the world a better place. Only love can do that. Only grace.

The convergence of it all—his family, Renee, innocence, judgment—made that brew erupt in his chest like a chemist's misguided recipe for catastrophe.

He walked to the bed and sat, unable to think beyond his own failure.

THE DOOR INTO Lamont's trophy room was open, and light spilled out onto his bed. I stood in the middle of our room, trying to decide what I should do. Call out? Go in?

Something wasn't right. I knew that. Danny had violated a sacred place, and I was afraid for him.

But Lamont's dead, Renee. Why are you so afraid?

I stepped forward, quiet as a mouse, and edged my head around the door that opened into Lamont's inner sanctum.

The heads were there, staring at me. The ropes still hung on the wall. A black bag sat on the desk, half open. Danny was here.

I looked around the room again. Nothing had changed. Everything was the way I remembered it. But then I saw that the door at the back of the trophy room was also open, and the light inside was on.

I had forgotten about that room. I don't know how I could have, because upon seeing the dim light I thought, *Oh no, he's gone into the inner sanctum to pay for his sins!*

Such a terrible fear welled up from somewhere deep inside that I started to shake. I wanted to rush in and save Danny. I wanted to turn and run away. I wanted to scream. I wanted to race upstairs and get my gun.

Instead I just stood there, unable to move, not daring to make the slightest sound.

Maybe Danny had already gone and I was left alone in this forbidden place—that thought was even more frightening than the thought of Danny paying for his sins.

I hurried forward, dreading each step. I placed one hand on the edge of the inner door frame to keep from falling. Then I stepped forward, peered into that secret room, and saw him.

Danny was sitting on my pink bed, facing the back wall. Unmoving. Like a man who'd been turned to stone.

It came to me then, like a whisper out of hell, that this room was a very, very bad place.

I don't know if it was the sight of Danny or the vague memory of my own torment in this room that bothered me more. The fear that had followed me into the room rose up like a monster and became a sorrow that swallowed me whole.

THE ANGELS WERE weeping. Danny could hear them floating around in the darkness of his mind, crying. For his mother. For his sisters. For Renee. But mostly for him.

They were crying for Renee's pain, but even more for his failure to save her. He'd failed as a boy. He'd failed as man. He'd failed as a priest.

And now that weeping was as unnerving to him as a scream, mocking him because he was indeed nothing but a priest with a graveyard to show for all of his pathetic attempts to fix this world.

If what he suspected about his last attempt to fix the world was in fact true, then he would rather be dead.

The weeping became a wail. A scream. Only then did the idea enter his clouded mind that it was a real sound, a high-pitched scream that had broken out of hell and come to mock him. Demons had been sent...

Danny abruptly turned. Stared at what he first thought was one of the screaming angels then immediately realized was not.

Renee stood in the doorway of the checkered room. Her frail body was trembling all over; her eyes were clenched; her mouth was parted in a scream. And on that scream rode the pain of a thousand demons, clawing at the jaws of hell in their desperate attempt to get out.

"Renee..." His voice was raspy, powerless.

Danny stumbled from the bed, rushed to her in three long steps, and reached to embrace her, desperate to bring comfort, forgiveness, love, grace—anything to stop her unbearable pain.

"Renee..."

She smashed his hand away.

"Renee?" She saw him as her tormentor? As Lamont?

Her hands formed fists that began to beat at him.

"Please, Renee."

Danny backed away but she followed him, flailing in weak objection. He grasped her wrists and tried to hush her. "It's okay, it's okay—"

"No, you can't..." Her face twisted with desperate anguish. "You can't see this!"

"But it's over! Whatever he did to you here is done. I'll protect you, Renee. Please."

He tried to hold her, but she pulled herself free and covered her face with both hands. She sank to her knees, lowered her face onto the pink comforter, and wept.

It's your fault, Danny. All of this is your fault. You are powerless. All he knew to do was kneel beside her, put one arm over her shoulders, and let her cry.

But there was even more here, wasn't there? Something even more horrifying than what he had learned in these past few minutes.

He couldn't be certain, but if what he suspected turned out to be the truth...

The pain Renee felt now might seem like a child's mere howling over a stubbed toe.

But only if.

He would know soon. Far too soon.

31

I WAS SO upset.

I realize that seems like an understatement, but sometimes the simplest explanations are the best. And at the time, my understanding of the situation was really very simple.

Danny was in trouble.

The law has a hard edge that can be respected only if it's strictly enforced, Lamont used to say. Even a dog with an electric collar needs to be shocked now and then to learn that there's a boundary.

I was thinking that Danny had crossed one of Lamont's very sacred boundaries, and now he would have to pay for it. There were never exceptions. I knew that because I'd crossed those boundaries, too, although I couldn't recall the specifics.

My own suffering in that room didn't really register. Or maybe it did and I mistook it for a fear of what might happen to Danny. After all, how would I know about the cost of crossing the law unless I'd paid the price? And why would I come so unglued, unless that suffering had been really terrible?

But I still had all that blocked out, and I thought I was weeping for Danny. He was mistaken about Lamont being the one who'd hurt me, but that was okay, he just didn't know.

Oh, I don't know, I was all mixed up, wasn't I? My mind was swimming with pain and sorrow and I wasn't clear about why except that I felt so sorry for Danny because he'd broken the rules and would be punished.

He knelt beside me for a long time and my crying began to ease. It occurred to me that we were still in the room. What if Lamont came home and found us here? Together!

We had to get out!

"We have to get out." I pushed myself to my feet, steadied myself to clear a spell of dizziness, then hurried for the door. "Hurry!"

The second I cleared the closet door I spun back and waved Danny through. "Hurry. Hurry!"

He ducked past me and I hit the switch. The wall rumbled. But the light inside was still on.

"He'll see the light!"

Daring to get my arm caught as the opening closed, I reached in around the corner, flipped the light switch down, and jerked my hand out. The wall closed with a soft *thump*.

I stepped back, shut the closet door, and stood still, thinking it had been a close call.

When I turned to face Danny he was watching me carefully. "Are you okay?"

I didn't want to break down again, so I turned away.

"Renee—"

"No, it's okay."

"He's gone, Renee," Danny said. "Lamont is dead."

I blinked. That was right. "Of course he is," I said. But I was still shaking. "I don't know what got into me. Sorry. I'm sorry."

"Renee. Please..."

His words washed over me like soothing oil, and my gratitude for him drew new tears from my eyes. I turned to him. Sank into his arms.

"Thank you, Danny. Thank you. I don't know what I would do without you."

Danny ran his hand over my hair. "It's okay. I'm so sorry, Renee."

"You're right, he's dead. He won't hurt you. He's dead."

"He can't hurt either of us," Danny said.

For a moment my sorrow was so intense, I couldn't get enough air to complete a breath. I used it all to whisper what was in my heart without thinking what it meant.

"I miss him so much, Danny," I said.

His hand stopped stroking my hair. His body stiffened.

"He was a monster, Renee."

Who was a monster? I still had not connected Lamont to any of the pain I felt. In my mind Bourque was a monster, and I'd just—

I jerked my head off Danny's shoulder and stepped back. "I shot him!"

"You shot Lamont?"

"What? No, I shot Bourque. I think he's dead. I shouldn't have gone, I know, but I couldn't help it, Danny."

My confession stunned him into silence.

"I had to do it! He was saying things about Lamont. Someone had to deal with him." I felt foolish trying to justify myself. "Please, Danny, don't be upset with me. Like you said, Bourque's a monster."

He blinked at me. "I wasn't talking about Jonathan Bourque."

"What do you mean?"

"I was talking about Lamont," he said. "I was talking about the man who locked you up in that room to punish you for not following his rules. I was talking about the monster who abused you here in this house for a full year."

I stared at him, still not sure what he was saying. "You can't really believe that."

"That's why I'm here, Renee. I found out——"

"Who told you that?"

"I spoke to Jonathan Bourque today. He——"

"No! He's lying. That's why I shot him! He's lying!"

"No, he's not lying. And it gets worse."

"What are you talking about?" I was horrified. It felt like a betrayal to me.

"I don't think Bourque killed Lamont."

Why was Danny taking sides with him? Unless...

A streak of hope lit my horizon. "You're saying Lamont's not dead?"

Danny's eyes were misted with tears, and for several long seconds he just stared at me. Then he walked over to the desk, opened his bag, pulled out a manila file, and turned to face me.

"The last man I killed was named Cain Kellerman. He lived in San Pedro, and the list of his crimes against humanity would make any sane person sick."

He opened the folder, looked at its contents, then lifted his eyes to meet mine. "Do you recognize him?" He flipped the file around.

A large photograph of a man with dark hair and black-rimmed glasses, eyes as blue as the ocean, was taped to the inside cover. I didn't recognize him.

"No," I said.

"Are you sure? Look closer," Danny said.

"I've never…" But then the man's mouth and nose triggered recognition. He was there, under that hair, behind those glasses.

I was looking at Lamont. Younger maybe, or older. His brother?

"Who is this?"

"You tell me."

I stared and now all I could see was Lamont, right there staring back at me. "That's…But Lamont had brown eyes. And blond hair."

"But it's him. It's Lamont, isn't it?"

It was, I could see that now. "Yes." My voice was a mere whisper.

Danny slowly closed the folder, his eyes on me.

"He had more than one name," he said. "To most he was known as Cain Kellerman."

"Cain? But you said he was Lamont."

"He was both. When he dyed his hair and wore the colored contacts, he went by the name Cain Kellerman."

"Cain Kellerman? The man you…" It was only then, staring into Danny's eyes, that I connected the dots. "You…you're saying that *you* killed Lamont?"

"He led two lives, Renee. One as an attorney named Cain Kellerman, the man I killed. The other as Bourque's man Lamont Myers, known only to a few."

My mind was exploding. Then it went black at the edges. I couldn't feel my fingers. I couldn't find my voice.

"I think Jonathan Bourque was planning to kill him, but I got to him first. Either way, the man who held you captive in his glass home is dead. He'll never hurt you again."

He said it as if he were holding up a trophy. One more head for the wall here in Lamont's room. Lamont's head.

"He…he saved me," I stammered.

"He was trolling that night, looking for a victim. He found you."

It was a lie. All lies!

My mouth was open, but I clamped it shut, I remember that. And it was almost as if the clamping of my jaw threw a switch somewhere in my head. A circuit had shorted in my drug-altered psyche.

I snapped.

My name is Renee, which means "reborn" in French, and I was reborn yet again in that moment. I went from being Renee the lover, who was falling for the priest named Danny, to Renee the killer, who despised Danny for killing Lamont, whose death I'd vowed to avenge.

I knew even then, in that first moment, that I would kill Danny.

However infatuated I might be with this hero who'd walked into my life, I couldn't accept that everything I'd lived for was just a big lie. Normal people just don't throw everything out like that. Staunch Republicans don't roll over and wake up Democrats. Buddhists don't snap their fingers and become Muslims. Muslims don't read an article and become Hindus.

I was reborn into Lamont's glass house. I owed everything to him. When he died, a large part of me had died with him, and what was left lived to kill the person who'd killed us.

My understanding was that simple, and the conviction ran as deep as any fundamental religious conviction.

"Renee, you've got to understand," he said.

I heard: *You're such a gullible little fool.*

His face sagged. "I want to help you," he said.

I heard: *I slit Lamont's throat so I could have you.*

He took a step toward me. "I know this is hard. You must hate me. I can see it in your eyes. I…"

I didn't hear the rest. The sound of my pumping blood had filled my ears. I turned on my heels and walked toward the door with only one thought on my mind.

My gun was in my kit. I had to get my gun.

I couldn't go for the gun in Danny's kit, because I could see the light in his eyes: He already knew my mind. He was a master and would stop me before I could take two steps toward his kit. But he didn't know that I had my kit upstairs.

So, I would get my gun and I would turn around and then I would shoot Danny Hansen in the head where he stood.

And then, after I had cried, I would leave the house and never return. Because then it would finally be over.

I had no other choice, see? All of this time I'd seen Danny as my new savior, but he'd been tricking me the whole time. He wasn't my savior, he was the man who'd *killed* my savior. That truth filled me with a kind of rage I'd never felt before.

Danny was the worst kind of viper.

"Where are you going?"

I didn't answer. I turned the corner into Lamont's bedroom, and the moment I cleared the doorway, I began to run.

32

DANNY STOOD ALONE in the trophy room, listening to the sound of Renee's feet pattering up the stairs, immobilized by a simple, surreal thought.

She's going to try to kill me.

Brother against brother; lover turned against lover. He'd been here before, when Orthodox Christians in Bosnia had killed Catholics and Muslims because they made a judgment.

Renee had become judge, jury, and now executioner. He, the priest, had judged and would now be judged.

The thoughts flogged his mind in the space of a few seconds before being summarily replaced by other, more practiced thoughts born of so many years in the field.

She killed Jonathan Bourque before coming here, probably by taxi. If she shot Bourque, she has her kit with her. Now she's going to get her gun out of the kit. Did she reload after shooting

Bourque? Nine rounds, how many left? Only one way to the top floor, up the stairs.

Under any other circumstance he would be moving already, focused on a clear objective, but now his aim was compromised by competing interests.

Was she the enemy? No.

Was he the enemy? Yes.

How was it possible that he could have become the enemy of that woman who'd swept into his life and stolen his heart? The answer was his death sentence: He couldn't possibly improve this world by judging others, not any more than Renee could improve her life by judging him.

Have you ever been tempted to judge, Father?

He was better off dead now. He would have been better off dead years ago, along with his mother and sisters.

But one thought rose above the others and he seized it. Only she mattered now. Only Renee, whom he did love in the only way he knew how to love. Whatever he did now had to be for her, not for him, and not for any ideal.

If by dying he could save her, he would.

If by living he could give her hope, he would.

If by taking her place in that hellhole and subjecting himself to madness he could bring back her sanity, he would bolt the door shut and strap himself to the bed.

Her feet padded on the marble floors over his head now. If she'd come by taxi, she would have brought her kit inside. It was likely by the front door, where she would have set it down upon entering.

Danny turned as if by rote, walked to his bag, and took his kit in his left hand. The gun was in the kit but he would not need it. He walked to the door that led to Lamont's bedroom and stopped.

Consider: That dear, precious girl was a novice. She was no match for him.

Consider: He could hide in any one of half a dozen places in the basement and take her out when she returned to kill him.

His mind seemed to stutter, then restart.

Consider: His mission had not failed, not yet. He was in business to better society by ridding it of the worst people who violated the innocent. He was given to that end for his mother's sake, for his sisters' sake, for his sake, and for God's sake. His mission had not failed, but it was now threatened.

Consider: Renee was only one person. The right moral choice is that which brings about the most good for the many, not the one.

Consider: If Renee killed him or in any way threatened his mission, he would be unable to save other victims.

Consider: She might be only one hundred pounds with skin as pale as the moon, but at the moment he would rather face a seasoned Serbian commando. Renee was going to kill him unless he stopped her.

Conclusion:

But that was where Danny's thoughts stopped. There was no conclusion this time. There was only fear and confusion. His earlier thoughts of dying to save her seemed vacuous now. Absurd.

The sound of her crying followed her footsteps. She was returning, gun in hand, to kill him. And he could do nothing but stand there.

But he wasn't seriously thinking that he should kill her. How could he? The notion was as ridiculous as dying to save her. She would not be saved by his death, only tormented by it. And there were all those victims he would fail to save.

Danny moved when her feet hit the top step. Snatching up

his kit, he hurried to the side of the bed, eased himself to the floor, and rolled under the frame. Then he scooted to the other side, closest to the door. The brown bed skirt effectively blocked his view.

The bag was a nuisance, but it contained evidence that might wreak havoc in the wrong hands. He couldn't leave it behind.

What did it matter now? What did anything matter?

She matters, Danny.

The mission matters now, Danny. Only the mission.

Renee sniffed back her crying as she reentered the room. Her feet whispered across the carpet.

Then she was breathing at the trophy room doorway. She'd already walked past him, but a move on his part now might give him away. He had to be sure she was inside the office before he rolled out.

"Danny?"

Her frail cry was muted by the separation of rooms—she had gone in. But the tone of her voice filled him with doubt. What if he'd misjudged the look on her face? What if she'd gone to retrieve a photograph of Lamont so they could be certain that Cain Kellerman was the same person? Or done something else that had nothing to do with killing him? She wasn't a killer by nature, so why should he assume she'd gone for a gun?

It was in Bourque's office that Danny first suspected there might be a connection between Cain and Lamont. There were too many similarities between the men to write off as coincidental. Both worked for Bourque. Both were attorneys who specialized in international affairs. Both felt threatened by Bourque. Both had vanished at the same time.

"Danny?"

He suppressed an urge to call out, *I'm here.*

"Danny!" Her voice carried to him from inside the trophy room.

Now. He rolled from under the bed, pulled his bag out behind him, and was turning to rush for the door when that familiar sound cut the stillness. *Phfftt!*

A bullet tugged at his left arm.

Pain flashed up his shoulder and he released the bag, which fell away from the bed. He dropped to his palms, keeping the bed between his body and the trophy room.

She'd shot him! It was only a surface wound, but that didn't change the fact that Renee had not only fooled him, but pointed her gun at him and pulled the trigger.

A small measure of clarity swept into his mind. The territory became a little more familiar.

"Renee, please! We can work this out."

"We are working it out, you lying piece of—"

"He wasn't who you thought he was." He had to distract her.

"He saved me!"

"He was a monster."

"He was my lover!" she screamed.

She marched around the end of the bed and fired again. The bullet clipped the heel of his right shoe. But in moving she'd made a mistake.

Danny rolled back under the bed, leaving the bag on the floor behind him. Quickly, to the far side of the bed. Past the bed skirt out into the open.

"How dare you call him a monster!" Another bullet whistled past his scalp. She'd dropped to her knees and was shooting under the bed.

Danny came to his feet, spun toward the office, and was through the doorway in three long steps. He would be trapped inside, but his only other option was to try to get past her. Certain suicide.

He leaped across the office, jerked the closet door halfway open, then took two steps and dropped into a narrow space between the desk and the wall. It had taken far too long, but she would likely approach with more caution this time, knowing that he was fully aware of her intent.

He crouched behind the desk, hoping that she would take the bait and be drawn to the closet first. If he had been willing to use his gun, this would already be over. She would be dead.

Maybe he should be willing. Maybe he owed that to the mothers and daughters he would save by living to administer more justice.

But his gun was out in the bedroom, safely tucked away in his lost kit. Even if he did have a weapon, could he use it on Renee? His hands began to shake.

You're going to die tonight, Danny.

The thought was simple and clear. He was on his knees at the mercy of an executioner who knew him for who he was. He'd escaped a thousand bullets in Bosnia, but he would not escape hers tonight.

She was sent to kill you, Danny.

"Danny?"

Inside now. Danny tried to hold his breath.

She must have seen the closet, because her words came bitter and under her breath. "You sick..." Her voice faltered.

It hadn't occurred to him that she would be afraid to approach the closet. But that only extended his advantage. Her attention would be swallowed by that space.

"Come out!" She fired her gun. Wood splintered. Then again.

Sweat trickled past his right temple, but now he regained some of his composure.

She was walking for the closet, striding with purpose, focused and deliberate so she wouldn't lose her nerve.

"You son of—"

Danny lunged for his exit while her words were still in her throat. He was halfway to the door when she saw him and spun.

She fired one round that went wide and plowed into the door frame. Then he was out of the trophy room and she was running for the doorway.

He slammed the door shut and twisted the dead bolt into place, locking her inside. He half expected her to crash into the barrier, crying out her rage. Instead, the room went quiet.

For the moment she was contained. She'd gotten off six shots that he knew of, and he wasn't sure how many rounds she'd put into Bourque. She could have as many as two left or as few as none unless she'd reloaded, which, given her state of mind, he doubted. She might try to shoot out the dead bolt, but these things were much easier said than done, especially with a metal door. Even if she managed to destroy this one, there was another at the top of the stairs.

He could retrieve his gun from his bag and lie in wait. Lure her out and shoot her then—

He was a monster!

Terrified by the thought, he sprinted for the door, scooping up his bag as he passed the far side of the bed. Dashed up the stairs, taking the steps two at a time. Closed the door to the basement. Locked it.

Silence poured into the glass house by the sea.

Danny stepped back, panting. So, now he was safe. At least for the moment. Until she managed to break out or was rescued. Then she would come after him.

And then he didn't know what. Nothing would be the same again. He'd honestly thought she would kill him down there, and yet here he stood, breathing, with only a bloodstained sleeve to show for all her bullets.

He had to gain control of his mind and consider his options with more clarity. These conflicting emotions, so strange to him after years of fighting, robbed him of logic.

He ran down the hall, exited through the front door, and stepped into the cool night air. A car drove by and vanished into the darkness. It was all good out here, no signs that anyone had heard a sound. He took a deep breath and eased the door closed behind him.

Slow down, Danny. Take your time. Find her taxi, check the exits. Think!

He withdrew his gun, slipped it behind his back, and set his kit behind the hedge that butted into the porch. It took him just over a minute to check the perimeter of the property, find the cab waiting down the street, and assure himself that there was no immediate threat outside the building.

Renee might have told the taxi driver to check on her if she didn't emerge within a given time period. Whatever Danny did, he could not afford to involve a third party.

You have to kill her, Danny. She will come after you and she will ruin everything sooner or later.

Danny had once known a man in Bosnia named Ruchov. Ruchov, the village butcher, had a wife and three daughters. He was liked by most, loved by his family. If someone had slit Ruchov's neck *before* the war, Danny's mother and sisters would still be alive today, because Ruchov was the man who'd killed them. Danny had learned all of this before he'd killed the man himself at age sixteen.

Would it have been right or wrong to kill Ruchov before he killed Danny's mother? All Danny knew was that he wished someone had.

If Renee stopped him from finding and killing the Ruchovs of the world, there would be a lot of weeping mothers and daughters.

He hurried along the side of the house, headed for the front entrance.

You're a monster for even thinking of killing her, Danny.

He couldn't rid his body of the shakes. The gun was there, at his back. He could wait for her to fall asleep. But no, the cabdriver might try to collect her before she fell asleep.

Danny retrieved his kit, slid back into the house, and closed the door.

All quiet.

He walked down the hall and stopped in front of the door to the stairwell. It was there that he heard the sound.

A faint high-pitched whine drifted through the air, the sound of something electrical, or of wind whistling through a vent. Then the sound ran out and began again.

Shivers spread through Danny's skin. He walked up to the door and placed his ear on the wood. The sound was coming from below and it wasn't electricity or a vent. It was the sound of terror and it was coming from a human throat.

Renee was screaming.

The sound ran down his spine like long, jagged fingernails. She wasn't trying to break out; she was down there screaming.

He twisted the lock and jerked the door open. The sound became louder, a wail of horror that raked his nerves. There was no anger in that cry, only raw fear.

Her panic spread to his nerves. How could he do this to her?

Danny ran down the stairs, thinking it was okay. It was okay because she was in the trophy room and she wasn't trying to shoot out the lock with her last bullets. She couldn't kill him as long as the door was locked.

He rushed into the bedroom. Her shrieking was that of a wounded animal. This from such a small woman.

But he knew why. Renee was screaming because he'd trapped her in her hell, and she was feeling all its dread. He'd locked her in that realm of punishment. Like Lamont had locked her in. He—Danny—had become her new law.

Yet he was sure that if he opened that door she would kill him.

Her screams would not relent. She was mindless in there, running around the room. Hitting the door with the gun and running more, trying to find a way out.

Like a fist, a knot filled his throat; tears spilled from his eyes. He could not do this! He almost took his chances and opened the door for her.

But there was something else happening. Renee was being confronted by a past she could not identify. Like an undiagnosed brain cancer, its symptoms were wreaking havoc and pushing her to madness.

He could rush in and try to tackle her to the floor before she shot him, but it would be risky. If he died she would either block out the incident and remain a captive of her past, or, realizing what she'd done to him, become a prisoner of guilt. His death would only enslave her from beyond the grave.

He felt utterly powerless.

Danny leaned his forehead against the door, overcome with anguish. *I am so sorry, Renee. I am so sorry.*

Still she wailed.

He turned, rested his back against the door, slumped down to his seat, leaned his head back, and silently wept for the woman inside who was losing her mind to a pain she could not understand.

33

I DON'T KNOW how it happened, really. I was furious at Danny for suggesting that he was ripping the cover off the ugly, hidden underbelly of my life. They were lies, all lies.

Then he tricked me and left me alone in the room. The sound of the door slamming was like a thunderclap. I'd fired at him twice and felt empowered, but with the door's booming bang, the gun felt stupid and heavy in my hand.

All I could think was, *He's left me?*

I heard him lock the door. Then run, up the stairs. I still hadn't moved a muscle when the distant sound of that door closing reached me through the walls.

Danny had left me alone with all those lies.

My anger was gone, replaced by something I'll never be able to properly explain. The walls seemed to close in on me, really close in, physically smothering me. They were magic and I was the dove in the box that was being forced into a small black hole.

I'd been here before. I did not like it then, and I didn't like it now. Terror flooded my mind in waves that crashed into me and sucked me under. I couldn't breathe, I couldn't move, I couldn't hold the dread back.

It was then that I first wondered if Danny had uncovered something. What if everything I'd believed was suddenly wrong? What if what I had mistaken for my life was actually a kind of death?

What if Lamont was a monster? My death? Maybe I thought I'd been saved by him, but I had only become his slave. This place of punishment had been my personal hell.

That was impossible! I did remember some things, like when Lamont wanted to flush out a piece of chocolate or something I'd eaten in a moment of weakness. He'd pour ten gallons of water down my throat using a funnel and make me throw it all up to rinse out my system. This often took more than a day. This was the kind of thing I learned to hate about that living hell.

But it wasn't Lamont's fault. He was only trying to help me. Danny had locked me up and gone.

It wasn't just fear that smothered me. It wasn't only the memory of pain. It wasn't simply sorrow or self-pity or humiliation.

It was the ruthless stripping of my human dignity that left me an empty, hollow shell. I was not worthy to be called a person, much less a woman.

When Danny locked me in that room, he left me alone with the horror of being nobody. I was the girl who had to be perfect under Lamont's laws in order to be somebody, which was impossible, which was why I was only *nobody*.

When Danny locked the second door at the top of the stairs, I lost myself. I blamed everything I felt on him.

On Danny. This was his fault, not Lamont's.

I don't even know what I was thinking, going berserk, banging into the door, pulling at my hair. I was screaming. A high-pitched sound that made me think something had broken in my head, which only filled me with more alarm.

I had to get away, you see. The sight of the open closet made me crazy with terror. I had to get out, and Danny was the only one who could help me get out. But Danny was the one who'd locked me in here.

This is why he locked you up, Renee. Lamont knew you were only a dog who would return to its vomit, just an animal who would run around and scream, just a worthless excuse of a life. That's why he was teaching you how to behave properly.

Eat the right foods.

Wear the right clothes.

Stay clean, clean, clean.

As the memories started to come in, my throat began to fail me and my wailing started to fade. I threw myself on the floor, facedown, dried of sobs. My face was in the corner where the walls met and I imagined that I could hide there, but that didn't help. Somehow I ended up in the middle of the floor, curled up in a tight ball.

I was nothing.

I think I stayed like that for at least an hour. Maybe two. But the human spirit is built to deal with everything, including nothing. Slowly, I began to accept my nothingness. Raw pain gave way to resolve.

I had put up with this before, right? Sure, I'd shut it all out of my mind, but I'd been strapped to the wall in that room back there for days at a time until I learned to smile and kiss Lamont and show him all the appreciation he deserved for being my "law unto life," as he liked to say.

Now it was going to start all over again, only this time it was Danny who'd locked me in.

My mind melted, thinking about that. Why Danny? I had been so sure that he loved me for who I was, not for who I could be. I thought he liked me. He'd been so kind and patient and showed me so many things.

My mind wandered in lazy circles, spiraling down to a place of familiarity. Lamont's early lessons came back to mind: the way he'd first treated me so nicely, feeding me drugs, always those drugs to keep me mellow. The lessons had ramped up slowly over several months.

I had been such a messy girl, and he'd only set up the laws to help me.

What a fool you are, Renee. You're here again, back where you started. It always comes back to the same thing—no matter how hard you try, you can never measure up. You will always be too fat or too stupid or too messy or too ungrateful or too mean or too rude or too talkative or a dozen other toos.

The thoughts bogged me down and I settled into a haze. I slowly slipped back into a more manageable state of mind, where denial and fancy head games were friends who led me to safety. I had been here so many times, hadn't I? I was an expert at this.

I wondered how long it had been since the office had been properly cleaned. Maybe I should clean it before Danny returned.

But Lamont was dead. Danny was the new law. And although I didn't really blame Lamont, I hated, hated, *hated* the thought of starting all over again with Danny.

More rules. More too this, too that. More punishment. I mean, look what Danny did to the worst of the monsters. He killed them!

I settled back down and stared at the corner where a spider was lowering itself on a long string of web. Normally I would have jumped up and killed the spider with a tissue, then thrown it in the waste can, but at the time I remember thinking that at least I had someone to share the room with.

A thought came out of nowhere and stopped me cold. *If Danny is the new law, then I have to kill him.*

I had to kill Danny because he had killed Lamont, and now he was the law and the judge just like Lamont had been, and I couldn't do that again, I just couldn't.

Really, those who demanded perfection when there wasn't any were the worst.

I pushed myself up and thought about that. Danny's law of punishing sin with death was the only thing in the world worse than his Pharisees. Wasn't that right? In fact, it made *him* a Pharisee. A viper.

I glanced at the door and saw where one of my bullets had gouged a hole in the wall nearby. My gun lay on the floor next to a sheet of paper.

That was odd. I didn't know where that paper had come from. The wind had blown it off the desk? But there was no wind. It had fallen out of Danny's kit? But he'd left his bag out by the bed.

The paper had been slipped under the door?

My pulse surged with a memory. Lamont used to slip me notes under the door sometimes. Usually to ask questions, like, *What did you do with the black paring knife?* That meant it wasn't where it was supposed to be, which in turn meant I was in even more trouble.

I crawled over to the piece of paper, picked it up, and read the brief note scrawled there: *I beg you, hear my confession. I'll be waiting.*

It was signed, *Danny*.

Confession? It sounded like some cruel trick. He expected me to hear his confession through this door? What that could possibly mean, I had no idea.

I don't need to hear your confession, Danny. I already know your sin. And you have the gall to accuse Lamont.

I picked up my gun and checked the clip. Empty. I tried to account for the shots. Three to Bourque. Which meant I had to have gotten off six more down here. I didn't remember all that, but I had a full clip in my kit upstairs, if Danny hadn't taken it.

I reached up and tried the doorknob just to be sure that it was still locked, an old habit from my past. The handle twisted and the door swung in and I jerked back like I'd been stung by a bee.

It was open!

The bedroom beyond waited in darkness. I scrambled to my feet, gun out, ready for his trick even though I had nothing. He'd believe I'd shoot. But when Danny didn't appear after ten or fifteen breaths, I dared to take a step forward.

"Danny?"

The empty house swallowed his name.

I walked out into the bedroom, but it was empty, too. I crept up the stairwell and stepped through the open doorway at the top.

There was no sign of Danny.

I checked the kitchen. Nothing. My bedroom. Empty. The only thing in the hallway was my kit, exactly where I'd left it.

The full clip lay on top of the kit. I couldn't remember putting it there, on top. I reloaded.

Then I tried the front door, opened the latch, and stepped out into a cool Southern California night.

Danny was gone.

Waiting for me at confession.

34

IT WAS ALMOST 9:00 PM when Danny pulled into the back of Saint Paul's on Long Beach Boulevard in Long Beach. The parking lot was vacant except for a maroon-and-white bus. The parish's name was stamped in big bold letters on the side, under a silhouette of a dove.

He parked his Malibu behind the bus and turned off the engine. City noise filtered into the cabin—the faint hum of traffic, the soft growl of a truck as it gunned its diesel engine through the intersection at the front of the building. A small dog barked and another returned the challenge.

But back here in the lot surrounded by the tallest trees on the city block, there were no other signs of life.

The church rose into the night sky, dark except for a lone bulb over the rear staff entrance. For the hundredth time, Danny questioned his decision to leave Renee at the glass house by the sea. Losing control of a situation so completely didn't come naturally to him, and he hadn't been in the clearest frame of mind. Maybe he really had thrown it all away this time.

But of course he had, hadn't he? Life as he knew it was over. What happened now was wholly in her hands. He was the puppet on her string. It was the only way. The right way. He'd come to that conclusion as he'd wept outside the prison he'd locked her in.

What if she didn't come? With each passing mile as he headed south, south, and farther south, the notion haunted him with increasing dread. Surely Renee wouldn't stay there in her torment, not knowing he'd unlocked the door. Surely she would come.

Surely he had made the right decision.

He'd left the house and approached the cab. A thousand dollars had persuaded the driver to wait an extra hour, two hours, three—all night if that's what it took. If Renee didn't emerge before sunrise, then he was to place a call to Danny's cell phone.

What if the driver didn't wait? Left a thousand dollars richer and no worse off for the gift? What if she passed out in the basement without finding his note? What if she found it but didn't understand it?

He'd told the driver to bring her to Saint Paul's, but what if she refused? Danny might have been better off waiting for her outside the house. He might be better off to return now. But he'd passed a point of no return the moment he hit the Pacific Coast Highway. If he missed her by even a few minutes she might reach the church ahead of him, find no one there, and leave.

Danny closed his eyes for a moment to still his spinning head. *Forgive me, Father. If you are there and you hear, bless me, for I have sinned.*

He reached for his kit, withdrew his Browning nine-millimeter, checked the load out of habit, then palmed it and stepped out of the car.

He took a deep breath, eased the gun behind his belt, and walked toward the lighted back door, aware of each footfall on the paved lot. It took him a full fifteen seconds to find the right key on his ring, because his mind was still back there in the basement with Renee.

It's the right decision, Danny. It's done, and it's the right thing.

He tried to insert the key and had to flip it three times before it slid in. Entering, he closed the door quietly behind him and started to twist the dead bolt. No, better to leave it open—she might come this way.

If she came. If he was right.

The hall brightened with a flip of a light switch. He'd leave this light on for her. She didn't know the way.

What you must do, do it quickly.

The church taught that a man who committed suicide did not go to heaven. Then again, by their reckoning, suicide was the least of the sins Danny would have to account for.

Danny took the side door into the main sanctuary. It was dimly lit by two rows of electric candles, which were mounted on seven pillars on each side of the empty pews. There would be no witnesses tonight.

Walking faster under the watchful eye of the crucified Christ, he crossed the foyer, stepped up to the large mahogany doors at the main entrance, jerked the brass bolt to one side, and unlatched a second restraining chain.

The church closed its doors at six on weeknights unless there was an evening service or social event. It was highly unlikely that anyone would try the doors this late into the night. The locals were accustomed to the schedule, and the area wasn't a hangout for tourists or night dwellers.

Danny cracked the door to be sure it was open, then eased it closed.

He walked to a bench along the wall, opened the seat's built-in storage compartment, and withdrew a hymnal. This he placed on its end against the front door. Any attempt to enter would knock the book flat on the wood floor. Then the empty halls would know. And the crucifix would know.

And he would know.

What you must do, do it quickly, my dear.

Danny retraced his steps through the sanctuary, then turned right and approached the confessional nearest the front. He entered the booth reserved for laity and lit a small candle reserved for show. If the wax gave out too soon, he would turn on the nightlight near the floor. But the occasion seemed to demand a flame.

There was a short bench in the booth, well worn by sinners seeking absolution over the church's twenty-seven-year history. Renee wasn't Catholic—he wondered if he should leave a note outside the booth instructing her to enter this side. The sign at the top of the door would have to suffice.

He backed out of the booth, closed the door, and looked around the sanctuary one last time before taking his familiar place inside the left booth. Releasing two small swivel latches, he freed the metal screen from the window between the two booths. Soft yellow light flickered through the wooden latticework that remained in place.

He rested his gun on the floor next to a two-inch gap that ran the length of the wall. A nudge from his foot would push the weapon into the next booth.

Now he would wait for the sound of the toppling hymnal, the telltale *thump* that would announce the beginning of the end. He took a deep breath, laced his fingers together, leaned against the bench's backrest, and waited.

After half an hour, he began to wonder if she might have killed herself in the basement. He'd been so focused on his own moral choice that he'd forgotten to consider the dangerous state of her mind. While he was down here in Long Beach, waiting to do the right thing, she was there in Malibu, dead on the floor.

He stood, fighting an urge to rush to his car and go back to the house. But if she came, he would be gone.

He sat and steadied his hands. No, this was the only course. The right choice. The moral path. A poetic and just if poignantly ironic ending to his journey.

You live by the law, you die by the law.

Lamont had lived and died by that law. Now it was Danny's turn. That Danny had even considered the possibility of killing Renee was the gavel that had finally sentenced him. It hit him like a brick as he'd wept on the floor.

He was as guilty as them all.

And now he would pay the price.

After an hour, he began to wonder if he'd misjudged Renee's nature. For his own sake, it was critical that the terms of their relationship be decided by the code that had put them in this situation. For Renee's sake, it was critical that she become what he'd made her: judge, jury, and executioner.

If she judged him and found him guilty, she must do what she must do.

After an hour and a half Danny began to sweat.

The hymnal did not fall.

35

I WAS GOING to kill Danny.

I was Judas, who was being paid in the silver of vengeance and justice. Danny knew it, and I knew it. In fact, I wasn't so sure he didn't want me to kill him.

He had killed the guilty in the name of justice, and by doing so he had become guilty. He had killed Lamont, and now in my mind he *was* Lamont. And although I didn't blame Lamont for the state of my life, I could not allow another law to take his place.

I had one chance to be set free and never look back. It was either that or Danny was waiting to kill me, and I was okay with that, too.

I stepped out on the curb in front of Saint Paul Catholic Church and walked away from the cab without looking back. But Raymond wasn't leaving, so I looked back and saw that he was watching me.

"You sure you're okay?" he asked.

"Yes," I said. Standing out there on the sidewalk I felt like a ghost who'd mistakenly walked into the real world. I was being watched from a hundred sides. I knew because I could hear the voices clearly again for the first time since I'd been chased down the alleyway by gunmen and saved by Lamont a year and three months ago. Only this time I was the one with the gun.

I gave him a halfhearted wave. "Thank you."

He nodded, then pulled away, and I walked up to the front doors. Not daring to look back in case someone was staring at me, I pressed the large thumb latch and pushed. The door opened. He'd left it open for me. Danny had always been such a gentleman. I had to love that about him.

I stepped in and shut the door behind me. My breathing was thick and my fingers were twitching, but inside the church I was safe from the street. Dim light glowed through the deadly quiet foyer. Someone had left a book on the floor. A hymnal.

Oddly enough, I felt more threat from the voices in my head than from Danny. My last real encounter with the voices had left me with a fractured mind and a broken, half-dead body. Danny, on the other hand, had never shown the slightest inclination to hurt me, not even when I was shooting at him. Yes, he did lock me in the room, but he probably could have killed me.

I didn't hate Danny. I didn't hate Lamont. I'm not even sure I hated Jonathan Bourque anymore. Instead, I hated that they had made me who I was.

I hated that I had to kill Danny, but there was nothing I was more eager to do than just that. An image from that movie *Apocalypse Now* flashed through my mind. A soldier went up a river during the Vietnam War to kill an army colonel named Kurtz, who'd gone off the deep end. Kurtz accepted his death willingly. He embraced the horror with as much boldness as he'd dished it out.

I was the soldier and Danny was Kurtz. There was an understanding between us, a nobility that most people would never get.

These lofty thoughts joined the voices whispering in my head, forming a strange, fractured soundtrack of terrible wonder. But above it all there was a much clearer sound, a voice that said over and over, *You're gonna kill him, Renee, You're gonna kill, Renee, You're gonna kill Danny, Renee.*

I really was finally doing what I had been born to do. Or at least what I had become reborn to do.

I set my kit on the floor, unlatched it, pulled out my gun, and stood up.

I would kill Danny or he would kill me. Then I would gladly die because I couldn't live anymore, not like this. I wasn't thinking about what I would do after I killed him. Escaping the police wasn't on my mind. How ending Danny's life would change me wasn't my concern.

I was simply doing what I had to do, because Danny deserved to die.

Maybe God would send another killer to kill me for killing Danny for killing Lamont. Maybe human nature is the ultimate assassin, finally taking every life because we are all guilty on one level or another.

I stood in the foyer for at least a minute, maybe two or maybe even five, swimming in a whirlpool of thoughts.

My resolve was interrupted by a sudden wave of regret and sorrow. Why did it have to be Danny? I thought I loved Danny. He was the kindest person I had ever known, other than Lamont, who turned out to be not so kind after all.

Maybe I had Danny pegged wrong, too. Or maybe I was attracted to monsters because *I* was a monster.

Or just maybe because I was meant to kill them.

I held the gun by my leg and stretched my fingers around

the butt, one at a time. Then I started forward, stepping lightly on my feet so I wouldn't make any sound.

It was time to hear Danny's confession.

THUMP.

Danny's heart jerked then stalled at the sound of the book slapping wood. A chill washed down his neck.

She'd come.

He heard the door close, just barely. He imagined more, breathing perhaps, a pounding heart maybe. But these were only from his own chest.

It was Renee and she was inside the church. Anyone else would be stomping around by now, calling out, mangling this eerie silence.

So...It was as he'd hoped. And dreaded.

For a long time, there was no other indication of her presence, and he wondered if she'd opened the door and peered through the crack only to close it without entering. But then the slight brush of shoes on the floor reached him, and he knew she was coming.

He would remove the figurative splinter from Renee's flesh. He would do it for her sake, not his own. He had to be sure she understood this before she killed him.

What if he failed? And then, what if guilt and shame destroyed her? He couldn't tolerate the thought that he might further wound that precious woman. She had to accept his death to save her life, but he would not allow it until he was sure she was absolved of all guilt.

Tears broke from both of his eyes and ran down his cheeks. What had become of him? He'd carried the burden of death and judgment on his shoulders for so many years, and now he would finally let it go.

He was so distracted by his own emotion that the grating of the door in the next booth seemed to come too early. She was entering.

He heard the familiar creak of the seat as she sat. And then it all went quiet again.

Danny reached up, gripped the knob on the small door between the booths, and slid it open. But he did not look into the adjacent booth. There was no rush.

She was in there, he was sure of it, but she didn't say a word. How could she, after all she'd suffered? She was only a shell of herself, having been emptied by his callous insistence that she know the truth.

When he couldn't stand the silence a moment longer he spoke out. "You came."

No response.

"Thank you."

Still not a word. Surely, it was Renee in there.

"Do you know what I want you to do?"

The voice finally came, soft and meek. Matter-of-fact.

"Yes."

That was all, just *yes*. But it was all he needed. Using his left foot, he nudged the gun under the partition into her booth.

"Tell me what I want you to do."

"You want me to kill you," Renee said.

Innocent. Distant.

"Tell me why," Danny said.

"Because you're no better than Lamont," she said. "You are two sides of the same coin."

"How is that?"

She hesitated. "I'm here to hear your confession, Father. You tell me."

Of course, that was how he'd intended it. He could see the butt of his gun on the floor. She hadn't picked it up.

"It's been three months since my last confession. I've never really believed that confession does much except make people feel better about themselves. It doesn't clean up the ugliness of this world. People hurt themselves and others and then they confess and then they hurt more people. It's the way we humans live."

"Yes," she said.

"I've taken a more direct path to cleaning up the world. I kill the worst offenders."

"Go on."

"I've been tempted to be good, the oldest and vilest temptation in the book, and I've been tempted to judge. And I'm afraid I've succumbed to these temptations in a monstrous fashion. I have ruined the lives of many. I have killed others."

He could hear her breathing now, steady and heavier than a moment ago. He had to say these words, if not for her then for himself.

"I thought I was right, living by an ethical code based on consequential moral reasoning, everything in perfect little packages. All of us are judged, and if found guilty we pay the price." Here it was then. "But today I learned that we are all guilty. I as much as they."

Why it had taken so long for this window in his mind to open, he didn't know. But now that it was gaping, he could hardly sit still in the light shining in on his dark soul.

"Tell me why you deserve to die," she said.

"In the name of the greater good, I have left hundreds of children fatherless and dozens of wives grieving. I have lived by the gun. I must die by that same gun."

"Tell me why I should be the one to kill you," she said.

Sweat broke from his hairline and tickled his right temple.

"Because I have given you permission. I give up my right to life to you, and you alone."

"Tell me why."

"Because I am judgment, and it was judgment that ruined your life. I have become the very monster that broke you. Now you must break me."

He could imagine nothing else now except dying by her hand. His heart was pounding and his hands were sweating, but it was remorse that smothered him, not fear. This was the right end to it all. This was justice.

"Please, Renee, I beg you." It was all he could do to keep from blurting out in desperation. His voice trembled. "I have done so much wrong. I have killed so many. I can't go on like this."

Still, she hadn't picked up the gun.

"You have everything you need to start over with a clean slate," he said.

For a long time nothing happened. He couldn't think of anything else to say. He'd made his point and couldn't think of a way to clarify it. His life was nothing more or less than an abscessed tooth that needed to be pulled from the world's mouth, and she was the one he'd chosen to do the pulling.

Renee started to cry in the other booth, and his heart began to melt with pain.

I WAS HOLDING my gun in my lap, knowing that I was going to shoot Danny. It was the right thing to do, because he'd given up his right to life and was begging me to do it. I was going to do it, because everything he said made perfect sense to me.

Danny was more than an evil man who'd killed so many other evil men. He was judgment itself—the very essence of humanity that made people hurt each other in the first place. That's what he was saying and I was sitting there thinking, *Yes, that's right. That's exactly right, Danny.*

But that didn't stop me from feeling sorry for him when I finally lifted the gun. He couldn't see me, of course, but I got the gun halfway up to the window when a new truth hit me.

Danny's my only friend.

A terrible wave of sadness swept over me and I started to cry. I lowered the gun, trying to reset my mind.

"No, Renee," Danny said. "You must not lose your nerve. Pick up the gun."

He was right, I knew that, and I told myself to get a grip. I sucked in tears, faced the window, pushed the long silencer through the lattice, and slid my finger around the trigger.

He wasn't in front of the barrel and I didn't turn the gun back to where I thought he must be sitting. Somehow I knew that I had gone far enough. I was offering him the barrel. It was up to him to take it.

I sat there, squared to the window, holding the gun in both hands, sobbing quietly.

SHE HAD HER own gun. His still lay on the floor. She'd come into the church with her own. This was the first thing that struck Danny when he saw the long black barrel slide through the latticework.

She had come intending to kill him.

He wasn't sure why this bothered him, only that it did. But then it made sense. He'd wounded her this deeply. Such an innocent young woman had been so ravaged by judgment that her only course was to extract her own judgment. It was a vicious circle.

Judge not lest you be judged.

She was trying not to cry, but her sobs were shaking the gun.

Danny slid off the bench, knelt on his right knee, faced the window, and held the long barrel against his mouth.

"Pull the trigger," he said.

A single bullet to the brain would do severe damage but might not end a victim's life immediately. A single bullet through the back of the neck, on the other hand, would separate the brain from the rest of the body as surely as if the victim had been beheaded.

He could see her now, facing him, tears streaming from her eyes, gun in both hands.

"Pull the trigger," he repeated.

She sucked in some air in an attempt to control herself. Her knuckles were white on the butt of the gun.

Danny felt his own face heat with a mix of emotions he couldn't place right away. Two thoughts crowded his mind as she stared into his eyes.

The first was that he loved her.

The second was that he was losing his nerve.

"Pull the trigger!"

"I don't think I can judge you, Danny!" If anyone else had been in the church they would have heard her cry. It was surreal, she with her gun against his teeth, Danny begging her to pull the trigger.

"You can! You can do it!"

"I don't think I can judge you."

"You're not!"

"What's the opposite of judging?" she asked.

Danny froze. The reverend mother's voice had spoken in this very confessional.

"Love?" Renee answered for him. "Isn't it love?"

I DON'T KNOW how it happened, but the moment I looked into Danny's eyes I knew that I couldn't pull that trigger.

I knew that I loved those eyes. That face. That man. In a way that I'd never loved Lamont.

He was still on his knees, staring at me as if I'd slapped him. I still had the barrel sticking through the latticework, and I was shaking—it was so strange. But we were both killers, and I suppose that part of us didn't know how else to behave.

"It's love, isn't it?" I cried.

He didn't seem to be able to speak.

"Tell me!" I screamed.

"Grace," he said.

"Grace?"

"It's...it's grace."

"And love?"

"And love." He said it softly and his eyes were shining as if he was saying something for the first time.

My world melted. I had the barrel pressed against his face and he was kneeling like a prisoner waiting for the final count, but my need to kill him flew out of my mind.

I didn't know much about grace, it sounded too religious for me. But love was a different story.

I thought I had loved Lamont. I thought he had loved me. But here in the confessional, I saw the truth: I had only feared him.

But Danny...I did not fear Danny.

I loved Danny. And Danny loved me, I mean, *really* loved me.

We both hated injustice enough to die for it, that was the thing. He was like me and I was like him. In fact, Danny was the only person in the whole world I could trust, a man I would rather die for than lose. He was beautiful and I loved him. I really, truly loved him.

Yet there I was holding a gun against his teeth...

Gasping, I jerked the gun back and dropped it onto the bench, where it landed with a loud *clump*. I spun for the door, managed to spring the latch, and flew around to his side.

Danny was coming to his feet when I crashed into his booth and threw myself at him, sobbing. He was a solid man twice my weight, and he absorbed me with only a slight stagger.

All I could think was that a few more ounces of pressure on that trigger and I would have blown him all over the booth. It was an agonizing realization.

I wrapped my arms around his neck and clung to him like a koala hugging a tree. "I'm sorry! I'm so sorry, Danny!"

I was kissing him on his neck and mouth and face as he stood still, caught completely off guard.

"Renee…" He was objecting, but he didn't know what to say.

"No, don't say anything more about that. I forgive you. You're not like Lamont. If you love me, tell me to stay with you. Tell me to run away with you."

"Renee, you don't know——"

"No, don't say that, Danny! Don't say I don't know what I'm saying!" I was still kissing him on his face and neck. "Take me away, please, just take me away."

"I…I don't know——"

"No, Danny!" I calmed myself. "Do you love me?"

I could barely see his eyes in the dim light, but I could see him blink.

"Tell me you love me."

"I love you." He could barely speak.

"Then tell me you'll take me away from here." I spoke in a rush, as eager for his words as for water in the desert. "Tell me you'll protect me and never let anyone ever hurt me again. Tell me that, please tell me that."

"I…" His voice was shaking. "I will never let anyone hurt you again."

"Tell me you will never kill anyone again," I said.

"I…Never…"

"Tell me we will always love each other."

He nodded and said it while kissing my forehead and my hair, returning my embrace. "Always. Always, always. I am so sorry, my dear. I am so very sorry."

"This is love, Danny."

Danny began to sob. "Yes!" I thought that he might either melt in all his tears or come apart in my arms because he was shaking so hard. "Yes..."

"I love you, Danny."

We stood in that confessional, holding each other like two lost children, and I knew then that all the lies were finished. Lamont had been a monster, I knew that now, and maybe Danny had been one, too, and I as well for that matter—all monsters.

But it was over. The law, the rules, the deceit to cover it all up, the failure, the revenge, the judging, the failure, the endless cycle of not being good enough—all of it was over.

Love and grace had found us finally.

We had each other, and even if our reprieve lasted only one night, it would be a night that would last forever.

I let Danny hold me close and we wept.

36

Three Months Later

I CAN REMEMBER some things about myself but not everything, because I've chosen to leave a few things in the past. My name, Renee Gilmore, is something I will never forget—how could I, after hearing it spoken by Danny so lovingly and so often, as if it were cotton candy and he was tasting it for the very first time.

Danny walked into the sunroom overlooking the valley, handed me a steaming cup of coffee, and settled into the chair next to mine. Our house was small, only nine hundred square feet, not including the porches or the barn. Our lives were simple, though we had more than enough money to last us many years. Our love was sure. "It's a beautiful morning," he said, gazing out the window. I'd awakened to the sweeping valley before us every morning for ten weeks, and I hadn't tired of the stunning view. It was all so green, with meadows that sloped up to a sharp tree line. The houses that spotted the meadows were white stone with shake-shingle roofs steep enough to shed the snow, because there would be a lot of it, Danny said.

"It's perfect," I said, taking his hand in mine.

I had been reborn many times in the last eighteen months. But not like the time both Danny and I found new life in the confessional at Saint Paul Catholic Church in Long Beach, California. We wept and we begged each other for forgiveness and then we collected what we had and fled the building.

Long Beach was only a memory. California was far behind us. We moved to a small town in Bosnia, not so far from Sarajevo.

"How much longer?" I asked a variation on that same question nearly every morning, not because I thought Danny knew, but because I wanted to hear his answer.

"A couple of months," he said.

"That's still a long time," I said.

"Not long enough."

"Not nearly." But it was enough for now. "And then what?"

He squeezed my hand and offered a comforting smile. "And then we will go to the authorities and confess our sins."

"What will they do to us?"

"They'll put us in prison."

We would make the front page, Danny had said. They would call us monsters. They would lock us up and Barbara Walters would ask for an interview. Life would never be the same. This said with a wry smile that always made me chuckle.

We'd been married in a small chapel in Sarajevo two weeks after leaving the States, one day after Danny got his requested discharge from the priesthood. He'd insisted, and I couldn't pretend I wanted to be together any less than he did.

"What if they give us the death penalty?" I asked.

"Then we'll die knowing that turning ourselves in was right," he said.

"They were all very nasty people," I said. "They deserved to die."

"They did. But then so do we."

"So do we."

This was our mantra and it usually ended here. But today I wanted to ask another question before we took our weekly walk down to the village square.

"Danny, do you mind if I make a confession?"

"I would be disappointed if you did not," he said.

"I mean, to a priest."

"Other than me?"

"You're no longer a priest."

He considered my question for a few moments. "And you would tell him everything?"

"If that would be okay with you."

Danny looked out across the valley. "Yes. Yes, it's the very least you deserve."

"Hmm..."

Did I tell you I like Danny?

"I love you," I said.

"And I love you, Renee."

His answer never changes. Danny is my rock and I will cling to him always. If that's only two more months, then those months will last me a lifetime.

CONFESSION

FATHER ANDRO STOPPED in front of his bookcase where he'd been pacing, finger on his chin, bound to my every word as I finished the story. His head turned toward me.

"And that's it?"

"That's not enough?"

He crossed to his desk. "Forgive me, of course. Yes, of course it's enough. Dear God."

It had taken me three long evenings to tell him everything and with each passing hour I felt my burden lift, if only because another person in a position of some authority had heard me without so much as judging either me or Danny once through the many hours. He said it was enough, but I actually think he was a little disappointed that it was all over. It's not often one hears such a gripping and true tale, not even in Bosnia.

"What do you think?" I asked.

Father Andro eased down into his chair, picked up his teacup which was long ago dry, and absently set it back down. He lifted his bushy eyebrows.

"As a priest?"

I shrugged. "As a man."

"I think that your Danny has finally learned what he set out to learn. I think he would now make an excellent priest."

"Hmm...Can a prisoner on death row function as a priest?"

"Yes, there is that."

"And what about me, Father?"

He studied me for a long time, then leaned back in his chair. "Honestly?"

"Honestly."

"I think Danny is a fortunate man to have learned such a hard lesson with such a wonderful person as you," he said with a gentle smile.

"Hmm...Seriously?"

Father Andro nodded once. "A very fortunate man indeed."